# Praise for *The Book of Ralph*

"This book is charming, sensitive, and at times flat-out hysterical. I knew kids like Ralph—and they scared me—but none of them had his heart, his humor, or ultimately his entertaining story. I hated to say good-bye at the end of the book."

—Mitch Albom, author of *The Five People You Meet in Heaven* and *Tuesdays with Morrie*

"McNally's writing is so compelling, not to mention funny, that you're often surprised by sudden, more tender moments. . . . His book has a depth that sneaks up on you. . . . It is McNally's ability to keep us interested in these characters beyond what they were to what they are that is the book's greatest strength."

—Sarah Dessen, *The News & Observer* (Raleigh, NC)

"There are times in *The Book of Ralph,* especially when McNally describes Hank's grade-school periods of restless angst and unrequited schoolyard crushes, when one is reminded of satirist David Sedaris."

—Stephen J. Lyons, *Chicago Sun-Times*

"Turn to nearly any page in *The Book of Ralph* and you will find a funny, moving, or outrageous set piece, usually with the hapless narrator, Hank, participating in some juvenile rite. . . . *The Book of Ralph* itself is much like Hank's father's project, a collection of strange and wonderful objects set out on the lawn, a carnival of vivid memories. . . . *The Book of Ralph* should earn John McNally the wider audience that his talent and wit deserve. Chicago-area readers, in particular, will have good reason to look forwar work by this native son."

—Porter Shreve, *Chic*

"McNally's talent for characterization and his lush sense of plac funny and oddly compelling reading."

"McNally knows how to balance the hair-raising with the better than any other young writer working today."

—*Virginia Quarte*

"*The Book of Ralph* is very funny. Ralph, the nutcase that holds these pieces together, is fabulously crazy."

—*The Journal News* (Westchester County, NY)

"There is not a single hazy recollection in this book, as McNally skillfully voices Hank's innocent, wandering and naïve thoughts with touching clarity: the type of depth not often seen in similar coming-of-age tales."

—*The Lantern* (Ohio State University)

"McNally is kind of like deep-dish pizza. He's one of the best things Chicago has to offer."

—*Newcity* (Chicago)

"I think you should read [McNally's] humorous book; a touch smart-ass, essentially meat-and-potatoes Chicago kind of story."

—Mike Danahey, *Chicago Sun-Times*

"Set mostly in 1978 Chicago, this sweet novel is a funny ode to juvenile delinquency and pop culture."

—*Chicago Tribune*

"In *The Book of Ralph* the reader gets this wild and crazy, skewed version of growing up. It's the 1970s with Tom Sawyer and Huck Finn and they're adventuring in the environs of the city. This is a city where the ghosts of Al Capone and gangsters hover in a benign way over Hank and Ralph, our heroes who make us laugh and sigh. They are absolutely irresistible!"

—*The Pilot* (North Carolina)

"Remember the CB radio craze? Cheap Trick? Pink Floyd? Organ stores at the mall? Head shops? Well, if you don't, you're not my age. Meet Hank, all-around nice kid. Meet Ralph, the eighth-grade troublemaker who befriends him. In the opening pages of John McNally's *The Book of Ralph*, it's 1978 and Ralph has found the 1974 Sears catalogue in which Patty O'Dell modeled Sears panties. Ten-four. Over-and-out. You will laugh so hard you'll forget you don't have air-conditioning."

—*Pulp* magazine (Pittsburgh)

"[T]his enjoyable first novel is a nostalgic trip back to late 1970s suburban Chicago and the foibles of eighth-grader Hank and his twice-left-back delinquent pal, Ralph. This lively novel will appeal to fans of Rich Cohen's *Lake Effect* or even Jean Shepherd's wistful fiction."

—*Publishers Weekly*

"The always reliable fascination of the good kid with the possibilities of the hood life knit together anecdotal memoirs set in the seedy southwest corner of Chicago in the late '70s and early '80s. . . . Harmless fun for the lads, courtesy of second-timer McNally."

—*Kirkus Reviews*

"John McNally's vivid, skewed characters, his vibrant prose and hilarious situations make *The Book of Ralph*, with its undercurrent of menace, a serious joy."

—Richard Russo, author of *Empire Falls*

"Wildly goofy yet touching, *The Book of Ralph* inhabits the same territory of growing up charted by Stuart Dybek and Tobias Wolff, and with as much warmth and terror as those masters. John McNally is sharp and smart and flat-out funny. The only time I stopped laughing was to marvel at his talent. And then he'd get me again."

—Stewart O'Nan, author of *The Night Country* and *Wish You Were Here*

"Populated with unlikely heroes, cast in the gray light of Chicago's South Side, McNally's book is wonderful, hilarious, and perfectly specific. By the end, I felt like I'd known Hank and Ralph my whole life."

—Haven Kimmel, author of *A Girl Called Zippy* and *Something Rising (Light and Swift)*

"John McNally brilliantly evokes childhood with all its love and loneliness, fear and sorrows, laughter and joy. His bold leaps through narrative time reveal our inability to fully escape the pressures of our past."

—Chris Offutt, author of *No Heroes*

"Hilarious, perverted, cartoonish, violent, absurd, disturbed, and, in the end, dead-on realistic, *The Book of Ralph* offers an authentic American hero in Hank Boyd—drummer of a struggling air band who becomes a murder-scene janitor. How can we withhold our love from someone so haunted by Chicago's most notorious serial killer, so lustily inspired by Cheap Trick ('I Want You to Want Me' . . .)? In *The Book of Ralph*, McNally more than cops a feel of his generation's psyche, he nails it."

—Julianna Baggott, author of *Girl Talk, The Miss America Family,* and *The Madam*

## Other Books by John McNally

### Fiction

*Troublemakers*

### Anthologies

*Bottom of the Ninth: Great Contemporary Baseball Short Stories*

*Humor Me: An Anthology of Humor by Writers of Color*

*The Student Body: Short Stories About College Students and Professors*

*High Infidelity: 24 Great Short Stories About Adultery*

# The
# Book
# of Ralph

A Novel

## JOHN McNALLY

**Free Press**
New York London Toronto Sydney

FREE PRESS
A Division of Simon & Schuster, Inc.
1230 Avenue of the Americas
New York, NY 10020

First Free Press trade paperback edition 2005

FREE PRESS and colophon are trademarks
of Simon & Schuster, Inc.

For information regarding special discounts for bulk purchases, please contact Simon & Schuster
Special Sales at 1-800-456-6798 or business@simonandschuster.com

Designed by Lauren Simonetti

Manufactured in the United States of America

10  9  8  7  6  5  4  3  2  1

The Library of Congress has cataloged the hardcover edition as follows:
McNally, John, date
The book of Ralph : a fiction / John McNally.
p. cm.
1. Teenage boys—Fiction. 2. Male friendship—Fiction. I. Title.
PS3563.C38813B66 2004          2003063054
ISBN 0-7432-5555-0
ISBN 0-7432-5777-4 (Pbk.)

Several chapters in this book first appeared, in somewhat different form, in the following magazines: "The Vomitorium" first appeared in *The Sun* and was reprinted in the *G. W. Review*; "Power Lines" in *Punk Planet*; "The Price of Pain" in *The Florida Review*; "Sheridan Drive-in" in *Punk Planet*; "Junk Heaven" in *Third Coast*; "Peacock Alley" in *Sleepwalk*; "Smoke" in *Sun Dog: The Southeast Review*; "South Side Records" on the website *bandit-lit: The Journal of Empirical Literature* (www.bandit-lit.com); "The Book of Ralph" in *The Idaho Review*; "You" appeared as "Duke's" in *Crab Orchard Review*; "The Bear at Your Front Door" in *Natural Bridge*; "Red's" in *Third Coast*; "The Grand Illusion" in *Chelsea*; "A Diagram of the Future" in *The Florida Review*; and "Brains of the Operation" in *New England Review*. Earlier versions of "The Vomitorium," "Smoke," and "The Grand Illusion" also appeared in *Troublemakers* by John McNally (University of Iowa Press, 2000). Reprinted from *Troublemakers* by John McNally by permission of the University of Iowa Press.

# ACKNOWLEDGMENTS

**E**TERNAL GRATITUDE TO THE George Washington University in Washington, D.C., for the Jenny McKean Moore Fellowship, a one-year gift of time, housing, and money. Much of this book was written during that year. Special thanks to Faye Moskowitz and David McAleavey of GW—and to that boy who created a disturbance, poet Dan Gutstein. Wake Forest University was generous enough to let me defer employment for a year so that I could take this fellowship. Thank you to Gale Sigal, Jane Mead, Paul Escott, and the English Department at Wake.

Many thanks to the tireless magazine editors who were kind enough to publish several of the chapters in this book. Please subscribe to their magazines!

Thanks to Holly Carver, publisher of the University of Iowa Press, for all her kindness and support. Thanks again to Megan Scott, also at Iowa, for her smarts and continued help.

I'm grateful to the many booksellers I've met over the years. Thanks, in particular, to Jim Harris, owner of Prairie Lights Bookstore in Iowa City; to fiction writers Dean Bakopoulos and Jeremiah Chamberlin, formerly of Canterbury Books in Madison, Wisconsin; and to Lisa Howorth, Richard Howorth, and Jamie Kornegay of Square Books in

Oxford, Mississippi. The inimitable Paul Ingram at Prairie Lights Bookstore deserves his own page. Thank you, Paul.

The troublemakers at Columbia College in Chicago have been especially supportive. My gratitude to all the ruffians connected to Columbia's Story Week, the best damned literary event in the country, but especially to Randy Albers, Patty McNair, and that true ruffian's ruffian, Don DeGrazia. Special thanks to Mae Governale of *F Magazine* fame. Thanks, too, to publicist Sheryl Johnston, who does amazing and wonderful work.

My dear friends Ted Genoways and Mary Anne Andrei have come to the rescue time and again.

My good friend Michael Honch has kept the endless supply of books arriving at my doorstep. He's a man who knows a good sentence when he sees one.

My old grade school buddy Terry O'Brien resurfaced after many years, just in time to jar my memory about a good number of things, including the day I gave him a battery-powered book that electrocuted him when he opened it. My apologies.

My agent, Jenny Bent, is a lifesaver. She is every author's dream, and I can't thank her enough.

I am grateful for the enthusiasm and support of everyone at Free Press, most notably publisher Martha Levin; my editor, Dominick Anfuso; and his assistant, Wylie O'Sullivan. Thank you, thank you, thank you.

No one has been more supportive over the years than my father, Robert McNally.

My wife, Amy Knox Brown, has read this manuscript more times than any one person should have to read anything, but it is a stronger book because of it, and I am grateful for her patience and intelligence.

# CONTENTS

for Joe Caccamisi

# AUTHOR'S NOTE

THOSE READERS FAMILIAR WITH the southwest side of Chicago may be curious about a few details. For starters, the vast majority of this book takes place in a city that resembles Burbank, Illinois, a southwest suburb that borders Chicago. I'll confess: I grew up in Burbank, so the resemblance is, at times, uncanny. Some readers, I realize, are sticklers for accuracy. To those folks, I offer an apology. As a fiction writer, I've played fast and loose with certain details. For example, I have relocated a few stores inside Ford City Shopping Center. The fact is, my characters, who are sometimes as lazy as I am, weren't always up for the long walk across the mall. I also fabricated some stores for convenience's sake. While the names of businesses and buildings, past and present, have sometimes been used in this book, they are fictionalized versions that bear only superficial, if any, resemblances. The characters are all fabrications—creatures of my subconscious. The great story writer John Cheever used to insist that fiction was not crypto-autobiography. To paraphrase him, as it applies to this book, the grade school may look vaguely familiar, the locker is my actual locker, but the people wandering the halls are all strangers.

# THE PRESENT: 1978–1979

# THE VOMITORIUM

**R**ALPH RAN A HAND up and over his head, flattening his hair before some freak combination of wind and static electricity blew it straight up and into a real-life fright wig.

We were standing at the far edge of the blacktop at Jacqueline Bouvier Kennedy Grade School, as far away from the recess monitor as we could get. It was 1978, the year we started eighth grade, though Ralph would have been in high school already if he hadn't failed both the third and fifth grades. He was nearly a foot taller than the rest of us, and every few weeks new sprigs of whiskers popped up along his cheeks and chin, scaring the girls and prompting the principal, Mr. Santoro, to drop into our homeroom unexpectedly and deliver speeches about personal hygiene.

"Boys," Mr. Santoro would say. "Some of you are starting to look like hoodlums." Though he addressed his insult to all the boys, everyone knew he meant Ralph.

Today Ralph pulled a fat Sears catalog out of a grocery sack, shook it at me, and said, "Get a load of this." The catalog was fatter than it should have been, as if someone had dropped it into a swamp and left it there to rot.

"I don't think they sell that stuff anymore," I said. "That's a 1974 catalog, Ralph. That was four years ago."

"Quiet," Ralph said. He licked two fingers, smearing photos and words each time he touched a page to turn it. "I'll show you Patty O'Dell."

"You found it?" I said. "That's it?"

Ralph nodded.

Rumor was that Patty O'Dell had modeled panties for Sears when she was seven or eight, and for the past two years Ralph had diligently pursued the rumor. If there existed somewhere on this planet a photo of Patty O'Dell in nothing but her panties, Ralph was going to find it.

"Here she is, Hank," Ralph said. Reluctantly, he surrendered the mildewed catalog. "Careful with it."

Ralph stood beside me, arms crossed, guarding his treasure. His hair still stood on end, as if he had stuck the very fingers he had licked into a live socket. I looked down at the photo, then peeked up at Ralph, but he just nodded for me to keep my eyes on the catalog.

I had no idea why Ralph and I were friends. I was a B+ student, a model citizen. Ralph already had a criminal record, a string of shoplifting charges all along Chicago's southwest side. He kept mug shots of himself in his wallet. The first time I met Ralph, he had walked up to me and asked if he could bum a smoke. That was four years ago. I was nine. I didn't smoke, but I didn't tell Ralph that. I said, "Sorry. Smoked the last one at recess."

The photo in the catalog was, in fact, of a girl wearing only panties. She was holding each of her shoulders so that her arms crisscrossed over her chest, and though I was starting to feel the first tremors of a boner, the girl in the photo was *not* Patty O'Dell. Not even close. After two years of fruitless searching, Ralph was starting to get desperate.

"That's not her," I said.

"Of course it's her," he said.

"You're crazy," I said.

"Give it to me." Ralph snatched the catalog out of my hands.

"Ralph. Get real. All you need to do is look at Patty, then look at the girl in the photo. They look nothing alike."

Ralph and I scanned the blacktop, searching for Patty O'Dell. It was Halloween, and I couldn't help myself: I looked instead for girls dressed like cats. All year I would dream about the girls who came to school as cats . . . Mary Polaski zipped up inside of a one-piece cat costume, purring, meowing, licking her paws while her stiff, curled tail vibrated behind her with each step she took. Or Gina Morales, actually down on all fours, crawling along the scuffed tile floor of our classroom: up one aisle, down the next, brushing against our legs, and letting us pet her. The very thought of it now gave my heart pause. It stole my breath. But only the younger kids dressed up anymore, and all I could find on the blacktop were Darth Vaders and Chewbaccas, C-3POs and R2-D2s, the occasional Snoopy.

The seventh- and eighth-graders were already tired of Halloween, tired of shenanigans, slouching and yawning, waiting for the day to come to an end. Among us, only Wes Papadakis wore a costume, a full-head rubber *Creature from the Black Lagoon* mask suctioned to his face. Next to him was Pete Elmazi, who wore his dad's Vietnam army jacket every day to school, no matter the season, and whose older brother was locked up in a juvenile home for delinquents because he'd beaten another kid to death with a baseball bat. There was Fred Lesniewski, who stood alone, an outcast for winning the science fair eight years in a row, since everyone knew his father worked at Argonne National Laboratory—where the white deer of genetic experiments loped behind a hurricane-wire fence, and where tomatoes grew to be the size of pumpkins—and that it was Fred's father (and not Fred) who was responsible for such award-winning projects as "How to Split an Atom in Your Own Kitchen" and "The Zero-Gravity Chamber: Step Inside!"

There were all of these losers, plus a few hundred more, but no Patty. Then, as a sea of people parted, Ralph spotted her and pointed, and at the far end of an ever widening path I saw her: Patty O'Dell. Ralph and I stared speechless, conjuring up the Patty of panty ads, a nearly naked Patty O'Dell letting a stranger snap photos of her while she stood under the hot, blinding lights in her bare feet. It was a thought so unfathomable, I might as well have been trying to grasp a mental picture of infinity, as complex and mysterious as the idea of something never coming to an end.

"You're right," Ralph said, shaking his head. "It's not her." He tossed the catalog off to the side of the blacktop, as if it were a fish too small to keep. He shook his head sadly and said, "Damn, Hank. I thought we had her."

Ralph had told me to meet him outside my house at eight, that his older cousin Norm was going to pick us up and take us to a party. Norm had just started dating Patty O'Dell's older sister, Jennifer, and with Norm's help, Ralph and I hoped to get to the bottom of the panty ads, maybe even score a few mint-condition catalogs from Jennifer, if at all possible.

"You got a costume?" Ralph asked.

"Of course I do," I said. "I've got all sorts of costumes. Hundreds!"

I had lied to Ralph; I didn't own any costumes. In fact, I'd had no plans of dressing up this year. But now I was trapped into scrounging up whatever I could, piecing together a costume from scratch.

My sister, Kelly—though disgusted by my choice and unable to conceal her revulsion—expertly applied the makeup.

"Of all the costumes," she said.

"What's wrong with Gene Simmons? What's wrong with KISS?" I asked.

"One day," she said, smearing grease paint from my eye all the way up to my ear and back. "One day you'll look back on this moment, and you'll consider shooting yourself."

"Okay," I said. "Whatever."

"Just let me know when you reach that point," Kelly said, "and I'll supply the gun."

I found hidden at the back of my parents' closet a stiff black wig hugging a Styrofoam ball. I sneaked a dinner roll out to the garage, spray-painted it black, then pinned it to the top of the wig, hoping it would look like a bun of hair. My parents didn't own any leather, but I found a black Naugahyde jacket instead, along with a pair of black polyester slacks I wore to church. For the final touch, my sister gave me her clogs. She was two years older than me, and her feet were exactly my size.

In the living room, in the shifting light of the color TV, my parents stared at me with profound sadness, as if all their efforts on my behalf had proven futile. My mother looked for a moment as though she might speak, then she turned away, back to the final minutes of *M\*A\*S\*H*.

Outside, I met Ralph. As far as I could tell, his only costume was a cape. A long black cape. One look at Ralph, and I suddenly felt the weight of what I'd done to myself. Ralph said, "What're you supposed to be? A transvestite?"

"I'm Gene Simmons," I said. "From KISS."

"Jesus," Ralph said. He reached up and touched the dinner roll on top of my head. "What's that?"

"It's a bun," I said.

"I can see *that*," Ralph said. "But why would you put a hamburger bun on top of your head? And why would you paint it black?"

"It's not *that* kind of bun," I said.

"Oh."

"At least I'm wearing a costume," I said. "Look at you. Where's *your* costume? All you've got on is a cape."

Ralph smiled and pulled his left hand from his cape. Butter knives were attached to each of his fingers, including his thumb.

"Holy smoke," I said. It was the most impressive thing I'd ever seen.

"I'm an Etruscan," he said, pronouncing it carefully while rattling his knives in front of my face.

"A what?"

"An Etruscan," Ralph said. "I've been reading a lot of history lately."

"History?" I said. This was news to me. Ralph hated school.

"Yeah," he said. "Stuff about the Romans."

"Romans," I said. I didn't tell Ralph, but I knew a little something about the Romans myself. I wrote my very first research paper in the sixth grade on them, though all I remembered was bits and pieces: the Gallic War, the Ides of March, some creep named Brutus stabbing Caesar to death. The idea of Ralph picking up a book and actually reading it was so preposterous, I decided to lob a few slow ones out to him and test what little he knew against what little I knew.

"So," I said. "What do you think about Caesar?"

"A great man," he said. "He brought a lot of people together."

"Oh really. How'd he do that?"

"Violence," Ralph said. I expected him to smile, but he didn't. His eyes, I noticed, were closer together than I had realized, and his eyebrows were connected by a swatch of fuzz. Ralph glared at me, as if he were thinking about punching me to illustrate what he'd just said. But the thought must have passed, and he said, "Etruscans were the original gladiators. Crazy but smart. Geniuses, actually. Very artistic."

"How'd you get the knives to stick to your fingers?"

"Krazy Glue," Ralph said.

I nodded appreciatively. I had always feared Krazy Glue, scared I'd accidentally glue myself to my mother or father, or to a lamppost. I'd seen such things on the news, men and women rushed to the hospital, their fingers permanently connected to their foreheads.

"What if they don't come off?" I asked.

Ralph said, "I thought of that. That's why I glued them to my fingernails. My fingernails will grow out, see. And then I can clip them."

"You're a genius," I said.

"I'm an Etruscan," he said. "Very brilliant, but violent."

Ralph's cousin Norm eventually pulled up in a Chevy Impala and motioned with his head for us to get in. He was twenty-five years old and ghoulishly thin, but the veins in his arms were thick and bulging to the point where you'd think they were going to explode right there. A spooky guy with spooky veiny arms, but he worked at the Tootsie Roll factory on Cicero Avenue along with Ralph's other cousin, Kenny, and he gave me and Ralph bags of Tootsie Pops each month, which made up in part for the spookiness.

I took the backseat; Ralph rode shotgun. Norm said nothing about our costumes. I reached up and made sure the bun on top of my wig was still there. Norm gunned the engine, then floored it. Blurry strings of ghosts, clowns, and pirates appeared and disappeared along the sidewalk. Pumpkins beamed at us from porch stoops.

A mile or two later, Ralph said, "Where we going, Norm?"

"I've got some business to take care of first."

"What kind of business?"

"I've got a trunkful of goods I need to unload."

Ralph cocked his head. If he were a dog, his ears would have stiffened. He loved the prospect of anything criminal. "Goods," Ralph repeated. "Are they stolen?"

"What do you think?" Norm said.

Ralph turned around, smiled at me, then looked at Norm again. "What kind of goods?" he asked.

Norm lifted his veiny arm and pointed at Ralph. "None of your business," he said. "The less you know, the better."

Ralph nodded. Norm was the only person who could talk to Ralph like that and get away with it. A few minutes later, Norm pulled into a White Hen Pantry parking lot. "I need some smokes," he said, and left us alone with the engine running.

Ralph turned around in his seat. "So what do you think's in the trunk?"

"I don't know," I said.

"Drugs," Ralph said. "That's my guess. Stolen drugs." He turned back to the White Hen to watch his cousin. He rested his hand with the knives on the dashboard and began drumming them quickly. "Maybe guns," he said. "A trunkload of semiautomatic machine guns."

Norm returned to the car, sucking on a cigarette so hard that the tip turned bright orange and crackled. He filled the entire car with smoke and said, "I ran into a little trouble two nights ago. Serious trouble. I'll admit, I fucked up. But hey, everyone fucks up every now and then, right? Huh? Am I right?"

"Right," Ralph said.

"Right on," I said. I lifted my fist in the air, a symbol of brotherhood, but nobody paid any attention.

"I had to get on the ball," Norm said. "Think fast. Figure out a way to come up with some money, pronto."

"What happened?" Ralph asked.

Norm looked at Ralph, then down at Ralph's fingers with the attached butter knives, as if he hadn't noticed them until this very second. He turned to me, squinting, raising his cigarette to his mouth for another deep puff. "Just what the hell are you guys supposed to be, anyway?"

Ralph said, "I'm an Etruscan."

"And I'm Gene Simmons," I said. "From KISS."

"The Etruscans," Norm said. "I never heard of those guys. They must be new. But KISS—" He snorted. "That's sissy shit. You should've gone as

Robert Plant. Or Jimmy Page. Or somebody from Blue Öyster Cult. Now, *that* I'd have respected."

Then Norm put the car in drive and peeled out.

The longer we sat in the car, the more I thought of Patty O'Dell wearing nothing but panties, and the more I thought of Patty O'Dell, the more I had to cross and uncross my legs.

Norm wheeled quickly into the parking lot of a ratty complex called Royal Chateau Apartments and said, "Give me a few minutes, guys. If the deal goes through, we'll party. If not, I'm screwed. Big time." He opened the door and got out. He slammed the door so hard, my ears popped.

Ralph turned around and said, "How's it going back there?"

I gave him the thumbs-up.

Ralph said, "Let's take a look and see what he's got in the trunk."

"I don't think that's a good idea," I said.

"C'mon," Ralph said. "Pretend you're Gene Simmons. What would he do in a situation like this?"

I leaned my head back and stuck my tongue all the way out, but the bun on top of my wig flopped over, cutting short my impression. A pin, apparently, had fallen out.

"I got the Krazy Glue with me," Ralph said. "You want me to glue it down?"

"I'm fine," I said.

Ralph reached over, turned off the car, and jerked the keys from the ignition.

"Hey," I said. "What're you doing?" But Ralph was already outside, leaving me with no choice. I got out, too.

By the time I reached the trunk, Ralph had already inserted the key in the lock. "Ready?" he asked. He turned the key, and the trunk hissed open. Slowly, he lifted the trunk's lid, as if it were the lid of a treasure chest and we were seeing whether the mutiny had been worth the trouble.

"Holy crap!" Ralph said. "Would you look at that?"

My heart paused briefly before kicking back in and pounding harder than ever. I'd never seen anything like it. The entire trunk was packed full of bite-size Tootsie Rolls. There must have been a few thousand. I dipped my hand inside and ran my fingers through them. Ralph scraped his knives gently across the heap as if it were a giant cat wanting to be scratched.

"Norm," Ralph said, frowning and nodding at the same time, clearly impressed with his cousin. "He's a real thinking man's man. He knows when to steal and when not to. Don't you see? This is perfect. I mean, when's the only time people start thinking bulk Tootsie Rolls? Halloween, man."

"Halloween's almost over," I said.

Ralph pointed his forefinger/butter knife at me and said, "That's the point exactly. People are running out of candy. They're getting desperate. Here's where Norm comes in. Bingo!"

"We better shut the trunk," I said.

"Not yet," Ralph said. "I'm hungry. Give me a hand. Start stuffing some of these babies in my pockets."

Ralph and I scooped up handfuls of Tootsie Rolls and dumped them into Ralph's cape pocket. Then Ralph shoved as many as he could into his jeans pockets. Twice, he accidentally poked my head with a butter knife.

"Watch it," I said. "You're gonna put my eye out."

"Count yourself lucky," Ralph said. "An Etruscan would've chopped off your head or thrown you to a lion by now."

We shut the trunk and waited for Norm. Using only his teeth and one hand, Ralph unrolled Tootsie Roll after Tootsie Roll and crammed them into his mouth until his cheeks bulged and chocolate juice dribbled down his chin. He started talking, but his mouth was so full I couldn't understand a word he was saying.

"Uh-huh," I said. "Oh yeah? Really? No kidding, Ralph," I said.

When he finally swallowed the boulder of chocolate, he said, "What's your problem? You're not making any sense."

Out of the corner of my eye I spotted Norm. I nudged Ralph. Norm was walking toward us along with a fat guy decked out in a red, white, and blue sweatsuit. The man's hair was sticking up on one side but flat on the other, as if Norm had woken him.

When Norm saw us, he shot us a look and said, "Get off the trunk, you punks." To the man, he said, "All I need are the keys . . ."

"I got 'em," Ralph said. "Here." He tossed them to Norm; Norm glared at Ralph, a look that said, *We'll talk about this later.*

"Didn't want to waste gas," Ralph said. "Remember when they had that shortage?"

The fat guy said, "I ain't got all day. Let's take a look."

Norm nodded, popped the trunk.

Where there had once been a mound of Tootsie Rolls was now an obvious trench. I didn't realize we'd taken that many. I looked at Ralph, but he just pulled another Tootsie Roll from his cape pocket and unrolled it with his teeth and weapon-free hand.

The fat guy said, "These are the small ones. I thought you were talking about the long ones."

"They're the same thing," Norm said. "One's just smaller than the other."

The guy shook his head. "Look, Slick. To make a profit, I got to sell a hundred of these for every twenty of the big ones. You see what I'm saying? Kids want the ones they can stick in their mouths like a big cigar."

"That's true," Ralph whispered to me.

"Okay," Norm said. "All right. You want to haggle? Fine. I respect that."

But the guy was already walking away, back to his Royal Chateau, saying, "No can do, Slick. No business tonight."

After the man rounded the corner, I looked up at Norm, afraid he was going to yell at us, but he was holding two fistfuls of his own hair and yanking on it. "I'm *fucked,*" he said. "Do you hear me? I . . . am . . . *fucked.*"

Ralph made a move to offer Norm a few Tootsie Rolls, but when I nudged him again, he thought better of it, slipping the stolen goods back into his own pocket, keeping them out of Norm's sight.

For an hour we sat in Norm's car and said nothing while Norm drove. Ralph started running his butter knives through his hair, giving himself a scalp massage. "Hey, Norm," Ralph finally said. "What do you know about Patty O'Dell posing naked for a Sears catalog?"

Norm said, "Would you mind shutting up a minute and letting me think?"

"Sure," Ralph said. He turned back to me and said, "Hey, Hank. Quit talking. Let the man think."

"What am *I* doing?" I asked.

"Both of you," Norm said. "Shut the hell up."

Norm drove us in circles, a loop that kept returning us to Seventy-ninth and Harlem, a corner Ralph and I knew well because it was the home of the Haunted Trails Miniature Golf Range (where Ralph and I enjoyed chipping golf balls over the fence and into heavy traffic). Behind Haunted Trails was the Sheridan Drive-in, where we could sneak through a chopped-out part of the fence and watch women take off their clothes on a screen the size of a battleship.

I liked any movie with martial arts, and Ralph liked disaster movies, but we both preferred movies about women in prison. We never heard any of the dialogue—we were always too far from the rows of cast-iron speakers—so Ralph would pass the night speculating about what was going on: "See that chick?" Ralph would say. "She probably killed her old man. That's why the warden pulled her pants down."

The seventh time Norm made the loop, I gave up any hope of ever getting to a party. When Norm finally deviated from the endless loop, he jerked a quick right into Guidish Park mobile homes. He stopped the car, killed the lights, and turned back to me.

"I need a favor," he said.

It was so dark, I couldn't even see his face. "What?" I said.

"I want you to take something to number forty-seven—it's about a half-block up there—and I want you to give it to whoever answers the door and tell them I'll get the rest of the money tomorrow. Okay?"

I didn't want to do it—my bowels felt on the verge of collapsing—but I was awful at standing up for myself, unable to tell someone older than me no, if only because my parents had trained me too well. I was dutiful to the end. So I told Norm okay, and when I stepped out of the car, he rolled his window down and handed over a cardboard cylinder. It was about a foot long. After walking away, I shook it but couldn't hear anything inside. Only when I passed under a streetlamp did I see what I was holding: a giant Tootsie Roll bank. It had a removable tin cap with a slit for depositing coins. I shook it again but couldn't hear any change.

At number 47, I knocked lightly on the door, two taps with a single knuckle. I was about to give up when the door creaked open and a man poked his head outside. He narrowed his eyes and inspected my costume. Without looking away, he reached off to the side and asked, "You like Butterfingers or Milk Duds?"

"Milk Duds," I said. "But actually, I've got something for *you*. It's from Norm."

Before I could smile and surrender the giant Tootsie Roll, I was yanked inside the trailer by the scruff of my Naugahyde jacket. He shut the door behind us and said, "Who are you?"

"His cousin," I lied.

"Uh-huh," he said, nodding. "So you're the famous *Ralph* I've heard so much about."

"I guess so," I said.

"My name's Bob. Can you remember to tell that to Norm? *Bob*."

"Sure," I said.

"I'm Jennifer's brother," Bob said.

"Jennifer O'Dell?" I asked.

"That's right."

"So you must be Patty's brother, too." I glanced quickly around the room for catalogs. Bob kept his eyes on me, then squeezed the giant Tootsie Roll as if it were my neck, until the lid popped off. He emptied it onto a card table. The best I could tell, there were three tens and a twenty, along with a note folded into a tight triangle, the kind we used in homeroom as footballs.

"Maybe I should go," I said.

Bob put his hand out as if he were a traffic cop and said, "Not yet. Follow me." We walked down a short and narrow hallway to a door at the far end of the trailer. When Bob opened the door, he motioned for me to join him inside the room.

It was dark, almost too dark to see, the only light coming from the room behind us. Two women were resting in bed, and at first I wanted to laugh, because one of the women was wearing Wes Papadakis's *Creature from the Black Lagoon* mask, and the thought of a grown woman lying in bed in the dark wearing a stupid rubber mask struck just the right chord in me tonight. Bob was trying to scare me, his very own Halloween prank, but I wasn't falling for it. I started snickering when Bob flipped on the light and I saw her face. I wanted to look away, but I couldn't. It kept drawing me in, like a pinwheel or a pendulum: *eyes so puffy she could barely see out . . . lips cracked open and swollen . . . the zigzag of stitches along her nostril.*

The other woman sitting on the bed was actually still a girl, and when I realized who it was, that it was Patty O'Dell, I quit breathing. She was wearing a long white T-shirt that she kept pulling over her knees, trying to hide herself from me. I knew it was the wrong time to think about it, I knew it shouldn't even have crossed my mind, but I wanted to believe that she was naked underneath that T-shirt. I tried imagining it, too: Patty lifting the shirt up and over her head, taking it off, until she was completely naked on the bed. But each time I got to the naked part, I would glance over at her sister—I couldn't help it—and the nude Patty in my head would dissolve into something dark and grainy.

When I finally gave up, I raised my hand and said, "Hi, Patty," but Patty turned away from me and stared at the wall.

"How much did he bring?" Jennifer asked.

Bob huffed. "Fifty bucks."

Jennifer looked down at her hands.

"There's a note, too," Bob said. He unfolded the triangle and said, "Oh, this is classic. You'll love this. He spelled your name wrong. He doesn't even know how to spell your name. Hey. Big surprise. The man's *illiterate.*" Bob laughed and shook his head. "Says here he'll try to get you the rest of the money tomorrow."

"Figures," she said.

Bob crumpled the note and said, "So what should we tell Gene Simmons? We can't keep an important man, a man of his *stature,* tied up all night."

"Tell Norm it's too late. He had his chance. That was the agreement. A thousand dollars or I'd call the police and file a complaint."

Bob looked at me. "You got that?"

I nodded.

"Good," Bob said. "Tell him to expect the police at his door in, oh, let's say an hour, two at the most. Maybe that'll teach the son of a bitch not to hit a woman."

My clogs clopped hollowly against the asphalt all the way back to the car. The night was officially ruined. I might not have been able to hold infinity in my mind, but I sure as hell knew the end of something when I saw it.

My stomach cramped up as if it had been punctured, as if my body were somehow poisoning itself. I was angry at Norm, certainly, angry at Norm for beating up Jennifer, angry at Norm for driving us around and acting like it was nothing, a mistake, a mistake anyone could make . . . but I was angrier at Norm for how Patty had looked at me then looked away, angry because I was close to something, I wasn't sure what, but each time I got within reach, I looked over at Jennifer, I saw her face, and it all disappeared. Norm had ruined it for me, whatever it was. For that I wanted to hurt Norm myself, but the closer I got to him, the more unlikely that seemed. I was thirteen. Norm was twenty-five. What could I possibly do?

Near the Impala, I heard someone gagging, trying to catch his breath. I dashed around the car and found Ralph bent over a pool of vomit next to a tire. Ralph's door was open, and the dome light inside the car lit up half of his face. Norm was slumped down, his hand drooped over the steering wheel, a cigarette smoldering between two fingers. The radio was on low. Ralph's fingers clanked together, and I thought of Brutus, his knife plunging into Caesar again and again.

"What did he do to you?" I whispered to Ralph. "Did he punch you in the stomach?"

"Who?" Ralph asked, still bent over, not looking at me.

"Norm," I said.

Ralph peeked up, fangs of vomit dripping from his chin. "Why would Norm punch me in the stomach?"

"You're throwing up," I said.

"I know. I ate too many Tootsie Rolls," Ralph said. "Besides, it's a Roman ritual. Eat till you puke. I wanted to see if I could do it. You should congratulate me."

After Ralph cleaned himself off with handfuls of loose dirt and the inside of his cape, we slid back into the car. Ralph said, "The first vomitorium on the South Side of Chicago. People will travel from miles around to come here and yak their brains out."

Norm revved the engine. He said, "So? What did she say?"

"She wants to talk to you," I lied.

"Oh yeah?"

"She wants you to go home," I said, thinking of the police at his door later tonight, knocking with their billy clubs. "She said she'll be there in an hour," I added.

"Really," Norm said, sticking the cigarette in the corner of his mouth and pounding the steering wheel with his palm. "What do you know about that? She's forgiven me."

"You bet," I said.

Norm shook his head and put the car in reverse. Back on Harlem Avenue, he said, "So where do you boys want to go?"

"Home," I said.

"Home it is!" Norm said. He said *home* as if it were an exotic place, like Liechtenstein or the Bermuda Triangle.

We drove in silence the first few miles. Then Norm said, "You think I should buy her some roses?"

"Nah," I said. "No sense wasting your money."

I could see Norm's eyes in the rearview mirror. He was watching me, but I couldn't tell if he knew I was lying. At a stoplight he turned around and said, "Gene Simmons, huh?"

"Gene Simmons," I said.

"From KISS," Ralph added.

Norm said, "When I was in high school, I went to a costume party dressed as Jim Croce. I glued on this big hairy-ass mustache and walked around with a cigar and sang 'Operator.' Chicks dug it." He smiled nostalgically until people behind us started honking. The light had turned green. "All right!" he yelled. "Shut the fuck up! I'm *going* already!"

Not far from the junior college, a pack of men and women wearing togas trudged along a sidewalk, hooting and raising bottles of liquor above their heads. "Would you look at that," Norm said.

Ralph cranked down the window for a better view. He said, "Stop the car."

"What?"

"Stop the car, Norm. I need to join them."

"Why?"

Ralph, peering out the window at the throng of bedsheets and olive wreaths, said, "My people."

"What people?" Norm asked.

"Romans!" Ralph got out of the car and yelled to the passing crowd: "Greetings!" He raised his hand with the butter knives in salutation, and the Romans went wild. They beckoned Ralph over, and he loped across the street.

Norm shook his head. "He's something else, ain't he? Half the time I forget we're related."

I had turned back to Norm, but Norm was still watching Ralph, amazed. I studied Norm but found no clues, no trace of what I was looking for, so I decided to ask him to see what he'd say. "Why'd you do it?"

Norm's eyes moved slowly from Ralph to me, focusing, his pupils seeming to grow. His brow furrowed, and he looked like he really wanted to answer me, as if the reasons were somewhere on the tip of his tongue. Then he shook his head and said, "Hell, I don't know. You lose control sometimes." He rubbed his hand up over his hair in such a way that it stood on end, the way Ralph's hair had stood on end this morning . . . a family gene, I suspected, a whole genealogy of screwed-up things inside him that he didn't understand, would *never* understand . . . and I thought, *Of course Norm doesn't know. Of course.* Not that the answer to my question was any comfort. Just the opposite, in fact.

Slowly we drove on, though a block away, as the last goblin of the night floated beside us, I couldn't resist. I turned and looked out the back window again.

The Romans were holding Ralph aloft, over their heads, and chanting his name. Ralph, floating above them, looked so content, so pleased, you could almost be fooled into believing he was leading his people into Chicago, as Caesar had gone into Gaul, to bring us all, by way of murder and pillage, together as one people, one tribe.

# POWER LINES

**T**HE POWER COMPANY IN Chicago wanted to do something nice for the kids, so they let the city construct parks where their power-line towers sat. Where I lived were three of these parks, each with a two-hoop basketball court, a swing set, a merry-go-round, a slide, and a couple of giant cast-iron insects that sat atop industrial-size springs, all in the shadows of wires, hundreds of them, strung from tower to tower like garland at Christmastime. Every few hours the power lines surged. The buzzing, growing louder, was the sound I imagined a man in an electric chair heard as his own sour spirit detached from his body, the way a large Band-Aid would sound peeled from a hairy leg.

I wasn't much of an athlete, but I liked throwing my basketball around at New Castle Park, one of the three parks with the power-line towers. Everyone I knew watched the Harlem Globetrotters on TV, and for a while it seemed that every kid in town owned a red, white, and blue basketball. At least once a day you'd see some poor kid trying to dribble a figure eight between and around his legs. It was embarrassing to watch—his bulging-eyed concentration, his rigor-mortis legs forming an upside-down U, the slippery ball flipped into the street, sometimes in front of a speeding car. My favorite Globetrotters were Meadowlark Lemon and Curly Neal, but I knew I'd never be able to do what they could do, and so I was satisfied with banging the basketball off the backboard, occasionally making a basket, all under the constant hum and crackle of the power lines. I threw that ball again and again, trying to empty my head of all thoughts. It wasn't as easy as it sounded, draining away your own past and future, trying to exist in whatever moment you happened to be in—not a second before and not a second after. This was how I imagined insects spent their days. I had stared hard into the eyes of a fly once, wondering if it ever, even for a second, thought about what it had done the day before. One time I stared at a grasshopper for thirty minutes, hoping for a sign, a look of reflection, but I wasn't so sure that it even remembered what it was doing when I first began looking at it. One thing I learned was that it was difficult to *not* think about anything, because thinking about *not* thinking was actually thinking about *something.* The idea of *nothing* fascinated me. I loved the idea of nothing, because it didn't seem possible. How could there ever be *nothing?* There couldn't! And so I'd throw the ball again and again, until I'd get a splitting headache trying to think of nothing but thinking about everything else instead. I always got a headache playing basketball, and I always took this as my sign to go home.

One fall day I saw Ralph trudging along New Castle Avenue, dragging a burlap bag behind him.

"What's in there?" I yelled from the basketball court.

Ralph stopped, then looked up and around, into the air, as if he'd been hearing voices his entire life.

"Over here!" I said.

Ralph turned, saw me. He didn't smile. He didn't wave. He nodded, which was about as friendly a greeting as a person could expect from Ralph, then he made his way over. His wallet was connected to a long drooping chain that rattled when he walked, and he was wearing a hooded sweatshirt with the hood up. The bag slid up the curb and bounced across the park's grass. He said, "What're you doing? Playing basketball by yourself?"

"You want to play some Horse?" I asked.

"Horse?" He narrowed his eyes as if the game might involve one of us riding the other around the basketball court. I hadn't really thought about it before, but I'd never seen Ralph in possession of any kind of sporting equipment. Since Ralph was two years older than the other eighth-graders, the principal wouldn't let him take gym class with us. I wasn't even sure what he did during that period. Ralph said, "You come here a lot? By yourself?"

"All the time," I said.

Ralph nodded. He said, "My cousins, they know a guy who knows a guy who knows something about electricity. See these power lines? This guy, the one who knows this guy that my cousins know, he said if you spend too much time around these things, you'll end up sterile."

"Sterile?" I said. I suspected that the look I was giving him was the same look that he'd given me at the suggestion of Horse. I knew being sterile meant I would never have kids, and I knew roughly what part of my body it had to do with, but I wasn't sure of the specifics. How, for instance, could something that didn't even touch me make me sterile?

"*Who's this guy?*" I asked.

"He's some guy who knows a guy who knows my cousins."

"And he's an expert on electricity?"

"So I've been told," Ralph said.

We stood there a moment without saying a word. The power lines sizzled above. I looked down at Ralph's burlap bag—a gunnysack, my mother would have called it. There was a lump in it about the size and shape of a small animal, like a possum.

Ralph said, "I better not stand here long. I normally don't even walk on this street."

"Afraid of getting sterile?" I asked.

I expected Ralph to laugh or at least smile, but he didn't. He nodded. "Don't want to risk it," he said.

Ralph, heading back to the street, dragged the lump behind him. I was about to yell out to him, to ask again what was in his sack, but a sharp pain tore through my head, causing me to drop the basketball. The ball bounced once, twice, a third time, each bounce closer to the last until it was vibrating against the ground, then dying and rolling toward the fence. To stop thinking about the searing pain inside my head, I tried imagining what was in Ralph's sack. A cat? A bucket's worth of sand? A couple of meat loafs? I shut my eyes and concentrated hard, harder than I had ever concentrated in my life, and while the power lines started to surge, the buzz growing so loud I was afraid that the towers themselves were going to burst into flames, an image of what was in the sack finally came to me: a baby, *my* baby, and Ralph, like some ghost from the future, rattling chains but spooked by his own sad mission, had come to show me what would never be.

# THE PRICE OF PAIN

**I** HAD SECRETLY HOPED that eighth grade would be different somehow, that a cute girl from another state would transfer to Jacqueline Bouvier Kennedy Grade School and fall insanely in love with me, maybe start stalking me all over Chicago's South Side, or that I would crack a joke on the playground, my best joke ever, and win over a whole new batch of friends, or that my clothes would fit better, that my teachers would take me under their wings, that for reasons I couldn't imagine yet, the principal, Mr. Santoro, would commission a bronze bust likeness of me to be placed in the school's entryway so all the new kids, from here on out, could walk respectfully past it and think, *So THAT'S what Hank Boyd looked like!* But as the school year wore on, I began fearing that eighth grade wasn't going to be any different from any other grade.

One cold, drizzly day in November, Ralph came springing nonchalantly toward me on the playground.

"I finished that list," he said.

"What list?"

"You know," he said, growing impatient. "The *list.*"

And then I remembered. On the last day of seventh grade, all the way back in June, he'd told me about a price list he was working on, prices he charged to do bodily harm to his fellow classmates. For a fee, he could be hired to take care of someone you didn't like. Now, as if the sun had set only once since we'd last talked about it, Ralph was telling me that he had finished it.

I held out my hand for the list, stifling a yawn. I really wanted to see it, but I didn't want to act too interested. It was dangerous to act too interested in anything that interested Ralph. As I unfolded the sheet, Ralph said, "You want me to take somebody out for you?"

"Maybe," I lied.

Ralph nodded. "Let me know and I'll write up an estimate."

I grunted.

Ralph launched into the history of the list, how his list was the exact same list that the meanest gang in New York City used in the 1880s, a group of thugs who called themselves the Whyo gang. I was about to ask him how he knew all of this when he unfolded another sheet that clearly had been torn from a book.

"Where'd you get that?" I asked.

"Library."

"You tore up a library book?" I asked. Tearing up a library book ranked right up there with flag burning and swearing in church. I loved the library. I would read a book about anything—kung fu, the Incas, silent movie stars with names like Fatty and Buster, the Loch Ness monster. We didn't have any books at home, and so I always felt the stab of anger when, at the library, I found a page scribbled on or a wad of chewing gum holding two pages together. And now here I stood face-to-face with the culprit himself. "Don't tell me you tore up a library book," I said.

Ralph shrugged. "I didn't have a library card. Listen. Forget the library, okay? Why are you always distracting me?"

"Why didn't you just get a card?" I asked.

Ralph stepped up so the tips of his shoes were touching the tips of my shoes. He said, "I don't know *why* I didn't just get a card, okay? Who cares. Listen. My *point* is that the leader of that gang had this exact same price list on him when he was arrested." He took a step back and said, "I thought about raising the prices, but after thinking about it all summer, I finally decided to keep them the same. It'll be part of my selling point; 1978 service at 1880 prices!"

For having been held back two grades, Ralph took great care in his own personal projects. His list—which he'd copied from the vandalized library book—had been carefully typed, with only a few blobs of Liquid Paper, raised like braille, covering the typos.

| | |
|---|---|
| • Punching | $2. |
| • Both eyes blacked | 4. |
| • Nose and jaw broke | 10. |
| • Jacked out (blackjacked) | 15. |
| • Ear chawed off | 15. |
| • Leg and arm broke | 19. |
| • Shot in leg | 25. |
| • Stab | 25. |
| • Doing the big job (murder) | 100. and up. |

"Wow!" I said. "Fifteen bucks for a chawed-off ear?"

"Ask around," Ralph said. "You won't find it any cheaper."

"How's business been?"

"Slow. But I wasn't expecting much in the fall. It takes a while for word of mouth to start working."

I handed the list back to him. I was impressed with it, but it also gave me the creeps to hold. I didn't know why Ralph and I were friends. The best I could figure, it was because I'd been taught to be polite. Everyone else was too afraid of Ralph to stand around and listen to what he had to say. But the more I listened to him, the more I liked him. If I were any smarter, though, I would have done what the other kids did—run full tilt in the opposite direction. For better or worse, it was too late for that.

"Hey," Ralph said. "You want to get an ice-cream cone and terrorize some kids?"

"Nah, I gotta get home," I said. "I'm supposed to go somewhere with my parents."

"Suit yourself," Ralph said, "but all week long I've had a craving."

"For ice cream?" I asked.

"Nuh-uh," he said. "For terrorizing kids." I expected him to grin, but he didn't. He folded the price list and tucked it away. Then he cracked his knuckles, one at a time, and took his place in line with the rest of the eighth-graders.

Before I could shut the front door behind me, Kelly yawned at my arrival, then delivered the news: "Grandma's been arrested." She said this without inflection, as if telling me what was on TV today, a new show called *Grandma's Been Arrested.* She was two years older than me and about as exciting as a fuse box.

In our family, Kelly was always the bearer of bad news. I was starting to think she *liked* delivering bad news, that bad news traveled through her like an electrical current, and to get too close to her was like sticking your finger into a light socket.

"*Our* grandmother?" I asked.

Kelly rolled her eyes. "Uh, *duh,*" she said, which had become her new favorite phrase. She'd say this to Mom and Dad, to our aunts and uncles, to our neighbors. I'd heard her say this into phones, into parked cars, to stray dogs and cats, to her stuffed animals, to people on TV. I had heard it through walls, from either the floor above or the floor below me, with screen doors separating us, from the opposite sides of picket fences, around grocery-store aisles, and once while passing a large bush. Lately, I'd begun to hear it in my dreams, and I was starting to wonder if Kelly was sneaking into my room at night and whispering it into my ear: *Uh, duh . . . Uh, duh . . . Uh, duh . . .*

I said, "What for?"

"What for *what?*"

"What was she *arrested* for?"

"Oh," Kelly said. "Stealing shoes."

"Shoes?"

"Yep. *Allegedly,* she'd go into shoe stores, try on some snazzy shoes, and then when the salesman wasn't looking, she'd walk out of the store wearing them. She was doing it all over town, so the owners set up a sting operation."

"A sting operation?" I said. "For Grandma?"

Before Kelly could answer, the front door banged open, causing me to jump and clutch my chest. Mom and Dad came in, but without Gramsie.

Dad said, "We have to wait until she's arraigned tomorrow morning, and then the judge will set bail. Bail! Jesus Christ. I can't believe what I'm saying. *Bail!* Do we have any beer? Kelly, go check the fridge and see if there's any beer."

I said, "Maybe we should get a good lawyer."

Dad said, "Is my last name Rockefeller? Do you see me throwing hundred-dollar bills in our fireplace to keep the house warm?"

"What fireplace?" I asked.

"Exactly," Dad said, cocking his head and squinting while firing up a cigarette.

Kelly returned with a beer for my father. She popped it open and handed it to him, and my father smiled at her, then poured half the beer down his throat. His eyes turned glassy. "Jesus Christ," he said, "sometimes there's nothing as good as a cold beer." He let his knees relax so he could drop, in one swift motion, into his recliner.

Kelly was the one who fetched things for Mom and Dad, who didn't ask questions, and so my parents liked her best. I was the one who interrogated, who was always setting one or the other of them off, and I wasn't so sure what they thought of me. In all of these years, I should have learned a thing or two from Kelly, but I hadn't.

My mother was busy in the kitchen, making Greek chicken. Gas hissed from the oven and I could smell oregano. Dad finished the rest of his beer and said, "Your grandmother, she's really put her ass in a sling this time. She's up shit creek without a paddle. That woman's made her bed, and now she'll have to lie in it."

I said, "Finders keepers, losers weepers."

Dad and Kelly looked over at me as if I'd just materialized in the room. Then Dad cut his eyes over to Kelly and said, "How's about another beer, sweetheart?" While Kelly played fetch, Dad leaned over and turned on his stereo. With his forefinger, he led the record player's arm to the 45 already on the turntable, Elvis Presley's "Suspicious Minds," a song my father played so often that you could barely hear the music over all the snaps and pops, but before long the two of us were sitting there bobbing our heads. When Kelly came in with Dad's beer, she started bobbing her head, too, and if someone who didn't know us had walked in at that precise moment, he'd have thought he was looking at three of the happiest people on this side of the planet.

The next morning at school, I buttonholed Ralph and said, "Get this. My grandmother got arrested for stealing."

"Whoa!" Ralph said. "What sort of places does she loot?"

"Shoe stores," I said.

"Shoe stores?" He laughed. "*Shoe* stores?" He thought about it for a minute. Then, holding his chin and nodding, he said, "Shoe stores," as if the idea of robbing shoe stores suddenly made perfect sense.

"She'd get a pair of shoes from the Goodwill for fifty cents, then go over to the shoe store, try on an expensive pair, and when the salesperson wasn't looking, she'd walk out of the store."

"If you're gonna steal shoes," he said, "that's the way to do it—one pair at a time." He rubbed the half-dozen whiskers on his chin and said, "Methodical. Patient. I bet she'd make a good safecracker."

"I think she's just a kleptomaniac," I said.

"Are you crazy? This woman knows what she's doing. She wants shoes. She's got a plan. Kleptos, they steal stuff, they don't care what. But your grandmother, she's like Clyde Barrow."

I nodded. I didn't know anyone named Clyde Barrow. Then a black Monte Carlo rolled up alongside the playground, a smoky window rolled down, and a guy in the passenger seat said, "Hey you. Yeah, *you.* Are you Ralph?"

Ralph leaned in to me and said, "Looks like business. Wait here, okay?" He walked over to the car, sort of bouncing on his way. I'd always suspected that one of Ralph's legs was an inch or two shorter than the other one, but it wasn't the sort of thing I'd ask him. Instead, I paid attention to the cuffs of his pants to see if one was higher than the other, but they were both already higher than they should have been, and since Ralph usually wore a different-colored sock on each foot, it was difficult to tell what his problem was.

The guy in the passenger seat looked about my father's age. I crouched down, trying to get a good peek at the driver, but he was wearing dark sunglasses and staring straight ahead. Ralph pulled his price list from his shirt pocket and handed it to the passenger. They exchanged a few words, then Ralph took out a tiny spiral pad from his back pocket and wrote something down. He tore the sheet from the spiral and handed it over. The passenger nodded, handed Ralph an envelope, and the two of them shook hands. As soon as Ralph started walking from the car, the smoky window rolled up and the driver pulled away.

"What did you give those guys?" I asked when Ralph returned.

"An estimate," he said. He sighed. "I wish they hadn't done that, though."

"Who?"

"Kenny and Norm." Ralph's cousins. I liked Kenny better than I liked Norm, but it was like choosing between two cough syrups: They both made the hair on my arms stand up.

"What did they do?" I asked.

"They told a few of their friends about my price list, then *those* people told more people, and now I've got more clients than I know what to do with."

"I thought you wanted business."

"I do," Ralph said. "The problem is, I don't even know these guys."

"I thought Norm was in jail."

"He copped a plea," Ralph said.

"Oh." This wasn't news I wanted to hear. "So what did those guys in the car want you to do?"

Ralph shrugged. "They want me to chew off somebody's ear."

"Hey, that's fifteen bucks, isn't it?" I asked, trying to boost his spirits. "Chawed ear, right?"

Ralph nodded.

"So?" I said. "Whose ear?"

"Roark Pile's," he said.

"Roark Pile?"

We both looked over at Roark Pile. He was one of our own classmates. Short and hunched, wearing bottle-thick eyeglasses, Roark looked more insectlike than ever as he stood alone at the far corner of the playground. We'd taken only one class together, a math class, and he had an asthma attack and was taken to the school nurse. I'd been going to school with him for eight years but hadn't ever said a word to him, and now that I thought about it, I wasn't sure anyone else had, either. He was flipping through his *Star Wars* collectors' cards today. He kept the cards rubber-banded together, and whenever there was a break before class, during lunch, or on the playground, he'd take off the rubber band and shuffle through them. He studied the cards with such intensity that you'd think it was a deck of naked ladies he was looking at, a buxom blonde in a hayloft instead of Chewbacca sitting in Han Solo's cockpit. At least three days a week he wore a T-shirt with an iron-on decal of Chewbacca on the front. He also had a *Star Wars* lunch box that prominently featured Chewey. I didn't care much for Roark, but I didn't care for him in the way that people don't care much for people they don't talk to, which is to say I didn't know why I didn't care for him. I just didn't. I'd never had any desire to chew off his ear, though.

"Roark Pile," I said. "Why?"

Ralph huffed, disgusted with me, and said, "I don't ask *why*. That's part of the deal. I get a job, I do the job. *Why* doesn't factor into it. I like to think I'm more professional than that."

"So," I said, "are you going to bite his ear off right now?" I didn't want to admit it, but I was curious to see how that would happen. Would Ralph walk up behind Roark, bite down on his ear, and start yanking on it? Or would he pin him to the ground first, secure his hands under his knees, and then try to chew it off?

"Are you *crazy*?" Ralph asked. "You don't just bite off someone's ear in broad daylight."

"Oh. Have you ever bitten somebody's ear off before?" I asked.

"Not for money," Ralph said, "no."

The first warning bell rang, and Roark Pile began strapping his *Star Wars* cards back together. In a few days he'd have only one ear, but for the time being he was probably unaware that he even had ears, let alone that it was a luxury to have two.

"Jeez," I said, shaking my head. Ralph and I joined the line heading back into school. "Who'd have thought someone was out to get Roark Pile?"

Ralph said, "Don't fool yourself. There's always someone out to get you."

When I arrived home from school, Grandma was in the living room recliner with her feet propped up. She wasn't wearing any shoes, and I wondered if the police had gone to her trailer and confiscated all of them, leaving her barefoot.

"Grams!" I yelled, but my father cut me off.

"Don't talk to her," he said. "She's grounded."

Grandma smiled at me, then shrugged. With her forefinger and thumb, she made like she was zipping her own mouth shut. For my benefit, she cocked her head at my father and rolled her eyes. My fear of her as a hardened criminal lessened at the greater fear that she had taken up mime.

Dad said, "She's unrepentant. She says it was an innocent mistake. Jesus Christ Almighty. My own mother, an unrepentant crook!"

I found my sister in the backyard with Mom. They were both sitting on rusty lawn chairs. I said, "Grams is home."

Kelly said, "Better hammer your shoes to the floor."

I was about to tell her to take it easy on the old lady when I noticed that they were both drinking fruity, icy drinks, and that both their mouths were bright red. "What are those?" I asked. "Slurpees?"

Mom said, "Not quite. Just a little something to take the edge off."

Kelly extended her arm over her head, then shook her hand like she was playing a maraca. "MargaRITA," she said.

"You're drinking *alcohol?*" I asked.

Mom said, "Oh, Hank, it's just a margarita. It's mostly ice."

"Well, then," I said. "Can I have one?"

"No," she said.

"Why not?"

"You're too young."

I looked inside through the plate-glass window and could see Dad pointing at Grandma, reprimanding her, but I couldn't hear what he was saying. Grandma sat stock-still, staring straight ahead, looking like a taxidermied version of her own self. Then her eyes began to move, slowly tracking toward me. When she finally spotted me, she started to smile but stopped. I could tell that she was worried I didn't like her anymore, the way everyone else seemed not to like her anymore, so I smiled to reassure her that this wasn't the case. For lack of something better to do, I pretended that I was leaning against something, the way a mime would. Next I acted like a heavy wind had swept through town, and it was all I could do to keep standing while walking into it. For my final routine, I pretended that I was trapped inside a box, and that it kept getting smaller and smaller. Grandma was laughing. My dad was in the middle of one of his *tell-me-what-I've-done-to-make-you-screw-up-so-badly* gestures when he turned and saw me outside being Marcel Marceau. The box that I was inside kept getting smaller, and I kept trying to curl tighter and tighter, lying on my side, pulling my legs up to my chest, then starting to convulse, as if the box were crushing me.

Mom turned, saw me, and yelled, "Oh my God, Hank's having a seizure!"

Kelly said, "We better put a pencil in his mouth so he doesn't bite his tongue off."

My father, though unable to hear either my mother or Kelly, lunged for the phone in the living room and started dialing.

But it was Grandma I kept watching, and I felt in that moment that we were reading each other's mind, and that she was the only person in this whole crazy family who'd ever really understood me.

Ralph and I spent the weekend trailing Roark Pile. I wasn't sure why I was trailing him with Ralph except that I was bored and I'd never trailed anyone before. When you trail someone, you learn how dull people really are. I guess I thought we'd be following Roark onto construction sites and into hollowed-out mounds of dirt that no one else knew about, or that he'd have secret knocks for getting into unmarked storefronts, or maybe he'd have a girlfriend from another school, a girl who reminded him, in some remotely hairy way, of his favorite *Star Wars* character, Chewbacca. But no: The Roark Pile of my imagination had nothing to do with the real Roark Pile. And what we already knew about Roark Pile from school—that he didn't have any friends and was obsessed with *Star Wars*—was all there was to know about him.

"Man oh man," I said. "This is one boring guy."

Ralph poked my shoulder with his forefinger and said, "Follow yourself around one day and see how interesting *you* are."

I wanted to ask Ralph at what point he had started taking Roark's side, but I let it slide. Following someone all day long can make you crabby. After several hours of hiding behind a thorny bush across the street from Roark's house, Ralph and I decided to call it quits.

Ralph said, "Is your grandmother out of the clink?"

"Dad sprung her yesterday," I said.

Ralph nodded. "She staying with you guys?"

"Until we can figure out what to do with her," I said.

At the corner where Ralph and I were to go our separate ways, he said, "Maybe you could set up a meet. You know, me, your grandmother, Kenny, Norm."

"Kenny and Norm?" I asked.

"Sure," Ralph said. "I told them about the old lady. The word *genius* came up ten times. I kept count. Of course, eight of those times Kenny and Norm were talking about themselves, but still . . ."

"I'll see what I can do," I said.

"You're a good egg," Ralph said, but then he punched my arm so hard that if I were an egg, I'd have splattered all over his fist.

When I got home, Dad was sitting at the kitchen table with six crushed beer cans in front of him and one sweaty can in his hand. Mom was curled on the couch, weeping. Kelly was staring blankly at a fuzzy TV show on the Spanish station.

"Hey, where's Uncle Fester and Cousin It?" I asked.

"Somebody tell Hank," Mom said.

"What?"

Kelly turned from the mustachioed bandito on TV and said, "Grandma's dead."

"She's *dead*?" I yelled. My first thought was that Dad had killed her, and I felt a strong urge to creep to the front door, then bolt for my life.

"She had a heart attack," Kelly said. "One minute she was eating oatmeal, the next she was dead. It was fast. Not entirely painless, but not too bad, I guess."

"Where's she now?"

"What, do you mean like *heaven?*" Kelly asked. "I guess that's where she is, but I don't know. I don't think she went to confession after stealing all those shoes, so she might not be in heaven. She might be, you know, some other place. It's hard to say. I guess we'd have to ask a priest."

I glared at Kelly before saying, "Where's her *body?*"

"Oh. An ambulance came and took her away." She cocked an eyebrow and said, "Any more questions, Sherlock? I mean, we're all a little broken up around here, since we were the ones who were here when it happened."

I could tell Kelly enjoyed having been here when Grandma keeled over. It made her one of the chosen ones. Later, she would cite this moment as more evidence of her superiority over me.

"I guess I don't have any more questions," I said. "Nope, I guess that's it for now."

The next time I saw Ralph, I told him about my grandmother.

Ralph nodded gravely. "They got to her," he said.

"Who got to her?"

"Shoe-store managers," he said.

"Actually, I think it was a heart attack. She was pretty old."

Ralph laughed and shook his head. "Hank, Hank, Hank. *Think* about it. What are the odds? The old woman goes to the slammer, right? She gets out, but before she has a chance to get back to work, *wham,* she falls over dead. And you think that's a coincidence? Hey, look." He put his arm around my shoulders. "I was born the same day Kennedy was killed. I *know* about conspiracies. It's in my blood." He removed his arm and said, "When's the funeral?"

"I don't know yet."

Ralph said, "When you find out, let me know. I'd like to pay my respects to the old broad."

"Sure. Okay."

Roark Pile emerged from his house, tugging on his Chewbacca T-shirt. He seemed especially buglike today, walking with his shoulders hunched and his head down, seemingly without a direction in mind, as though feeling his way across town with a pair of antennae. We followed him for hours—past New Castle Park, where the power-line towers buzzed so hard your teeth would start to zing; to the Haunted Trails Miniature Golf Range, where, on the first hole, you had to putt the golf ball between Frankenstein's legs; to Dunkin' Donuts, behind which the police had once found a chopped-up body of a boy who'd disappeared from a church carnival months earlier. We ended up at the city reservoir, which was a bone-dry cavern alongside Eighty-seventh Street. Another boy was down there waiting for him. It was the first time, to my knowledge, that Roark had made contact with another human being his own age.

"What are they doing?" Ralph said.

I pulled out my father's binoculars, a fancy pair with zoom that I controlled with my forefinger, only today I couldn't seem to focus and zoom at the same time. I hadn't used them much before except to zoom in on my sister's face at close range and start screaming, causing her to yawn and say, "Puh-*leaze*."

"Look," Ralph said. "They're making an exchange of some kind. I bet it's drugs."

"I can't see," I said, zooming in and out, trying to focus.

"Roark Pile, drug kingpin," Ralph said. "No wonder they want me to bite his ear off. He's probably horning in on their territory. It's finally making sense."

"Wait, wait," I said, capturing Roark in my sights. "Okay, I got him."

Ralph said, "Well?"

"They're trading *Star Wars* cards," I said.

"Sure they are," Ralph said.

"No, I can see them. It's *Star Wars* trading cards."

Ralph said, "Why the hell are they meeting all the way down there, then? And who's that kid? Do we know him?"

Across Eighty-seventh Street was a different school district, meaning that there were a dozen more grade schools and another high school, our rival high school, and it was possible that one of their kids had slipped across the border to make this exchange with Roark. I told Ralph my theory.

"I wish I had a high-powered rifle," he said. "I'd shoot the cards right out of their hands. Scare 'em a little."

"So," I said. "Are you going to bite off his ear or what?"

"I don't know," Ralph said. "I mean, I guess so. I don't have any good reason *not* to bite it off. Something's not right." He stood from his crouch and said, "I wish I knew *what*, though."

My mother took me to Robert Hall to buy a suit right off the rack, just as the commercial advertised. My last suit was from 1975, a sky-blue leisure deal that my mother had thought looked nice with a dark blue turtleneck, but every time I put that turtleneck on, I thought I was going to choke to death. It jacked up my body temperature a notch or two, and my face and ears would turn dark red if I wore one for too long.

"Ugh, I can't breathe," I'd say in a raspy voice through labored breaths.

Kelly would roll her eyes, and Mom would say, "Hank, cut it out before someone decides to choke you for real."

Today Mom pulled a dark blue leisure suit off the rack and said, "Now, *this* would look nice with a light blue turtleneck."

"No turtlenecks!" I yelled. "They CHOKE me! You don't BELIEVE me, but they DO! They cut off the circulation to my HEAD, and then I can't BREATHE!"

A few customers stopped what they were doing to stare at me. Other kids' mothers looked disgusted to see someone my age whining.

"Okay, okay," Mom said. "Keep your voice down." To quiet me, she pulled from the rack a three-piece forest-green suit and promptly located a matching tie. Suit in bag, we stopped next door at Kinney Shoes for a new pair of wing tips.

"Hey," I whispered to Mom. "Is this one of the places Grandma knocked over?"

"Shhhh," she said. "Quiet."

Since Mom hadn't answered me, I assumed my guess was correct. When a large man burst through the saloon-style doors that separated the customers from the stock in back, I thought of Ralph's conspiracy theory, how the shoe-store managers were probably involved in Gramsie's death.

"I see we're doing a little shopping today," the big guy said. "A Robert Hall suit!" He nodded at the bag. "And what's the occasion? You look a little young to be getting married!" He winked at me.

"A death in the family," my mother explained. "His grandmother."

"Oh. Oh, well, I'm very sorry," the man said. He cleared his throat. "I didn't know."

*How COULD he know?* I thought. *Why would he say he didn't know unless he DID know?* I said, "We think someone killed her."

"Hank!" Mom said.

The salesman cocked his head and squinted at me, sizing up the situation. "Murder?" he asked.

"Maybe you heard of her," I said. "Ruth Boyd." I waited. The man didn't say anything, so I continued. "She got herself mixed up with some people she shouldn't have."

Mom took hold of my elbow, squeezed it as hard as she could, and said, "Enough!" I was about to say more when she yanked my arm hard enough to put a dislocated shoulder back into place. With the salesman eyeing both of us now, my mother smiled bravely and said, "What kind of dress shoe do you have in a size eight?"

That night Ralph and I started trailing Roark Pile, but Roark spotted us and took off running.

"I think he's onto us," Ralph said.

"I don't know why you don't just bite his ear off," I complained.

Ralph said, "How'd you like it if somebody hired me to bite your ear off? Now, let's say they hired me for all the wrong reasons. It seems to me that a little investigative work might save you your ear, right? And that's all fine and dandy if it's *your* ear I've been hired to bite off, isn't it? But not if it's someone else's. No! You want me to bite a guy's ear off without doing any legwork. Who knows what chain reaction I'll start if I bite somebody's ear off for the wrong reason? Jesus, Hank, your head's so thick I'm surprised it's not in a laboratory being weighed even as we speak."

Ralph was wearing an old turtleneck that had been eaten by moths. I hadn't meant to set him off, so I changed the subject. "I can't wear turtlenecks. They choke me."

"Choke you?" he said. "What, like *this*?" He reached out and grabbed my neck, and although he was only joking, he choked me for a good five seconds before letting go. He snickered and, mocking me, said, *"They choke me!* You know what? If I had a little spare time, I'd bring a lawsuit against the school and make a case that *you* should've failed two grades, not me."

I could tell that this business of biting off Roark Pile's ear was troubling Ralph, and that this was why he was snapping at me. I decided not to take any of it personally, but I also didn't want to get choked again, so I said, "I better go, Ralph. People are still grieving back home."

Ralph nodded. "Yeah, well," he said. "It's not like Roark Pile's ear is going anywhere, now is it?"

"Apparently not," I said.

Grandma's wake was held at night at Vitiriti and Sons Funeral Parlor. I'd never seen a dead person before, and I was secretly looking forward to it until I actually saw my own grandmother in the casket. I couldn't help myself. I burst out crying.

Kelly came up to me and whispered, "Geez, Hank, are you okay?"

My shoulders shuddered, and I couldn't catch my breath. My crying reached the point where it didn't seem to have anything to do with Grandma anymore. I was feeling lightheaded, the way I felt lightheaded around gasoline pumps, and like those dizzying moments at the Standard Oil with my dad or mom, when I'd suck in the fumes as fast as I could, I started to enjoy the act of crying, the giddy way it made me feel, and I wasn't sure I could make myself stop even if I wanted to.

My mother came over and said, "Oh, my poor Hank," and hugged me until her blouse was soaking wet from tears.

My father eventually stomped over and said, "You're scaring everyone, Hank. Go outside and get some fresh air." He nudged me away from the casket.

Outside, in the dark funeral-home parking lot, I found Ralph and his cousins, Norm and Kenny. Norm was wearing a tuxedo T-shirt. Kenny was wearing a powder-blue tux he must not have returned after his senior prom five years before. Ralph was wearing the same moth-eaten turtleneck he'd worn yesterday.

"Hey, hey! Look at you," Norm said, tugging at my new suit and sniggering. "Somebody die?" Kenny punched him, and Norm said, "Oh yeah. *Sorry.*"

Ralph said, "You forgot to tell me about the wake, Hank. I had to look it up in the newspaper."

I hadn't told him on purpose, but I acted surprised. "I didn't tell you?"

Ralph leaned toward me and said, "Hey, you been crying or what?"

"Nah," I said. "I'm allergic to perfume."

Ralph said, "You look like a blowfish. Doesn't he look like a blowfish?"

"He looks like a blowfish," Norm said.

Kenny nodded. "He looks like a blowfish."

I needed to change the subject, so I asked Ralph if he'd bitten off Roark's ear yet.

"Soon," Ralph said. "Tomorrow, maybe." He nodded as if imagining the crucial moment that his teeth would sink into the lobe. He said, "You going back inside?"

"I don't think so," I said.

"Okay," Ralph said, "I guess it's time for us to pay our respects."

Kenny and Norm nodded solemnly. Ralph slapped me on the back. Kenny pinched my cheek. Norm trapped me in a bear hug and said, "Don't ever forget her, man." He smelled like beer and Italian sausage. For a second I thought Norm had fallen asleep on my shoulder, but then he stood, straightened his tuxedo T-shirt, and said, "All right, dudes, let's do it."

The next morning at school, Ralph said, "I'm biting Roark's ear off tonight, six o'clock, no matter where he is or what he's doing."

"Thank God!" I said.

We were on the blacktop, waiting for the bell to ring. Ralph, glaring at Roark, ground his molars so hard, I thought I heard them squeak. When the bell rang—a noise that always made my heart clench—I started making my way toward the eighth-grade line, moaning with each step.

"What's your problem, Hank?" Ralph asked.

"My mother pitched my old tennis shoes," I said. "She thought they were getting ratty. So until I get some new ones, I have to wear these." I pointed to the wing tips from Kinney Shoes.

Ralph said, "Sure your grandmother didn't leave those for you in her will?"

I shrugged. No one had said anything about a will. All Dad ever talked about these days was having to go over to Grandma's trailer and, as he put it, "sift through all her shit." Last night, after dinner, he lit a cigarette. Staring at the flame rising from his Bic, he said, "A little Jewish lightning would make my life a hell of a lot easier. Yessiree!" He sucked on his cigarette, coughed a few balls of smoke, then dropped the lighter next to his ashtray. I didn't ask what Jewish lightning was; I didn't want to know.

"Tonight," Ralph said. He reached over and touched my ear, and I shivered.

Before I met up with Ralph, my father took me over to Grandma's trailer. It was in a park across the street from the Haunted Trails Miniature Golf Range, and from her bedroom window, you could see the looming head of Frankenstein, the bolts sticking out of either side of his neck. I'd been inside the trailer a few hundred times, but I'd never noticed until today how small it was or how little Grandma had owned.

"Well, hell," Dad said, peeking under the bed, then tipping the cedar chest up to see if anything was underneath. "This won't take much time at all. Guess I won't have to burn the place down after all."

"There's not much *to* burn," I said, and opened the closet door. Hundreds of pairs of shoes came tumbling out, an avalanche large enough to grip my ankles.

"Son of a bitch!" Dad said. "Goddamn it!"

There were slippers, white orthopedics, high heels with straps, stilettos. There were Hush Puppies, Candies, Spaldings. I'd never really thought much about shoes before, but looking at these, I thought I understood her fascination. It was no different from my own desire to save every issue of *TV Guide*. There were things you collected for no other reason than that you wanted to collect them. I couldn't explain to anyone why I owned more than two hundred issues of *TV Guide*. I just did.

On our way home, Dad said, "Your grandmother sort of lost her mind near the end. Went a little cuckoo."

"I don't think she was all that crazy," I said.

Dad didn't say anything until he'd stopped at a red light. Then he turned to me and said, "What do you know about crazy? Huh? You've never seen anything in your life except civilized behavior. Hell, we're practically the Cleavers. Your mother's June, I'm whatever-the-hell-the-dad's-name-is, your sister's Wally, and you're the Beav. Did they have a dog? I can't remember. Doesn't make a difference for the point I'm making. But here's my point—"

A car behind us started honking. The light had turned green a while ago, and now it was already turning yellow again.

"Ah, Christ," Dad said, and punched the gas. We barely made it a block when a cop pulled us over and wrote my father a ticket for failing to yield.

"Have a nice day," the cop said, swaggering back to his cruiser.

I waited until we were almost home before speaking again. "You were about to make a point," I reminded him.

"What?" He seemed startled to discover that I was in the car with him.

"You said 'Here's my point' before that guy honked his horn."

My father looked up at the ticket pinned under the visor, then cut his eyes to me. "A point? What point? I don't know what you're talking about, Hank." He parked the car in the driveway, snatched the ticket, and said, "Hold on to your hat, son. Here's where the shit hits the fan."

I checked my watch. I was already late meeting Ralph. I walked behind Dad, but as soon as we stepped over the threshold, I turned around and walked back outside, shutting the door between us.

Ralph was in front of his house, jabbing the shattered sidewalk with a stick. All along the sidewalk were places where blunt instruments had slammed down, leaving cobweb patterns in the concrete, and I wondered if Ralph came out here at night with a ball-peen hammer and smashed the sidewalk himself.

Ralph said, "Where were you? We're supposed to be at the hardware store right now. My surveillance information leads me to believe that Roark will be there."

"Surveillance information? *What* surveillance information?" I wasn't sure I liked the idea of Ralph having the equipment to listen in on people. I knew he'd tap my phone in a heartbeat if he had the means to do it.

Ralph said, "I don't want to give away all my tricks, but if you really want to know, I took a drinking glass and held the bottom of it up to their living room window last night, and then I stuck my ear to the mouth of the glass. I got all sorts of good stuff, including this business about going to the hardware store." He winged the stick into the neighbor's yard, causing a cat to yowl and run up a tree. He stood and brushed dirt from his already permanently stained pants.

Dellagado's Hardware was all the way across town. For long stretches of the walk, I didn't think I was going to make it. My new shoes were chopping away at my ankles, and I cringed each time my feet hit the pavement. Though we made it there before closing, the manager was already pushing the last of the marked-down lawn mowers back inside the store.

"You kids better hurry up if you want anything."

Ralph saluted the man, then rolled his eyes at me.

Loitering in the row of pesticides, I asked, "Do you think Roark was already here?"

Ralph picked up a box of weed killer and said, "Am I carrying a crystal ball? How should I know?" He set down the weed killer and was reaching for a can of wasp spray when the bell above the front door jingled and Roark lumbered inside with a man who looked creepily like what you'd imagine Roark to look like in thirty years.

"Is that his *father*?" I whispered.

"Gee, I don't know," Ralph said. "Here, let me get my crystal ball out again." He gently smacked my face with a flyswatter.

"Ouch! *Sorry*," I said.

Roark's father walked up to the manager, who said, "What's new in the world today, Roark?"

Ralph and I looked around for Roark Pile, but he had already abandoned his father.

The father said, "Same ol', same ol'."

"Oh, shit," Ralph said. "The old man's name is Roark, too."

"Two Roarks?" I said.

Ralph and I didn't have to say anything more. We both knew the truth: The men who had hired Ralph were after Roark's father and not Roark. I was about to suggest we leave when Roark Jr. rounded the corner and nearly slammed into us. He froze but didn't say a word. A sound came from his throat like he was having a heart attack, but then I realized that it was just Roark breathing. We were so close that I saw the intricate details of his ears. They were small and pink. The lobes were attached to his head instead of dangling, like mine or Ralph's. I could even see the ear's network of veins and the blue blood that shot through them. He must have sensed that I was looking at his ears, because he reached up and scratched one before turning and leaving us alone in the bug-spray aisle.

"What are you going to do?" I asked. "Are you going to bite an ear off of each Roark?"

Ralph shook his head. "I don't believe this." Without so much as baring his teeth at either of them, he walked past the two Roarks and out of the store.

I followed. I said, "I better call home for a ride. My shoes feel like they're made out of razor blades."

Ralph ignored me. He kept walking. When he finally stopped, he said, "If I'd known it was *this* Roark Pile, I'd never have agreed. I have age limits. I won't bite off the ear of anyone eighteen years old or older. I mean, I'd *love* to bite the guy's ear off, don't get me wrong."

"Can't you make an exception?" I asked.

Ralph shook his head. "A man sets up rules, he has to stick to them. If I make an exception today, what's to stop me from biting off, say, *your* father's ear? Or your *mother's,* for that matter."

I shrugged. "Nothing, I guess."

"That's right." Ralph sighed. "I don't know. I was thinking of getting out of the business, anyway." He took his price list from his shirt pocket and said, "Here. Maybe you'll want to take it over. The money's good, and the hours are flexible."

"I don't think anyone's afraid of me," I said.

Ralph said, "You're right. People *aren't* afraid of you. But once they know you've got this price list, that'll all change."

"Thanks," I said. I tucked it into my pants pocket. Ralph started walking away, but I couldn't bring myself to follow, limping instead to the nearest pay phone so I could beg my mom for a ride home.

The next morning at school, a long dark Monte Carlo rolled up alongside the playground. A tinted window crept down, and a man with dark sunglasses motioned Ralph over.

Ralph said, "Time to break the news." He sauntered over to the car, crouched, and poked his head through the open window. I could see a lot of hand gesturing, but I couldn't hear anything.

"So?" I asked when Ralph returned.

"They weren't happy."

"It was a misunderstanding," I said. "I mean, how were you supposed to know there were two Roarks, right?"

"Actually," Ralph said, "I spent their money."

"They paid you up front?"

Ralph nodded.

"It's only fifteen bucks," I said. "Can't your cousins loan you fifteen bucks?"

"The problem," Ralph said, "is that they gave me a hundred."

"A hundred?" I said. "For chawing off an ear?" I pulled out the list that Ralph had given to me. I was right: *Ear chawed off. $15.* One hundred dollars was for doing the big job. *Murder.* I looked back up at Ralph.

Ralph said, "They didn't say *exactly* what they wanted, so I was going to mix it up a little, make it come out to a hundred bucks' worth of service. You know, chew his ear off, then punch him forty-three times."

"And you think that would have been okay with them?" I asked.

"Probably not," he said.

Roark Pile quit coming to school. An entire week had come and gone without a sighting of him.

"Where do you think he is?" I asked.

"Hold on," Ralph said. "I think I left my crystal ball in my locker."

At week's end, my mother showed me a newspaper article and asked, "Do you know this boy?" She pointed to Roark Pile's name. The article was about how a local man named Roark Pile, age forty-five, had disappeared one night after taking out the garbage. The son, Roark Jr., was so upset that he had stopped going to school.

"He goes to your school," Mom said, "and he's in your grade."

I shrugged. "I don't think I ever heard of him before. I think I'd remember a name like Roark Pile, don't you?" Later that night, I cut out the article.

When I saw Ralph again, I showed him the article and asked what he thought had happened to Roark's father.

Ralph was chewing on a toothpick, moving it from one corner of his mouth to the other. "They'll find him one day," he said. "A leg here, an arm there. One thing's for sure. No one's coming out of this one happy."

There were times I wondered if Ralph'd had anything to do with the disappearance of Roark's father, but he seemed as disturbed by the news as I was, maybe more so. There were other times I wondered if Ralph's cousins Kenny and Norm were involved, but they didn't seem capable of carrying out a successful grocery mission, let alone a kidnapping or a murder.

It didn't take long for the rumors to take root and sprout. Kelly thought Roark Sr. was having an affair and ran off with a rich woman in town, this despite the fact that there weren't any rich women in town. Kelly didn't know who this woman was, but that didn't stop her from making up names and histories for her. "Mrs. Dorchester," she'd say. "She owns a pink poodle and a pink Cadillac. She lives in the cul-de-sac by the country club."

"What country club?" I asked. "And what the hell's a cul-de-sac?"

Kelly rolled her eyes and said, "Uh, *duh*."

Mom had a similar theory, except that in her version it wasn't a rich society woman named Mrs. Dorchester; it was some trailer trash named Doreen or Lorelei, and it was Doreen's or Lorelei's trailer-trash husband, Lloyd or Ewell, who chased Roark out of town on a rail.

"Grandma lived in a trailer," I said. "Was she trailer trash, too?"

Mom said, "Don't go saying bad things about your own grandmother, Hank, you hear me? The poor woman's no longer here to defend herself."

My father thought both theories bordered on the insane. "Women!" he said. "They always think it has to do with love. This guy, he probably owed someone a lot of money. Probably got in too deep with the wrong folks. A juice loan. Something like that. And if you think things like that don't go on around here, think again, my friends. Think again."

I didn't know what to think. The only image that came clearly into focus was that of a dark sedan rolling up to the curb and waiting for Roark Sr. to drag his garbage cans to the curb. Beyond that, what happened was anybody's guess.

Throughout Roark's entire absence from school, my feet continued to ache from the new shoes. In a spiral notebook I charted their metamorphosis, how they went from being baby soft to bloody stumps, from slightly toughened to bloody stumps again, from callused to bloody stumps again, and so on. The garbage can next to the washer and dryer was stuffed with bloody socks.

Mom said, "I thought you'd eventually break them in, but I guess that's not going to happen. You're costing me a fortune in new socks."

In the end, it wasn't the pain so much as the cost resulting from the pain that finally persuaded my mother to give me ten bucks for a new pair of sneakers. She was too embarrassed to go with me after our last adventure, so one Saturday I limped all the way to Kinney Shoes by myself. Aisle after aisle, I picked up sneakers and tested their durability by bending them toe to heel. For fun, I imagined how much it would hurt if my foot were inside and someone were bending my foot the same way that I was bending the shoe. I was making the face of someone in excruciating pain when the big salesman from my last visit appeared behind me and said, "You want to give it a whirl? Try it on for size? See how it works for you?"

"Sure!" I said.

I tried on both shoes, walking up and down the aisles, first bouncing on my toes, then walking on my heels. I was about to tell the salesman that I'd take them, but the front door opened and Roark Pile, Jr., walked in with a woman who must have been his mother.

"What kind of dress shoe do you have in a size eight?" the woman asked the salesman, and it was like a fist jabbed square in my gut, hearing the same question my own mother had asked when we were looking at shoes for Grandma's wake—and though it was possible that Roark and his mother were here for no other purpose than to buy shoes, I couldn't help wondering if the police had finally found Roark's father, and if, as Ralph predicted, they'd found him in more than one piece. I knew it was ridiculous, but I started feeling that I was to blame for the man's disappearance. At the very least, I knew things other people didn't. Because of this, I really didn't want to be in the same store with Roark and his mother. It didn't seem right.

I was at the far end of an aisle, watching from the greatest distance possible. Roark began looking around, so I stepped out of sight behind a tall shelf of shoes.

The salesman said, "Let me round up a few choices," and I heard his feet slapping the carpet, the slap getting louder and louder, until he was upon me. "How're those sneakers working out?"

"They're pretty nice," I said. "Comfy."

"It's your lucky day," he said. "They're on sale. Nineteen ninety-nine."

I nodded. I had only ten bucks, not a penny more.

"Genuine leather," he added before heading for the back room.

I peeked around the corner. Roark was heading down my aisle. I walked one aisle over so another tall shelf of shoes separated us. I could feel his presence, so I tried miming his moves, taking a step when I heard him take a step, moving slowly toward the exit when he moved slowly toward the stockroom. It was like some kind of magnetic force pulling us together, and midway down the aisle, I knew that he was directly opposite me on the other side of that shelf. I tried not to breathe, hoping he wouldn't know I was there, but then I saw him looking at me through a cluster of perforated holes in the shelving unit, the way a fly looks at someone with its many eyes.

"Why do you keep following me?" he whispered. "Everywhere I go," Roark said, "you're there."

I wanted to explain, but to say anything in my defense would only prove Roark right: I *had* been following him. Maybe not today, but on all those days with Ralph, I'd trailed Roark's every move. So I didn't say anything. I tiptoed away, toward Mrs. Pile, toward the entrance, and the magnetic grip started to loosen. Each step became easier than the last.

Mrs. Pile had parked herself on a bench. As soon as I reached the door and turned to nod at her, the salesman came out of the stockroom holding several shoe boxes. He froze when he saw me at the door, as if fearing he had lost a customer, but then he looked down at the new pair of shoes on my feet and realized what was about to happen. Roark was still looking through the perforated shelf, waiting for me to answer his question. Mrs. Pile was watching her curious son as if trying to figure out how he had become what he had become. The salesman, eyes narrowing, didn't say or do anything. Nobody said or did anything, and I saw that whatever was going to happen hinged on my next move.

"Roark!" I yelled, startling myself. Roark looked up, confused to see me by the door. "Is that you?" I asked, smiling and looking around. Everything that happened next seemed beyond my control. I strode over to Roark, trapped him in a hug, and said, loud enough for everyone to hear, "Where've you been hiding? We haven't seen you in school. Is everything okay?" As Roark tensed in my embrace, I peeked over my shoulder. The salesman had resumed delivering the new shoes to Mrs. Pile; she was staring at Roark and the friend she didn't know he had. Clearly I had made her day. Her son had friends! Who'd have guessed?

I turned back to Roark, patting his shoulder. I was about to let go when I felt him relax. His grip on me, however, tightened. I wanted to say something, a word of comfort, but when I opened my mouth, nothing came out. I just stood there holding the poor kid. Was he crying? I couldn't tell. "Here, here," I said, but it was more for myself than for Roark, because suddenly *I* was the one who felt like crying. I didn't know why, either. For my grandmother? For Roark's father? For standing in this shoe store, not knowing what would happen next? I really couldn't have said. I patted Roark and listened for the telltale signs, the sniffles, the sobs, but the only sounds I could make out were Roark's asthmatic breaths and my own thumping heart, as if one depended upon the other to keep the two of us alive.

# SHERIDAN DRIVE-IN

THE SHERIDAN, AT THE corner of Seventy-ninth and Harlem, was our nearest drive-in movie theater. It was a dusty parking lot with a few hundred lead posts poking up out of the gravel. Each post held a cast-iron speaker. At the center of the lot was a low-to-the-ground concrete bunker where concessions were sold and the projectionist ran the movie. When my parents took me and Kelly to the Sheridan, we sometimes had to drive around to find a speaker that worked. My father, cursing each time one wouldn't click on, would eventually say, "I'll try one more, and if *that* one doesn't work, I'm getting a refund." But the last one always worked, maybe because the odds were leaning in our favor with each bad speaker, or maybe because we'd end up parking several rows behind everyone else and the speakers back there hadn't been used much.

When we first started going to the Sheridan, my parents owned a Rambler. My father didn't like to run the heat during the movie—"We'll burn up all our gas," he'd say—so on cold nights we'd bring blankets and pile them on top of us. Kelly would kick me under the blankets and then blame me for starting it.

"*Both* of you better cut it out," our father would say, "or this is the last thing we'll ever do together as a family, you hear me?"

The truth is, it was the only thing we ever did together besides live in the same house, but the threat always hinted to other, more interesting things, all of which would vanish if we didn't cut it out. I wanted to ask if there were things I was forgetting, but I knew this question would set our father off. I was always setting one or the other of my parents off with questions I'd ask before I really thought them through.

During our dozen years of going to the Sheridan, we saw probably fifty or sixty movies, but the ones I remembered best were *Easy Rider, Planet of the Apes, The Chinese Connection, Beneath the Planet of the Apes, Buster and Billie, Escape from the Planet of the Apes, Walking Tall, Conquest of the Planet of the Apes, Enter the Dragon,* and *Battle for the Planet of the Apes.* The two times I made the mistake of going with someone else's parents, I saw *The Love Bug* and a movie called *Gus* about a mule that played football.

Every night was a double feature. The first movie was always the one that everyone in the world wanted to see, but I liked going to the Sheridan for other reasons. For starters, I liked intermission. A black-and-white movie of a clown pointing to a ticking clock showed how much time you had left to buy hot dogs. On those rare occasions when my father would give me money to get everyone a hot dog, I would walk by the projectionist's booth and look at the man inside. It was the same man each time, an old guy with a pencil-thin mustache, the kind of mustache Bud Abbott had, and he would always be smoking a cigarette and reading a magazine. One time I walked in front of the concession stand and jumped up with my arm in the air, and the shadow of my hand appeared on the screen, magnified to at least twelve feet high and three feet wide. When I got back to the car, I wanted to ask if anyone had seen my incredibly big hand, but my father was complaining about how little ice was in the cooler, and how his beer, sitting on top of everyone else's drinks, was too warm to enjoy. Kelly, sound asleep or pretending to be sound asleep, was nothing more than a lump under the blankets. I handed my mother the hot dogs, each one slipped into a shiny aluminum bag and looking like a miniature rocket ship.

"If Kelly doesn't wake up," Dad said, "I'll eat her hot dog. She'll never know, right?"

The other thing I liked about going to the Sheridan was the second movie, because there were always a lot of naked women in them. My parents liked to believe I had fallen asleep by the time the movie had gotten to the racy parts, and I'd even go so far as to shut my eyes.

"Are they asleep?" my father always asked at the appearance of the first naked woman.

My mother would turn around and say, "Kelly's asleep. I can't tell about Hank. He's still sitting up." She'd call out to me in a heavy whisper: "*Hank. Are you asleep? Hank. You're not watching this, are you?*"

As soon as she turned back around, I'd open my eyes just a little so that they were narrow slits through which I could watch the movie. Usually, the movies were about women who'd gone bad, women who were in prison at the very beginning of the movie, or women who weren't bad to begin with but ended up bad in prison. I imagined girls from my school—Mary Polaski or Peggy Petropulos—handcuffed and put together in a dark jail cell. I imagined myself as a prison guard smacking my billy club against my palm, walking back and forth in front of their cell, waiting for one or the other of them to pee. Peeing always played a big role in these movies.

No matter how hard I tried not to, I would fall asleep at some point, dreaming of girls from my class, all of them now in prison, and when I woke up, I was either slung over my father's shoulder or already in my bed, my body curled like a fist. Only once did I wake up during the movie, and my mom and dad were in the front seat kissing. I'd never seen them kiss like this, on the mouth, the way men and women kiss in movies. On the screen behind them was a woman who, having escaped from prison, was being chased by a pack of vicious dogs. I couldn't actually see the face of the woman being chased because we were seeing everything through her eyes. The dogs were barking behind us, getting louder, catching up to us, while jagged tree branches scratched our arms and fallen tree trunks caused us to trip and stumble. My mother said to my father, "Okay, that's enough," and my father sat up. Without a word, he rolled down the window and returned the speaker to its hook. Then he started the car and backed out of the space.

Was this what they did each time we went to the movies? Did they kiss until my mother said they'd had enough?

As Dad circled the parking lot, I could still hear the tinny barks and growls of angry dogs. I had to swivel in my seat to keep watching the movie, but as my father pulled out of the Sheridan and turned onto Harlem Avenue the screen got smaller and smaller, until finally it all disappeared, leaving the four of us alone—me; my sister the lump; my mother picking up trash and stuffing it into a too small bag; and my father, behind the wheel. My father's eyes kept darting up to the rearview mirror, and I imagined the pack of dogs, having jumped from the screen, was following us, gaining on us, and my father was doing what needed to be done to save us, but you could tell by the haunted look in his eyes that he feared he would fail.

# JUNK HEAVEN

**O**UR NEIGHBORHOOD WAS PINCHED on two of its four sides by factories. My father worked at the 3M plant, the one that made tape. I couldn't have told anyone exactly what it was my father did there, but every few weeks he'd bring home rolls of Scotch or packing tape or a box of packing peanuts, in case we ever needed to mail something fragile, which we never did. One year he came home with six hundred rolls of shrink-wrapped duct tape. "Bastards don't give us a Christmas bonus," he said, "so I thought I'd give one to myself. What the hell, right?" Since it normally took us two years to use up a single roll of duct tape, my parents doled out the extras to our friends whenever an occasion to give gifts came up, but even this left us with more than five hundred rolls. As far as I knew, *nobody* had that many friends.

I'd never really thought much about the things my father brought home until the winter of '78, the year I was in eighth grade. That December, three weeks before Christmas, my father came home with a large but severely crooked pine tree he'd found poking up out of a Dumpster behind Dunkin' Donuts, where he stopped off each morning for coffee.

"It's a perfectly good tree," he said, standing with the front door wide open and pointing to it on the sidewalk. During winter in Chicago, opening the front door was like opening the door to a walk-in freezer, and the first icy gusts of wind caused me to shiver. Snow whirled into the house as my father dragged the tree inside. A few dozen branches caught on the door frame and snapped off along the way. He said, "I figure somebody took an early vacation and threw this baby out."

Mom said, "You found it in a Dumpster? It's probably crawling with vermin, Frank." Instead of helping with the tree, she turned and headed for the kitchen. Whenever she was mad, she loved to pretend that she was cleaning the cabinet that held the pots and pans. She could clang around in there for hours.

"Vermin?" Dad called out over the racket. "In *December?* I didn't see any *rats*, if that's what you mean." He rolled the tree across the living room and into a corner. He sat on the edge of the sofa, lit a cigarette, and stared into the tree. "First real tree we've ever had," he said, "and your mother's putting up a stink."

Kelly had begun walking everywhere barefoot. I almost always heard her before I saw her, and tonight it was her voice I heard first *("What's all the noise down there?")*, followed by stomping. Then she appeared, tromping down the stairs. The living room carpet was jungle-dense green shag, and when her bare foot met the main floor, a pine needle inserted itself into her sole. Kelly screamed and fell to the carpet as if she'd stepped on a land mine, only to have another needle jab her knee when she landed. "Oh my God," she said, afraid to move, staring up at us. And then she started bawling.

Mom ran into the living room, looked at Kelly, and said, "Did something bite her?"

Dad didn't answer. He blew smoke out his nose and prodded the tree with his foot, as if testing it for vermin.

The next night my father came home with a set of plastic reindeer. One reindeer was completely flat, as if a semi had run over it. Another was missing a head. All had been smeared with a mysterious dark soot.

"Where on earth did you find those?" my mother asked.

"Oh, next to the highway. They were just lying there, so I pulled over and threw them in the back of the truck."

Kelly came downstairs wearing combat boots she'd bought earlier that day from an army-surplus store. She took one look at the reindeer and said, "They're deformed."

"You're getting gunk all over the carpet," Mom said to Dad, touching the soot with her forefinger, then holding her finger under a hundred-watt bulb to get a better look.

"Okay, okay," Dad said, dragging the reindeer, which were connected by wire, out of the house. "Hank," he yelled to me, "give me a hand here. I want to put these on the roof."

"Are you sure?" I asked.

"Of course I'm sure. It's Christmas!"

The next night my father came home empty-handed, but the night after that he showed up with a long rectangular piece of sheet metal that was curled on one end and spray-painted red.

"What's that?" I asked.

"Whaddya mean, *what's that?* It's a sleigh. Haven't you ever seen a sleigh before? Me and some of the guys at work, we were screwing off on our break when I spotted some scrap metal. Next thing I knew, we had ourselves a sleigh. Want to give it a whirl?"

"I don't think so," I said.

"Want to watch your old man give it a whirl?" He smiled and waggled his eyebrows.

I shrugged. We lived on a flat street, and the only incline anywhere around was the city's empty reservoir. Once the snow started, the reservoir became the closest thing to a ski resort that we had, and although no one I knew owned skis, they used sheets of corrugated cardboard or metal garbage lids, anything that could be sat on, to slide down the slope. Chances were I would see kids I knew there, and I didn't want my father joining them with his curled-up piece of sheet metal.

"What's wrong with you people, anyway?" my father asked, smiling. "Where's the holiday spirit?" He shook his head from side to side. He had the look of a man who'd stepped off a plane only to find he'd taken the wrong flight. "Okay, give me a hand putting this on the roof behind the reindeer, then. You can do that, can't you?"

Over the next week and a half, my father brought home all kinds of garbage he'd found at the side of the road or in a trash can or behind the factory where he worked: J-shaped plumbing pipes that he claimed looked like silver candy canes; a couple of foot-high Troll dolls with pug noses and rainbow-colored hair that could double as Santa's helpers; and a piece of chicken wire that he bent to look more or less like a camel.

"A camel?" I asked.

"You know," he said. "The Three Wise Guys? The Gift of the Rabbi? *You* know the story. They were sort of like the first Federal Express, only they used a camel instead of a truck."

"Have you been drinking?" Mom asked.

Dad said, "It depends on what you mean by drinking."

Thursday night, after he'd come home from work and eaten dinner, Dad suggested that we search our neighbors' trash to see what we could find. It was the night before garbage pickup, and the streets would be lined with fresh trash.

"You'd be surprised to see what people throw out," he said.

Mom said, "You're *not* letting our son pick through other people's garbage."

From another room, I heard Kelly say, "Gross," and then she appeared, combat boots on. She pulled a pair of binoculars from behind her back, looked at me through them, and said, "No telling what kind of bacteria you'll find. You better burn your clothes when you're done, Hank."

Dad draped an arm over my shoulders and said, "We're not going to be tearing into sacks, if that's what you girls think. We're just going to see what they've left by the curb. The bigger items. Isn't that right, Hank?"

I nodded. It was easier to agree than to disagree, so I found myself agreeing to all kinds of things I really didn't want to agree with.

After the two of us settled into the pickup's ice-cold cab, Dad pulled a can of beer from his coat pocket. I'd always liked the sound it made, the hiss, when he popped one open. He said, "Women," and took the first loud slurp.

Unlike other dads I knew who bought plastic holders for their drinks, the kind that hung from inside their car-door window, my father used a roll of duct tape. It sat next to him on the seat, and he placed the can of beer inside the tape's hole. It was heavy enough so the drink wouldn't slip around, and the can was a perfect fit—not too tight, not too loose.

Using the roll as a drink coaster was ingenious, really, and I wondered how a man who could think up something that brilliant could come up with some of his other hare-brained ideas.

When my father lifted the beer for another sip, I asked, "What if people don't want us messing with their trash?"

My father laughed. He set down the drink and dug into his shirt pocket for a cigarette. Cigarette smoke always burned my eyes, but whenever I mentioned this, my father would tell me to crack a window. It was so cold tonight, though, that I needed the window up to keep my teeth from chattering.

My father puffed several times to get the cigarette going. He said, "Listen. Garbage is fair game. You throw it out, it's no longer yours, pal. The United States has some of the best garbage in the world. You're living in junk heaven, and don't ever forget it."

At first we stopped to examine only the big stuff, as promised, but when the big stuff wasn't panning out, Dad made me untie garbage sacks while he used a flashlight and a tire iron to poke through it.

"Good God," he said. "The things people eat!"

"I don't think this is a good idea," I said. "Why don't we go home?"

"Maybe you're right," he said. "Looks like a bad week for garbage. But don't go thinking that's a poor reflection on our fine country."

A block from our house, my father spotted three white beanbag chairs next to a trash can, piled one on top of the other. "Bingo!" he said.

"They're losing their beans," I said. "They look sort of, I don't know, *deflated*."

"Don't you see what they look like, though?" he said.

"What?"

"It looks just like a freaking snowman!" he said. "You can't see that?"

"Not really," I said. "No, I guess not."

"Use your imagination," Dad said. "Don't they teach you to use your imagination in school? A little paint for a face, and it'll look just like a snowman. And the great thing is, it won't melt. All of our dipshit neighbors will have to worry each and every time the sun comes out, but not us, no sir."

While my father revved the engine, I heaved each beanbag chair into the bed of the pickup, where they looked more like a giant albino insect from a horror movie than a dozing snowman. A radioactive ant, I thought. The sort of thing that might push open our front door, shimmy inside, and eat our whole family alive.

Friday night my father came home with a copy of the *Southtown Economist* and opened it up so that it covered the food Mom had put on the table. He said, "Look at this, ladies and germs." Steam from a plate of chicken legs was starting to make the paper sag, but Dad just snapped it back into shape and said, "A contest for the best holiday decorations on the South Side!"

Kelly said, "I can't get to the rolls, Dad."

Mom, frowning, said, "Where'd you find that paper?"

"Huh?"

"The paper? Where'd you get it?"

It was a good question; Dad never read the newspaper. "Lucky's," he said.

Lucky's was the neighborhood tavern, and this past year my father had earned enough points from all the beer he'd bought there that the bartender presented him with a wooden stein with his name on it. I'd never seen it because the stein, according to my father, remained on a shelf behind the bar, along with all the other steins presented to those who had earned the right. It was, Dad said, the highest honor Lucky's bestowed upon its customers.

"That paper's probably filthy," Mom said, "and now it's touching the food we're about to eat."

"Huh? Oh." Dad raised the paper higher, but one of its corners curled over, as if trying to lick Dad's plate. "Look," he said. "The deadline's next Friday. The winner gets five hundred bones. I don't want to knock our good neighbors or anything"—here my father snickered; he hated our neighbors—"but the way I see it, any frickin' idiot can go to the Kmart and *buy* decorations." He looked at me. "Am I right, Hank? Sure I am. But not everyone can turn nothing into something. Which is what we're doing. The entry fee is only, let's see . . ." He rattled the paper a few times, leaning over and squinting. "Ah, here it is. Twenty-five bucks." He looked up and said, "Not a bad investment for a five-hundred-dollar payday.

But me and Hank, we've got a hell of a lot of work to do before next Friday, don't we?"

I nodded.

Dad reached over the table and cuffed my shoulder. "My little apprentice," he said, then rolled up the dirty newspaper and swatted the top of my head with it.

Early Saturday morning, before anyone else was awake, I looked out my bedroom window and saw Ralph standing in the middle of the street, staring at our house. He wasn't wearing a coat. He was squinting and nodding, but I couldn't tell what he was thinking. Ralph lived in a shingled shotgun house with his mother, but since I'd never actually seen his mother, I sometimes wondered if he lived there alone, coming and going as he pleased. It was possible, I supposed. I wasn't going to ask, though. I was too polite to ask. Politeness, I was coming to understand, was my downfall.

"Ralph," I said after stepping outside, bundled up in my snorkel parka, the hood pulled up and unrolled so that it funneled out from my face at least a foot, narrowing into a small porthole and ending in a wreath of fake fur. "Is everything okay?" I asked through the hood's long tunnel.

"What?"

"IS EVERYTHING OKAY?" I yelled.

Ralph nodded.

I was standing next to the beanbag snowman, but I tried not to notice it. I expected Ralph to ask what was happening to our house, but he didn't say a word. He shuffled toward me, but his eyes were busy recording everything my father and I had done. A slight wind whispered past, and three dangling candy canes made out of plumbing pipes banged over my head. My father had brought home red book-binding tape from work, and he wrapped the tape around each pipe to create the swirls of candy canes, but they still looked like plumbing supplies.

Ralph said, "I'm broke, Hank. Dead broke. And then last night I saw some Christmas carolers going door-to-door, and I had an idea."

I cringed. I always feared Ralph's ideas. I pictured myself, Ralph, and

Kenny and Norm knocking on people's doors and singing "Jingle Bells" for money. I didn't want any part of it.

"Look," I said. "I can't really sing, Ralph. I'm sort of tone-deaf, if you want to know the truth."

Ralph said, "What are you talking about? We're not *singing*. Are you crazy?"

"Good," I said. I rolled back the tunneled hood so I could see and hear Ralph better.

Ralph said, "Actually, I was wondering if you wanted to help me *jump* them so we could take their money."

"You want me to help you mug the Christmas carolers?" I asked.

Ralph shrugged. "Mug. Jump. Whatever."

"Do people give them money?" I asked.

"Sometimes," Ralph said. "Tips and whatnot. Plus, they probably have a little spending money of their own. You know, for juice or candy bars."

I wasn't going to help Ralph mug Christmas carolers, but when I asked how old they were, Ralph perked up. "Fourth-graders," he said. "Fifth grade, tops. I promise. The way I see it, we'll be outnumbered—there's got to be at least six of them—but two of them are chicks, and all of them are at least three years younger than you and five years younger than me."

Going door-to-door and shouting "Jingle Bells" off-key suddenly didn't sound so bad after all. "I don't know," I said. "I don't think it's a good idea."

Ralph said, "Yeah, well, maybe you're right. I guess six of them could do some damage to us, especially if they're carrying weapons."

"Weapons? What kind of weapons would a bunch of carolers have?"

"I don't know," Ralph said. "Could be anything. Steak knives, corkscrews, ice picks. Kids these days'll turn anything into a weapon." He sighed and shook his head. He seemed to be reconsidering the plan.

Relieved, I leaned against the beanbag snowman, which was a mistake. Ralph's eyes had followed my elbow, stopping at the snowman's head. He reached out and, using his fingernail, scraped the face my father had painted on yesterday after a late night at Lucky's. The paint was too thick in places, dripping at the corners of the snowman's eyes and mouth, causing it to look like a beanbag version of Alice Cooper. After chipping off some of the thicker clumps of paint, Ralph tucked his hands into his pockets.

I said, "Dad's entering the house in a Christmas-decoration contest. The winner gets five hundred bucks."

Ralph, frowning and nodding, said, "So *that's* what's going on here."

"What did you *think* it was?" I asked, acting offended.

"No, no," Ralph said. "I can see it now." He was walking backward to take in the whole house at once. He said, "It looks like something Picasso would do."

Only last week our class had taken a school field trip all the way downtown to the Art Institute of Chicago to see the Picasso exhibit, but we were all bored out of our skulls, and no one paid much attention. The next day at school, our art teacher said, "You should be ashamed of yourselves. All of you. You were looking at the work of a genius, but what did you care? You were bored, right?" I had made the mistake of nodding.

I assumed that Ralph, who had failed two grades, would have been even more bored than the rest of us, but apparently this wasn't the case.

"Picasso?" I said. "You think so?"

"Absolutely," Ralph said. "Your father's a genius."

"*My* father?" I said. "A *genius?*"

Ralph nodded. He said, "But don't expect the judges of the contest to recognize that. That's the whole deal with being a genius. No one realizes you're one until you're dead."

I turned around and looked at the house. I wasn't sure that I saw what Ralph saw, but then I wasn't sure what the big deal was about Picasso, either, so what did I know?

Ralph said, "Listen. About the mugging. If you change your mind . . ."

"I don't think I'll be changing my mind," I said.

"You never know," Ralph said. "All I'm saying is, if you decide you *do* want to jump a bunch of little kids who can't sing worth crap, come and get me."

It was getting colder, so I rolled out the snorkel parka and yelled, "WILL DO!"

The week before Christmas I asked the art teacher, Mrs. Richards, if I could borrow one of her books about Picasso. She eyed me suspiciously but looked anyway, digging through a pile of brushes, crepe paper, chunks of plaster, and globs of clay until she found the book. "I expect this to be returned to me in the condition I'm giving it to you," she said.

That entire week I had a hard time staying awake in school. I normally had problems staying awake, but this week I couldn't keep my eyes open because I was up until at least midnight every night helping my father.

Dad brought home sheets of plywood from work—"They'll never miss it!"—but since we didn't own the appropriate tools for doing fancy edge work, like curlicues, everything we made looked as though it had been attacked by a blind man swinging an ax. *This*, I was starting to see, was part of Dad's genius.

"There!" he said. "Why don't we paint a holiday message on one of these. Not your usual holiday message. Something original."

I said, "What about 'Happy Christmas and Merry New Year'?"

Dad narrowed his eyes at me. He could tell there was something wrong with what I'd said, but what I'd said wasn't so different from the original that he couldn't immediately tell *what* was different about it. A dozen empty Schlitz cans sat along a sawhorse. Artists, I'd read in the Picasso book, were tortured by demons, and they often sought the company of alcohol and other substances. This explained why Dad had earned the beer stein at Lucky's. He was a tortured artist.

"No, no," Dad finally said. "Here. Hand me the spray paint." Before I could offer another suggestion, he started shaking the can. "Tell me, kiddo," he said after he'd stopped shaking. "What's the first thing that comes to mind when you think of Argo?"

Argo was two towns northwest, our football archrival, home to the Argo cornstarch factory. On a day with only the slightest of breezes, the wind picked up the stench and carried it from town to town, causing those who didn't live with the cornstarch smell on a daily basis to gag and run inside. It was the sort of smell that lodged itself into your nose and stayed there for days.

"Well," I said, "it stinks, if that's what you mean."

"Exactly." He ruffled my hair, then started spraying. He sprayed so close to the board that the first letter looked like a blazing sun of hot tar, but then he backed up and tried again. "What do you think?" he said when he'd finished. In large block letters, the sign read: JINGLE BELLS, ARGO SMELLS!

"You sure you want to put this outside?" I asked.

"Absolutely," Dad said. "What this shows is town pride. That's always good for a few extra votes."

"Okay," I said. I helped Dad drag the enormous sheet of jagged-edged plywood out to the curb, and we leaned it against the mailbox.

Dad stood in the street to take a look. "That oughta do 'er," he said.

I imagined whole books written about my father and his art, each including a chapter about his son, Hank, and how he was the only one in the entire Boyd family who had understood the old man, and how much that meant to the genius on his deathbed.

The next night Dad said, "What have I been thinking? We keep checking the garbage in our own neighborhood when what we should be doing is checking out the hoity-toity neighborhoods."

"You're right!" I said, nearly yelling to show my enthusiasm.

We waited until dusk to tool around the suburb of Beverly, a place I didn't even know existed. Some houses were smeared in stucco and had roofs made of orange tiles, the kind that looked like flowerpots cut in half. I'd seen houses like these on TV shows set in California or Florida, but I'd never seen any in Chicago. The streets had been plowed all the way to the concrete, and the excess snow lugged away. I couldn't imagine where it had been taken. The curbs were lined with garbage cans—large squarish plastic cans placed neatly side by side. No slumping Hefty bags. No punctured Glad bags oozing intestines of spaghetti. But there were also no large items—no appliances, no bicycles. Did these people buy things that didn't break so easily? Or had someone already beaten us here, someone who knew the best time to swoop in and pick through the hoity-toities' trash?

Dad said, "We better take a closer look. No telling what they're storing in those trash cans."

"Really?" I said. "You think?"

"Hell, yeah. I didn't burn all this gas to come here and admire their lawns."

"I don't want to pick through garbage anymore," I said. A whine had crept into my voice.

"Oh, okay," Dad said. "I see. You're embarrassed to be with your own father."

"No, that's not it," I said.

Dad held up his hand, palm out, as if to say, *Halt!* He said, "I didn't think it would ever come to this, but I don't know why not. I was embarrassed of my old man, too. He was senile and sometimes went out in public without his pants on, but maybe I should have gone a little easier on him, the crazy bastard."

The knife stab of guilt punctured me. Who was I to thwart my father's project? Picking through garbage was a small price to pay for being in the company of genius, so I told him okay, I would do it.

"No, you don't have to," he said. "I wouldn't want to embarrass you."

"Stop it," I said. "I said I'd do it."

Can after can, I raised the lid while my father aimed the flashlight inside. Each and every bag was neatly shut with twist ties, so my father gave me his Swiss army knife with its pair of minuscule scissors for me to snip the heads off, allowing him to poke about with his trusty tire iron. The tire iron was such a useful tool, I was starting to wonder why I didn't own one myself. I was about to ask my father if I could have one for Christmas when a police cruiser rolled up and flipped on its swirling lights.

My father, whose face alternated between blue and red, said, "Goddamn it all to hell."

The cop got out, shining a flashlight into our faces, and said, "How are you gentlemen doing tonight?"

My father shined his flashlight into the cop's face and said, "Just fine. And yourself?"

"Put your flashlight down, sir," the cop said, squinting. "*Now!*"

Under his breath, my father said, "They don't like it when you do to them what they do to you." He lowered the flashlight.

The cop came over, took a good long look at me, then looked down at the Swiss army knife in my hand. He cut his eyes to my father and said, "Looking for food?"

My father laughed. "What, do we look like hoboes? Do we look like vagrants? Ha! That's a good one. No, my son and I are looking for *junk*."

"Junk? What kind of junk?"

"The kind of junk a person can use to decorate his house."

The cop nodded. It was clear he didn't know what my father was talking about. He said, "Look, sir, I'm going to let you go with a warning. But you can't be coming here, rooting around other people's trash. The people here, they don't like it."

"Tough titty," my dad said. "The law says that once you throw something out, it's fair game. Isn't that the law where you live, too? I bet it is. Unless, of course, you live in one of *these* houses. Hank, do you think the officer lives in one of these houses?" Though the question was directed to me, my father didn't move his eyes from the cop. He snorted and, before I could answer, said, "Nope, I don't *think* so."

"Don't get smart," the cop said.

I snickered. Little did he know that he was telling a genius not to get smart.

The cop said, "I see you're raising your kid well, too."

While the cop lectured my father, I reached into one of the garbage cans and pulled out a photo of a family. The photo had been glued onto a piece of artificial wood so that it would look like a slice of tree. In the photo were a father, a mother, a daughter, and a son. Amazingly, the family looked like my family. It was dark out, and I couldn't see it all that well, but I could tell that the boy was about my age and the girl was about Kelly's size and shape. The parents, though better dressed, could have been my parents. I looked at the house where the photo had come from, but the lights were out, and I couldn't see anyone moving around inside.

"Ah, fuck it," my father said to the cop. "We'll go. There's no good junk around here, anyway. Isn't that right, Hank?"

I nodded.

The cop wrote up a warning and handed it to my father. He told us he didn't want to see us around here again.

"Not a problem," my father said. As the cop walked back to his cruiser, my father looked down at the photo I was holding and said, "What the hell's that?"

"A family portrait," I said, handing it to him. "Look familiar?"

Dad studied it a moment. "Nope," he said, and tossed it back in the trash.

Inside the truck, my father handed me the warning and told me to stuff it in the glove compartment. I popped it open, and a dozen other warnings sprang out onto my lap. My father said, "Don't make a mess, you hear? Just cram everything inside and slam it shut." He reached under his seat and pulled out a can of beer. Then he reached down and pulled out another can. "Here," he said. "We've had a tough night, kiddo. You deserve this one. Yes indeedy. We *both* deserve it."

I couldn't sleep that night because of the beer. Every few minutes I needed to pee. Eventually I ran out of pee but still felt like I had to go. When I couldn't fall back asleep, I stood up and touched my toes a few times. Our gym teacher had told us that a good way to keep in shape was to do some sort of exercise whenever you were bored, and since I was bored all the time, I was always touching my toes. There were times when my mother or father would be talking to me, and I'd reach down and touch my toes. Lately, every time my sister opened her mouth to say something, I'd reach down and touch my toes before she could get the first word out. Tonight I touched my toes three times. When I raised up the third time, I saw Ralph standing across the street and taking notes. I had no idea how long he'd been there. It was two in the morning. I knocked on the window. Ralph looked up, saw me, and quickly folded his pocket notebook.

I put on my snorkel parka and shoes, then tiptoed downstairs. "What are you doing here?" I asked, shivering in the street.

"The house is looking sweet. How's Pablo?"

"*Who?*"

"Your dad," Ralph said.

"Oh. He's okay." Since Ralph seemed to know so much about art, I decided to impress him by quoting a line of Picasso's that I had committed to memory. I cleared my throat. "You know," I said from inside the cave of my snorkel hood, "'we all know that Art is not truth. Art is a lie that makes us realize the truth, at least the truth that is given to us to understand.'"

"Whatever," Ralph said. "Hey, listen, I was wondering if you'd thought anymore about jumping those carolers. We're only a few days away from Christmas, so our window of opportunity is, you know, shrinking by the second."

"That's why you came by?" I asked.

"Naw. I came by to check out the house, see how it's coming along. But now that you're out here, I figured I'd see where you were leaning on the issue of the carolers." Ralph grinned, waiting.

"I don't think I'm up to it. I've been working a lot of late nights." I nodded toward the house.

Ralph said, "Yeah; well; I figured as much. The thing is, I've got a backup plan to make some money. It's a long shot, though. Not like the carolers. The carolers were a sure thing."

My fingers were starting to feel like icicles attached to larger blocks of ice. I said, "I better go inside."

Ralph nodded. "Go ahead. I'll only be a few more minutes."

Back in my bedroom, I peeked out my window again and saw Ralph scratching out a few more notes. What was he writing? Before I could shut the curtain, he caught me watching him. I started to wave, but he tucked the pad into his pocket and headed toward home.

The day before the judges were to drive around and evaluate the houses, my father stayed home from work to put on the final touches. My parents' voices occasionally floated up through the vents, and I heard my mother say at one point, "Frank, you can't afford to stay home from work."

"Don't worry about it," Dad said. "I've got enough sick time built up to get a fair-size brain tumor removed. Trust me. It's no biggie."

I had woken up that morning coughing and shivering, unable to concentrate on any one thing for over a second. The flu had come to visit me in the night. I tried touching my toes, but halfway down, I felt like puking. I ran to the bathroom and locked myself inside. Later, Dad came pounding at the door.

"Ready to give me a hand, big guy?" he asked.

"I don't feel too good," I said.

"Very funny," Dad said. "The judges'll be here tonight. I need your help." When I opened the door, my father took a step back. "Whoa! Don't tell your mother I gave you that beer, okay? In fact, you better not even let her see you like this."

"It's the flu," I said.

"The flu?" he said. "Thank God! Whew!" And then he was out of my room, yelling down the stairs, "Hey, your son's got the flu! He looks like death warmed over!"

When Mom finally came up to check on me, she was carrying a bowl of hot soup and four Flintstone chewable vitamins. She pulled out a thermometer, shook it a few thousand times, then stabbed the underside of my tongue with its silver point. When she slid it out, she said, "Poor kid. One hundred and three." I groaned. Mom said, "Here, drink your soup and take your vitamins. I've got to make sure your father doesn't set the house on fire. That man's driving me to an early grave, I swear." Before she left, she said, "Call me if you need something." As I popped two Freds, a Barney, and a Wilma into my mouth, I heard Kelly say, "You're faking it," and then she appeared to appraise my illness. She was still wearing army boots, but she'd added a camouflage jacket and matching pants. All she needed was some green and black makeup, and we could throw her into a jungle somewhere. "What excuse did you and Dad cook up today?" she asked. "The flu?"

"Listen, GI Joe," I said. "I don't have to prove to you that I'm sick. I have a fever of one hundred and three."

She rolled her eyes. Then she took a step closer and said, "Why aren't you outside helping Dad destroy the house we live in?"

"Destroy?" I said. I laughed. It wasn't worth explaining to her about Picasso, about the tortured nature of artists, about how great art always goes unappreciated at first.

Kelly, without any inflection, said, "I've always wanted to be the laughingstock of the neighborhood. I'd like to thank you and Dad for helping me to achieve that goal."

"No problem," I said. "Anytime. But you didn't really need our help," I added.

Kelly stuck both hands into her camouflage jacket, and I worried that maybe she'd bought an army-issue pistol, a sleek black job with a silencer, but she kept her hands hidden and backed out of the room, ghostlike, leaving me to shiver and hallucinate in peace.

Periodically I'd peek out the window to see what Dad was up to. Twice a black Monte Carlo with tinted windows crept past the house. A judge, I thought.

All day I drifted in and out of sleep, freezing one minute, boiling the next. Mom occasionally poked her head in to check on me, though I was pretty certain I had hallucinated some of those times, especially when the door opened slightly and I saw only an eye, part of an arm, and the first few inches of a foot, Mom's body broken apart like one of Picasso's paintings, nothing whole, nothing as it should have been.

It was after midnight when my father finished with the house. I waited for Dad to come get me so we could look at it together. I waited and waited, but apparently they thought I was too sick. Everyone had already gone to bed by the time I made my way downstairs in my pajamas. "Hello?" I whispered. "Anybody awake?" I was dizzy from the flu, dizzy from being in bed all day, dizzy from not eating as much as I should have, but I really wanted to see the house, so I put on the first coat I found—it turned out to be one of my mother's, knee-length and insulated—and slipped on a pair of my father's too big mukluks.

As soon as I stepped outside, wind blew sheets of snow at me, pelting my face, and I had to duck my head just to make it into the street. Snow blew up the legs of my pajamas, but I still had a fever, so the cold air felt sort of good. I shut my eyes and turned around, preparing myself to take in the whole house at once, and then I opened my eyes. The moon, full and low, lit up our house.

"Holy smoke," I said. I shivered hard, but it wasn't from the cold. Dad had transformed our house into a masterpiece. As with most masterpieces, it was hard to put into words *why* it was a masterpiece; it just was. I had read in the Picasso book that modern art wasn't scientific, and it wasn't intellectual; it was visual. When it came from the eye of a genius like my dad, even fools should have been able to see they were looking at the real deal. As best as I could tell, Dad's vision was this: Christmas gave everyone a good beating—the way the flattened reindeer leaned against the TV antenna, or the way that the plumbing-pipe candy canes swung heavily in the wind, or the trolls, which could barely be seen, appeared to be climbing down the drainpipe at the corners of the house, as if escaping the long hours of Santa's workshop.

It was chilling. I found myself wanting to weep right there at both the beauty and the sadness of it all, but before I could squeeze out the first tears, the black Monte Carlo with its smoky windows came rolling up to the house. The judges could finally look at Dad's vision of Christmas and see for themselves how great it was, but when they put the windows down, I saw that the people inside weren't judges at all. It was a group of high school punks.

The doors opened, and all four guys got out. They walked over to our Christmas greeting, and the driver said, "'Jingle bells, Argo smells.'" He looked up at me. "Argo smells, huh?"

I wasn't sure what to say. It *did* smell. I said, "Sort of."

"*Sort of?* Well, *we're* from Argo, and *we* don't think it smells." He kicked our sign.

I was about to tell him how sometimes you couldn't smell something bad when you were standing in the middle of it, and I was going to give him a few examples, when one of the guys pushed me.

"Look," he said. "He's wearing a woman's coat. He's making fun of the place we live, and he's wearing a woman's coat."

"It's my mother's," I began explaining, but a fist met my stomach with such force that I was knocked clean out of my father's mukluks. Before I could plead with them, I was surrounded by the rest of the thugs, and more fists landed against my ribs and my back. Oddly enough, it wasn't as bad as I'd expected, and after they had sped off in their car, I didn't feel hurt so much as sleepy. One minute I was sitting in a mound of snow, leaning against the busted ARGO SMELLS sign, considering taking a nap. The next minute the police were at our house, I was inside with a blanket wrapped around me, and some guy with a stethoscope was shining a penlight into my eyes. My father was pacing the living room and yelling about how he was going to kill the sons of bitches who broke his sign.

"What's wrong?" I asked.

"Oh, honey," Mom said. "Oh, sweetie. Are you okay?"

"I'm fine," I said.

My father said, "I want blood!"

A short and stocky cop who looked like he might have been a high school wrestler said, "Mr. Boyd. You're going to have to calm down, sir."

Another cop—this one older and with a walrus mustache—came inside, blowing into his palms to warm up. He said something, but you couldn't see his lips moving because of the thick mustache bristles. He looked around as if maybe he'd stepped into the wrong house, then said, "There's another little problem we'll need to discuss."

"What's that?" my father asked.

"It's a matter of the, uh, *junk* you've got lying around."

"Junk? What junk?" Dad asked.

"Let's see." While the cop looked at his notepad, he tapped around the bottom edge of his mustache with the tip of his tongue. I'm sure it was an old habit, checking for crumbs, and I could imagine his wife saying, *Honey, you've got a chunk of cake on your . . . right there . . . good . . . you got it!* He said, "Those three old beanbag chairs? That violates the upholstered-furniture ordinance. That loose sheet of metal up on the roof is a hazard. A good wind could take that down and slice somebody's head off. As for that huge wooden spool, it appears to be the property of the telephone company. Do you work for the telephone company, Mr. Boyd?"

"I don't see your point," Dad said.

"The point," the cop said, "is that I have a list here. It's about four pages long. There are ordinances about maintaining your property, and you're in violation of most of them."

"Maintaining my property?" my father said. "What, are you *crazy?* Those are decorations!"

The cop looked down at his notepad again. "I think maybe we're talking about different things here," he said. "What I'm talking about is all that *junk* out there. I can show you the list, but I don't think you need to see it. I called the department, and according to our records, we issued a warning last week."

"You did?"

The cop nodded. "It's supposed to be cleaned up by tomorrow. There's a stiff fine if it's not." He stuck out his tongue as if to do some more checking, but then thought better of it. He nodded, looked around the house as he'd done when he arrived, then walked backward to the front door and let himself out. It was like watching a movie in reverse.

"Clean it up?" I yelled. "You *can't* make him clean it up. My dad's a genius! What's wrong with you people?"

The stocky wrestler-cop pivoted his torso toward me, sizing me up. He said, "The poor kid's still delirious."

My father, using a stage whisper, said, "Hank, take it easy there, pal."

"He must have suffered some brain damage." This came from Kelly. She was sitting in a corner wearing an army helmet I'd never seen before, knees pulled up to her neck. Had she been there the whole time?

"This is what the Nazis did to artists," I said. "I bet they're going to make you burn everything, too."

"Oh, no," the cop said. "No one's setting anything on fire. We've got rules about burning stuff, too. Better you just pile it up neatly for the garbageman."

My mother said, "What about my son? What are you going to do about that?"

"Oh yeah. Right. Well, sounds like a bunch of teenagers from another town and, well, there's not a lot you can do. If you see them again, though, give us a call."

My mother nodded, but her fists were clenched.

After the police left, my father said, "Cops! I bet both those sons of bitches have their own houses entered in the contest. You just watch when the results come in." He put on his coat and headed outside with a crowbar. "Wouldn't surprise me one bit, no sir."

When I woke up the next day—the day the judges were to visit each house—I thought I had dreamed all that had happened the night before, but when I stood up and felt my bruised muscles, the ache in my ribs, I knew all of it had really happened. I opened my curtains and gasped. Next to the curb were all the decorations that Dad and I had carefully selected. Piled that way, it looked like what it really was—*junk*.

Downstairs, I asked Mom where Dad was.

"Work."

"Work?" I said. The idea of Dad doing something as ordinary as going to work depressed me.

"He gets time and a half today," Mom said. "That's nothing to sneeze at."

"I need to go somewhere," I said.

"Oh, no," Mom said. "Yesterday you had a temperature over one hundred. You're not going anywhere today, mister."

I wanted to argue, but I knew who'd win. The more you argued with Mom, the harder she dug in. Before you knew it, you'd be locked in a room and chained to a bed, wishing you'd kept your mouth shut.

"Okey-doke," I said.

I waited until Dad had come home, until we'd all finished eating, before sneaking away. While everyone thought I was calling it an early night, I slipped out the back door and put on my snorkel parka, which I had dumped behind some bushes earlier that day. What I hadn't counted on was the parka freezing. The arms were stiff, and I was colder with it on than off. I might as well have tied it to a rope and stored it in Lake Michigan.

I kept it on, though, hoping my shivering would generate some heat, which it did. I needed to see Ralph. He was the only other person who'd understand what an outrage it was that my father had been forced to ruin his masterpiece.

As I rounded the corner of Ralph's street, the first thing I saw was Ralph's cousin's Nova. Both cousins, Kenny and Norm, were sitting on the trunk and drinking beer. They each lived in apartments furnished with things they'd made in high school shop class. Kenny had a lamp whose shade was a Budweiser can with the top sliced off. Norm had a plywood coffee table covered with *Playboy* centerfolds and then lacquered. I liked Kenny better than I liked Norm, but I liked Norm's place better. I'd never even seen a *Playboy* except for the shiny pages that were part of Norm's coffee table, and I found that the longer I stared at the table, the harder it was to walk away.

Tonight Kenny and Norm had a cooler next to the bumper, half sunk into a mound of snow. When I got closer, I saw that Ralph had decorated his mother's house for the contest. What wasn't immediately apparent was what holiday he had decorated the house in honor of.

Oil drums with ten-foot flames shooting out lined the sidewalk. A glowing six-foot statue of Jesus held a Roman candle. I was about to yell out to Ralph, but a Roman candle shot from Jesus' hand and whistled into the sky. Ralph then removed a bedsheet to reveal a life-size manger. Painted on the side of the manger was what appeared at first glance to be an angel but on closer inspection was actually the logo Led Zeppelin had used for their Swan Song record label.

"I did that," Kenny said, pointing.

Inside the manger was a statue of a Cherokee Indian that used to stand atop a building in town. Next to it was a blow-up Frankenstein doll.

Norm said, "Indians and monsters together. *That's* the real spirit of Christmas, folks."

"What's it mean?" I asked.

Kenny said, "It means that life is fucked up. It means that life is weirder than any of us ever imagined." He finished his beer, tossed the can into a neighbor's yard, and said, "Hand me another one, little man."

Jesus shot off four more Roman candles, but when one of the still-sizzling fireworks came spiraling back down and hit the manger, the whole thing went up in flames.

"Holy shit," Kenny said. "Get a fire extinguisher."

Norm said, "No, no, man. It's working. This is the way it should be."

By the time the fire trucks arrived, the manger had burned to the snow, and the fire had all but extinguished itself. Ralph stood next to me while the firemen hosed off the oil drums.

"I figured it'd come down to me and your father for first and second place," he said. "Your old man's stiff competition, though."

"Not anymore," I said, and I explained what had happened.

I expected Ralph to get more worked up, but all he did was shake his head and say, "Bastards." Then he slapped me on the back and said, "At least it's good to know that genius runs in your family. From what I've read, it skips a generation, but think about your kids, Hank."

The two cops from the night before walked over to Ralph and handed him a ticket. "You're lucky we're not taking you to jail, pal." The cop with the walrus mustache squinted at me and said, "Haven't I arrested you before?"

"No sir," I said, but the cop didn't believe me. On his way back to the patrol car, he turned to look at me twice, as if trying to remember my crime.

"*Now* what am I going to do?" Ralph said. "I sort of counted on that prize money." He shook his head and sighed. "Give your old man my regards. From one artist to another."

I nodded. "Will do," I said. Ralph and I shook hands, then he wandered over to Kenny and Norm, who were taking stock of the frozen but smoking lawn.

On my way home, I passed house after house with strings of blinking lights, the occasional illuminated Santa waving from a front stoop. I hadn't considered until now just how dull people were, how dull and unimaginative. I was so mad that I wanted to break every window sprayed with fake snow. I wanted to set fire to every wreath on every door. I started packing a snowball when I heard them—their voices glorious, angelic—and then I saw them, pudgy faces red from the cold but beaming, eyes shining in the moonlight, eight boys and girls at the height of their musical powers. Carolers! I was at one street corner; they were at the other. My arms went limp, and the snowball fell from my hand. I'd thought they were coming in my direction, but then they turned, heading where I had just been, marching joyously toward the smoke and the smell of sulfur. I wanted to warn them about Ralph and his cousins, but as soon as one song ended, they began belting out another without pausing to catch their breath. Their singing was mightier than ever, and the smallest of the eight children, ringing his bell loud enough to rouse even the shyest of ghosts, turned and waved at me, and I waved back.

# PEACOCK ALLEY

**R**ALPH WANTED ME TO meet him at Ford City Shopping Center. "The entrance to Peacock Alley," he added. "Do you think you can do that? Can you handle it?"

"Sure," I said. "Why *couldn't* I handle it?"

It was the dead of winter, and Ford City was a good hike from where I lived. Even when it wasn't skull-numbingly cold outside, walking to Ford City was dicey. Part of the way, you followed a fence that separated you from several factories. Attack dogs—Dobermans and rottweilers— bared their teeth and trailed you from their side of the fence, growling the whole way. Eventually you'd cross over into another grade school's territory, where kids would crouch between hedges for the sole purpose of jumping those not from around there. To make matters worse, high school boys and girls were always walking to and from Ford City, and sometimes this meant having to cross all four busy lanes of State Street to avoid running into a group of infamous thugs who hadn't had their day's fill of pummeling. If all of this wasn't enough, you still had to cross Cicero Avenue, an eight-lane road that separated Ford City from my neighborhood, and you had to dodge traffic to get from one side to the other. Sometimes the traffic was so bad you'd end up stranded on the ridged island, fearful that two semis heading in opposite directions might crush you. There were dozens of factories up and down Cicero, and semis sped by all day long. I wanted to think that arriving at Ford City would be like stepping into Oz or some other promised land, but in truth it presented a whole new batch of problems, namely that the thugs were even tougher, and the landscape of concrete and asphalt was more brutal.

My father liked telling the history of Ford City because, for him, a person who'd spent his entire life in Chicago, it was hard to imagine what Ford City had become. We lived only a few miles south of Midway Airport, and during the start of World War II, Ford City had been a government building where Chrysler made B-29s, something called the Superfortress, and engines for bombers. Sometime in the late '40s, a man named Tucker made automobiles there, the Tucker Torpedo, but that didn't last very long. A few years later, during the Korean War, the Ford Motor Company moved in and manufactured jet engines. Not until the early 1960s did a man named Harry Chaddick buy the property and turn it into Ford City Shopping Center. It opened on August 12, 1965, a week before I was born, and my father took my mother, who was full to bursting with me, and my sister, only two years old at the time, to join more than two hundred thousand other people who had gone there to watch the Grand Opening Ribbon-Cutting Ceremony and, more importantly, to catch a glimpse of Mayor Richard J. Daley, a man as famous in Chicago as the pope.

My father didn't see Daley that day, and he took it personally, holding his grudge against Ford City Shopping Center. Each time we drove by, he'd say, "If you ask me—and mind you, nobody has—the damned place still looks like a factory," or "Talk about your eyesores," or "One big red pimple on the ass of our fine city!"

He was right: It *did* still look like a factory. Even though names like Wieboldt's and Montgomery Ward adorned the building's various entrances, you could easily imagine those names gone, and, instead of shoppers, streams of women with goggles pushed up on their heads and lunch pails tapping against their thighs, all filing inside for a day of work on the assembly line, probably already waiting for the shrill whistle when they could finally take a lunch break.

The parking lot, with its long jagged cracks and poked-up dandelions, reminded me of an abandoned airport runway, and if a plane happened to be overhead while I was crossing the lot, I pretended it was a Japanese fighter jet with a blazing red sun painted on either side and a kamikaze pilot inside, spinning the plane toward the mall, spinning like a gyroscope, prepared to take out the entire bomber assembly line. Sometimes, when I was alone, I would even yell, "Banzai!" and then whistle the plane's dark descent, ending with a muffled explosion: *"Kuh-pkkkkkkkkkkkk."*

Ford City Shopping Center was divided into two sections: the main building, with its dozens of stores; and then another strip of buildings across the parking lot, with several more businesses, each of which you entered from outside: the General Cinema movie theater, the bowling alley and pool hall, a fabric store that only old ladies went into, and a few other stores that no one could ever remember because they looked so dull.

I headed for the main building today, the indoor part of Ford City.

Certain stores fascinated me. The store that sold Wurlitzer organs, for instance. I always peeked inside because there were never any customers and because the salesman, bored, could be found playing "When the Saints Go Marching In" with a rumba backbeat. Late at night, with the hope of luring in some of the younger kids, he'd play Yes's "Roundabout" or the Doors' "Light My Fire." It never worked, though. He was greeted by confused looks and the occasional insult. Tall and bony, he wore a white short-sleeved shirt, black slacks, and a long, skinny black tie that made him look like a preacher from one of the fuzzy UHF stations I'd flip past on Sunday mornings while desperately searching for cartoons. I'd never seen a customer pushing an organ out to his pickup truck, so I couldn't imagine how they stayed in business.

Woolworth's was another place. It had an oval-shaped diner that took up a good part of the corridor outside the store. It was an old diner, with old people working there and old people eating there, and a spaceship landing inside the mall wouldn't have seemed any more foreign to me. I'd never eaten at a diner, ever, but I was spellbound by this one—the steaming grill, the dozen hamburgers sizzling at once, the outrageous mountain of hash browns. Men with fedoras sat at the counter and read the newspaper. Since none of my friends' fathers wore fedoras, I wondered where these men came from and why they read the newspaper here rather than at home. I asked my father once about the newspapers, and he said, "Don't get me wrong, I love your mother, but let's just say it's nice to go somewhere where no one's riding your *ass* all day long," and then he winked at me. Each time I walked by the old men at Woolworth's, I imagined old women at home chasing them around with brooms, sweeping them from room to room, accusing them of this or that, until they couldn't take it anymore and rode the city bus down to Woolworth's. Since these were their few precious moments of peace, I always tiptoed by and tried not to stare too long.

Today I walked over to the Peacock Alley entrance. Peacock Alley was an underground mall that you entered from a dank stairwell in the main mall. Painted on the stairwell's walls were the names of various businesses that were supposed to be in Peacock Alley, but I recognized only a few of them. The rest, like Chuck's Fine Photos or Betty's Boutique, were long gone. Since Ford City had a previous history, it was hard to say what Peacock Alley used to be. The narrow hallway was dimly lit, and it twisted all the way beneath the parking lot to the movie theater and the bowling alley. The rumor was that a tunnel ran from Ford City to Midway Airport, and this was how the engineers and mechanics transported important parts for their bombers during wartime. I always looked for secret entrances or walled-up corridors but couldn't find any. In places, the hallway did thin into a tunnel with no stores, and if a large enough family was walking toward you, you'd have to suck in your gut and turn sideways to let them pass.

It was in one of the tunnels that I saw a high school boy kicking another boy in the stomach with his steel-toed boot. This was two years ago; I was in sixth grade. My parents and my sister were shopping upstairs. It was almost closing time, so not many people were left in Peacock Alley. I needed to walk through the tunnel to get back to the mall itself, but I didn't want to walk by the boy with the steel-toed boots, so I turned around and took the exit that led outside. The only thing more dangerous than a Peacock Alley tunnel was the Ford City Shopping Center parking lot at night, but I didn't have a choice. I never knew what happened to the high school boy with the boots, or the boy who was getting kicked, but I made it safely across the dark parking lot, entered

Montgomery Ward from outside, and found my family in the large home-appliance section, where my father was arguing with the salesman about the prices being jacked up and about how he was getting dicked over. "When it comes to my hard-earned money," he said, "I hate getting *dicked over*." My mother was tugging his elbow, trying to get him to drop it. I was dripping sweat, but no one noticed, not even Kelly, who had stuck her entire head inside one of the ovens. When she saw me out of the corner of her eye, she said, "A thirteen-year-old girl with her head in a gas oven and nobody cares." She reached out of the oven and turned one of the knobs higher. I peeked behind the oven. "It's electric," I said, "and it's not plugged in." Kelly emerged, her face red as though she'd been holding her breath, and said, "That's *not* the point," and walked over to a deep freeze, into which I imagined she might crawl and then shut herself.

Today I waited a good twenty minutes for Ralph before heading down into Peacock Alley to look for him. The deeper you went into Peacock Alley, the dizzier you got from the incense that burned in about a third of the stores, incense with names like Jasmine, Funky Cherry, or the Sea of Tranquillity. Some stores used strobe lights to lure customers inside. Down here, teenage girls still wore leather vests with long leather fringe circling their soft bellies. If you looked closely, you might even see a belly button, and although I tried not to give away that I was looking, I always checked to see if it was an innie or an outie. For reasons I couldn't quite put into words, my favorites were the outies, though maybe this was because mine was an innie. On no fewer than five nights, I had fallen asleep to the thought of a girl pressing her outie into my innie.

The first store at the bottom of the stairs sold nothing but wicker furniture. I looked but couldn't see Ralph. The next store was what my mother called a head shop. Teenagers hung out there, slumped at the counter, sometimes smoking cigarettes or looking, as my mother liked to put it, "doped up." Dad told me that if he ever caught me in there, he'd skin me alive. My father had never hit me—not really—but the punishments that he threatened varied in their degree of severity, depending upon the offense. *I'll whup your butt so hard, you won't be able to sit down for a week* was the least serious, probably because of the words *whup* and *butt,* but also because my dad usually said this without any emotion, sometimes not even looking up from whatever he was doing. Next in seriousness was *How'd you like the belt?* Only once did he go so far as to unbuckle it, jerk it from his pants, and double it up, but that was enough to send me running and screaming, as if it were an ax he'd revealed and not the belt I'd bought for him at Kmart for Father's Day. Finally, there was the threat of being skinned alive, which scared me for three reasons. Number one: He'd threatened me with it only four times in my life, and *less* carried more power than *more.* Number two: He always looked me in the eye when he said it, and since he almost never looked me in the eye, this scared the wits out of me. Number three: I'd read a Scholastic book about Indians skinning their enemies, so I knew how much pain my father was talking about. I imagined him going so far as burying me up to my neck in the dirt on a hot day and then pouring honey over my skinned head, letting ants and wasps have a field day with me. The result of the threat was that I wouldn't even look at the head shop, let alone step inside. The first place of business that I would step inside was the record shop, which was blocked off from the hallway not by walls but by a wrought-iron gate that was as high as my hip.

In the record store, where they burned incense not so much by the stick as by the pound, I looked at the Roxy Music album covers because there were naked women on them. I also looked at the Rolling Stones' *Sticky Fingers* album because it had a real zipper on the front of it. In addition to being one of the strangest things I'd ever seen, it was the first time I saw how two things that weren't alike at all could come together to surprise everyone who came into contact with them. An album cover with a zipper! Who'd have thought it was possible? I looked at Linda Ronstadt and Olivia Newton-John albums because I had crushes on both of them, and then I looked at Styx albums because they were from the South Side of Chicago. I loved flipping through the posters, too. One of my favorites was of W. C. Fields wearing a stovepipe hat and peeking up from a handful of fanned cards. I also liked the one from *Easy Rider* with a guy riding a chopper. I liked how choppers looked and wanted to turn my three-speed bicycle into a chopper, but when I asked my father if I could use his blowtorch, he asked me how I'd like his belt. The poster that I saved for last was Farrah Fawcett-Majors in a red swimsuit, her white teeth practically glowing, her loopy signature in the bottom right-hand corner. I didn't look at her teeth or swimsuit or signature until I had studied, with my forehead almost touching the poster itself, Farrah Fawcett-Majors's nipples, the way you could see them in amazing detail through her swimsuit. They seemed to be an optical illusion, a trick of the eye, and it was for this reason and this reason alone that I studied them so closely and for so long, a sincere attempt to determine if they were real or if the photo had been tampered with. I couldn't ever come to a satisfying conclusion and was forced to continue my investigations each time I visited Ford City. I never bought anything from the record store because I never had any money, but looking was good enough. Sometimes looking was as good as getting something free.

After the record store came Nickelodeon Pizza, where high school boys sat at the counter and flirted with the waitresses. It was a different planet, a different *solar system,* from the Woolworth's diner upstairs, and I wondered if the customers of one place even knew about the existence of the other. I doubted it. Beyond Nickelodeon Pizza was a gag shop that sold rubber masks of Richard Nixon, Gerald Ford, and Jimmy Carter. My father once suggested that the four of us go as presidents for Halloween one year.

"But I see only three presidents," I'd said.

My father shrugged. "One of us could go as the Wolfman, I suppose."

The masks were expensive, and I knew my father would never fork over that kind of money for four rubber masks, but it bothered me for days on end that he couldn't see how wrong it would be for only *three* of us to be presidents while one of us was a monster. Why couldn't he see the problem with that?

I sauntered through the tunnel, still hoping to bump into Ralph, but the longer I went without seeing him, the less likely it was that we were going to meet up. Maybe I had the wrong time. Maybe we were supposed to meet tomorrow.

The end of the tunnel meant that the smell of incense would be replaced by the rich stench of perm solution. Ford City Beauty School was where my mother took me for haircuts. They charged half of what other places charged so that the girls, who weren't yet licensed to cut hair, could experiment on a bunch of different cheapskates' heads. Sometimes the haircut looked pretty good, but more often than not, one of my ears looked higher than it should have, or I appeared to be in the first stages of going bald, or, thanks to crooked bangs, one eye seemed an inch lower than my other eye. I didn't mind because the girls, who weren't much older than me, only four or five years, would press into me while they snipped away, and I had to be careful not to think about Farrah Fawcett-Majors and, failing that, not to let the girl cutting my hair see the rising drop cloth on my lap. The few times this had happened, I was reminded of magicians who made blanketed girls levitate, an image that only made matters worse.

I loved the beauty school. I'd never been to a fun house, but I suspected that getting my hair cut wasn't so different: I was strapped in a chair, raised and lowered, tilted back, and surrounded by so many mirrors that I could look nearly anywhere and see myself disappearing into infinity. I always left the beauty school knock-kneed—the lights had been so bright, the perm solution so dizzying, the beautician's body so warm that my own temperature rose a few notches—and the whole time I wouldn't say a word. I'd just sit there, breathing heavier and heavier, until the girl I had fallen in love with, whichever girl happened to be cutting my hair, untied the drop cloth and set me free.

Ford City Beauty School was the end of the road, the last main attraction of Peacock Alley, and then came the stairwell to the parking lot, up into the first shaft of light. Climbing the stairs, I imagined that I was a coal miner who'd spent the better part of the day underground and was eager to see all my loved ones again. I took the steps two at a time, sometimes three, straining, making a bigger production than necessary, until I reached the top, where, blinking and shivering, I had to shade my eyes from the blinding piles of snow and wait for everything to come back into focus.

"Where the hell have you been?" a voice asked. I heard him before I saw him, but when I turned around, there he stood. Ralph! Arms crossed, eyes narrowed, he was waiting for an answer.

"Where've *I* been?" I said. "I was looking for *you.*"

"*Me?* I've been *here* the whole time."

"*Here?*" I said. "Why *here?* You told me to meet you at the *entrance,* not the *exit.*"

"This *is* the entrance," he said, and we both looked toward it for an answer, as if a sign might be posted, proving one of us right, but there was no sign. "Ah, forget it," he said. "It's not worth arguing about." He unfolded his arms and walked toward me. "I just don't know about you, Hank."

"Me?" I said. "What about *you?*"

Ralph, ignoring my question, started down the stairs. I was about to tell him that I'd already seen everything that I needed to see, but then the smell of perm solution hit me again, and I suddenly didn't mind working my way backward. I knew that every minute I lived was one less minute I'd be alive, but returning to Peacock Alley was different: It was like stealing time, getting back what I'd lost. It was quite a feeling, really, being thirteen years old and cheating death.

# SMOKE

**M**OM SAID SHE NEEDED to talk to me—"this minute," she said—that it was really important and couldn't wait, but I said, "Not now." I opened the sliding glass door, walked outside, and found Tex, my dog, who'd spent the better part of this past week digging up the backyard. He held a bone lengthwise in his mouth, his fourth one today. He dropped it onto a small, neat pile next to the grill. He licked my hand, and I pointed at his nose and said, "*Sit! Give me a paw!*" But he tilted his head, then ran away.

We found Tex two weeks ago, smack in the middle of a downpour, a wet pup the size and color of a meat loaf. He was limping across the expressway, his dark head hung low, too depressed by the rain and lightning to care about the cars and trucks speeding toward him. Dad pulled over and Mom opened her door, and together we lured him into our car and into our lives with the promise of a good home and table food.

"He *smells* like a dog," my father had said. He snickered and called him a dog's dog—a joke I didn't get, though I liked how it sounded.

"Tex!" I yelled, but Tex was digging where I couldn't see him. Our house was small, our front lawn tiny, but the backyard stretched away forever—one of the few in the city that did so, but only because if you kept walking you'd run into a fence, and beyond that fence was an industrial park that nobody wanted to live near.

I sat on the crooked chaise longue, just beyond the rim of the bug light's light, and I watched and listened to the moths and june bugs and what-have-you touch down on the bulb, then flap crazily to get away from it. In the mornings I liked to walk outside barefoot and check the yellow bulb, see the wings glued to the glass, and touch what was left of the bugs who wanted too much of a good thing.

I was beginning to focus too intensely on the bulb, a dim yellow hole burning into my field of vision, when I caught Kelly glaring at me from the kitchen. She looked perfect under the outrageously bright kitchen lights. *Slinky*, I thought—a word I liked to say alone in bed before I drifted to sleep. She slid open the glass door, glared harder, and said, "Hank, is that you?"

"No," I said. "It's John Gacy, serial killer!"

Kelly stared blankly in my direction. She never laughed at my jokes, never thought what I said was funny. Dad called her a literalist. *A dog's dog*, I thought. She stepped outside, leaving Mom alone at the kitchen table, and shut the door behind her.

"Where's Dad?" I asked.

"Va*moose*," she said.

"Bowling?"

"Yeah; right," she said, as if she knew things about Dad that I didn't, but I decided not to press. Kelly walked over to where I was sitting and, without looking at me, said, "I'm depressed."

"Me, too," I said, smiling.

"No you're not," she said. "*I'm* depressed." From her back pocket she pulled a folded, soggy sheet of paper. She handed it to me and said, "I'm manic-depressive."

What she'd given me was a photocopy of a page from the dictionary, the definition for *manic-depressive*, only she'd enlarged it eight or nine times, and the letters hung on the page like fuzzy caterpillars artfully shaped into words.

"Wow," I said, impressed by the jumbo letters, blurry on the paper.

"It's chemical," she said.

"So," I said. "You're a depressed maniac."

"A manic-depressive, you clod."

"Who knows," I said. "Maybe I'm a manic-depressive, too."

She rolled her eyes and said, "I don't think so."

"How would you know?"

She sighed and took back her definition, refolded it carefully, and stuck it in her pocket. "A manic-depressive can always spot another manic-depressive," she said. "And you're *not* a manic-depressive."

"Maybe not," I said. "But I'm double-jointed." I showed her my knuckles and began popping one in and out of place.

She groaned and said, "Good-bye," though it had come to mean something far more than *good-bye*—a word so weighted, it was meant to send me off somewhere far away from her.

"My slinky sister," I whispered, and Tex, collector of bones, walked into the semicircle of light, another bone clamped in his jaws, his eyes glowing red like those of the sole demon in a bad family snapshot.

Ralph hopped a fence whose gate he could've simply opened. He walked over to the chaise and nudged me with his foot. He was starting to grow wispy sideburns. The shadow of a weak mustache clung to his upper lip. Today he was wearing a skintight lime-green T-shirt that said SOUTH SIDE IRISH, though technically we lived on the south*west* side of Chicago, and Ralph was Lithuanian.

"Ralph," I said. "The fence has a latch."

"Latch snatch," he said, speaking a language I knew and didn't know at the same time. He walked over to the sliding glass door to peek in on my mother, who was staring at the table. Whenever she did this, she reminded me of Superman boring holes through steel with his eyes.

"What's wrong with *her?*" Ralph asked, serious now, backing slowly away from the house.

"I don't know," I said. "She's probably a manic-depressive or something."

Ralph nodded as though he'd heard of such things. He shut his eyes and let the full impact of my mother's life soak into him like a hot breeze. Then he pulled a Fluffernutter sandwich wrapped in cellophane from his back pocket, peeled back the plastic, and stuffed half into his mouth.

"My *sister* is a manic-depressive," I said. "Do you believe that?"

Ralph's jaw went slack, and in the dark hollow of his mouth, I saw swirls of Marshmallow Fluff and peanut butter and long strings of spit connecting his tongue to his teeth like cobwebs.

"Unless she's pulling my leg," I added.

"Oh," Ralph said, and shut his mouth as if amazement and disappointment were the pulleys working his jaw. "You want to know something?" he said. "I wouldn't mind boning your sister."

Ralph was always talking about boning my sister—this was old news—so I yawned, then said, "What's the game plan tonight, Ralph?"

"Well," Ralph said, "my aunt and uncle and their idiot kid are on vacation, and they asked me to feed their dog."

"They asked *you?*"

He stuffed the last of his sandwich into his mouth, wiped his palms on his jeans, and said, "Yeah. They asked *me*. What're you sayin'?" He pushed me hard with both palms.

"Nothing," I said.

"What's wrong with somebody askin' *me* to take care of their ugly, mangy, flea-infested pet, huh?" He pushed me again.

"Cut it out, Ralph."

Ralph smiled and winked at me. He was like that. He'd beat you up one minute, buy you an ice-cream cone the next. "Let's go," he said.

It was seven o'clock and dark, the last splotch of light disappearing even as we spoke. Ralph and I headed down Menard, walking fast as always, hands jammed deep into our pockets.

"Know what I heard?" Ralph said. "I heard Janet likes you. I heard she wants to get you in the sack." In a low growl, he said, "*Janet.*"

"The Planet?" I asked, then caught myself. Janet the Planet was twice my size, but this didn't matter. I would no longer play favorites. The name of each girl in the eighth grade had begun giving my heart an equal surge, a jolt in the dark of night. I promised myself right then and there never to call Janet "The Planet" again.

"Know what else I heard?" Ralph said.

"What?"

"All fat chicks give head."

"Where'd you hear that?" I asked.

"It's a fact," Ralph said. "Don't tell me you never heard that before."

"Never."

Ralph punched my arm too hard and said, "Check into it, my friend."

We walked to the part of town where people left junk all over their yards and porches—washers and dryers, Big Wheels with broken handlebars or cracked seats, roofing shingles piled against houses—a part of town where things were either missing or broken.

Ralph bent over and picked up two rusty nuts and a screw. He gave me one of the nuts, and I began rubbing it between my two palms.

"You know Veronica Slomski?" he said. "Know what I heard about Veronica?"

"She likes me?"

"No. Get this. You know Lucky's?"

"Lucky's Tavern?"

"Yeah. You know the alley?"

"Behind Lucky's?"

"Yeah. You know what Veronica does behind that alley?"

"What?"

"She smokes guys."

I stopped rubbing the nut between my palms. I wanted to ask Ralph to repeat what he'd said so I could listen to how he said it, figure out what he meant. "She smokes guys," I said.

"Five bucks a smoke," he said.

"When?" I asked.

"Every night," he said.

"School nights?"

"My cousin told me."

"Norm?"

"No. My cousin Kenny. You know Kenny."

"Yeah," I said.

"Veronica smokes Kenny?" I asked.

"Shhhhhhh," Ralph said. "Watch this."

A small boy was approaching on a rusty Schwinn Continental, his legs barely long enough to reach the pedals. When he got close enough, Ralph stepped in front of him and raised his palm the way a traffic cop would. Then he took hold of the kid's handlebars and said, "Hey. Where'd you get this bike?"

The boy said, "It's my brother's."

"Uh-uh," Ralph said, shaking his head. "It's *mine*, and I think it's time you give it back." Ralph walked behind the boy, looped his arms under the boy's armpits, pressing his palms firmly against the boy's neck, then lifted him off the bike. It was a smooth move, and though I didn't think Ralph should have done it, it was as impressive as anything I'd seen lately on Sunday-afternoon wrestling.

Ralph sat on the bike, squeezed the brakes twice, and said, "Hey, Hank. Watch this." He pedaled hard up and down the street, yelling, *"Look! I'm Evel Knievel!"* He popped a wheelie, rode it high for a long time, then fell completely backward off the bike, cracking his head against the asphalt. The Schwinn wobbled a ways before smashing into a parked car.

"I think I've got a concussion," Ralph said. He stood and brushed himself off. His hair was matted to the back of his head. Silently, without any warning, he started walking away.

The boy, still on the ground, kept sobbing. I looked at him and shrugged.

Ralph scratched his head several times where a dark stain had begun to grow. I kept up with him in case he died. Ten blocks later, I said, "You shouldn't have done that."

"Done what?"

"Scared that kid."

"What kid?" Ralph asked. "I don't remember any kid."

"No one likes a bully," I said.

Ralph said, "Are you still talking about that kid?"

We slowed down to a shuffle and stopped at a tree. Ralph touched his head lightly and said, "Want to go watch Veronica?"

"Why?" I asked. "You want to put her in a half nelson?"

"Maybe," Ralph said. "But I thought we could watch her smoke a guy first."

I grunted. The truth of the matter was, I wanted to check out this smoking business. And I wanted to go to Lucky's. "I guess so," I said. "If you want to."

Lucky's Tavern was on the far edge of town—"a *dive*," my mother called it, "a dive where nothing but a bunch of ignorant rednecks go." Whenever Mom said this, Dad laughed. Dad spent a lot of time at Lucky's, and the idea of rednecks going there apparently cracked him up. I'd never been inside Lucky's, but every time we drove by, I stared through the dark-tinted windows beyond the beer advertisements, hoping to see what a bunch of ignorant rednecks looked like. The few times I could see in—hot nights when the door was propped open—what I saw were two old men sitting at opposite ends of the bar, and the bartender perched on a wooden stool next to the cash register, his head tilted back to watch the TV suspended above him, nobody moving. It reminded me of a display I might have seen behind glass at the Field Museum downtown, a slice of history frozen in time and place: LUCKY'S TAVERN, the sign would read. A BUNCH OF IGNORANT REDNECKS. 1979.

When Ralph and I arrived at Lucky's, the alley was empty.

"No smoking tonight," I said.

"Take a load off," Ralph said, and he sat next to the Dumpster, hiding behind a stack of flattened boxes and a large wire rack of some sort, probably for magazines. He said, "Give me the lowdown on your sister. We're practically the same age, you know." Ralph shifted on the gravel, stretching his legs, trying to get comfortable. When it came to Kelly, Ralph believed anything I told him, and normally I told him the truth. Today, however, I decided to make things up, saying whatever came to mind.

"She's got only one kidney," I said.

"No shit."

"She wet her bed until my mother bought her a rubber blanket."

Ralph said nothing, savoring the thought.

"She sleeps on her back and snores like a pig."

"I like that," Ralph said. "I wouldn't mind listening to that sometime, if you can arrange it."

I said, "She's really only my half sister. We've got different fathers. Mom married some other guy first. Then she fooled around with my dad, and *whammo*, she got knocked up."

Ralph said, "So what happened to Kelly's dad?"

"Who knows. He was a drifter."

Ralph said, "Now that you mention it, I can see your mother with some drifter freak. No offense, but she's the type."

"Yep."

"Jesus," Ralph said. "Your family's more twisted than mine."

But then I couldn't go on. I couldn't keep the lie inside, smothered where it belonged. So I told Ralph the truth, smiling as I did, and when I finished, he reached over and grabbed me by the throat. He choked me harder than I expected, pushing his thumb into my windpipe, blocking the passage of air. When he let go, he said, "You shouldn't lie about your mom." And that was all he said.

At Ralph's insistence, we waited another hour, but nothing happened. My throat kept throbbing, phantom fingers squeezing my neck between heartbeats, giving me the creeps. Then, at long last, the back door creaked open, though all that appeared at first were four fingertips clutching the door's edge.

"I should go over there and bite them," Ralph whispered. He bared his teeth like a werewolf and moved toward my forehead. I yelled, and the man stepped around the door, a beer bottle dangling next to his leg from the tips of his fingers, a cigarette bent upward from his lips the way FDR smoked. It was my dad. He stood there in the light, squinting at us, until he recognized us and smiled.

"Hey, guys," he said. "What's going on?"

"Hi, Dad," I said.

Ralph said, "Hey, Mr. Boyd."

Dad didn't seem a bit surprised to see us there, all the way across town, half underneath a Dumpster. He said, "How're you boys doin'?"

Ralph said, "Just hanging out. Watching people *smoke*."

Dad chuckled, but I doubt he knew what Ralph meant. No one ever seemed to know what Ralph meant.

Dad shook his head and flicked away his cigarette butt in a long, high arc, soaring like a bug on fire, landing in somebody's backyard. Whenever Dad did this, I was afraid he was going to set the whole city on fire, the way Mrs. O'Leary's cow had set the city on fire a hundred years ago. Dad said, "Son of a bitch pulled a straight out of nowhere. Do you believe that? Out of *nowhere*. And to think I *dealt* it to him."

"Snake eyes!" Ralph yelled. "The doctor! Bingo!"

"A straight!" my father said, wagging his head.

"Yowza!" Ralph said. He raised his palm into the air, as if to high-five my father, and said, "My main most man!"

My father pointed his forefinger at Ralph and fired it like a gun. Then he looked at me and said, "Are you gonna be home later tonight?"

It was a stupid question: I'd never not come home for the night. But I nodded and said, "Yeah. Sure."

"We need to talk, son," he said. He raised his arm to wave good-bye and said, "We'll talk tonight," then stepped back into the bar, the heavy door slamming hard behind him.

"Jesus," I said. "Everyone wants to talk to me."

"You're like Ann Landers or something," Ralph said.

"I don't think so," I said. "I don't think they want my advice."

We took alleys to Ralph's aunt and uncle's house, and when we reached it, we approached from behind. Ralph tried the back door, then jerked a screwdriver from his pants.

"What's that for?"

"They forgot to give me a key," Ralph said. He jammed the screwdriver between the door frame and the door and started prying.

"Hey," I said. "Don't do that. You'll bust up the woodwork."

"Listen, Einstein," he said. "What do you think they'll be more upset about—a broken door or a dead dog? Huh?" Ralph continued wiggling the screwdriver back and forth, pushing with all his weight, until the door finally popped open. He stepped inside and said, "Voilà!"

Ralph switched on a light and began searching the house. I stood in the kitchen, looking around for the dog-food bowls, the dog food, and the dog. I checked the kitchen countertop for a note, directions on dog maintenance, but couldn't find one. I went to the living room and said, "Here, pooch. Here, poochy-pooch."

The house looked exactly like all of my Italian friends' houses—furniture covered in see-through plastic; bisque figurines decorating the end tables; a three-dimensional Last Supper hanging above a humongous TV console.

"You sure we're in the right house?" I yelled. "Nothing personal,

Ralph, but this doesn't look like the sort of place where one of your relatives would live. It's too clean."

I stepped into the bedroom to keep giving Ralph a hard time, but he wasn't listening. He was rifling through drawers, pulling everything out and throwing it over his shoulder. He stood up and said, "What a dump."

"*You're* the one messing it up," I said.

Ralph walked back into the living room, picked up a figurine of an old man wearing a straw hat and holding a fishing rod, and said, "Look at this crap. A houseful of junk. And how much does this TV weigh? A gazillion pounds, probably. At *least* a gazillion."

"I can't find the dog," I said. "What kind of dog is it?"

Ralph pulled a newspaper clipping from his pocket, uncrumpled it, and said, "Hey. Go out front and tell me what the address is. We might be in the wrong house."

"You're *kidding*," I said. My heart began pounding.

"Hank," he said, looking at me for the first time since we'd entered the house. "You see anything that looks good?"

"What do you mean?"

"Cassette deck, turntable, ham radio?"

"Ham radio? What's a ham radio?"

"Forget it," Ralph said. "Just go check the address, okay?"

"Ralph," I said. "Where's the dog?"

"What dog?"

I pointed to his newspaper clipping and said, "What's this?"

He handed it to me and said, "Here. I'm gonna look around some more. Now go see if this address matches the one outside. Is that too hard or *what*? Jeesh."

Ralph walked away, and I smoothed out the clipping. It was an obituary for a woman named Nadine Lorenz. Outside, I studied the dead woman's address, looking for a mistake, but there was no mistake: This was her house. I stepped back inside. If the clock on the wall could be trusted, visitation hours at the funeral home were in full swing this very second.

When Ralph returned, he said, "So what's the verdict?"

I waved the clipping at him. "This is *her* house?"

Ralph said, "Technically, no. Not anymore."

"Ralph," I said. "Let's just go, okay?"

He let out a long, disappointed sigh, the kind of sigh my father liked to make, and said, "You're right. There's nothing here but a bunch of old-lady crap." On his way out, he picked up a waffle iron and said, "How much you think these things go for?" He lifted it high into the air, over his head, and said, "This would make a great weapon. Someone screws with you, you pull this baby out and say, 'Hey. You want a waffle?' Then *boom.* You smash the dork in the face with it."

We stepped into the fresh air, and Ralph shut the busted door.

"She was *dead,*" I said. "Jesus, Ralph. You broke in to a *dead* woman's house. That's the lowest thing I ever heard of."

The waffle iron dangled beside Ralph's leg as we walked, and every so often he chuckled, but I didn't feel much like talking anymore. Each time he chuckled, I had a gut feeling Ralph wasn't long for this world, and that I would have to make a decision over the weekend: keep hanging out with Ralph or cut my losses. There were pluses to both sides. *With* Ralph, no one would mess with me; they'd know better. *Without* Ralph, I might stay alive longer, and my chances of doing any serious jail time would be kept to a minimum. These were the benefits, short- and long-term, and though the decision should have been easy, I knew it wasn't going to be. I liked Ralph. That was the sad part.

Ralph stopped in the middle of the street as though he'd read my mind, sensing his own mortality, and he touched his hair, sticky-looking from the blood. He said, "I got hit on the head once with a sledgehammer."

"Really," I said. "Did it hurt?"

"Nuh-uh."

When we got to Ralph's house, he opened the gate and went through, then shut it without offering to let me come inside. I'd never been any closer than where I stood today, and I'd never seen his mother, though I always suspected she was in there, peeking out from between the thick crushed-velvet curtains, watching our every move. He lived in a small house with pebbly gray shingles covering the sides and black shingles on the roof. The lawn was mostly dirt.

Ralph said, "You know why it didn't hurt?"

"Why?"

"It knocked me out cold," he said. "You know that tunnel of light everyone talks about? Let me tell you, pal, it's true. I saw it. I kept walking deeper and deeper into this bright light, and then I started getting pulled back, away from it, and the next thing I knew, I was awake and in bed. It changed my life, Hank. No shit. From that point on, I decided to be a different person."

"What kind of person was that?"

He grinned and said, "A mean one."

Ralph walked away, and as he reached for the screen door, I said, "How old were you, Ralph?"

"Eight," he said. He waved at me with the waffle iron, then disappeared into his house.

I wasn't feeling so good anymore. I held my gut and walked quickly along the dark streets. I was in a part of town that made me queasy, an area my mother always told me to stay away from. When I was in the first grade, a high school boy was killed on this very street, clubbed to death with a baseball bat by one of his own classmates, Karl Elmazi. But the scary part of the story wasn't that a guy had gotten beaten to death with a Louisville Slugger. It was that Karl Elmazi had ten of his buddies with him, and none of them, not a single one, tried to stop the beating.

For my mother, this was a powerful story with a good moral. "Pick your friends carefully," she liked to say, especially after one of Ralph's visits.

When I reached my driveway, the dome light was on inside Dad's car, and Kelly was slouched in the driver's seat. I crept up on her, hoping to scare her, but I didn't. In fact, she moved only her eyes, as if my being there deserved just the barest of movements.

"You still depressed?" I asked.

"After looking at you," she said, "I've become suicidal."

"What're you so depressed about, anyway?"

She reached over to the ashtray and picked up a lit cigarette I hadn't noticed. She said, "Everything and nothing. But I don't expect you to understand that."

I nodded; I didn't understand. It didn't seem possible. I pointed at her cigarette and said, "You don't smoke," and when I heard what I'd said, I reached into the car and placed my palm on top of my sister's head, just to feel it. I'd heard that 90 percent of a person's body heat escaped out the top of the head, and this was what I felt: searing heat rising like a ghost from Kelly's scalp.

"Who says I don't smoke?" Kelly said, ignoring my hand. Then she snuffed out the cigarette in the ashtray.

I took my hand away and said, "What're you doing out here?"

"Waiting for Mom," she said, and this time I did understand. It was nearly midnight; Dad had been home only a short while. I could tell because the car engine was still ticking. "We're going for a ride," Kelly said. "She says she wants to talk to me about something important." She rolled her eyes.

"Good luck," I said, and made my way around the house to the backyard. From a safe distance, I watched Mom and Dad through the sliding glass door. As usual, they were arguing. Tex came up behind me, his paws crunching the grass with each step. He was lugging a long, bent bone in his mouth, thin at one end, thick at the other.

"Tex," I said. "Holy smoke. What's *that?*"

Tex dropped the bone and jogged away, as he'd been doing all week. I picked up the bone and held it close to my face to get a good view. It looked like a leg. I walked over to the pile of bones next to the gas grill, crouched, and spread them out before me.

"Tex," I said, but I was whispering. I was too close to the house, too close to the bug light, the swarm of bugs; too close, it seemed, to everything. I made my way across the backyard, looking for Tex, listening. The yard was too large at night, and I couldn't see him or hear him. No doubt he was flat in the high grass, resting, listening to crickets, distant dogs, and the power lines sizzling high above us, before going back to work.

My parents were still arguing, but they looked so small from out here that it was impossible to take them seriously. If only they could've seen themselves, they might actually have laughed. Instead, Dad pointed at Mom, and it looked as if he was saying, *Sit! Give me a paw!;* and Mom, as though she'd read my mind or sensed what I had sensed, lifted her purse off the floor and left the house. A moment later, the car started. Dad stood alone in the kitchen while Mom revved the engine too hard, gunning it, trying to blow it up. When she finally let up on the gas, she backed out of the driveway, headlights spraying across our house before she aimed her car down the road that would eventually take her away from us for good.

"Tex," I said. But Tex wouldn't answer.

Dad opened the sliding glass door and walked outside. I took a step back: Though I knew he couldn't see me, he was staring right at me. He pulled a pack of cigarettes from his shirt pocket and smacked it against his palm. I'd seen him do this thousands of times, but only now did it register that here was a man smacking a pack of cigarettes into his palm, and I had no idea why.

Dad stood on the back porch, exhausted, lighting a cigarette, the weight of everyone's life crushing his head, this man I knew and didn't know. A *dad's dad,* I thought, and tried snickering, but I'd never snickered before and couldn't do it. Dad looked deeper into the backyard, searching for the sound he had heard, my half-snicker. He tried to see but couldn't and gave up. Leaning forward, he rested his hand on the gas grill for support. At first I thought he was fainting, collapsing from stress. A heart attack, I thought. A stroke. I was about to run toward him, to help him, then realized he wasn't dying at all—not yet, at least—but looking down at the bones Tex had found. He eased himself down on his knees and began messing with them, arranging them like so, as if they were pieces of a puzzle. Then he leaned back and studied what he'd done. I couldn't see it, but I knew that he was crying. There was something about his posture, and about the way he touched the bones and simply stared.

He said something I couldn't hear, and I stepped back farther into darkness. I sensed Tex close by, behind me, and I stepped back again, but I fell this time, my leg suddenly deep inside a hole.

Tex nudged my arm with his cold nose, his gesture of need. I pulled my leg from the hole and reached into the ground.

"Dad," I whispered, but Dad couldn't hear me.

Dad was sitting now, resting against the grill, moving his hand through the air. He was petting the ghost of a dog he'd once known, and all the way across the yard, I was touching that same dog's skull, still lodged in the earth. I tried to imagine the sorts of things firing inside Dad's head, so I looked at Tex, concentrating on the bones beyond his fur and skin, beyond the Tex I knew—the dog *beneath* the dog—but I couldn't imagine anything at all. There was no dog beneath the dog. There was only Tex.

When Dad finally looked up from the bones, he peered out into the dark of the backyard and called my name. "Hank? Is that you out there?" he asked. "Hank. What are you doing?"

I didn't say anything. I was already filling in the hole, clawing frantically, trying to cover the skull.

"You okay?" he asked. "You hurt or something?"

I flattened out, placing my head against the ground, staying as still as possible.

"They're all against me, Hank," he said, more to himself than to me. "Not you, too." He took a long drag off his cigarette, and while smoke escaped his nose and mouth, momentarily blanketing his face, he shook his head, then stepped back into the nervous quiet of our house.

# SOUTH SIDE RECORDS

**I** **USUALLY DIDN'T HAVE** enough money to buy any, but I loved albums and 45s. When South Side Records opened, a tiny store with narrow aisles, I'd visit it once a week to see the new arrivals. The albums, set in row after row of plywood bins, were a buck fifty less than what you'd pay for them at the local Kmart or Zayre, but I still couldn't afford them. Each week, though, you could pick up a free list of Chicago's top-selling music, the top ten albums listed on the left side, the top forty singles on the right. On the back was a photograph of a Chicago DJ. It always scared me to see how different DJs looked from what their voices had led me to expect. Whenever my father had a disagreement with someone who wasn't particularly attractive, he'd nudge me afterward and say, "Talk about a face that was meant for radio." I never knew what he meant until I saw those photos.

The man who owned South Side Records was an old hippie, except that he'd trimmed his wiry beard and cut his wiry hair, grooming habits that probably didn't sit well with other hippies, the ones who still wore moccasins and leather-fringe vests, who bathed only once a year and called everyone and everything (man, woman, child, or animal) "man." When I went into South Side Records, I started calling everyone "man" so the owner would understand that I'd have been a hippie, too, if circumstances were different.

"How's it going, man?" I'd ask as soon as I had stepped foot inside, and the owner, whose name was Larry, would say, "There he is!" as if everyone had been waiting for me. Larry hired only pretty high school girls, and since he seemed to have different employees every couple of weeks, I made it a point to show the new girls that Larry and I had this special bond. Sometimes, after asking how he was doing, I'd point at him, wink, and nod all at once, and Larry would call me something new and startling like "The South Side Messiah!" or "Little Big Man!" or "The Merchant of Venice!" I loved hearing what he called me. I imagined that these names came to him from all his early hippie years of doing drugs, funny words and combinations of words still bubbling inside his head, starting to overflow.

One day, in the spring of my eighth-grade year, Larry said, "If it isn't Mr. Clean himself! How goes things for the almighty bald one?"

I pointed at him, winked, and nodded. The two girls giving Larry a back massage giggled.

"Listen," Larry said, shrugging off the girls. "I was thinking. You come in here all the time, but you never buy anything. Why is that?"

Hippies on TV shows called money *bread,* so I shook my head and said, "Bread, man. No bread."

Larry nodded. "No *moola?* No *dinero?* That's no way to go through life, pal. Tell you what. How'd you like to trade a few hours a day for an album of your choice? You come in, do a little sweeping in the back room, maybe unload a few boxes, and I'll let you pick whatever album you want."

"Really?"

"Absolutely. But here's the catch." He leaned on the counter so his head was level with my head, and said, "You can't tell your folks."

"Not a problem!" I said. After an argument with his boss, my father had quit his job at the 3M plant, and since my mother spent her time being mad at him, I went pretty much wherever I wanted without either of them noticing.

"I mean it," he said.

"No, really," I said. "They don't even know I'm here right now."

At this revelation, Larry's eyes widened. "Good!" he said. "That's terrific."

On my first day, Larry led me to the back room. It looked as though someone had opened up the service door and thrown a couple of grenades inside. The floor was entirely blanketed with empty and half-empty boxes, soda cans, broken albums, Styrofoam peanuts, and crumpled posters of rock bands. Taped to the far wall was a poster of the Bee Gees wearing white sequined jumpsuits. Someone had written underneath them, THESE THREE MUST DIE FOR THE GOOD OF EVOLUTION!!!

Larry saw me looking at the Bee Gees and said, "You realize I'm kidding, of course. I'd never kill anyone." He paused. "You don't *like* them, though, do you?"

"Nuh-uh," I lied.

"Good man."

After explaining the various chores and showing me where he kept the broom, mop, and cleaning solvents, he left me alone. It wasn't easy figuring out where to begin. I needed a strategy, so I began dividing up the junk—boxes in one corner, shattered albums and torn album covers in another, posters stuffed into the room's only garbage can. At the end of the day, I picked out Elton John's *Goodbye Yellow Brick Road*.

Larry frowned when I handed it over. He said, "That's a *double* album, my friend. Single albums only. Sorry." I returned it to the bin and brought up KISS's *Dressed to Kill*. "Is *this* what you want?" Larry said. "*Really?*" I nodded. He said, "Hey, it's your hard-earned money, pal, not mine." He slipped the album into a sack and handed it over.

Before reaching home, I slid the album up under my shirt so my parents wouldn't see it. I wasn't sure why, but I didn't think they would have approved of me working. My mother might have wanted me to start paying for my own groceries; my father might have thought I had taken a job just to make a point about him quitting *his* job. But when I stepped inside the house, I saw that no one would have noticed if I had come home wearing a leopard-skin loincloth, holding a spear, and dragging a king cobra behind me. My mother had locked herself in the bedroom— I could see the light on under the door—and my father was sitting at the dining room table reading *1001 Best Jokes of the Century*. Every once in a while he'd chuckle. Even when I couldn't see my mother, I knew that the sound of Dad's chuckling multiplied her anger. It wasn't enough that he'd quit his job, but now he was in a good mood, walking around and smiling! I knew my mother. I knew that each chuckle was like a hot iron tapping the back of her neck.

In my bedroom, I put the album on my turntable and kicked back to listen, but the album skipped every few seconds, the needle jumping and landing with an amplified thud each time. I wanted to exchange the album, but since I wasn't sure what kind of return policy Larry offered, especially given our arrangement, I decided not to say anything.

The next day at work, as I studied a vandalized promotional photo of John Travolta, whose eyes had been cut out, someone began pounding hard at the service entrance. I opened the door and was surprised to see not a person but a custom van with a person inside. Everything inside the van was carpeted. A Middle Eastern man with a thick mustache was sitting inside the shaggy van, smoking a cigarette and thumping, with one finger, the fuzzy dice that hung from his rearview mirror. His window was rolled down, and he blew a cloud of thick smoke at me. It was the first time I'd ever seen anyone knock on a door while still in his car, so I wasn't entirely sure how to greet him. I expected him to have an accent, but he didn't. He said, "Tell your boss that Ghassan is here." Before I could turn around, though, Larry was yelling, *"As-sallaamu-alaykum,* my brother. *As-sallaamu-alaykum!"* But Ghassan wasn't having any of it. He flipped his cigarette half a block away. With the engine still running, he opened the van's door and slid out.

"Gotta lay low for a while," Ghassan said. "Feds are cracking down. I got a friend who pirates Disney shit, and they arrested him last Saturday at the Twin Drive-in."

The Twin Drive-in was a flea market on weekend mornings. Nothing I'd ever bought there worked—sparklers, a transistor radio, a windup toy car—but I couldn't bring myself to throw any of it away. I stuffed all the broken junk into a dresser drawer full of old socks with gaping holes. I couldn't bear to throw my socks away, either.

Larry turned to me. "Give our friend Ghassan a hand."

The back of the van was packed full of thousands of black concert T-shirts, and I helped carry hundreds of them inside. They were grouped first by musician, then by size. After Larry had handed over a fist of cash to Ghassan, and after Ghassan had driven away, I held up a Nazareth T-shirt and said, "These are cool, man."

"They're bootleg," Larry said. "I get 'em for a buck, sell 'em for four. If

I went through the promoters, I'd be lucky to make fifty cents. You can't live with a profit margin like that. You do what you got to do. Remember that, buddy."

The album I took home that night had a long scratch that ran from the label to the outer edge. It was deep enough that the song popped on every rotation. I knew I'd have a hard time convincing Larry that every album I took home, every *new* album, was damaged before I even opened it, so I filed it under my bed with the other damaged album.

The next day brought more pounding at the service entrance. By this time I had cleared a path to the door, but there were concert T-shirts piled everywhere, narrowing the room's width. I expected to see Ghassan sitting in his van again, but it was a guy in his early twenties with long greasy hair and whiskers sprouting from his pimples. He was sitting on a girl's bicycle. Pink and white plastic tassels hung from each handlebar. He handed over a stack of rubber-banded tickets and said, "Tell Lare-O this was all I could score. Tell him I'll do better when Nugent comes to town." When he saw me looking at the girl's bike, which had a tiny license plate that said BECKY, he said, "Found this leaning against a Dumpster. I'm taking it to a pawnshop right now."

I nodded and shut the door, glad I didn't have to look at him any longer. I took the tickets to Larry and relayed the message.

"Pink Frickin' Floyd, and this was all he could get me? Okay, tell me again: What *exactly* did he say?"

Both girls behind the counter—new girls—gasped. "You got *Floyd* tickets?" one asked, and the other one, who was wearing several long bird feathers clipped in her hair, said, "Kick *ass!* We're going to *Floyd!*"

"Whoa," Larry said. "Easy, girls, easy. I was expecting more tickets than this. I mean, *shit.* I've got bills to pay."

After picking out my album for the night—the sound track to *Rocky,* good music for jogging in place and punching the air—I found Ralph and told him what I'd seen these past few days.

"Bootleg T-shirts and scalped tickets?" he said. "You better watch your back."

"You think?"

"Do I *think? Yes,* I *think.* That's heavy stuff. And if you ask me, I bet it's just the tip of the iceberg lettuce, so to speak."

At home, my father peeked up from his joke book and said, "*You're not mad at me, are you?*"

"No," I said.

"Good. Because I want to tell you a joke. Are you ready?"

I nodded.

"Okay," he said. "Here we go." I had a hard time following, but it had something to do with a priest walking into a bar and complaining to the bartender about his boss. Once the bartender realizes that God is the priest's boss, he gets sort of disturbed by the conversation. The joke didn't end there, though. It went on and on. My father kept going back and telling some of it over. He paused a few times, trying to remember what happened next. When he finally finished, he opened his eyes wide, waiting for my reaction.

I said, "Is that from your joke book?"

"You don't think it's funny?" he asked, but before I could answer, he said, "Did I leave something out? Maybe I forgot part of it."

I excused myself, fearful that he'd start telling the joke again.

In my bedroom, I listened to *Rocky*. Amazingly, the album itself didn't have any problems, but it was missing the inside sleeve. You could tip the cover and watch the naked LP roll out. But at least it didn't skip or pop. I was happy about that.

On my fourth day at work, I walked into the back room and found Larry making out with one of the girls who worked the cash register. He was sitting in a metal folding chair, and she was sitting on his lap. Her name was Connie Donadio. She was a pudgy girl who wore thick eyeglasses, and when she looked up at me, her lenses were steamed over. "Who is it?" she asked Larry, and Larry said, "It's our little friend." "Oh," Connie said. "Hello, little friend."

"I can come back later," I said, but Larry held his palm up toward me. A few minutes later, they were both gone, and I was alone.

By the end of the week, I had quit greeting people when I walked into the store, and they had quit greeting me. No more "Little Big Man!" from Larry. No more winking, pointing, or nodding from me. I'd simply walk past everyone and head for the back room. The sooner I could start working, the sooner it would be over. The way I saw it, I wasn't getting paid for the time it took to chat. In fact, I wasn't getting paid at all anymore. I'd lost interest in picking out an album each night. Something was always wrong with it, so it didn't seem worth the extra time that I spent in the store looking. More depressing than the wasted time was the disappointment that swallowed me each time I played an album and heard its fatal flaw. I found myself holding my breath until the first angry pop, and then I'd feel as though I'd stepped off the side of a cliff. My heart actually hurt from pounding so hard.

On my seventh day at work, I was dragging all the trash out to the Dumpster in the alley when a milk-delivery truck pulled up beside me.

"Go get Larry," the driver said.

I didn't like getting ordered around—especially now that I was working for free—but I wasn't good at talking back to someone older than me. Besides, the driver was one of those fat guys who was hairier than an ape and looked as though he'd run me over for sport, so I trudged to the front of the store and found Larry behind the counter, smoking a Tiparillo. A new girl was sitting next to him, blowing on a stick of incense, watching the red ember glow, then dim.

"Someone wants you," I said to Larry.

"Who?"

"How should I know who?"

The girl blowing incense stopped blowing, peeked up, and cocked her head the way a dog does when it hears a high-pitched whistle. "Dude," she said. "*Chill.*" She shut her eyes and resumed blowing.

My father used to come home from work and, after telling us a story about someone who annoyed him, say, "One of these days I'm going to reach over and *choke* that son of a bitch." Whenever he said it, which was several times each week, I feared he'd eventually choke one of his coworkers and end up in jail. It had never crossed my mind as a customer at South Side Records to hurt anyone who worked here, but as an employee, I had an urge to reach over the counter and choke the girl with the incense. The urge passed as quickly as it came, but nothing during that split second would have made me happier.

Cracking my knuckles, I followed Larry through the store and into the alley. "Aha!" Larry said when he saw the milk-delivery truck. He turned to me and said, "We need your help, maestro."

I stood at the back of the truck while Larry and the driver handed milk crate after milk crate down to me. Each crate, crammed full of albums, was as heavy as a cinder block, so I could carry only one at a time. I lugged each one to another room in back, a room I hadn't even been inside before today, and I set all the crates against a wall. Larry gave the driver a thick wad of money, and then the two men began talking as if I weren't standing there with them.

The driver said, "Where's that cute girl you used to have working back here, the one with the pigtails?"

"Marcy," Larry said, and sighed. "She didn't work out."

The driver said, "The boy, *he's* working out? You turning acey-deucey on us or what?"

"I needed to make a distinction," Larry said, "between work and pleasure. The boy, he's a worker. The girls, they're here for pleasure. It took me a while to realize that you can't have girls here for pleasure and then ask them to work."

The driver nodded. "Look at me. All work, no pleasure. Maybe I should open a store across the street and run you out of town." He laughed. "Yeah, maybe I'll do just that." He put the truck in gear and rumbled down the alley, his axles creaking with every shallow hole, thick blasts of exhaust appearing each time the truck coughed.

Larry's eyes, after following the truck, landed on me. "Oh. There you are," he said. "C'mon, kiddo, let's see what Santa brought us, shall we?" Inside, squatting, he pulled stacks of albums from milk crates, resting them on his thighs and flipping through them. "Not bad. Hey, look. The new Van Halen."

"Getting into the used-record business?" I asked.

Larry laughed. He explained to me how all of these albums were recent returns at other stores, how he had connections, and how his connections made more money by selling the returns to him than if they returned them to the distributor. "And I've got this machine here," he said, pointing to a contraption in the corner of the room, "that'll shrink-wrap these babies so they look like brand new."

It took a moment for Larry's words to sink in. "So all your new albums are already old?" I asked.

"I wouldn't say they're *old*," he said. "People buy albums, and for one reason or another, they sometimes decide they don't want them. Most stores have a thirty-day return policy, so they're not *that* old. Thirty days, tops! My return policy is twenty-four hours. I can't afford returns. Who would I return them to?" He started explaining to me how the shrink-wrap machine worked, but I told him I needed to go. Larry said, "Hold on, big guy. I need these puppies on display by tomorrow morning. You can't stay a bit longer, help out your old friend? I could probably swing that double album you wanted."

"Nah. I don't think so."

"Well, shit," he said. "Go, then. Scram." He was trying to make me feel guilty, but I wasn't falling for it. As the door of the back room shut behind me, he yelled, "Don't come back! And don't take an album today! You hear me?"

I didn't take an album. I grabbed three concert T-shirts instead, and when I reached the front counter, I walked behind it for the first time.

The girl at the cash register quit blowing on the stick of incense. She pointed the red-hot tip at me and said, "Did Larry say you can come back here?"

"Actually," I said, "Larry wanted me to tell you something."

When I didn't say anything, the girl said, "Well? Do I look like I have all day?"

"Larry told me to tell you that you're fired."

"What?"

"You're fired," I said.

The girl put the stick of incense on the glass countertop. The tip, still on fire and radiating a circle of heat, started to leave a black mark on the glass. The girl narrowed her eyes as if unsure whether to believe me, but then she looked toward the back room, holding her gaze on the wall as if the power to see through drywall might suddenly possess her.

"Who came to see him?" she asked.

"I don't know her name," I said, "but she has pigtails. Marcy, I think. Yeah. Marcy!"

"Is she back there with him right now?"

"They're in that other room," I said. "The small room." In case this wasn't conjuring the right image, I added, "The room with the *shrink-wrap* machine."

Her eyes, filling with tears, lost focus on the wall. She walked around the counter, shot one last glance at the back of the store, then walked out, a tiny bell jingling cheerfully over her head. I almost followed her outside to tell her I was lying, but I didn't. I stood on a stepladder, slid two Pink Floyd tickets from the grip of their rubber band, and tucked them into my back pocket. With my new T-shirts draped over my arm, I walked out of South Side Records for the last time.

I hadn't realized how bad work had been making me feel until this very moment. I was breathing easier, grateful for all the free time ahead. I walked down the exact same streets I walked down every day, but the way that everything looked so new, so strange, I might as well have been walking on a different planet. Quitting the job was like being pulled from the tight confines of a deep and narrow well, but when I started to picture the scene—rescue workers huddled around the opening and pulling on the rope—I was surprised to see that it wasn't my own head emerging from the well but my father's, and the poor guy, blinking at the sunlight and smiling, had never looked happier.

# THE BOOK OF RALPH

**O**N THE LAST DAY before spring break, Jesus showed up at Rice Park, next to our school. He kept his distance, slinking around the monkey bars, looking pretty much like every drawing I'd ever seen of him: dingy white robe, long brown hair, well-kept beard with a neatly trimmed mustache. I was in eighth grade, and none of my classmates knew what to do about him, so we loped around the blacktop with our hands jammed inside our pockets, occasionally shooting him a look that said, *Yeah, okay, we see you, but we're not all that impressed.*

Ralph nudged me and said, "Check out his feet. He's wearing flip-flops. Who does he think he's fooling?"

Ralph's voice had recently dropped two octaves, and the speed at which hair appeared on him reminded me of scenes in *The Wolf Man* when Lon Chaney, Jr., watched his own arms turn from man to beast.

By recess, Jesus had moved to the seesaw, and he started luring over some of the eighth-grade girls. One by one, the girls sauntered over with their heads bowed, returning minutes later to relay his messages. "He says he's the son of God," Gina Morales said. "He says he died for us," Mary Polaski reported. Lucy Bruno, the class weeper, returned weeping. "He says it was time for him to come back to earth because there's too much cruelty."

When Mr. Santoro, our principal, finally spotted Jesus, he lifted his battery-powered bullhorn, pressed the mouthpiece to his lips, and clicked it on. *"Stay away from that man!"* Mr. Santoro yelled. *"He could be armed! He could be a child molester!"*

Terrified of the bullhorn, we fell silent as the word *molester* echoed across the blacktop. Jesus merely stood from his crouched position at the seesaw and waved at us, as though from the deck of a departing ship.

Mr. Santoro was by nature a nervous guy, but lately he'd had good reason. It was 1979, and four months before, in December, police had removed twenty-seven bodies from the house of a man named John Wayne Gacy. Gacy's house was only twenty miles away, in a northwest suburb of Chicago. Where I lived, on the southwest side, it wasn't unusual for a kid to get jumped by a carload of thugs from another neighborhood, but what we saw on TV each night about Gacy was altogether new to us. Between Christmas and New Year's Day, from a house nicer than ours, men carried out body bag after body bag; and just when we were starting to think that they'd found all they were going to find, winter gave way to spring, the rock-hard ground softened, and police discovered even more bodies. At last count, they'd found the remains of thirty-three men and boys.

Mr. Santoro clicked on the bullhorn and reassured us that everything would be okay if we followed his instructions. Then he ordered us to form a single-file line and head for the building. "Chop, chop!" he said.

"You know what I'd do if I was him?" Ralph said, nodding toward Jesus. "I'd show up here with a burning bush. I'd probably have some sort of speaker rigged up inside the bush, maybe bury the wire underground, and then I'd have *you*"—he jabbed me in the chest—"hidden somewhere talking into a microphone. You know, saying things the bush might say."

"What would a bush say?" I asked.

"I don't know," Ralph said. "Maybe 'Hey, look, I'm on fire! What do all you peckerheads think of *that?*' You ask me, a burning bush would have some attitude. It wouldn't just stand around and say a bunch of cheeseball things like *this* bozo."

The word *bozo* made me cringe. It seemed a blasphemous thing to say until we had a little more information on the guy.

Ralph, shaking his head, turned away from Jesus. He said, "Listen. Kenny and Norm had to bail on a side job. I told them we could do it." Since both of Ralph's cousins had spent stretches of time in jail, the idea of filling in for them for anything made me queasy.

"I don't know," I said. "What kind of job is it?"

"It's an acting job," Ralph said.

"They're actors?" I said. "What about their jobs at the Tootsie Roll factory?"

Ralph said, "They're not *professional* actors."

I waited for Ralph to explain what *not professional* meant, but he didn't. "What kind of acting job is it?" I asked.

"We'll find out tomorrow morning. Kenny'll pick us up."

"Why's Kenny picking us up?"

"Because," Ralph said, cocking his head and pausing after each word, as if speaking to an alien. "He's. The. One. Who's. Taking. Us. To. The. *Job!*"

"Oh," I said. "And where's that? The job?"

Ralph said, "Would you quit asking so many questions?"

I couldn't ever seem to get a handle on Ralph. For starters, I didn't understand how he could agree to do something without knowing what it was that he was agreeing to do.

"Okay," I said, meaning that I would quit asking questions, but Ralph took it to mean that I would do the job with him.

"Good!" he said, cracking me on the back. "I knew we could count on old Hank."

After recess, Mrs. Davis quizzed us on Stephen Crane's "The Bride Comes to Yellow Sky." I hadn't read it, but even the brainy kids, distracted by the arrival of a squad car, weren't participating. The cops had come to haul Jesus' sorry butt away.

"This is *exactly* what happened to him the first time!" Gina Morales cried.

Lucy Bruno began weeping. "It's starting all over again," she whined.

Mary Polaski, who was in my weekly CCD class at St. Fabian's Church, looked pleadingly at Mrs. Davis. "Can't you *do* something? Can't you *stop* them?"

Mrs. Davis ordered the girls away from the windows. She said, "The young man outside is nothing but a hippie. He could be a pedophile." No one knew what a pedophile was, but it scared us anyway.

Earlier that month I had fallen insanely in love with Mary Polaski. She had long blond hair parted in the middle and feathered like Olivia Newton-John's. She was seeing a jug-eared high school boy named Chuck McDowell, and she spent the better part of her days in school drawing bulbous hearts with their names lewdly intertwined inside. Just a week ago I had sent Mary an anonymous love letter. Alluding to her evenings spent with Chuck, I quoted at length my favorite Journey song: "Lovin', Touchin', Squeezin'."

In a careless moment, I had shown the letter to Ralph's cousin Kenny. He read the letter, turned it over to see if I had redeemed myself on the opposite side, then flipped it back again. He said, "Were you *stoned* when you wrote this?" He sniffed the letter a few times. "You should have quoted Zeppelin, man. 'Whole Lotta Love.'" With his air guitar, he started playing the opening riff: "Nuh, nah, nuh, nah, NAH *nuh-nuh* NAH *nuh-nuh* NAH *nuh-nuh* NAH . . ."

Since sending the letter, I'd begun calling more attention to myself. For the past eight years I'd been a quiet kid, a solid B+ student, but now that my grade school career was careening to an end, I had become, in my father's words, a "Class-A wisenheimer." But no one ever laughed at my jokes, and today wasn't any different. Lucy Bruno sat in front of me, and after my sixth wisecrack in a row, her arm shot up.

"Mrs. Davis!" Lucy said. "I just wanted to let you know that if you're hearing any snide comments, they're not coming from me, they're coming from *him!*" She turned around and pointed at me. I turned around, too, as if searching for the real perpetrator, but since I was surrounded by girls, it was clear that I was the *him* in question.

"Enough!" Mrs. Davis said. "All of you. You may think because you're graduating in a few short weeks that you don't have to take these assignments seriously anymore, but let me assure you that nothing could be further from the truth. Keep in mind, if you don't pass this class, you will *not* be graduating with your fellow classmates. Have I made myself clear?"

A grim silence fell over the room. We knew Mrs. Davis wasn't bluffing. All we had to do was look at Ralph. He served as our constant reminder of how bad things could get.

"Good," Mrs. Davis said. "Let us continue, then."

Most of the houses in our neighborhood looked alike, but the house Ralph lived in with his mother was at least thirty years older than the others and covered on all four sides with roofing shingles. Long and narrow, it was what my father called a shotgun shack. Since I'd never stepped foot inside the sagging fence, let alone the house, I waited by the gate tonight, hoping Ralph would look out a window and see me. I never told my parents that I was going over to Ralph's, because I knew my mother would sigh loudly and say, "Just remember: You're judged by the company you keep." To which my sister, Kelly, would add, "You are what you eat." The sad fact was that I *was* worried about being judged by the company I kept, so I was always walking a razor-thin line—being Ralph's friend on the one hand, while pretending to everyone else that we weren't friends. My family would be disappointed in me if they knew I was friends with Ralph, and Ralph would be disappointed in me if he knew I told people that we weren't. My stomach ached just thinking about it.

Ralph finally opened the front door and said, "Jesus, Hank, I thought you were a Mormon or something. What do you want?" He bounded down the front stoop and walked over to the gate, but as usual, he didn't invite me inside. He was wearing a too tight T-shirt with a decal that read CLASS OF '73. It was 1979, and Ralph hadn't graduated from anything yet. The shirt was probably a hand-me-down from one of his cousins.

"Have you talked to Kenny again?" I asked.

"Kenny? Why?"

"The job," I said. "I was wondering what kind of acting we need to do. Do you think we'll need to memorize any lines?"

"Memorize lines?" Ralph said. "What for?"

"For the *parts* we're going to play," I said.

"Go home and get some sleep. Tomorrow'll be here before you know it." He shook his head and said, "Christ, Hank, sometimes I don't know what to make of you." He huffed, then turned and headed for his house, his T-shirt creeping farther up his back with each step.

The very next morning, the first day of spring break, Kenny roared up in front of my house in the souped-up Nova he'd been working on since I'd started grade school. Each time Kenny pressed down on the accelerator, toxic clouds exploded from the dual exhaust pipes. Coughing, eyes watering, I was reminded of the air-pollution movie we were forced to watch in Science every year, a movie about the year 2000 and how the few remaining people on earth would be wearing spacesuits with oxygen tanks, thanks to inconsiderate people like Kenny. I was going to tell him about the movie, but when the Nova violently backfired and Kenny, clutching his stomach, said, "Excuse me, boys," as if the noise had come from him, I no longer saw the point in bringing it up.

Ralph was sitting in the passenger seat; I rode in back next to two overstuffed Hefty bags.

"What's in these?" I asked, poking one.

"Our costumes," Ralph said.

"Costumes?"

Kenny, peeking into the rearview mirror to look at me when he spoke, explained how Frank Wisiniewski, owner of Frank Wisiniewski Ford, had hired him and Norm to greet customers at the grand opening of their remodeled car lots, but Norm was temporarily incarcerated, and he, *Kenny,* had decided at the last minute to attend a rally at Comiskey Park dedicated to the immediate annihilation of the disco movement. Here was where Ralph and I stepped in. The job would last all day, and we'd get paid six dollars an hour.

"Six bucks an hour?" I yelled. "Just to greet people?" I'd never heard of anyone making six bucks an hour. Minimum wage was $2.90.

Ralph whispered to Kenny, "I told you he'd wet his pants, didn't I?"

I poked the bloated Hefty bag again. "So," I said. "What are the costumes?"

"*You,*" Kenny said, pointing at me in the rearview mirror, "are going to be Big Bird. And Ralph, here, he's the elephant from that show."

"Snuffleupagus?" I asked.

"Whatever," Kenny said.

"You're going to be *Snuffy?*" I asked Ralph.

Ralph said, "I know, I know. People like elephants better than they like birds, but since I landed us the job, I figured I could pick first. Don't worry, though. People like birds, too."

The way Ralph was talking, I wasn't sure he'd ever actually seen *Sesame Street.* On *Sesame Street,* it was clear who the star of the show was, and it wasn't the elephant. Snuffleupagus was Big Bird's imaginary friend, a giant brown elephant that only Big Bird could see, and while Snuffy certainly enjoyed his own cult following, Big Bird was nobody's sidekick. The fact was, I *wanted* to be Big Bird, but I was worried I wasn't tall enough. I was about to say something about my height when Kenny issued a warning: "I had to put a deposit down on those suits, so if either of you damage them, I'll come knocking at your door with a lead pipe." Then he pulled into Wisiniewski Ford and told us to beat it.

Ralph and I, abandoned at the dusty outer edge of the parking lot, each held a Hefty bag. Ralph said, "Let's find the john and suit up."

We lugged our bags through the showroom to the restroom, where, locked inside, Ralph stripped out of his clothes, including a pair of gray Fruit Of The Looms and mismatched tube socks. Buck naked and hairy in a way that only wild animals were, Ralph shimmied into his Snuffle-upagus costume. I considered telling him that I didn't think people wore full-body costumes without any clothes on underneath, but then, hold-ing Snuffy's head as if it were the prize trophy from an African hunting expedition, he asked me to zip him up.

"Okey-doke," I said. Working as fast as I could, I snagged some of the hair on his back with the zipper's teeth.

"Ouch!" Ralph yelled. "Watch it, for chrissake." He lifted Snuffy's head and placed it over his own. Except for slight modifications— instead of four legs, he had two legs and two arms—the Snuffleupagus in front of me looked like the Snuffleupagus from TV, and my feeling of re-vulsion melted into warmth. Here was this make-believe creature I had spent my early grade school years watching. I'd even had my own Snuffy hand puppet, and I had almost gotten teary-eyed at the thought of this part of my life coming to an end when Ralph, through the head of Snuffleupagus, said, "What are you dicking around for? Put the bird suit on."

As fast as possible, and with my underwear and socks still on, I slipped into the Big Bird costume. On my hands, I wore yellow gloves made of felt. Each hand had only three triangular fingers to give the illusion of claws. The most gratifying part of the transformation was placing Big Bird's head over mine. I had assumed I'd be staring out of Big Bird's eyes, but it was through a sheet of wire mesh inside his beak that I looked. The wire mesh was painted black and worked like a two-way mirror. I could see out, but no one could see in. The extra headroom made it possible for me to be taller than I really was. The beak, however, remained permanently open, which didn't seem particularly authentic.

We unlocked the door and stepped out of the bathroom. A mechanic waiting his turn flinched at the sight of us. Ralph said, "Sorry for the wait, bud," and I nodded my beak at him.

The owner saw us before we saw him, and he called out from his office: "There you two are!" It was Frank Wisiniewski himself. I'd seen him on TV my entire life, a razor-thin baldheaded man with bulging eyes who was always yelling about zero-percent finance charges and no money down. What I remembered most from those commercials were his hands. They never stopped moving, like a pair of battery-powered toys that wouldn't shut off. Frank said, "Norm and Kenny, right?"

Ralph scratched his trunk and said, "At your service."

"Well, listen. I want this grand opening to be something special, okay? I want each family to leave here with a Ford automobile and memories to last them a goddamn lifetime."

People passing by the glass-walled window of Frank's office slowed down at the sight of us, and I was starting to get a taste of celebrity. I sat down in one of Frank's overstuffed recliners and casually crossed my feathered legs, but Ralph motioned with his elephant head for me to stand back up.

Frank rubbed his palms together quickly, as if trying to warm up. Then he clapped a few times, snapped his fingers, and, dedicating a hand to each of us, pointed at me and Ralph. He said, "Big Bird stays here at the new-car lot. Snuffy goes across the street to the used lot. Wave at the passing cars. Later, we'll have one of you come inside and let folks get their photos taken. We've got a professional photographer scheduled from noon to five. Any questions? None? Great! Let's go out and sell some friggin' cars."

Back in the showroom, Ralph said, "What if someone wants to buy a new car from the elephant? It seems screwy to have me all the way across the street."

"I don't think we're actually going to be *selling* the cars," I said.

"Yeah; well," Ralph said. "All I'm saying is I don't think it's a savvy business move, putting the elephant across the street."

I took my position at the curb next to the highway. Ralph attempted to cross over to the used cars, but a VW van quickly turned a corner and nearly took him out. Ralph, frozen in the middle of the road, lifted his shaggy brown arms over his head and swore at the van.

The rest of the morning wasn't much of an improvement. Adults driving by didn't notice me, while carloads of teenagers flipped me off. After an hour of abuse, I waited for the next offensive finger to appear from a passenger's window. When it happened, I bent down two of my three felt claws, leaving only the middle triangle. I did the same with my other claw, all the while crouching and leaning back, giving them a double dose of their own medicine. I was feeling better, too, until I turned and saw three little girls in the parking lot watching me. The two youngest looked about to burst into tears. Here was Big Bird doing something they'd never seen Big Bird do on TV. I considered waddling over and putting on an impromptu show for their benefit, but then I thought, *Why should I?* What harm had I done? Wasn't it a worthwhile lesson to show kids that Big Bird wasn't going to take any crap from anybody?

The girls ran to their parents, clutching belt loops and legs. I peered across the street to see how Ralph was holding up, but Snuffleupagus was lying on a grassy strip next to the highway, apparently taking a nap. I yelled across the traffic, trying to wake him up, but he wasn't budging. The elephant, it appeared, was out for the count.

No one ever came to relieve me for lunch. Meanwhile, the grand opening, fueled by free hot dogs and Canfield's sodas, gained momentum. In under an hour, I was surrounded by dozens of women and children. They touched me, poked me, hugged me, and prodded me. Everyone wanted a piece of Big Bird, and in the course of this frenzy, I worried loose several of my own feathers. Ralph was finally coming to, but other than a beefy salesman sitting in a lawn chair, no one was over there.

Frank Wisiniewski came out to work the crowd. He raised his arms in the air as if conducting an orchestra, and yelled, "Who wants their picture taken with Big Bird?"

A dozen hands rose. "Me!" the kids yelled back.

"All right, then," he said. Frank looked into my beak and said, "You're doing great, big guy. Follow me." Before we headed inside, Frank glanced across the highway at Ralph, who was sitting with his shaggy legs over the curb, swatting flies with his trunk. Frank was about to say something but didn't.

I was concerned about the authenticity of my costume, afraid some of the kids might decide to call me on it—the beak, after all, didn't move, and I couldn't speak because my voice didn't sound anything like Big Bird's—but to my surprise, the kids didn't want their picture taken with me so much as their mothers did. These mothers were all quite a bit younger than mine, and each time one sat on my lap, slung an arm around my neck, and cooed into my ear, I feared they would feel something poking into them and, upon realizing what that something was, let out a bloodcurdling scream. But this didn't happen. Big Bird seemed to be doing something for them, and I soon began to view my job as one with a greater purpose, even though I wasn't exactly sure what that was.

Not that I didn't have my suspicions. When I began going to CCD in the first grade, the teacher told us the story of Adam and Eve, and of the Garden of Eden, and then she showed us drawings of a nearly naked man and a nearly naked woman, explaining how giving in to temptation had ruined the innocence of God's work, which I took to mean the naked body. Back then, in 1971, the nightly news featured stories about nudist camps, which seemed to be gaining in popularity, and I started to mix these two ideas together in my head—the Garden of Eden and the nudist camp—and in those edgy moments before falling asleep, I imagined myself a naked boy surrounded by a sea of naked girls, and all these naked girls were older than me, and I was always the center of attention. These girls, these gorgeous naked girls, would pick me up and pass me around as if I were no heavier than a beach ball, or they would let me sit on their lap, all the while stroking my hair. For years I lulled myself to sleep with these fantasies, and now I was actually living that dream, or the closest thing to it, the main differences being that I was wearing a Big Bird costume and that the women weren't naked.

"He's so *cute*," one of the young mothers said, stroking the side of my head. "Look at those big eyes!"

I shifted under her weight, trying not to startle the poor woman. Then Lucy Bruno, holding a helium-filled balloon in one hand and a hot dog with relish in the other, came waltzing over with her mother. Her mother had the sour look of someone who'd just stepped in dog poop. Lucy sized up the situation with the same sour look before joining the line. When her turn to sit on my lap came, she gave me the once-over and said, "You're a little *short* to be Big Bird, aren't you?"

I shrugged. I was still steamed about her finger-pointing in Mrs. Davis's class, a traitorous act, so when she sat on my lap, I took the quill of a feather that had come loose and poked her in the ass with it. Lucy yelped and hopped off.

"He stuck me with a pin!" she yelled.

When I opened my arms to hug her, she screamed and ran to her mother.

Moments later, Frank Wisiniewski marched over. He offered his TV grin to the others in line, then crouched and whispered into my beak, "You drew blood on that kid. I don't want any lawsuits, you hear?"

By three o'clock, I was starving, but with people getting off work at the mall, the line grew even longer. At one point, a fat man stepped up to me, gave me a long look, then plopped down on my lap. My legs felt about to snap in half, but I kept quiet. The man claimed that he wanted to take a good look at my costume up close, and that he wanted a photo so he could study it later at home. "Tell me, pal, what's the beak made out of, *plaster?*"

"I don't know," I said. "I'm only renting." These were the first words I'd spoken in hours, and my voice was hoarse.

The guy said, "I bet I could make one of these costumes myself. They sell the eyes in any half-decent arts-and-crafts store. The feathers, hell, they would be a cinch to get. But the *beak*. I'd have to make that myself, I suppose. Papier-mâché, you think?"

"I really don't know," I said. The circulation in my legs had been cut off under the crush of weight, the initial pain dissolving into numbness with occasional bursts of tingling.

Before he heave-hoed himself up off my lap, he took one last look and said, "Yep, I think I could piece me together a costume as good as yours."

"Good luck," I said.

I watched him walk away. I wondered if he was a John Gacy type. John Gacy had been a big fat clown in his killing-spree heyday—Pogo was his clown name—and seeing all those body bags night after night made me curious about grown men who wore makeup. What were they *really* up to? Here was some guy three times my age and six times my weight, talking about making a bird suit for his own private use. *For what?*

By the end of the day, the bird suit stank, and just as the stink was reaching new heights, Mary Polaski appeared in the showroom with a throng of other girls from our class. When she saw me, she squealed. "Oh-look-oh-look!" she said. "I *have* to get my picture taken with him."

Mary Polaski was the very last person in line, and when her turn came to hop in my lap, my feathered crotch bulged. Already overheated, my breathing growing heavier and heavier, I sounded more like Darth Vader than Big Bird.

While the photographer loaded a new roll of film into the camera, Mary squirmed for a better position until she settled onto the bulge itself—and then she froze. Blush darkened her face. Her ears turned pink. All I heard was the sound of my own labored breath. Mary turned her head and stared dreamily into my beak. Her eyelids were heavy, as if she had woken from a deep sleep, and I was starting to think she could see through the perforated holes of the wire mesh, and that she could tell it was me, Hank, whose hard-on she was balancing herself upon. But then she reached into my beak and, with the tip of her finger, tapped the screen twice. "Who's in there?" she whispered. "Who's the real Big Bird?"

I said nothing. I held my breath. I wanted to lean forward and kiss her, but I'd have engulfed her entire head with my beak if I tried.

"Talk to me," she said. "It must get lonely in there."

I knew I had to say something—I couldn't let the moment slip by— so I said, "Break up with Chuck McDowell. You can do better than that."

She leaned back. "You know Chuck?" she asked.

Before I could answer, the photographer interrupted: "Let's give Big Bird a smooch!" When Mary put her lips against the corner of my beak, the photographer squeezed the rubber bulb, and a flash of light exploded.

Blinking, Mary put her finger back inside my beak, resting it on my petrified tongue. She was about to speak when a group of tiny kids rushed over to pluck my feathers. Then Ralph, still dressed as Snuffle-upagus, stepped into the showroom, his trunk swaying like a pendulum. When he patted himself down, mushroom clouds of dust erupted from his costume. A few flies buzzed endlessly around his head. He looked over at the kids and said, "Beat it, you punks. The bird's ride is here."

Mary Polaski hugged me hard and said, "Thanks for the advice. You're absolutely right. I *can* do better." On her way out the door, she turned and said, "You're a sweetheart!" She winked, then bounded joyfully out the door and into the ever gray Chicago spring.

After changing into my clothes and stuffing the costume into my Hefty bag, I found Ralph and told him the restroom was all his.

"I'm fine," Ralph said. "Kenny's already here. Waiting."

"You're not going to take the Snuffleupagus costume off?" I asked.

Ralph wagged his head.

Kenny's Nova was parked where he'd dropped us off this morning. Ralph and I took our usual seats, though Ralph's fit was tighter now, and he spilled over onto Kenny's seat.

"So?" Kenny said. "How'd it go, girls?"

I told Kenny what a great time I'd had; how I was surrounded all day by women who kept sitting on my lap, and how, at the end of the day, Mary Polaski had sat down on me and flirted.

"But she didn't realize it was you," Kenny said.

"Doesn't matter," I said.

"It *does* matter," Kenny said. "I know that kind of chick, the kind who'll flirt with a guy inside a bird suit. She didn't care who was inside. Could've been *me* in there. You can't trust a girl like that. Listen to your uncle Kenny. I know. Believe me, *I know.*"

Kenny wasn't my uncle, and I didn't want his advice. To change the subject, I asked, "How'd the disco thing go?"

"It wasn't a *thing*," Kenny said. "It was disco demolition, and we kicked some serious ass. We made this gigantic bonfire on the pitcher's mound, and then fifty thousand people tossed in every kind of disco shit you could imagine. Platform shoes. Mirror balls. Cardboard cutouts of John Travolta. I threw in my ex-wife's copy of Donna Summer's *Bad Girls.* You want your disco inferno? There it is, man. In spades. That fire must've been two hundred feet high."

At the mention of fire, Ralph turned his elephant head toward Kenny and nodded as if taking it all in, but he didn't say a word the whole way home. At one point I thought I heard him snort, but since he was still wearing his costume, it was possible that he'd fallen asleep and was snoring.

Kenny slammed on the brakes in front of my house and said, "You'll have to take the costume back yourself. Return the deposit to me in full, and I'll pay you for the job. You got that? Good. I guess me and the elephant are outta here."

After I got out, Ralph turned to face me, but the pull of my instincts being stronger than my logic, I stared into the huge fake eyes, waiting for recognition, instead of looking into the mouth, where I knew Ralph's face was. The recognition never came, and then Kenny peeled away, wrapping me in a cocoon of exhaust.

I rubbed my eyes and saw dimly, through the smoke, my parents looking at me from the picture window. They must have wondered what was making all the noise, but what they found was their son materializing out of vapor, as if I'd returned home from another world. I started to wave, but my mother reached up and yanked the drapes shut, making me wonder if they'd even seen me at all.

The next day, at Waldo's Trick Shop and Costumes, Waldo pulled the costume from the Hefty bag and carefully inspected it. "You lost some feathers," he said, and pointed at Big Bird's crotch. He opened the cash register and counted out half of the deposit money—fifty dollars. My entire paycheck would be forty-two dollars, meaning that I would owe Kenny eight dollars for my day of work. I knew Kenny would make me pay it, too. I wanted to argue with Waldo, but what could I say? I'd lost so many feathers that anyone could easily see the nylon bodysuit beneath. It looked worse than I remembered, so I took what little money he offered.

That night Mom waited until Dad came home before serving dinner, and when he did arrive, three hours late, it was clear he'd been at Lucky's Tavern for a few drinks. He was grinning at everyone and everything, a clear sign that he'd lost a boatload of money playing poker. I already braced myself for the argument that I would hear later, muffled behind my parents' bedroom door.

"These are great green beans!" Dad said, nearly yelling. "Are they FRESH?"

"No," my mother said. "They're canned."

"Green GIANT?"

"No. Generic."

"Oh." Dad took another spoonful. I hated generic green beans. They were too green, still had the stems, and felt like tubes of rubber on my tongue. Dad looked up at me and Kelly, then waggled his eyebrows, trying to make us smile, but we weren't falling for it. His eyes widened and he said, "Oh, shit, I almost forgot. I saw the damnedest thing on the way home. Actually, I'm not sure *what* I saw, but it looked like an elephant walking down Seventy-ninth Street."

"You've been drinking," Mom said. "Don't scare the kids."

"No, listen," Dad said. "It wasn't a *real* elephant. It was sort of rust-colored, and it was walking on its hind legs."

Mom stood up abruptly, gritting her teeth. She scooped her food into the trash and slammed her plate in the sink. Then she went to the bedroom, locking herself inside.

Dad helped himself to more green beans. He said, "An elephant on the prowl. It was the damnedest thing I've ever seen. Honest to God."

School may have been out for the week of spring break, but CCD was still in session on Thursday night, as usual. As far as I knew, everyone in Chicago was Catholic. All of my classmates, except for Hani Abdallah, were Catholic, so all the parents in the neighborhood—except Hani Abdallah's—sent their kids to CCD. No one knew why we had to go to

CCD, though. "Why do I have to go?" I'd ask my mother. "I'm missing *The Bionic Woman!* How can I follow what's going on in *The Six Million Dollar Man* if I'm missing *The Bionic Woman?*"

"Your job," my mother would say, "isn't to ask why. Your job is to do what I tell you to do." So far as I could tell, that was what everyone's parents were saying. I suspected Hani Abdallah and his parents knew something the rest of us didn't, but I never asked him. I wasn't sure I wanted to know.

The only good thing about CCD this year was that Mary Polaski was in my class. The bad thing was that this was where she had met Chuck McDowell, a latecomer to Catholicism. Tonight, though, they were sitting at opposite ends of the room, a sight that made my palms moist and my heart thump faster. She had taken my advice and broken up with him, and now she was on the lookout for someone better—possibly *me.*

My CCD teachers, mostly single women, were getting more than they had bargained for. They'd taken the job because they liked kids, but they had not anticipated that kids in theory were always more appealing than real live kids, particularly when those kids would rather spend their Thursday nights doing nearly anything else—drilling holes in walls, for instance, or breaking boards over their own heads. I wasn't any better. I yawned too much, cracked lame jokes, barely listened.

Tonight the teacher talked about Jesus baking loaves of bread and catching fish. Hoping to prove to Mary Polaski that I was a serious student of the Bible, I tried to concentrate, but all I could picture was the Jesus who'd shown up at our school, handing out loaves of Wonder bread and cans of StarKist tuna. Before long, my brain clicked off, as if controlled by a thermostat, and I drifted away. My eyelids were starting to flutter when someone yelled, "Look!" and pointed out the window.

Crossing the church parking lot was Snuffleupagus, except that it was hard to tell that it was actually Snuffy. His fur was matted, and his trunk seemed to be held on by a long thread.

"What *is* that?" Chuck McDowell asked.

"It looks like an alien," another boy said.

Mary Polaski said, "I've seen it before, but I can't remember where."

I wanted to announce that it was just Ralph, but I wasn't sure it *was*

Ralph. Ralph might have returned the costume, and someone else might have rented it. Or maybe the guy who'd sat in my lap, having lived up to his promise of making his own costume, now spent his nights haunting church parking lots.

The teacher, already irritated, told us to ignore him. "It's a bum," she said. "What he wants is your attention. If you ignore him, he'll go away."

The rest of spring break, I paced our house with nothing to do, feeling out of sorts inside my own body. I'd hoped Frank Wisiniewski would call Kenny and say he wanted us back for another day. I'd have done it for free. I was that bored.

Next to a curb, I found half of a soggy newspaper opened to a story about John Wayne Gacy. Gacy was still in the news every day. Today's story included a long list of items that investigators had found inside Gacy's house shortly before they arrested him. Among the suspicious items were an address book, a scale, a stained section of rug, and clothing much too small for Gacy. Inside my own house, I found an address book, a scale, a stained section of rug, and clothing much too small for me. But on Gacy's list were also a pair of handcuffs with keys, seven erotic movies made in Sweden, and books with titles like *Bike Boy* and *Twenty-one Abnormal Sex Cases*. I looked around my bedroom, but the only suspicious items were a copy of *Frampton! An Unauthorized Biography*, a poster of Elton John wearing a mink coat and eyeglasses shaped like two grand pianos, and three yellow feathers extracted from an extraordinarily large bird costume. What conclusions, I wondered, would investigators draw? *Who*, they might ask, *was this Hank character?*

On Saturday a letter arrived for me, a genuine letter with a local postmark, and I was hoping it was from Mary Polaski, but it was a bill from Kenny for the damaged costume. He wanted twenty bucks. Thanks to taxes, social security, and other deductions, my paycheck was less than I had calculated, resulting in me owing Kenny even more money.

I was eager to see how much he'd charged Ralph, so I biked over to Ralph's house. I waited by the gate, as usual, but apparently he didn't see me. It was possible that he was staying with Kenny, which he sometimes did, but I didn't have Kenny's number, and I wasn't sure I'd have called even if I'd had it.

When school resumed on Monday, Ralph wasn't there, either. It wasn't like Ralph not to be at school. He'd already failed two grades, and I knew he didn't want to fail a third.

Lucy Bruno, however, was there, limping dramatically into class and easing herself into her chair. Mary Polaski was there, too, honking into Kleenex and drawing fresh hearts, inside of which she wrote JESUS LOVES MARY. I wasn't sure if she meant the Jesus who'd shown up at our school or *Jesus* Jesus. I needed to clarify what I'd meant when I told Mary she could do better than Chuck McDowell. What I meant was that she should dump Chuck for me. What I *didn't* mean was that she should dump Chuck for Jesus Christ, our savior.

In art class, when Mrs. Welch gave each of us some chicken wire, papier-mâché, and a small coffee can full of water for dipping, I rolled up my sleeves and got to work, shaping chicken wire until my fingers were raw. I stuffed newspaper inside the chicken-wire sculpture, and I started slapping down one strip of papier-mâché after another, trying to finish my project by the end of the hour. I was making Big Bird's beak, as the guy on my lap had suggested, and I was doing a pretty good job. It looked like a beak, except it wasn't painted, and it wasn't attached to the rest of Big Bird's head. Still, it was a beak, and when I had finished, I tried getting Mary Polaski's attention.

"Psssst," I said. "Hey, Mary. Psssst."

Mary glanced up, her hands draped with strips of gooey newspaper. She looked like the Mummy starting to unravel.

"Mary," I whispered. "Does this look familiar?" I held up the beak, hoping she would make the connection and understand what I had meant.

Mary stared at it, but there were no burning signs of recognition.

"Remember?" I asked. I held it up as an extension of my own mouth.

Mary smiled, but there was a faraway look in her eyes. Around her neck hung a gold cross I'd never seen before. The beak had been my last chance to win her over, but it was too late. Mary Polaski, for all practical purposes, was a goner.

I spent the better part of recess kicking a lumpy chunk of concrete from one end of the blacktop to the other until a crowd began gathering at the far corner. I figured Jesus, released from jail for loitering, had returned to Rice Park, so I wandered over to catch a peek, hoping to see what sort of stunts he was going to pull today, but it wasn't Jesus. It was Ralph.

Ralph was standing by the monkey bars, where Jesus had stood, only no one knew that it was Ralph because he was wearing his Snuffleupagus costume. But no one recognized him as Snuffleupagus, either. The head was crushed on one side; his trunk appeared to have been severed, doing away altogether with the idea that he was an elephant; both eyes were gone; and patches of fur were missing, as if he were suffering mange. To confuse matters further, this new Snuffleupagus had a cigarette dangling from his humongous mouth. Ralph had somehow rigged it so the mouth opened and closed, allowing him to smoke.

Mr. Santoro rushed over to see what was going on, and when he saw Ralph, he lifted the bullhorn to his mouth. But then he squinted and cocked his head, as if unsure what he was looking at, and lowered the bullhorn, waiting along with the rest of us to see what would happen.

I was about to yell out to Ralph when a wall of feedback hit us, causing everyone to jump back and clutch their ears. Next came a voice through a PA system, but the words sounded slow and warped, the way Ralph spoke to me when he was irritated, carefully pronouncing each syllable, as if I were an alien. The problem today was with Ralph's portable cassette player and the size-D batteries inside that were running out of juice. Even so, the effect was haunting. The voice, distorted and amplified, said, "You. Want. To. See. Something?"

We waited, looking around. When nothing happened, someone said, "See *what?*" Then the voice came back, louder this time, answering the question.

"Watch. *This.*"

With one mittened paw, Ralph removed the cigarette from his huge mouth and threw it into a nearby bush. The bush burst into flames. The amplified voice said, "Do. You. Know. Who. I. Am? Well. Do. You?"

No one knew, not even me. I knew that it was Ralph, sure, but beyond this I didn't know what Ralph was doing or who he was supposed to be. And there was no way to know whether he was getting the reaction he wanted, but every last one of us stared at him in horror. No one doubted that what we were seeing was something otherworldly, and I suppose at first it could have gone either way—Ralph as angel of mercy or Ralph as messenger from hell—but the longer we stood there watching Ralph squirt the burning bush with lighter fluid, flames so high that the catalpa branches over his head were catching fire, the clearer it became from which sad and unholy world this visitation had come.

# YOU

**D**UKE'S WAS WHERE MY dad took me to pick up the best Italian beef-and-sausage sandwiches on the southwest side of Chicago. The building wasn't much bigger than a hut, but the lines sometimes snaked out its two side doors. Once you were within reach of the counter, ordering food turned from a spectator sport into a competitive event. The men and women who worked the counter would yell out, "Hey, YOU. Whaddya want?" or "Who's next? Are YOU next?" Sometimes they pointed randomly and yelled "YOU" over and over until someone claimed to be the YOU in question.

The closer my father and I got to the counter, the harder my heart pounded. I hated being pointed at or yelled at, but at Duke's the chances were good that both of these would happen, possibly several times, even after you'd ordered. And once you were picked, you'd better know what you wanted, and you'd better know how to order it. Ordering had its own language, and it took years of listening to my dad to understand what all of it meant.

"Gimme two beefs, extra juicy, a sausage, make it bloody. Gimme two dogs."

"What'll it be on the dogs?"

"The works."

"You want the beefs dipped?"

"Yeah, soak 'em."

"You want peppers on those beefs?"

"Yeah, gimme peppers."

"Hot, mild, or both?"

"Both. Extra cukes on those dogs."

"You got it."

One time a really fat guy ordered about half the menu. By the time he left, he was sweating like mad, three bags in each hand, forcing everyone to smoosh together so he could reach the door. As soon as he was safely out of earshot, we all looked at one another and sort of snickered and shook our heads, partly because he was so fat and partly because he'd ordered so much food, but mostly out of admiration for a guy who could eat that much.

"Must have an appetite, that guy," someone said, and someone else said, "I wonder how much he spends on groceries, huh? How much you think a guy like that spends?" And then a few people whistled, and one guy added, "Shit, I wouldn't even want to guess." This was how conversations unraveled in Chicago: One minute you'd be standing in line with a few dozen people you didn't know; the next, everyone would be laughing and talking. All they needed was a topic, but once that topic revealed itself, there would be no stopping them.

My father never pitched in. He never added anything. He wouldn't even smile or look at the people talking.

On our way home, I said, "Man, that guy was *fat.*"

My father said, "YOU," and poked me in the shoulder with his forefinger. "*You* know better."

"Whaddaya mean?" I said, but my father didn't have to say anything. I could hear the answer in my own voice, the way I'd shot back my reply, and it scared me.

The next time we went to Duke's, the fat guy was there again. Dad and I went to Duke's the same time every week, so our schedule must have started overlapping with his. I watched the fat guy order. I watched him dig through his pants pockets for money, then pay for his food. I watched him make his way out the door, mumbling, "Excuse me," as people pressed into one another to make room.

I always wondered who would be the first person to speak up, who would get the ball rolling, so when no one stepped forward, I decided to give it a try. I cleared my throat. Louder than I meant to, I said, "Man, that guy was F.A.T., *fat!*" I looked around. When no one responded, I said, "Did everyone see that fat guy? *Whew!*"

I had expected someone to echo what I had said, to add to it, to spin off of it and start his own riff, but no one said a word. They exchanged looks, or they glanced from me to my dad and then back again. Beads of sweat appeared on my dad's forehead. I tried picturing the man from last week who had called the fat guy *fat,* but then I couldn't remember anyone actually calling him fat. What they'd said was that the guy had an appetite. But what was the difference? Wasn't saying that a guy had an appetite and then laughing about it the same as calling him fat?

Outside, my father and I each carried a sack of food. I could hear distant birds, the low squawks of their approach, but when I looked up, the sky was clear, not a bird in sight. I turned and saw that the noise was coming from Duke's, from the men and women inside, and I knew that fat wasn't the topic. *I* was the topic. I wanted to go back inside and protest, I wanted to make my case, but I knew it wouldn't help. Everyone eventually got their turn. Yesterday it was the fat guy. Today it was me. The next day it might have been my sister or my mother or my father. It might have been anybody, really. It might have been you.

# THE BEAR AT YOUR FRONT DOOR

IN APRIL, AFTER MOST of the snow had melted, my parents had a garage sale. It was too early to have a garage sale, still too cold outside, but that didn't stop my mother, who'd been talking about it all winter.

"We need the space," my mother said. "This stuff is just gathering dust."

Each time my mother set something on a card table with a price tag, my father would pick it up and say, "Are you *sure* you want to sell this?" It didn't make a difference what it was—a spatula, an old transistor-radio speaker, a bald tire. "Think carefully," he'd add, "before you conclude the transaction. Once it's gone, we'll never see it again."

"That's the point," Mom said.

I sat outside the first day, shivering, working the cash register. The cash register was a shoe box with a lot of dollar bills and pennies inside. At the end of the first day, after we'd brought in ten bucks, Ralph and his cousin Kenny pulled into the drive. They got out of Kenny's Nova as if they lived here.

I nodded at Ralph; he nodded back. Since a business transaction might occur, I didn't want to be too friendly.

"Look at this," Ralph said, and he pointed at the CB beneath one of the tables.

Kenny said, "I've always wanted a CB. How much?"

Ralph lifted the box and held it close to his eyes. "Twenty bucks! What an outrage!"

"No kidding," Kenny said.

Ralph looked at me. "Twenty bucks? For this hunk o' junk?"

"You want to buy a new one?" I said. "Go right ahead. Be my guest."

Kenny said, "We'll give you five."

I laughed. I bent over, holding my stomach, and said, "Good one!"

"Okay," Ralph said, "seven-fifty. Our final offer."

"Ten," I said.

Ralph and Kenny consulted, then began emptying their pockets, flicking the occasional piece of lint from their fingers into the air.

"All right, all right," Ralph said. "Ten it is. It better work, though."

"It does."

Ralph handed over the money, and without looking at anything else, the two headed back to their car as if they had found the very thing they had been in search of. Only after they were gone did I suffer a surge of regret. The CB! *My* CB. For a measly ten bucks. What was I thinking? But Dad was right: It was too late now; I'd sold it; it was gone for good.

Nearly two years earlier, during the summer of 1977, when I was be-tween the sixth and seventh grades, my father wanted to install a CB beneath the dashboard of my mother's Ford Maverick. Mom didn't want a CB, couldn't see how a CB was going to make our lives any better, and wouldn't stay in the room if anything about CBs came on TV.

I started noticing a pattern. One minute we'd be sitting together in the living room, a complete family unit; the next, we'd have a missing person on our hands. *Where's Mom?* became the catchphrase that sum-mer. There were times that she'd be standing right behind me, but before expending the energy it took to crane my neck, I'd ask, "Where's Mom?" If our lives were a sitcom, *Where's Mom?* would have been followed by peals of laughter, growing louder and longer as the season wore on; but since we weren't a sitcom, the eerie way that one of us would ask but no one else would answer or even, it seemed, hear the question, started to make the hair on my arms raise, the skin goose-pimple.

The CB argument ping-ponged back and forth for a month, and every night Dad would have a new reason why we should own one. On the night of his final pitch, Dad said, "Listen. We *need* this CB for when we take trips."

"What trips?" Mom asked. "We don't take trips."

"We'll *start* taking trips!" Dad said, grinning. He looked over at me and Kelly for support. I wanted the CB—everyone in the country had one except us—but I could see Mom's point. We'd never gone anywhere. Dad was still smiling, but a crazy gleam had appeared in his eyes, like that of a man trying to talk his way out of a shoplifting charge. This was how things worked around here: Dad always wanted to spend money, while Mom reminded him that we didn't have any money to spend. I knew I should side with Mom, that siding with Mom would be the practical thing to do, but I usually sided with Dad. The sad truth was, I wanted to buy things as much as, if not more than Dad.

"I'd like a CB," I said.

"You see," Dad said, "the kids want one, too."

Kelly stood up to take objection at being lumped in with me, but I nudged her in the ribs. I didn't want her to spoil the momentum. As far as I could tell, spoiling the momentum was her one true talent.

Mom said, "We didn't need a CB before, why do we need one now?"

Dad's smile vanished. He was going to do what he wanted to do; he always did. He just felt better if Mom granted him permission. When she didn't grant it for the CB, Dad gritted his teeth and said, "Jesus *Christ*," then stomped away. "This house. I swear!" he said on his way out the door. An hour later, he returned home with a giant shopping bag from Radio Shack.

Once Dad started installing the CB, I could tell that Mom's resistance to it was more than money. The Maverick was her first new car—it was one of the cheapest cars on the market, and Dad had managed to swing a good deal on one of the previous year's models—and so Mom didn't want Dad drilling holes all over it.

"See if you can find a smaller bit for me," he said to me. He was on his back on the floorboard, and I was looking at his head upside down, which gave him an odd expression of surprise. "Hurry up, now," he said. "I'd like to get this baby put in before it's too dark to see."

With the CB installed, Dad then mounted a twelve-foot fiberglass antenna onto Mom's trunk. "That oughta do 'er," he said.

I stayed up late that night, using a flashlight to study the booklet of CB lingo. *Bird dog* was a radar detector. *Chicken coop* was a weigh station. *Alligator* was a piece of blown-out tire in the road; from a distance, it looked like an alligator sunning itself. The idea of using words that didn't mean what they usually meant appealed to me. I wasn't sure why, except that the idea of talking, which was something I hadn't thought about much before, suddenly became a lot more interesting.

I woke up early the next morning, took my mother's keys out of her purse, and headed for the car to listen in on what everyone had to say. Channel 19 was where the truckers were, and since we lived only a few miles from Interstate 55, I could pick up an endless stream of staticky conversations. When one faded out, another faded in. I could picture the huge trucks barreling toward our house, then retreating.

"Roger," one of the truckers said, "I just got shot in the back."

My heartbeat quickened. I quickly flipped through the CB booklet. Getting shot in the back meant that you'd driven past a cop operating radar from an exit ramp.

"Hey, good buddy," another trucker said, "you got yourself a bear at your front door."

A bear at your front door meant that a cop was driving somewhere ahead of you.

Around lunchtime, my mother pounded on the car window, causing me to jump and drop the booklet.

"Hank," she said. "Have you decided to move into my car? Let me know so I can start piling all your stuff in the backseat."

Later that day, my father sauntered up to the car with a plate of spaghetti and meatballs. With his fist, he gave me the international symbol for *roll down your window.* "Hey, Hank," he said, "the neighbors are starting to wonder what you're doing in there. Mrs. Rybicki just called to see if you've asphyxiated yourself."

The edge of Mrs. Rybicki's property sat against our driveway, allowing her to see everything that went on at our house. Ever since her husband had died last fall, she spent all her time at home. She couldn't hold down a job because she had Tourette's syndrome and would frequently make faces or call the person she was talking to a name. Her bosses had never heard of Tourette's, so they didn't believe that it was a medical condition. According to Mrs. Rybicki, her bosses thought it was an excuse she'd made up so she could swear at them.

"She called to see if I'd done *what?*" I asked.

"Asphyxiated," he said. "You know." He bugged his eyes out and looked sort of dead. I wasn't sure if he was doing an impression of Mrs. Rybicki or trying to define the word for me.

"I'm fine," I said.

"Okey-doke, pardner," he said, and handed over my dinner.

When Kelly came home from a night out with her friends, it was already pitch black. She took one look at me and said, "They say it's addictive."

"What?"

"That!" she said, and pointed at the CB.

"I can leave anytime I want," I said.

She took a good long look at me. She shook her head. "Nope," she said. "You're already a goner. I can tell. Sorry to be the one to break the news."

That night, in my dreams, a grizzly bear showed up at my front door, pushed me aside, and mauled my family to death. I hid inside the chicken coop in my bedroom, and while the bear ripped apart the house around me, leaving claw marks along the walls, I peered out my bedroom window at the thousands of alligators crawling the streets and sidewalks.

It took my mother pounding on my bedroom door and yelling my name to wake me up.

"What?" I said.

"Open up. I don't want everyone on the block to hear me."

I dragged myself to the door, muttering the whole way. My eyes were still partially sealed shut from sleep glue. When I opened the door, Mom was tapping her finger on the wall, sizing me up.

"What?" I said. She didn't say anything. "*What?*" I said again.

"I've been out here for ten minutes knocking. What time did you finally go to bed?"

I looked at my wrist where a watch might have been, something my father did a million times a day, but I didn't own a wristwatch, so I looked back up and shrugged.

"One of these days," Mom said, "I'll get on a bus, ride it out of here, and *then* let's see how long everyone will last."

I never knew what to say when Mom said things like this. "She's just talking," Dad always told me, but I didn't see how that was supposed to make me feel any better.

Mom said, "Do you want Count Chocula for breakfast?"

"Sounds good, big mama."

"What did you say?"

"Sounds good," I said, shaking my head, trying to clear the night's cobweb of faceless voices from my brain.

After breakfast, I found my mother's car keys and headed outside. As soon as I flipped on the CB and heard its static, its first mumbling voices, I melted into the car's front seat, soothed. I must have looked the way my mother looked when she took the first drag off her morning cigarette. I could always see in her eyes how much she had wanted that cigarette, and I could see, when she took that first puff, how everything about her softened, as if all the sharp edges of the world suddenly blurred into something fuzzy and inviting.

Today I was listening to truckers talk about a bunch of plain wrappers at a yardstick, or, as best as I could tell, several unmarked police cars parked by a mile marker. Kelly knocked on the passenger-side window. Against my better judgment, I rolled it down.

"Look at you," she said. "Hank, the voyeur."

"What do you mean?" Everyone was trying to confuse me with new vocabulary words. First Dad; now Kelly.

"You might as well ask for a subscription to *Playboy* for your birthday," she said.

I liked the idea of a subscription to *Playboy* for my birthday, but I didn't tell Kelly this. "Did a screw come loose inside your head?" I asked. "Let me know, and I'll go get Dad's socket set."

"You don't fool me," she said. "You sit out here and act like you're listening to truckers, but I know what you're really listening to, you big perv."

"Well," I said, "now that you know, I guess you can leave me alone."

Kelly narrowed her eyes at the CB as if it were the centerfold of a girl she knew but didn't like, and said, "Disgusting."

Mrs. Rybicki poked her head out her bedroom window and said, "How are you today, Kelly? Having a nice summer?" Before my sister could answer, Mrs. Rybicki barked out, "*PIG LICKER!*"

Kelly liked to lecture everyone in the family on Mrs. Rybicki's condition, how it was medical and how no one should take what she said or did personally, but I suspected that Kelly used Mrs. Rybicki to show how much better she was than the rest of us, how much more understanding, when the truth of the matter was that Mrs. Rybicki's name-calling actually got under her skin—only, of course, when she found herself on the receiving end. Today Kelly's neck tightened, but she smiled and said, "I'm having a *wonderful* summer."

"Good," Mrs. Rybicki said. "Enjoy it while you're young. *SLUT!*"

After studying the booklet some more, I gathered my courage to try out the CB. I cleared my throat. I waited for a pause in the conversation, then held down the microphone's button. "Breaker, breaker," I said. "Anybody out there got the ten-thirty-six?"

What I was asking for was the time, and I had to wait no longer than a second before someone clicked on and said, "Ten-thirty-six is one-thirty-seven."

The proper way to say "I appreciate it" was to run it all together into one word, so I said to the trucker, "Preeshaydit." I waited ten minutes, then clicked back on. "Breaker, breaker," I said. "Can anybody out there give me a ten-thirty-six?"

The same trucker clicked back on. "Ten-four. Ten-thirty-six is one-forty-seven."

"Preeshaydit," I said. I wanted to wait the full ten minutes before asking again, but I couldn't help myself. In five minutes, I clicked back on. "Anybody out there kind enough to give this good buddy a ten-thirty-six?"

There was a pause this time. Then the same trucker clicked back on. "What's your handle?"

I hadn't thought of a handle, so I used the first word I saw, the make of my mother's car: Maverick. "Ten-four. You got the Maverick here."

"Maverick," the trucker said. "Do us all a favor, wouldja? Read your mail and quit your jabberin'. You got that?"

"Ten-four," I said. "Got it and preeshaydit."

According to my booklet, reading your mail meant listening to the CB without talking. I waited ten minutes. I really wanted to click back on for another ten-thirty-six, but I took the trucker's advice and waited a full twenty minutes. This time no one answered when I asked.

Around lunchtime, Mom burst out of the house, her purse banging against her knee. She was always in a hurry. Whatever she held banged against her when she walked. "Hank, I need to go to the store," she said.

I stared at her a moment, then looked down at the CB and back up at her.

"We need groceries," Mom said. "Unless you don't need food anymore."

I hated going to the grocery store and tried not to go whenever possible, but I didn't want to leave the CB, so I scooted over.

"You're going?" Mom asked.

"I'll stay in the car," I said. "You know, keep an eye on everything while you shop."

Mom nodded, then gave the CB the exact same look Kelly had given it yesterday.

Before Dad had installed the CB, I could have taken it or left it, but now that it was here, I couldn't imagine how we'd lived without one. How had I spent all of my previous summers? I must have been bored completely out of my skull and not even known it.

Mrs. Rybicki appeared around the corner of her house, holding a rake. She yelled out to my mother, "Beautiful afternoon, isn't it?"

My mother groaned so that only I could hear. To Mrs. Rybicki, she said, "I suppose."

"Nice day for yard work," Mrs. Rybicki said. "Not too sunny. Uptight *MONKEY!*"

My mother waved at her, then slid into the car. "I'm in no mood," she said, "to listen to that woman today. *No* mood." She backed out of the driveway, smiling and nodding at Mrs. Rybicki the whole time, then jerked the shift into drive and burned rubber in front of our house.

Normally, Mom was a good driver—a defensive driver, my father called her—but on this particular trip, I noticed a variety of potential dangers, and my palms grew moist with sweat. For starters, a cop had taken a U-turn and was now behind us, speeding up. I clicked on the CB and said, "Breaker, breaker. This is the Maverick. A city kitty just did a flip-flop and is westbound and hammered down."

My mother cut her eyes over to me, but I gave her one of my wait-a-sec looks.

"Roger, Maverick," a trucker said. "We hear you loud and clear. You got a ten-twenty on that kitty?"

"Roger, good buddy," I said. "Kitty's westbound on Eighty-seventh just past Austin."

There was a pause. Then "Roger, Maverick. You want to give us a mile marker?"

"No mile marker," I said.

"Roger. What's the *big* road you're travelin' then, Maverick?"

"No big road," I said. "We're in the 'burbs. Roger."

Mom said, "Hank! What are you doing?"

"Just trying to help out," I said.

The sound of static filled the car, and just as I thought that something had gone wrong with the radio, the trucker who'd given me all the ten-thirty-sixes earlier clicked on and said, "Rubber Chicken here with a PSA. Our friend Maverick, he's a four-wheeler. And he'd do himself a *real* big favor by finding another station to play trucker on. Roger."

I clicked on the CB and said, "Preeshaydit, Rubber Chicken. This is Maverick signing off. Over and out." I turned off the CB.

"You better watch yourself," Mom said. "Sometimes people don't want your help."

"That's a big ten-four," I said. "I hear you loud and clear."

In the parking lot, alone, I clicked the CB back on and started flipping through the stations. Some were emergency stations and some were for cops only, but after my second time around, I found one where the people talking sounded like kids. Older than me, maybe even older than Kelly, but still kids. They were using CB lingo, but the way they dragged out their words, or the way they clicked on only to laugh (*heh-heh,* like someone clearing his throat) made them sound more like late-night disc jockeys than truckers.

I slumped down to listen.

A boy said, "Hey, sexy, what's your handle?" and a girl answered, "Dream Weaver. What's *your* handle?" and then the boy answered, "You really want to know? It's a *long* handle. A handle you could really wrap your hand around."

At this another boy clicked on, coughing out a sly laugh: "*Heh-heh.*"

Dream Weaver said, "Okay, big boy. Give it to me. I can take it." She sounded like she was blowing smoke out her mouth and talking at the same time.

"Rough 'n' Ready," the boy said.

Dream Weaver said, "Ooooooo. I like that. But you know what? It's not as *long* as you made it sound."

Again that laugh: "*Heh-heh.*"

So this was what Kelly was talking about: the Citizens Band station for pervs! I didn't want anyone in the grocery-store parking lot to think I was a sex maniac, but I didn't want to turn it off, either, so I lowered the volume and crouched down to catch what was being said. Moments after I had finished contorting myself so that half of me fit underneath the dashboard, an elderly woman appeared at the car next to ours and started putting away her groceries. She looked over, squinted, then leaned toward the car to see if what she was looking at was what she thought she was looking at. When she concluded that I was a living person, she gasped and straightened up. The Maverick's windows were rolled all the way up. I was dripping sweat and breathing slowly. The woman was old enough to be my grandmother. She mouthed, *Are you okay?* and I gave her the thumbs-up.

By the time my mother returned to the car to load grocery bags into the trunk, I'd listened to Dream Weaver and Rough 'n' Ready tell each other all the things they wanted to do to each other, and I was worked up like I hadn't ever been worked up. Afraid of getting caught, I snapped off the CB. I crossed my legs and shifted in my seat. Mom opened the door, slid behind the wheel, and said, "Thanks for all your help, Hank."

"No problem," I said.

Mom looked over at me. It was a look I was used to getting. Mom, Dad, and Kelly all gave it to me several times a day. It was the same look you'd give a person who looked almost exactly like someone you knew but who wasn't actually that person. The only people I ever gave that look to were strangers in department stores, who, in turn, gave me their own looks, looks that said, *What the hell are YOU looking at?* It was a look that made my knees start knocking together.

Mom shook her head. She said, "Did the CB break?"

"Nope," I said. "I just got bored."

"Too bad."

My head buzzed all the way home with phantom conversations. Listening to that station had been like picking up a telephone from another room and hearing things no one wanted you to hear, a phone call from one darkened bedroom to another darkened bedroom, but there was something different about the CB: Everyone talking must have known that at least a few dozen other people were listening in. I'd spent my life in constant fear that girls could read my mind. It had never occurred to me to say out loud precisely what I was thinking. It seemed even crazier to broadcast these thoughts to anyone who wanted to listen. But it was this craziness that made listening in so thrilling. During pauses in their conversations, I heard my own heart thumping.

That night I asked Kelly what she knew about the station.

"Horndog Central?" she asked.

I nodded. "Do you know anyone who uses that station?"

"Puh-*leeze*," she said. "Why would I know anyone who uses that station? What do I look like to you? A nymphomaniac?"

I didn't know what she was talking about, so I told her to forget it, that I was only asking.

"Hank. Go look at yourself in the mirror," she said. "You're looking kinda creepy these days. In thirty years you'll be flashing little kids at Rice Park. I'll tell Mom to get you a raincoat for Christmas, okay?"

"Sure," I said, "I could use a new raincoat."

Kelly gave me that look, but I gave her a look back, the look that said,

*What the hell are YOU looking at?* and that was all it took. A shiver rippled through her. "Creepy," she whispered, walking away.

I couldn't sleep, so I sneaked out of the house, lifting my mother's key ring along the way. It was after midnight, and the only sounds outside were crickets and Mrs. Rybicki's barking. Ever since her husband died, Mrs. Rybicki would sleep off and on throughout the day, then stay awake at night, smoking and watching the Late, Late Movie, occasionally barking at the TV—always three individual barks, followed by three quick ones: Arf! Arf! Arf! *Arf-arf-arf!*

I slipped the key into the ignition and turned it partway, and the CB, sputtering and hissing, began to glow. I turned the dial slowly, my ear turned toward it. I must have looked like a safecracker waiting for the tumblers to fall. All I needed were rubber gloves and a stethoscope. After some fine-tuning, I finally found it. *Horndog Central!*

The first voice I heard was that of the girl who sounded like she could blow smoke and talk at the same time. She was still talking to Rough 'n' Ready, telling him she wanted to meet him, that they should "hook up." "I want to see," she said, "if your handle's really as long as you say it is."

"*Heh-heh.*"

Then Rough 'n' Ready said, "Roger, Dream Weaver. I'll show you my handle, but what are you gonna show me? Over."

Someone clicked on and said, "Maybe she can show you her double nickels."

"*Heh-heh.*"

"Or maybe," someone else suggested, "she can show you her meat-wagon."

"*Heh-heh.*"

I knew from my booklet that double nickels was a speed limit of 55 and a meatwagon was an ambulance, but I was getting their drift.

"How about it?" Rough 'n' Ready asked. "Do you want to show me your meatwagon?"

Dream Weaver clicked back on, blowing smoke, getting ready to talk, but then I made the mistake of looking up. Mrs. Rybicki's face hovered outside my window. She waited until I had finished screaming before she knocked. I clicked off the CB and caught my breath, then rolled down the window.

"Can't sleep?" she asked.

"Naw. Thought I'd come outside," I said.

Mrs. Rybicki looked at the CB. She said, "What's the big appeal of those things, anyway?" Her face tightened, and I braced myself. "*STINKY BOY!*" she said. "*SHIT FOR BREATH!*" Her face softened again. Some days were better than others for Mrs. Rybicki's Tourette's, but tonight her left eye was twitching an awful lot.

"Well," I said, "you get to listen to what other people say."

"And do people say interesting things?"

"Sometimes," I said. "But they talk in CB language. Like code."

"Code, huh?" She twitched. "How about those *COW PIES?*"

I nodded. "Yeah, codes. Like ten-four. That means *okay.* But there are better words. Like meatwagon."

"Meatwagon? What's a meatwagon?"

"An ambulance," I said.

Mrs. Rybicki leaned her head into the car a bit too far and started sniffing. She leaned back out and said, "Maybe I should get one. Give me something to do."

I imagined Mrs. Rybicki sitting in her car, calling truckers names. "Sure," I said. "It'd be a lot of fun."

"All right, Hank. I better get going. I'll see you tomorrow. Good night."

"Good night, Mrs. Rybicki."

I turned the CB back on, but everyone was gone. I clicked on and said, "Breaker-breaker. Breaker for a radio check." I waited, but no one was there. When Mrs. Rybicki started barking—"Arf! Arf! Arf! *Arf-arf-arf!*"—I decided it was time to call it a night.

Saturday, over breakfast, Dad started talking about this new machine he'd heard about. It was like a cassette recorder, only the cassettes were larger than music cassettes, and you could record shows from the TV.

"Beta-something," he said.

"Betamax?" Kelly said.

"Bingo!" Dad said, and winked at her.

Mom, cutting to the chase, said, "How much do they cost?"

"Oh, I don't know," Dad said. He sawed a link of sausage in half. "I think they're a little over a grand."

"A thousand dollars?" Mom asked.

Dad forked the sausage, inserted it into his mouth. "Mm-hm," he said.

"Well," Mom said, "we're not getting one. Where would we get a thousand dollars?"

"Did I *say* we were getting one?" Dad asked. He sawed the next link, only he kept sawing after his knife hit the plate. "I was just talking. I was just making conversation."

Mom smiled. Whenever she didn't believe my father, she smiled. She smiled a lot these days. "Good," she said. "I'm glad to hear you were just talking."

Dad said, "The TV store in the mall, they have in-house financing."

Mom dropped her silverware so that it clanged against her plate. She stood up.

"For Christ's sake," Dad said, "all I'm saying is that they have financing. I'm not saying that I was going to finance one." But Mom was already in the bedroom.

Kelly, eyes filling with tears, pushed her plate aside and ran to her room.

"Look at us," Dad said to me. "Your mother's going through menopause, and your sister's starting puberty. We're no match for them. We don't have a prayer. It's like watching a bare-knuckled fistfight between Muhammad Ali and Mahatma Gandhi. No match. You know what I'm saying?"

I'd heard of puberty but didn't know what the big deal was. I'd never heard of menopause. "*What's* Mom going through?" I asked.

"Menopause. Sounds like a racehorse, don't it? Men o' Pause." He snickered, but I could tell that even he didn't think it was too funny. "She can't have kids anymore," he added.

"Did she *want* more kids?"

"Hell, no!" Dad said. He said this so fast it made me wonder if maybe they already had one more than they wanted. Kelly was always proposing this notion to me, and since I was the youngest, that extra kid would have been me.

"Then what's the big deal?" I asked.

Dad pointed his fork at me and said, "Exactly. Only it's more complicated."

"You mean, it's harder to buy what you want?" I said.

Dad jabbed the fork at me, causing me to jump back. *"Exactly,"* he said. "And the funny thing is, the worse things get, the more I want to buy. Now, isn't *that* a pisser?"

I preferred Mom's car to my bedroom, the people on the CB to the people inside my house, static to silence. Everyone would probably get along a lot better if they never saw one another, if they spent their days speaking into microphones and listening to voices coming out of speakers. Maybe the CB radio was a glimpse into the future, a sign of how the world might operate in twenty years. I'd already heard of houses with PA systems installed, so it seemed possible.

Inside the Maverick, lying across the front seat with a pillow under my head, I listened to the perv station for hours, until nearly everyone had clicked off for the night. I was starting to drift to sleep when a voice I hadn't heard before, the voice of a girl, woke me up.

"Hello?" she said. "Is anyone still out there?" I picked up the mike. I waited, figuring she had moved on, but then she said, "If anyone's out there, talk to me."

I clicked on the mike. "Breaker, breaker. This is the Maverick. What's your handle, sweetie pie?"

"I don't have a handle," she said.

"Roger," I said. "Did everyone hear that? We got ourselves a no-handle here. Over."

The girl said, "Where do you learn to talk like that?"

"Roger," I said. "Like what? Over."

"Like *that*. CB talk. I don't know what half of it means."

"Ten-four," I said. "I hear you loud and clear, No-Handle. I can teach ya. Over."

"I'd like that," she said.

"Roger," I said. *"Meatwagon* is an ambulance. *Double nickels* means fifty-five miles per hour."

The Laugher unexpectedly keyed the mike and added his two cents: *"Heh-heh."*

"I thought we were alone," the girl said.

"Negatory," I said. "Over."

"Maverick?"

"Yeah?"

"Maybe you'd like to teach me in person?"

The Laugher clicked on and tried to laugh but started coughing instead. The speaker inside my CB sounded like it might explode until the Laugher clicked back off.

"Sure," I said. "I mean, ten-four. A *big* ten-four."

No-Handle said, "Where should we meet?"

"Uh, I don't know," I said.

"How about the corner of Seventy-ninth and Narragansett?" she said.

"Ten-four," I said.

"How about Monday? Around noon?" she asked.

"Okay," I said. "I'll be there. Preeshaydit."

"Don't let me down," she said.

"Roger on the not-letting-you-down part."

"Sweet dreams," she said. "I'm really tired."

"Forty-two, Bubba. See you in a short short," I said, and clicked off the CB before the moment was spoiled.

The next day, while I was hosing down my bike and using Dad's Turtle Wax on the frame, Mom came home with a giant box.

"What's that?" I asked.

Mom smiled, but it was the same smile she gave Mrs. Rybicki, so instead of smiling back, I braced myself. I followed Mom inside the house and watched her set the box on the kitchen table in front of Dad.

"What the hell's this?" Dad asked.

"Open it."

Dad took the butter knife he'd been using on his toast and pried loose the humongous staples. Then he reached in and pulled out what looked like a giant cassette player. A clock, the kind where one number rolled slowly to the next, was mounted on top.

"What is it?" I asked. "A giant alarm clock?"

"It's a Betamax," he said.

"It's what you wanted, isn't it?" Mom asked.

Dad set it gently back inside the box and said, "Why did you get this? Huh? Why?"

"You wanted it, right? Well, there it is. It's yours."

I knew Dad was being toyed with. Kelly, sitting on the couch, knew Dad was being toyed with. Worst of all was that *Dad* knew he was being toyed with.

"What's your point?" he asked. "What does this prove?"

At this Mom laughed. She said, "It proves that I can sink us just as fast as you can. It proves that I can spend money as fast, if not faster, than you. *That's* what it proves."

"God*damn* it," Dad said. He picked up the box with the Betamax as if he were going to throw it, but then he set it back down. If Mom hadn't brought one home, I knew Dad would have bought one, but now that Mom had brought one home herself, he'd have to return it. Until now I hadn't understood how Mom thought, but I saw that she had a game plan that was larger than all of us. Her game plan was to keep all of us afloat. It wasn't any more complicated than that, really.

Mom said, "Enjoy," and headed for the bedroom.

I reached into the box and pulled out the instructions. "How does this thing work, anyway?" I asked, hoping to cheer up Dad, but he ordered me to put the instructions back in the box.

"Kelly," he said. "Go find me some tape. Who wants to go with me to the mall?" When no one answered, Dad said, "Hank, get your coat," even though it was summer, and I felt a sudden sickening emptiness in my stomach that my father couldn't even remember what season it was.

Nearly two years later, a few days after our garage sale, I spotted Kenny and Ralph driving around in Kenny's Nova, the fiberglass antenna swaying in the wind. I waved, and Kenny did a U-turn, pulling up beside me. Ralph rolled down his window.

"How's it going?" I asked.

Ralph said, "We can't find anyone on the CB."

"No one?"

"Not *no one*," Ralph said. "No one *interesting*."

Kenny said, "Hey, Hank, do you remember a station where chicks talked to dudes? You remember that?"

I wasn't sure what to say. Of course I remembered. I nodded. I said, "Kelly told me something about it."

Kenny said, "Well? Where the hell is it? Do you know? What station?"

"That was two years ago," I said. "I think they're all gone."

"Gone?" Ralph said. "GONE?"

"No one talks on CBs anymore," I said. "Unless you're a trucker."

Ralph and Kenny silently regarded each other, then turned back to me. I expected them to ask for their ten bucks back, but they didn't. Kenny said, "I don't believe that. I think you're wrong."

I shrugged.

"Keep trying different stations," Kenny told Ralph. Before I could say good-bye, Kenny floored it, leaving me in a cloud of dust.

On the morning of the day I was to meet No-Handle, the girl of my static-filled dreams, I made for the Maverick but saw, even before opening the door, that all of it was gone—the CB, the mike, even the bracket that held the CB. At first I thought someone had stolen it, but then I turned around and saw that the antenna was gone, too. I couldn't help it. I screamed. I didn't want to scream, but I did anyway. I screamed and kicked one of the car's tires. "No!" I yelled. "NO! NO!" After some searching, I found all of it inside the garage, half hidden behind a strobe light, a box containing Dad's old karate uniform and nunchakus, and my broken Evel Knievel Scramble Van.

There was too much to do, too much to think about. I needed to listen to the CB, see if the girl without a handle had tuned in this morning; I had to get ready for our date; I had to think about what to say when I met her. The last thing I needed was a problem with the CB. I wasn't sure I knew how to hook it up myself. When I'd helped Dad, I wasn't paying attention to anything he did; my sole job had been to hand him tools, which was what my job always was.

When I stepped out of the garage, Dad nearly knocked me over. I hadn't even known that he was still home. It was Monday; he should have been at his new job.

"There you are!" he said. I was about to ask about the CB, to demand its return, but Dad said, "Where's Mom?"

"Who?" I was always momentarily confused when Dad called Mom *Mom*. "Oh," I said. "Mom. *My* mom. I don't know."

"Huh," he said.

Behind us, a woman called out my name. It was Mrs. Rybicki. She was heading up our driveway.

"Goddamn it," Dad said under his breath. "This is all I need."

Mrs. Rybicki said, "Hank, I was wondering if you could give me a hand with a few things." She turned to my father as if seeing him there for the first time, then leaned toward him. The closer she got to him, the more her eyes bugged out. Then she leaned back, and her eyes returned to normal. She did this several times. For reasons I couldn't figure out, Mrs. Rybicki never called my father names. She just made faces at him. Occasionally, though not often, she'd make farting noises out the corner of her mouth. Normally I looked forward to hearing them, but I wasn't in the mood for them today.

"I'll be there in a sec," I said.

My father said under his breath, "Jesus Christ, that woman gives me the creeps."

"It's a medical thing," I said. "She can't help it."

Dad nodded. "Yeah; well; I can't say that I one hundred percent believe that. You'd be surprised how many women use *that* one as an excuse."

I was hoping that Mrs. Rybicki had bought a CB and wanted me to show her how to use it, but the help she wanted was nothing like that. For starters, I had to climb up on a stepladder, which she was afraid to do, and change a lightbulb in her hallway.

"Mrs. Rybicki," I said. "I need to go."

I was running late. I hadn't even figured out what I was going to say to the girl when I met her. Should I introduce myself as the Maverick? Should I bring her a box of Whitman's chocolates, even though all I could afford was the one that held four pieces of candy?

"Just one more thing," Mrs. Rybicki said. "It'll take a second."

An hour later, on my way home, after Mrs. Rybicki thanked me and then called me *shit for brains,* Kelly stepped out from behind a tall hedge, nearly causing me to wet my pants. There were times that she reminded me of the ghosts in *A Christmas Carol,* my favorite movie. I was about to suggest that she start dragging some chains around with her, but she cut me off.

"So, pervert," she said, "what are you going to do now that your perv machine has been taken away?"

I shrugged.

"You *are* a perv," she said. "You realize that, don't you?"

I grunted.

"Listen to you," Kelly said. "You even *sound* like a pervert." She shook her head. "Hey. Where's Mom? You can point, if you like. Point and grunt."

"I don't know," I said. "Dad's home, though."

Kelly snorted. "You and Dad. You two don't think about anyone except yourselves, do you?"

"How can you say that?" I asked. "I think about other people!" I tried to remember what I spent my days thinking about, but I couldn't remember thinking about anyone unless I was in the picture, too. But didn't everyone think about only themselves? Why would you spend your days thinking about other people? The way I saw it, other people were already thinking about themselves and didn't need me thinking about them, too.

"What time is it?" I asked.

She looked at her watch. "Noon. Why?"

"I'm late."

"See!" she said. "It's always about you!"

I started for my bike, but I yelled behind me, "I'm me! Why *shouldn't* it be about me? I don't even know what you're talking about. You're crazy. Did you know that? You're *nuts!*"

I zipped out of the driveway, past Kelly, past Mrs. Rybicki's house, pumping the pedals faster and faster. I hadn't changed clothes. I hadn't even glanced in the mirror to make sure I looked okay. I took the corners fast, almost wiping out but managing not to. By the time I reached my destination, sweat covered my entire face, as if I were in the first stages of melting. I stood there wiping my forehead with my sleeve, but new sweat instantly replaced the old sweat. My shirt was covered with dark wet patches.

We hadn't settled on a specific place to meet. The corner of Seventy-ninth and Narragansett was a major intersection with cars and trucks continuously ripping past. What had I been thinking? All day yesterday, based on nothing but her crackling voice, I'd tried picturing her. She would be older than me, maybe four or five years, but I wouldn't mind. She would have straight brown hair. She'd be wearing cutoffs with fringe around her tanned legs. She'd probably have on a white shirt that sort of ruffled out at the bottom, the sort you liked to see girls wear on windy days, the kind hippie girls used to wear, hippie girls who didn't care if everyone saw their belly buttons. I was eleven years old. I *liked* belly buttons.

I was getting pretty worked up, thinking about her. When I held my hand Scout-style to shade my eyes from the sun, I spotted a girl at the ice-cream shop across the street. She was standing at the outside counter and talking to the man who worked there. It's her, I thought. It's her, and she's asking the man if he's seen me. I inched my bike closer to the street so I could cross when the traffic cleared. I was about to yell out and wave, but then she turned around, and I saw that she wasn't a girl at all. She was my mother.

Mom walked away from the ice-cream shop toward the intersection. I expected her to be holding a cone, but what she held was a cigarette. She flicked away the ashes. The cigarette, however, didn't seem to be working its usual magic on her. She didn't look relaxed.

What was she doing here? Had she found out about my date? Was she here to stop it before it even began—to nip it in the bud, as she would have said. *Mom*, I thought. *Mom*. I pressed my lips together, but the word *Mom* caught inside my head. And then I saw the reason why Mom was here: A bus was heading toward the ice-cream shop. A bus. The sight of it rolling toward us caused my gut to ache, as if someone had sucker-punched me right after breakfast.

Mom dropped the cigarette. She blew a long stream of smoke, and it attached to her mouth like a comic-strip balloon. If this were the funnies, my name would have appeared inside—HANK!—but the balloon dissolved as fast as it had appeared.

I opened my mouth, but instead of words came howls: *"Ah, wooooooo. Ah, wooooooo."* Was this how Mrs. Rybicki felt, stray words and sounds prowling the dark knot of her brain like packs of werewolves, the rabid ones overpowering the weak and then escaping? I wanted to speak but couldn't. I howled louder: *"AH, WOOOOOOO! AH, WOOOOOOO!"* My mother looked behind her, above her. She looked everywhere except where I was standing. The bus pulled up, blocking my view, and I started to bark: "Arf! Arf! Arf!" I barked faster, louder, desperately. "Arf! Arf! Arf! *Arf, arf, arf!*" I barked and barked, hoping my mother wouldn't get on the bus, that she would see me and call out my name, but the only reply came from dogs, dozens of them. They were pacing backyards. They were inside houses, peering out picture windows. They were telling me their own sad stories, each and every one, and as the bus started to pull away, first hissing, then groaning, I held my breath, waiting to see what hope, if any, I could offer in return.

# RED'S

**R**ALPH AND I CALLED it Red's, though its real name was R&D's. We started calling it Red's, I guess, because neither of us had bothered to look closely at the sign. Not that this made a difference. It was one of those places nobody knew by name. If people called it anything at all, they'd call it "that ice-cream joint on the corner of Seventy-ninth and Narragansett" and leave it at that.

At least once a week during the spring of our eighth-grade year, Ralph and I would agree to meet at Red's. A husband and wife ran the place. The husband was there by himself all morning and for a good part of the afternoon, and then the wife came to help out with the nighttime rush. She brought her poodle and kept it in their car, a Ford LTD, with the windows rolled down partway. The dog usually stood on an armrest and watched everything going on. If it started to bark, the wife would poke her head out the service window and tell it to shush.

The husband and wife were older than my parents, probably in their fifties. They never smiled; they never talked to each other. If I said hello, the husband would say, "What can I get you?" The wife didn't help with anything but the ice cream. The husband took all the orders, he fixed all the hamburgers and hot dogs, and he dealt with all the customer complaints. He always wore a white T-shirt tucked into dress pants; she always wore a pink polyester dress that could have been a waitress's uniform she'd taken from another restaurant years ago. An old electric fan, spray-painted black, ran all the time, turning creakily one way and then the other.

Ralph and I went there only after it got dark out. By then the owner would have flipped on the yellow bulb where bugs of every kind met and hung out. That's how things were there at night: swarms of customers in the parking lot, swarms of bugs in the air. There were always bugs I'd never seen before, one with extraordinarily long legs and a flimsy, almost see-through body; or a metallic-looking beetle, twice the size of any other beetle, with pincers that looked ready to chop off a small child's finger. The poodle in the car watched me watch the bugs, and whenever I'd look over at the poodle, it would let out a little whimper. Its breath steamed the glass, and tiny pawprints dotted the window's bottom edge.

One time Ralph asked, "Why do you like this place?"

"I don't know. Don't you like it?"

Ralph didn't answer.

The counter outside, the one where I rested my money while peering through the sliding screen door to watch the man inside make my hot-fudge sundae, had been painted so many times that you could sink your thumbnail in and watch the paint bubble up somewhere else. It reminded me of blisters I'd had, still full of goo. If my mother had been with me, she'd have told me not to touch it, how many thousands of other people had touched it, and how many of those thousands were filthy. But since I always came alone or with Ralph, I couldn't help it: I touched it. I pushed my thumbnail in and watched the paint bubble up. It was revolting, but I didn't have a choice in the matter. Sometimes I'd tell myself that I wasn't going to touch it, and I'd try holding out as long as possible, but at the last minute, as the husband finished up my sundae or turned to get my change, I'd dig my thumbnail all the way in, trying to pop through the paint but leaving only a deep quarter-moon gouge.

One particularly busy night, the husband was working all by himself. The wife wasn't back there with him. The car and the poodle weren't in the parking lot. The husband was sweating, working like a madman in a laboratory, and when he did something that required only one hand, like making change, he'd dial the phone at the same time, and you could tell that whoever he had called wasn't answering, that the phone kept ringing and ringing. Twice he gave teenagers the wrong change, too little each time.

"Where do you think she is?" I asked Ralph.

"Who?"

"His wife."

"His *wife*? What, you know these people personally? They're family friends?"

"What do you mean?"

Ralph sighed. He said, "How do you know they're married?"

I thought about it a minute; I didn't know. I finally said, "They have a poodle."

"What poodle?"

"The poodle they keep in the car."

"What car?"

"The LTD," I said. I pointed at the empty spot, but the fact that the spot was empty confirmed for Ralph that he was right.

As the teenagers in front of us got their orders, the husband kept the phone cradled on his shoulder, pinned by his ear and chin. Ralph and I stepped up to order, but the moment I brought my thumbnail to the counter, the husband flipped the OPEN sign to CLOSED and then pulled down the shade.

"What the hell?" Ralph said. Behind us came mutters, curses. Ralph said, "Anyone got the time?" No one gave Ralph the time. It was a question that didn't need an answer. Someone answered Ralph by saying, "No kidding."

I biked to R&D's the next day, but it was closed. I biked there every day for a week, but each day was the same. Then one day a Realtor's sign appeared on the corner. Six weeks later, a new business moved in, an insurance company, and they bricked up the hole where we used to order ice cream. It looked odd because the bricks were a slightly different color. The counter with the hundreds of layers of paint was gone, too.

In June, on the first hot day of the year, one week before eighth-grade graduation, I walked inside the insurance company, and a blast of ice-cold air-conditioned air hit me. It felt so good that I wanted to sit down and stay there, but I couldn't: The two girls who worked in the office were studying me as if I were a raccoon who'd wandered in hunting for food. They were both young and pretty, and one of them was snapping a wad of gum. They were probably only a few years out of high school, not that much older than me. The shorter of the two, the one who wasn't chewing gum, smiled and walked over to the counter where I stood.

"Can I help you?"

I'd never done anything like this before, walk into a place where I didn't belong, and I suddenly felt that I'd made a mistake, but it was too late now. I said, "I was wondering if you know what happened to the ice-cream place that was here."

The short girl turned to look at the gum snapper. They both shook their heads, then the short one turned back to me. "No, I'm sorry. We don't." The one with the gum blew a huge bubble just then. It popped, then wilted, hanging out of her mouth like a shriveled tongue.

"Thanks for your time," I said.

"Maybe," the short one said, "we can interest you in some life insurance?" The other girl started to giggle but caught herself.

"Nah," I said. "I don't think so." But before I could turn to go, the short girl had come around the counter. To my surprise, she wasn't any taller than me. She took my arm and led me to the desks where she and her friend did their work.

"Here," she said, and handed over a brochure. "Now, sit down."

The one with the gum said, "*Tracy,*" and then laughed, covering her mouth with the back of her hand.

I looked through the brochure. It didn't make a lot of sense. The best I could tell, I would have to pay a little bit of money each month while I was still alive, but when I died, someone else would hit the jackpot. I kept thinking I was missing something, that maybe I was misreading it. I felt something touch my ankle, and when I reached down to brush it away, I saw the tip of the short girl's shoe rubbing against me.

"Well?" she said. "Can we offer you some insurance? Shall we write up a policy?"

"I don't know," I said. "I guess I don't get it. Why do I need insurance?"

The girl with the gum pulled up a chair and sat next to me. She leaned in to me, whispering into my ear, "Because life is full of surprises." The shorter girl leaned toward me, her palms resting on my knees, and said, "Because you never know what's going to happen from one minute to the next."

# THE GRAND ILLUSION

**I** **GRADUATED FROM EIGHTH** grade the summer Cheap Trick introduced America to Budokan. That was 1979, and at graduation I leaned forward and whispered into Lucy Bruno's ear, "I want YOU to want ME."

Lucy spun around and said, "Not if I live to be a hundred. Not if I'm old and blind as a bat and smell like potted meat."

Ralph said, "I love potted meat. I eat two cans a day."

Lucy Bruno shivered, then turned away from us.

Ralph, having failed both the third and the fifth grades, was the oldest person ever to graduate from Jacqueline Bouvier Kennedy Grade School, an honor he hoped the principal would note during his commencement address. He sat next to me during the ceremony, a cowlick rising off the top of his head like a giant question mark; the wiry beginnings of what he insisted on calling "porkchop sideburns" sprouted on either side of his face.

I looked above and beyond Lucy's nest of hair to Gina Morales, our valedictorian, standing onstage and smiling into the day's last great blast of sunlight, her braces winking each time she moved her brainy head. I'm not sure what came over me, but every girl that day made my heart lurch. I wanted to whisper into the delicate whorls of each girl's ear what I had whispered into the delicate but unforgiving ear of Lucy Bruno: I want YOU to want ME.

Two days after graduation, plans of monumental proportions were well under way. Styx, it was rumored, was going to perform a surprise concert in our city's reservoir. The reservoir was bone-dry, used these days for drainage, the perfect spot for a full-blown rock concert. Members of Styx had grown up on Chicago's South Side, and the word on the street was that they wanted to give a little something back to their hometown fans. The only mystery was the concert's date. Every night a procession of cars crawled around the reservoir, watching for the arrival of Styx's road crew. Our classmate Wes Papadakis had vowed to camp out until Styx arrived, and some nights you could hear the faint reverberations of "Come Sail Away" or "Lady" floating up from the reservoir's concrete basin, where Wes, clutching his boom box, lay like a castaway atop his bicentennial inflatable mattress, waiting.

I went over to Ralph's house to see what he knew about all of this, but when I got there, he was on top of his mother's garage, peering through a magnifying glass. I made my way around to the alley, found the ladder, and climbed up. "Ralph," I said, tiptoeing across the lumpy tar, afraid of falling through. "What are you doing?"

He pointed at Mr. Gonzales, his next-door neighbor, and said, "I'm trying to set that son of a bitch on fire." Mr. Gonzales was sitting in a chaise longue and drinking a beer, naked except for a pair of Bermuda shorts. He was unemployed that year and almost always outside, as naked as you could get without actually being naked. Crushed beer cans decorated his lawn, glinting in the sunlight, while a tiny speck of light from Ralph's magnifying glass seared into his bare shoulder blade.

"Why?"

"Shhhhh," Ralph said. "Watch this. Here it comes."

Mr. Gonzales twitched a few times, then reached up over his shoulder and swatted the dagger of light, a phantom mosquito.

"Jesus," I said. "How long have you been doing this?"

"Two weeks," Ralph said. "I put in at least an hour a day. Some days, two. Every once in a while I think I see smoke."

"But *why?*"

"Why what?"

"Why do you want to set him on fire?"

Ralph reached into a grocery sack and pulled out three Big Chief notepads. A thick rubber band held the batch together.

"What's this?" I asked.

"It's my revenge list," he said. "It's a list of everyone I'm going to get even with."

"Really," I said. I removed the rubber band, eager to read the list, expecting to find our teachers' names sprinkled among Ralph's schoolwork and doodles, but what I found was a much more frightening and detailed accounting. On each page were twenty names—I saw Lucy Bruno's, and Gina Morales's not far from her—and each notepad, according to its cover, contained a hundred pages.

"Ralph," I said. "There must be six hundred names here."

Ralph jammed his magnifying glass into his back pocket. He said, "Look. I've met a lot of people since the third grade, okay?"

The pages listed everyone I knew, including my parents—everyone, as far as I could tell, except for me and my sister, Kelly.

"Geez, Ralph. Who's *not* on this list?"

Ralph shrugged. "Are you done reading that yet?" he asked. He snatched the notebooks away and stuffed them deep inside his grocery sack.

I liked Ralph, but danger always lurked close behind him. Sooner or later he was bound to drag me with him into the swamp of low-life crime, and I'd been meaning all year to break off my friendship with him, only I couldn't figure out how to do it without repercussion. His revenge list confirmed what I'd feared all along, that Ralph wasn't going to make it easy for me.

"Styx," he said after we had climbed down from the roof and I had told him why I'd stopped by. "You want front-row tickets to the reservoir concert? I'll talk to my cousins, see what I can scare up."

"Great," I said. "I appreciate it."

Kelly had her first real boyfriend that summer, a skinny bucktoothed kid named Unger. Unger was not at all the sort of future in-law I had ever imagined. The only way I ever pictured him in our family tree was dangling from a rope. I suppose I made my feelings clear by pulling out my Mortimer Snerd ventriloquist doll each time Unger came over, settling the doll on my right knee and yanking the string that opened its mouth, out of which came "Hi, my name's Unger," or "Boy, my girlfriend, Kelly, is one hot babe. I can't imagine what she sees in me," or "What's an orthodontist?"

For her part, Kelly quit speaking to me, except to hurl insults. "*Your* problem," she liked to say, "is that you're a sexually confused boy whose only friend is a hoodlum."

Sadly, she was more or less right on both points. Ralph *was* a hoodlum, and sex *did* confuse me, especially the particulars, even though Ralph had once smuggled onto school property a color photo of a naked man holding an upside down naked woman.

Ralph slipped the photo to me one day during history class and whispered, "This is what it's going to be like day and night once we get out of school."

The activity in the photo looked like some new kind of calisthenic, something Mr. Mica, our PE teacher, might have forced us to do prior to a savage game of Bombardment, the main differences being that we'd have been wearing our regulation gym clothes and there would have been no exotic parrot in the background watching us. Nonetheless, the photo raised more questions than it answered. Was this what Kelly and Unger did together when I wasn't around to abuse him with my Mortimer Snerd doll? Was this what my parents did at night while I was upstairs trying to fall asleep?

As for Ralph, I was still determined to break things off with him, but the next day he called to say that he had a surprise for me, and when I showed up at his house, he appeared on his front stoop grinning, a giant tie dangling from his neck. He met me at the gate and said, "Here," pressing into my hands another necktie, equally large. "Put it on."

"What?"

"Put it on. I know where Dennis DeYoung is having dinner tonight."

Dennis DeYoung, Styx's lead singer, was the man who gave meaning to our otherwise useless summer. "You're kidding," I said. "*The* Dennis DeYoung?"

"No," Ralph said. "Dennis DeYoung the child molester."

"How do you know he'll be there?" I asked.

"Sources," Ralph said. Ralph's sources were Kenny and Norm. In addition to working the Tootsie Roll assembly line, they apparently doubled as music insiders, privy to the secrets of the world's most successful rock stars. For instance: Robert Plant couldn't have held a note if not for the electronic vocal augmenter installed in each of his microphones and controlled by a man working a soundboard. Gene Simmons had had a cow tongue surgically attached to his own. After *Frampton Comes Alive!* became the best-selling album of all time, Peter Frampton ballooned up to four hundred pounds and moved to Iceland, too fat to play his guitar anymore; his new albums, all flops, were written and performed by his identical twin, Larry Frampton.

Though I was wearing a yellow T-shirt with an iron-on decal of a gargantuan falcon, our school's mascot, I slipped the already looped tie over my head and tightened the knot. We walked nearly two miles to Ford City Shopping Center, then over to Ford City Bowling and Billiards, home to a few dozen pool-hustling hooligans who liked to pick fights with adults and flick lit cigarettes at kids. Next door was a Mexican restaurant: El Matador.

"You sure this is where Dennis DeYoung's supposed to be?" I asked. "It's sort of rough around here."

Ralph adjusted his tie's knot. "This is the place. From what I hear, he loves Mexican."

We stepped into the crushed-velvet dining room, decorated with sombreros and strings of dried red peppers. A fancy acoustic guitar hung on the wall next to our booth.

"You think he'll play a song while he's here?" I asked, pointing to the guitar.

"Maybe," Ralph said. "I wouldn't mind hearing a little 'Grand Illusion' tonight. A cappella," he added.

"No kidding," I said. I had started humming "Lorelei" when I noticed that Ralph's thoughts were elsewhere. He seemed to be staring beyond El Matador's walls and into some blurry vision of his own past. Years ago, Ralph had admitted to me that he wanted to do something that would make our classmates remember him, and for a fleeting moment, while playing the bongos in Mr. Mudjra's music class, hammering out his own solo to Led Zeppelin's "Moby Dick," Ralph had succeeded in winning the hearts of twenty-one seventh-graders, one of whom was me. We watched, awestruck, as one of our own moved his hands in expert chaos, keeping up with the music in such a way that we were not quite sure *what* we were watching. Veronica Slomski and Isabel Messina, sitting in the front row, wept after Ralph had finished.

I had a feeling Ralph was rolling those ten minutes over in his head right now, so I asked him if he was okay, but he just cut his eyes toward me and said, "Of course I'm okay. What the hell's *your* problem?"

"Nothing," I said.

When the waitress arrived, we ordered drinks and several appetizers, along with our main courses and dessert—everything at once. I had never ordered my own food at a restaurant (my mom or dad always took care of it), so I was unprepared when it began arriving in droves, plate after plate, way too much for a single table. Even so, Ralph and I scarfed it all down until our bellies poked out and we could no longer sit up straight in our booth.

I groaned and then Ralph did the same, only louder. I spotted Lucy Bruno and her parents on the other side of the restaurant. All three were staring at us, so I lifted my glass of pop in a toast, while Ralph carefully peeled back his eyelids and stuck his tongue out at them. Lucy shrieked and looked away.

Ralph said, "I can't get that potted-meat insult out of my mind. I friggin' *love* that stuff."

"When do you think Dennis DeYoung's gonna get here?" I asked. "I'm not feeling too good."

"Maybe he's not coming tonight," Ralph said. "Maybe he ate Chinese tonight. I hear he likes Chinese, too."

When the check came, Ralph said, "It's on me." He pulled a bent pen from his back pocket, flipped the check over, and wrote, *I.O.U. a lot of money. Thanks!*

"Good one," I said. "We can hide the money under an ashtray. Give her a heart attack until she finds it."

Ralph stood from the table, stretched, then started walking away. I had to grip the edge of the table and brace myself to stand. For the first time in my life, I felt like a fat person. "Hey, Ralph," I said. "Don't forget to leave the money."

Ralph turned and shot me a look that said, *Shut up*.

I didn't have any money, so I had no choice but to follow. My heart felt swollen, pounding so hard it hurt: food and fear, a lethal combo. Outside, beyond the Ford City parking lot, I asked Ralph what exactly had just happened.

"We didn't pay for our food," he said.

"Why not?" I asked, my stomach starting to gurgle more dangerously.

"Listen," he said. "Restaurants work on the good-faith system. They give you a check, and you're supposed to put the money down. You wave to the waitress on the way out, and she waves back. 'Have a nice day,' she says, and you say, 'Will do.' Well, they got stiffed this time. The way I see it, I'm teaching the whole industry a lesson."

"What lesson's that?"

Ralph grinned. "Not everyone's honest," he said.

"Oh. I see," I said, but I didn't.

After the restaurant incident, I avoided Ralph, afraid he was going to land me in jail, where I would grow old and rot. A few days later, while concocting hair-raising scenarios in which the cops came roaring up to my parents' front door looking for me, I walked into my bedroom and found Unger holding my Mortimer Snerd ventriloquist doll.

"What the hell are *you* doing in here?" I asked.

He pulled the string at the back of Mortimer Snerd's head, and its mouth opened. Unger messed with the string some more until Snerd's teeth chattered. Then, in a high-pitched voice, without moving his lips, Unger repeated what I had said: *"What the hell are YOU doing here?"*

"Hey," I said. "That's pretty good. You can throw your voice."

Mortimer Snerd turned its head first left, then right. *"Hey,"* the doll said. *"That's pretty good. You can throw your voice."*

I felt silly for all those times I'd used Snerd to insult Unger, not so much because I'd insulted him but because I had made no bones that it was me doing all the talking. I had never bothered to change my voice, and I had always moved my lips. Unger, on the other hand, reacted to everything the dummy said. He asked it questions, treating it as a creature beyond his control, which is what drew me into his show. For their finale, Unger drank a tall glass of water while Snerd sang "You Light Up My Life."

When Unger set Snerd aside, I stood up and applauded. "Jesus," I said. "You should go on *The Gong Show*."

"I've thought about it," Unger said.

"Seriously," I said. "You've got talent."

Unger blushed. I didn't think I'd ever seen another boy blush before, so I quit complimenting him. "What are you doing here, anyway?" I asked. "Where's Kelly?"

"Oh, she's still at pom-pom practice," he said.

"Pom-pom practice?" I said. "What the hell's that? I didn't know Kelly did anything at school."

Unger smiled and said, "There's a *lot* you don't know about Kelly." He tried to look mischievous when he said it, but then he blushed again, and I had to turn away. It embarrassed me too much to watch.

"Listen," I said. "I don't want to hear about you and Kelly. If I want to watch a horror movie, I'll stay up and watch *Creature Features*, okay?"

Two days later, I found Unger in my bedroom again. "What the hell?" I said.

Unger blushed, but Mortimer Snerd said, "*I hope you don't mind. We were just practicing.*" And then Snerd laughed: "*Uh-huck, uh-huck.*"

"Hey," I said. "That sounds just like him, Unger. Seriously."

Unger set Snerd aside. "I found some of my dad's old Charlie McCarthy records. I worked on it all weekend."

I stared at Unger; I didn't know what to say. I didn't know anyone my age who spent all weekend working on *anything*.

Unger said, "I came over to tell you about this great idea," and then he told me about how he and a few of his friends were going to start a band, an *air* band, and how they needed a drummer.

"I can't play the drums," I said.

"It's an *air* band," Unger said. "All you do is pretend to play. We'll put together a tape with a bunch of songs, and we'll play them at parties."

"Whose parties?" I asked.

"Anybody's parties," he said. "This is the best idea ever. People will pay us to come over and play. They'll think we're a hoot."

*Hoot* was a word only my grandparents used, but I tried to ignore it. Maybe he'd picked it up over the weekend, listening to Charlie McCarthy. "People will actually *pay* us?" I asked. "Are you out of your mind?"

"There's nothing out there like this," he said, "and that's what you need these days, a gimmick."

He seemed so sure of success, I couldn't help getting a little excited. "What'll we play? You think we could play some Styx?"

Unger frowned. "Maybe," he said. "I don't know. I'd have to talk to the other guys. We were thinking about some cutting-edge stuff, like Roxy Music or Elvis Costello or the Knack." He stared at his shoes and said, "The thing is, we need a place to practice. Do you think we can use your basement?"

I laughed. "Are you kidding? My parents would never let a band practice in their basement." Unger stared at me patiently, waiting for my brain to catch up to the conversation. "So what you're saying," I said slowly, "is that *no one* would actually be playing any instruments?"

"Right."

"Would I need a drum set?"

"Nothing," Unger said. "All we need is a boom box, and Jimmy Cook has that."

"And you want *me* to be the drummer," I said.

"You'd be perfect," he said.

"Okay," I said. "Sure. I'll do it. Why not?"

After I joined the air band, Kelly quit talking to me for good. She thought the whole thing had been my idea, a ploy to keep her and Unger from seeing each other. The rehearsals, as it turned out, were pretty grueling—two hours each night, five nights a week.

"We have to practice," Unger told her, a whine creeping into his voice. "How are we going to get any good if we don't practice?"

I felt totally ridiculous at first, the five of us pretending to play instruments that weren't even in the room: Joe Matecki tickling the ivories,

Howlin' Jimmy Cook belting out the lead vocals, Bob Jesinowski sawing away on the electric guitar, Unger dutifully plucking the bass, while I went nuts on the drums. But after a few weeks, an odd thing happened: I started getting into it. The more I picked up on the quirks of different drummers, the more I lost myself to the music. And when I shut my eyes, an amphitheater rolled out before me, thousands of crazed girls screaming, crying, throwing themselves against the stage, their arms in the air, stretching and arching toward me. It was as if I were holding a gigantic magnet, and the girls—weighted down with silver bracelets, pewter rings, and stainless-steel watches—couldn't help being pulled into my circle of energy.

Once, in the midst of such a vision, my arms flailing wildly to the Who's "Won't Get Fooled Again," I opened my eyes and saw Ralph standing at the foot of the basement stairs. My mother must have let him in and told him to go on downstairs. The other four guys in the band were lost in their own private worlds, twitching or swaying. Unger was bouncing up and down, eyes squeezed shut.

"Ralph!" I yelled over the music. My voice startled the other band members. They looked up, saw Ralph, and stopped playing. Someone reached over and turned down the boom box. No one knew quite what to do with their hands now that their instruments had vanished. Jimmy violently scratched his head, using the tips of all his fingers. Joe rubbed his palms so hard against his jeans, I thought he was going to spontaneously combust.

"Hey," I said to Ralph. "The porkchop sideburns are looking good. They're really coming in." Ralph didn't say anything. He looked from one musician to the next, squinting, sizing us up. "Ralph plays the bongos," I said, hoping to snap Ralph out of whatever trance he appeared to be falling into. "I've never seen anyone play the bongos like him, either," I added. "You should've seen him last year in Mr. Mudjra's class. *Man!* You guys would've dropped dead." I smiled at Ralph, shook my head. "Hey, listen. I got an idea. Why don't you play the bongos in our band? That'd be okay, wouldn't it, guys?"

Unger said, "I don't know. We'd have to talk about it. I mean, we've been rehearsing and everything. Our first gig's next week."

"Well," I said, "he can sit in, though, can't he?"

"Sure," Unger said. "You want to sit in with us, Ralph?"

"C'mon, Ralph. Sit in with us," I said.

Ralph's focus seemed to widen to include all of us. Then, without so much as a word, he placed a business card of some kind on my dad's toolbox, turned, and walked back upstairs, disappearing into the light above.

"Okay," Unger said. "Back to work."

After everyone had left, I walked over to my father's toolbox. What Ralph had left behind was not a business card. It was a ticket for the Styx concert. The ticket was made of blue construction paper with black ink that had bled until each letter looked sort of hairy. It said, STYX: LIVE AT THE RESERVOIR. NO CAMERAS. NO RECORDING DEVICES. RAIN OR SHINE. There was no date on the ticket. No time, either. No seat number, no address. I kept it with me, though, tucked inside my back pocket, ready at a moment's notice to be there, to be a part of history.

Bored, I went upstairs to my room and made a few dozen crank calls to Lucy Bruno, asking her if it was true that she liked Hugh G. Rection. After the fourth call, Lucy fell headfirst into the teeth of my trap. Angry, she blurted out what sounded like, "Whose huge erection?" and I yelled back, "Mine!"

This game went on until her parents picked up another extension and announced that the line was tapped, and that the police would be at my house in short order. I didn't believe them, of course. After all, I had deepened my voice and put a couple of tube socks over the mouthpiece, but their threats caused me to question what I was doing. Why was I making prank phone calls in the first place? What sort of person was I turning into?

For the band's first gig, we were to play in the rec room of a new condo on the far edge of town, and from the looks of it, everyone at the party was at least five years older than Unger, who was sixteen.

"Who set this gig up?" I asked.

"Jimmy did," Unger said. "These are his brother's friends."

A man wearing a powder-blue tuxedo came over and introduced himself as Chad. "Bad Chad," he said and laughed. "What do you guys call yourselves? The Air Band? Is that what your brother told me, Jimmy?"

"Yeah, that's right."

"What sort of shit do you play?"

"Anything," Unger said. "You name it."

"Disco?" Chad asked.

"You bet," Unger said. "We play disco all the time."

Chad was one of those white guys who tried but failed to pull off an afro. From a distance, it appeared that a small toxic cloud—a vapor— had attached itself to the top of his head. He'd also jammed a jumbo pitchfork of a comb in the 'do to give it that final touch, but each time he nodded, the comb wiggled wildly.

Chad said, "You can set your equipment up over there."

"Cool," Unger said.

While Joe set up the boom box, the rest of us took our positions. We had made several specialty tapes: Hard Rock, Disco, Punk, even Country. I knew from all our weeks of practice what to do and when to do it, so I shut my eyes for dramatic effect. "Play That Funky Music" was the first song on our disco tape, opening with the electric guitar and followed by vocals. Then came the drums, a simple but seductive beat.

Moving my head in and out like a turtle, finding the groove, I played well over a minute before opening my eyes. No one was dancing. No one was singing along. The audience stood in groups of two or three, watching us. The only people getting into the song were the other guys in the band, who were clearly as lost in the music as I had been. Chad—*Bad Chad*—ran the tips of his fingers along his suit's lapels. Our eyes met, and I stopped playing.

Somewhere along the way there had been a misunderstanding, and the very thought of the gap between the audience's expectations and what we were actually doing made me instantly queasy. They had expected a real band; we hadn't even brought instruments. The gap couldn't have been any wider.

Chad motioned with his head, so I reached over and turned off the boom box. I might as well have been a hypnotist clapping my hands: Joe, Jimmy, Bob, and Unger suddenly came to, shaking their heads and looking around, bewildered. As simple as that, I had snapped them back to the here and now.

Chad took two steps forward and opened his mouth as if to scold us, but nothing came out. He shut his eyes and shook his head, then stopped and glared at us again—crazed this time—before throwing his arms into the air, turning around, and stomping toward the keg at the back of the room.

Summer was winding down, and I hadn't seen Ralph in over a month. Kelly and Unger had broken up, but Unger still came over to practice throwing his voice. Meanwhile, our air band was put on indefinite hold.

One night at the beginning of August, with a tornado watch in progress, Unger and I sat in my room, and I watched him put on a show with my Mortimer Snerd doll. I had to admit, his new act was pure genius. Using his boom box, he played Rolling Stones songs, and while Mortimer Snerd lip-synched the lead vocals, Unger sang backup. It was dizzying to watch. I couldn't even begin to imagine how much time he'd spent at home figuring out the logistics of it all.

Every few minutes my father would bang on my bedroom door to upgrade us on the status of the approaching storm. "The watch is on until ten o'clock," he said the first time. "That's for *all* of Cook County"; then, in an hour, "It's been upgraded to a warning, guys. Eighty-mile-an-hour winds. Hold on to your hats."

Initially all we heard was the soft patter of rain, though not much later, our lights started flickering while fists of hail pounded the house. Somewhere a window shattered.

"Wow," I said.

"Sympathy for the Devil" was playing, and Unger kept singing the "oooooo-ooooooo" part until an explosion nearby caused us to jump.

"One of those giant transformers must have blown up," I said, though before I finished saying it, our lights shut off for good. "Great," I said. Unger didn't say anything. His battery-operated boom box chugged on, and Mick Jagger continued singing. It was my favorite part of the song, the part where Mick asks who killed the Kennedys, so I closed my eyes.

While Mick's words rumbled through me, I felt a hand touch my knee, then Unger's breath against my face, then his mouth against my mouth. Before I understood what was happening, his tongue swiped across my lips.

When he sat back, I screamed. When he put his hand against my mouth to quiet me, I bit down, sinking my teeth into his knuckles, then *he* screamed. My father bolted into the room with a high-powered flashlight, yelling, "What's wrong? You guys all right? What happened?"

"We're all right," I said. "Nothing happened."

My father swung the flashlight toward Unger. "Cut your hand?" he asked.

"Nah," he said. "I'm okay."

"Jesus Christ," Dad said. "The two of you had better quit screwing around. This house is under *siege*. The basement's flooding, and a tree's down out back. I sure as hell don't need any extra horseshit on top of it."

"No problem," I said.

Much to my horror, my mother insisted that Unger spend the night. She put him up in my bedroom, so I took the couch in the living room and wrapped myself in a quilt. I didn't know what time it was when I finally fell asleep, but I woke up the next morning to my father nudging me with his foot.

"Don't you know this kid?" he asked. He pointed his big toe at the TV.

I was so tired I could barely make sense of where I was or what was going on, but when I finally did, I saw my father in his La-Z-Boy, holding a bowl of cereal, still nudging me with his foot; my mother and sister, side by side, staring at the TV screen; and Unger, who blushed when I looked at him.

"I remember him from back when you were in Cub Scouts," Dad said. "Isn't that the same kid?"

On TV was Wes Papadakis, and he was being interviewed by Walter Jacobson of channel 2 news. The interview had been conducted late last night, and it was the hottest story on all the stations. Later I would hear the whole thing, how Wes had been sound asleep at the bottom of the reservoir when the storm hit, waiting there—as he had been every night—for the arrival of Styx. Apparently he'd fallen asleep listening to *Pieces of Eight* when the first ball of hail cracked him on the head. Not much later, he noticed water pouring over the sides. The sides proved too muddy for climbing out, leaving him, as he saw it, with only one option: to ride the storm out. And that was exactly what he did. Clutching his bicentennial inflatable mattress, with all the city's flooded streets draining toward him, Wes floated twenty, thirty, forty feet, until he reached the upper lip of the reservoir and, swept along by a heavy current, rode his raft down Rutherford Avenue all the way home.

"It's a miracle," my mother said, "that he's alive."

Kelly, tears in her eyes, turned and asked if I had his phone number.

"*No,* I don't have his phone number," I said. Until last night, Wes had been a mere shadow on the playground, a bit player at recess. Could his life really have changed that quickly?

"They should give that kid a medal," my father said.

"A medal?" I asked.

My father turned his head slowly, to point his chin at me. *And what have you done lately?* was what this look meant. Then, disgusted, he turned away. "Hell," he said. "They should at least give him a key to the city."

My mother agreed. "That's the *least* they could do," she said.

I didn't see Unger anymore until I started high school. For those last few weeks of summer, I couldn't shake the thought of Unger's mouth against my mouth, his tongue swiping my lips. Panicked, I called Lucy Bruno three times in three days, finally persuading her to go with me to the Haunted Trails Miniature Golf Range, where, much to my own amazement, I chipped a fluorescent green golf ball off Frankenstein's head. The manager promptly asked us to leave, I walked Lucy home, and we never spoke again. Whatever Lucy Bruno had thought of me before our date was proved in spades by my recklessness with a golf club, by the threat I posed to society, and by the fact that I was far more amused by what I had done than anyone else at the golf range.

The day before the first day of high school, I stuck my Mortimer Snerd ventriloquist doll and a hacksaw into a grocery sack with the general plan of sawing off Mortimer's head. I walked to the reservoir, where I intended to perform this act. Carefully, I made my way down the slope. I had never been down before, but after everything that had happened with Wes, I wanted to see it.

Styx, of course, had never shown up, and now that I was down here, I couldn't imagine how it would have happened. There were no electrical outlets, the sides were too steep for people to sit, and the acoustics were awful. What had Wes been thinking? What had *any* of us been thinking?

"HELLO," I yelled for fun. "HOW ARE YOU?" I listened to my voice hit the wall and come back to me. It bounced off another wall, then came back again. This continued for a while, my voice bouncing up behind me, to the side of me, or head-on, fainter and fainter, until it became a bunch of half-words and grunts, then nothing at all.

"HELLO," I yelled again. Someone from above yelled, "HELLO," and together our voices surrounded me, one voice answering the other, overlapping, mocking each other. I looked up. A cop was peering down at me. With his billy club, he motioned for me to climb out of the reservoir. After I'd struggled up to him, he said, "What's in the bag?"

"A ventriloquist doll and a hacksaw," I said.

He nodded. "You see this sign?" He tapped it with his club. NO TRESPASSING, it said.

"No," I said. "I've never seen it before."

"It's there for a reason," he said. "Kid almost drowned a few weeks ago."

"Wes Papadakis," I said.

The cop regarded me as if what I'd said made absolutely no sense to him. He said, "Got to start teaching you kids the meaning of laws. Got to start somewhere."

I guess I thought he was simply talking out loud, because I was smiling when he read me my rights and pulled out his handcuffs. He asked me to set my bag down, then he cuffed my hands behind my back. I was still smiling, but I was starting to get the chills, too.

"What's so funny?" the cop asked.

"Nothing," I said.

"Well," the cop said, "I wouldn't be smiling if I were you."

"I'm cold."

"It's August," he said. "You can't be cold. It's ninety degrees."

"I'm freezing."

With his hand on top of my head, the cop guided me into the back-seat of his cruiser. "You know what? All you kids are nuts." He shut the door. After settling himself into the driver's seat, he set my bag down beside him and said, "That kid who almost drowned? He was nuts, too. Kept saying he was down there waiting for *sticks*, whatever the hell *that's* supposed to mean. Now look at him. A goddamn hero. You ask me, this whole city's nuts."

At the police station, the cop uncuffed me and returned my bag before pawning me off to a woman cop who sat at a desk, smoking a long, thin cigarette. "Identification?" she said.

"I don't have any."

"How old are you, honey?"

"Thirteen."

"Boy," she said, "they get younger every day." She stood up and said, "Hold your horses, okay?"

I passed the time looking over some mug shots, until another cop, a bald one, lugged Ralph in, shoving him hard into a chair. Like me, Ralph was holding a grocery sack. The cop said, "Don't do anything that would require us to shoot you. You got that?"

Ralph yawned.

"I wouldn't hesitate to use force," the cop said, leaving the two of us alone.

"Hey, Ralph," I said. Ralph looked over, and I smiled at him. "They got me, too," I said. I expected him to get up and come over, but he didn't. Instead, he narrowed his eyes at me, as if I were the witness called in to point him out in a lineup.

"I'm under arrest," I said, and laughed. "Do you believe that?" I shook my head, unable to believe it myself. "Hey! You shaved off your pork-chop sideburns. Why'd you do that?"

Ralph touched the side of his face as if he no longer remembered what had been there. "What's in the bag?" he asked.

"A ventriloquist doll and a hacksaw," I said. "What's in yours?"

"My revenge list."

"Oh yeah," I said. "That's right. I forgot about that." I knew, of course, that my name had been added to Ralph's revenge list—how could it not have been?—and the very thought gave me goose bumps. "So," I said, changing subjects. "What'd they get *you* for?"

"Skipped out on a restaurant without paying the bill."

My heart sped up. "El Matador?" I asked.

"Nuh-uh. They never caught me for that one." He grinned, pleased that we'd gotten away with it, and I relaxed. "*Last* week," he said, "they nailed my cousins for selling fake Styx tickets. Styx's management heard about what they were doing and set up a sting operation." He shook his head and said, "Norm and Kenny. They're *screwed*."

Had Ralph forgotten he'd given me one of the tickets? Had he known all along that it was a fake? I didn't tell Ralph, but I still had the ticket; I kept it on display in my bedroom, sealed under the glass top of my dresser, between a stub for the only White Sox game I ever attended and a stolen ticket for a Pink Floyd concert that my parents wouldn't drive me to.

"What they nail you for?" Ralph asked.

"Trespassing," I said.

Ralph snorted.

"They caught me in the reservoir," I said, "you know, where Wes Papadakis almost drowned."

Ralph nodded, then turned away. He crumpled shut the top of his grocery sack and waited for his officer to return. We both seemed to know that this would be our last conversation, and Ralph must have seen no point in prolonging it. I feared deep down that in a few years our classmates would not only *not* remember the day Ralph had played his bongos in Mr. Mudjra's class, but they would have a hard time remembering Ralph at all. He was old enough to drop out of school, which I'm sure he was planning to do. I worried, too, that it would be only a matter of time before he moved through the town like a ghost, invisible even to those who had once known him.

It was possible, though, that I was worried about my own self and not Ralph. Whatever any of us had done before, whatever accomplishments we'd achieved, it all paled by comparison to Wes Papadakis's. Wes had become the South Side's very own Noah. His journey out of the reservoir would be passed along to children for generations, as powerful as any

Bible story—more powerful, since he was one of our own. No one would ever forget the morning they first saw Wes on TV, his raft blown up to look like the American flag. Rain pelting the umbrella above his head, lightning snapping in the distance, Wes looked directly into the cameras and into our homes and told us his story.

The bald cop returned and said, "Looks like we'll have to put the two of you in a holding cell until we get your parents on the horn. Come along, now. Both of you."

Ralph and I walked side by side down the corridor, trailing the cop. Our grocery sacks rubbed together, and when we passed the exit, Ralph looked out the glass door into the sunlight, as if considering making a break for it. I had decided in that instant that if Ralph bolted for the door, I would bolt with him. I was hoping he'd do it. Nothing had ever been as real to me as that moment, waiting for Ralph's decision. But Ralph faced ahead, setting his jaw in grim defeat, and I remained beside him, already sorry for knowing who between us would be the first one set free.

# THE PAST: 1975

# A DIAGRAM OF THE FUTURE

**I**N **1975, THE YEAR** I fell in love with Miss Martz, the school's new li-
brarian, Ralph was forced to spend an hour each week with our fifth-
grade class because there was no other place to put him.

Ralph and I had exchanged grunts and nods on the playground before, but I didn't really know him back then. I knew *about* him, but
everyone knew about him. What I knew was that he'd failed both the
third and fifth grades, and that he scared people, old and young alike.
There were rumors, of course, about the things he'd done—acts of violence, mostly—but I didn't know anyone who'd ever seen him do anything. What scared *me* about Ralph were the smaller details. For
instance, he always wore old faded T-shirts, and from the droopy opening of a sleeve's cave, you could see a bush of hair under his arm. When I
mentioned this to my sister, Kelly, who had once, many years ago, been
classmates with Ralph, she rolled her eyes and said, "Ralph had hairy pits
back when we were in kindergarten."

"Really?"

"And he was growing a mustache, too."

"A mustache?" I said. "In *kindergarten?*"

Kelly nodded. She liked knowing things that I didn't. "Unless his lip was always dirty," she added. "But I don't think so. We were all pretty sure it was a mustache."

It was rumored that Ralph now had his own private teacher, and this teacher, an otherwise patient and good-natured man, needed daily hour-long cigarette breaks somewhere far away from Ralph. Normally someone like Ralph would be sent to the principal's office for that hour, but our principal, Mr. Santoro, was, as he himself put it, at the end of his rope when it came to dealing with Ralph. Everyone who dealt with Ralph eventually felt at the end of his or her rope—which is why, I supposed, he was sent to Miss Martz. She was new to our school. She still had some rope left.

But it was before Ralph arrived in our class that I fell in love with Miss Martz. Miss Martz had long brown hair, perfectly straight and parted in the middle, and although she wore dark sweaters and dark skirts, she also wore jewelry with large colorful insets, like turquoise or red coral. I fell in love with her because one of her teeth—a tooth next to one of her two big teeth on top—was crooked in the exact same way that mine was. I sat all through class, waiting for her to smile, and when she did, I shut my eyes and imagined myself sitting on her lap and pressing my tooth against her tooth, the two of us comparing whose was more crooked. Sometimes we playfully argued, going back and forth: *Mine's more crooked . . . No, no, MINE'S more crooked.* We were naked, too. We were always naked in my fantasies.

What I wanted more than anything was to prove to Miss Martz how special I was, how everything in the world fascinated me, how knowledgeable I was about most things. I wanted her to look at me and shake her head in sheer amazement. *My little genius,* she'd think. The age difference worried me, of course, but with my genius factored in, that would seem paltry when weighed against what she'd gain by spending time in my presence. This, at least, was my hope. My fear was that she'd find out the truth, that I wasn't really a genius, that I was faking it.

During the first week of fifth grade, before Mr. Santoro dumped Ralph on us, I walked up to Miss Martz's desk and said, "I've been thinking a lot about Mr. Dewey lately."

Miss Martz smiled. When I smiled back, I saw her eyes travel down to my crooked tooth, and I was certain she understood in that moment that we were destined to spend our lives together. She said, "Who?"

"Dewey. The guy who invented the Dewey Decimal System of Classification."

"Oh, yes. *That* Dewey." Her expression grew serious. I suspected she was thinking about the enormity of my brain. She said, "What precisely were you thinking about Mr. Dewey?"

"I was just wondering . . . do you think he had any friends?"

Miss Martz considered this. I had an irrational urge to reach out and pinch her nose and then pretend I had captured it between two of my fingers. But I didn't. She frowned, not unkindly, and said, "I don't know. I imagine he did. Why?"

"It's tough," I said, "being a genius and all. I bet he was a pretty lonely guy." I nodded thoughtfully at my own observation, then headed back to my table, keeping my head low and, like a lonely guy, refusing to look at any of my classmates.

At the center of each table was a revolving bookcase crammed full of dictionaries, yearbooks, and encyclopedias. It worked on the same principle as my mother's lazy Susan: You spun it around until you found what you wanted. So I was spinning the bookcase at my table, one way and then the other, trying to appear deep in thought, when I spotted fresh graffiti. Someone had carved into the wood: *Miss Martz has a hairy twat.*

I wasn't sure what the sentence meant, but my not knowing didn't stop my palms from pooling with sweat or prevent the shiver that caused my entire body to convulse. I had an idea of what it meant, and I didn't want Miss Martz to see it. More importantly, I didn't want Miss Martz to think I was the one who had written it. I spun the bookcase around so it faced Gina Morales, who sat directly across from me, but when she looked up and saw the carving, she wrinkled her nose and said, "You're disgusting, Hank," and spun it back around. I didn't want to call any more attention to it, so I pulled out my king-size permanent marker from my school supply box and began filling in the carved letters, hoping that the words would blend into the woodwork. It wasn't until after I had filled in the last *T* that I leaned back and saw how much worse I'd made it. Instead of making the words disappear, I had highlighted them.

We attended library class only once a week, and it was the following week when Ralph was led into our classroom. For the other days of the week he would be palmed off on somebody else, but on Wednesdays at eleven o'clock, Ralph would be all ours. At the mere sight of him, a couple of girls gasped, while several boys avoided making eye contact. Ralph was wearing a too tight T-shirt, and on it, Wile E. Coyote was choking the Roadrunner. The caption underneath read, BEEP, BEEP, MY ASS! Ralph had a droopy upper lip, though it probably looked droopier due to the wisps of facial hair, and his arms seemed unusually long, though the problem may have been that his legs were unusually short.

The tables in the library were square, each one seating four people. There were four students seated at every table in the room, with the exception of my table which had two empty chairs.

Gina lowered her head and ripped through three abridged Hail Marys, but it was too late. "Over there," Mr. Santoro said, pointing to us.

Ralph appraised the situation. He turned to Mr. Santoro and said, "Looks good. Well, old man, I really appreciated the company. We should get together sometime. I think you'll find we have a lot in common." He offered his hand to Mr. Santoro, but the principal was already shaking his head and walking away.

Ralph sauntered over to our table and plopped down. The first thing he did was spin the bookcase around, tilting his head so he could read the various graffiti, but when he reached what had been written about Miss Martz, he bent forward, his nose practically touching the wood. He read it a few more times, then squinted at Miss Martz. Then, nodding with his bottom lip poked meditatively out, Ralph turned to me and said, "Huh!"

I shrugged.

Miss Martz, treating Ralph's presence as a perfectly normal occurrence, began to explain how she wanted each of us to check out a book from the science-fiction section, where there were many excellent novels. After reading our books, we were each to build a diorama of the future.

She stroked the turquoise stone on her dangling necklace while she spoke, as if it had magical powers, and I imagined her stroking it a certain number of times in order to transport us, her and me, to a nudist colony where we would live for the remainder of our days. I was imagining the two of us buck naked and knocking a huge beach ball back and forth when Ralph nudged me and said, "What does she want? A *diagram* of the future?"

"No," I said. "A diorama."

"A what?"

"A *diorama*," I said.

Ralph furrowed his brow, read the graffiti one more time, then gave Miss Martz a sour look, as if nothing about his day was making sense.

Miss Martz said, "The question to ask yourself is 'What will my neighborhood look like in the future?'"

Ralph's arm shot up. A pain, originating at my heart, radiated throughout my entire chest. I feared whatever Ralph might say.

Ralph cleared his throat. "Where do you live?" he asked.

Miss Martz, smiling, tilted her head as if she hadn't caught his question.

Ralph continued, "You want us to diagram what your neighborhood'll look like in the future, right? Well, I need to know where you live."

Miss Martz said, "Not *my* neighborhood. *Your* neighborhood."

"Oh," Ralph said. "My hearing must be going." He stuck a finger inside his ear and rattled it around a few times.

On our way out of class, Ralph nudged me and said, "Do you think it's true?"

"What?"

"The hairy business."

"I wouldn't know," I said. I thought of Ralph's own hair, those tumbleweeds covering each armpit.

Ralph said, "I wonder who wrote it."

I shook my head.

Ralph said, "I bet she has an ex-husband, and I bet he broke in here one night, after the school was closed, and carved it. Don't you think?"

I didn't say anything. I didn't want anyone to see me having a conversation with Ralph. I *really* didn't want anyone to think we were friends, so I started walking.

The next week Miss Martz stepped out of her little office behind the circulation desk, wearing a black turtleneck and a matching black skirt.

Her earrings were two different planets. The red one was clearly Mars, but I couldn't identify the other, somewhat larger one. I decided I would check out a book on astronomy so I could learn everything there was to know about planets.

Before Miss Martz could say anything, Ralph raised his hand. "What year?" he asked.

"What?" Miss Martz said.

"What year in the future? I started working on my diagram, and I was thinking 2050 seemed like a good year, but then I did the math. I'd be eighty-seven years old. Most of us would probably be dead. *You'd* be dead for sure. So then I was thinking maybe that was too far in the future. You see what I'm saying?"

Miss Martz, pinching Mars, then rocking it back and forth, stared at Ralph. She finally said, "How about 2001? Does that sound good?"

Ralph nodded. "So, not everyone here will be dead by then. Some of us, probably, but not most of us. Okay. Sounds good." He looked around the room. "Any other questions?" he asked, as if he were the teacher. "Nothing? Okay. Good."

The following week, Ralph said to Miss Martz, "I've got a question."

Constellations hung like chandeliers from Miss Martz's earlobes. Like me, she had the kind of earlobes that dangled. I had a theory that people with dangling earlobes were smarter than people with earlobes that were attached to the head. Since the first grade, I'd been studying dangling-eared people versus attached-ear people, and while my theory wasn't true 100 percent of the time, more times than not, the person with the dangling earlobe was of a higher intelligence than the poor soul who could only dream of earlobes that dangled.

Miss Martz sighed. "Yes, Ralph?"

Ralph stood up. "Does anyone in here have any extra balsa wood or know where I can get some balsa wood?"

I didn't know what balsa wood was. Apparently nobody else knew, either.

"Okay," Ralph said. "Just thought I'd ask." He sat down.

That night I began my project in earnest. Naturally, in order to secure a life with Miss Martz, I had wanted my diorama to be the best, the most original, but I knew that to achieve this, I would have to create a vision of the future so enticing, so mind-boggling, that Miss Martz would want to corner me day after day to ask the infinite questions that my project had raised, not only about the future but about the imagination from which it had sprung. I wasn't able to begin construction, however, until my mother had collected enough cardboard tubes from our toilet-paper and paper-towel rolls, and it took a few weeks to gather as many as I needed. The future, as I saw it, would be full of tall and short buildings, all of them cylindrical, each one shiny, almost blinding to the unprotected eye. To achieve this effect, I wrapped each cardboard roll in tinfoil, then I glued each one upright on a flat sheet of cardboard that was also covered in tinfoil. The city needed other touches, but I wasn't entirely sure what those touches should be or how to achieve them.

Each week in class, I worried that Miss Martz would walk over to our table and see the graffiti about her, so I kept my science-fiction novel propped up and open, covering it. I suspected one of the eighth-grade thugs had carved it, a cheap pocketknife clutched in his sweaty, possibly hairy, palm.

"I was talking to my cousins," Ralph said, standing up at the beginning of class, "and they thought I should ask you about scale."

"Scale?" Miss Martz asked.

"Ratio," Ralph said. "What're we looking at here? Ten to one? Fifty to one?"

"Ralph," Miss Martz said. I imagined her reaching for more rope but finding only the frayed end. "I don't know," she said. "You shouldn't be worrying about these things."

"My cousins," Ralph said, "they used to build model airplanes, so they know all about things like scale and ratio. They're going to lend me some of the glue. They don't build airplanes anymore, but they still buy the glue." He scratched behind his ear a few times, fast and hard, the way a dog would.

Miss Martz said, "I haven't given any thought to scale or ratio, so do whatever you think is best, Ralph."

Ralph said, "Maybe if I got an idea of what everyone else is doing." He looked around. "Anyone want to tell me about their city? What kind of ratio are you guys working on? What're we looking at here?" No one would make eye contact with Ralph, so he sat back down.

Throughout my other classes, I tried to imagine what my life was going to be like in the year 2001. I would be taller, better-looking, and always wearing a silver suit that would protect me from radiation. Miss Martz and I would be married, naturally, and she would fly to school each day in a car that recycled garbage for its energy. Each morning before she left for work, I would tromp outside in my silver suit and stuff the remains of last night's dinner into Miss Martz's gas tank/garbage compactor—chicken bones, potato peels, gravy. In it would all go, and then I'd start the car, shooting fire from the exhaust pipes. I'd rev the engine a few times and then mess with the thermostat so the car would be toasty warm by the time Miss Martz left. We would be happy in the year 2001, Miss Martz and I, as happy as any couple living in the future.

The next time I went to the library, I brought a jar of my father's wood putty. I brought a putty knife, too. I swiveled the vandalized bookcase around so the graffiti faced me. I kept the putty jar between my thighs, and when I didn't think anyone was looking, I filled in one of the letters with putty. Each time I repaired a letter, I moved my book over to block it.

Gina Morales's science-fiction novel, the cover of which showed an alien shaking hands with a boy who looked eerily like me, had put her into a deep trance, but there was no way I could repair the bookcase without Ralph seeing what I was doing.

Ralph followed my knife each time it dipped down between my legs and came up with a fresh glob of putty. He didn't say anything, even when our eyes met. What he did do was act as my lookout. Whenever he thought Miss Martz was about to head over, he'd raise his hand, palm down, for me to pause. When the coast was clear, he'd lower his hand and nod for me to continue. When the bell rang, I moved my book to see how the repair job had turned out.

"Holy crap," I said.

The bookcase's wood was stained dark, while the putty I'd used was light tan. Instead of erasing the graffiti, I'd made it glow. Anyone walking by would be able to see it.

Ralph, admiring my work, said, "Good job. Real professional. I like it."

I wanted to explain to Ralph what it was that I was trying to do, but everyone was filing out, and I didn't want to linger behind and call attention to myself.

That night I was too nervous to do much work on my neighborhood of the future. I pasted a few cotton balls around my cylindrical buildings and then painted the cotton green with my tempera paints, but they looked less like shrubs and more like a bunch of fat Martians lounging around outside. All they needed were cigarettes to make them resemble disgruntled employees taking a break.

Each night I fell asleep thinking about myself sitting on Miss Martz's lap, and each night the fantasy would roll on, twisting in new and interesting directions. After we had joked about our crooked teeth, Miss Martz would lean back and say, "You're the smartest boy I've ever met. Did you know that? You are. The smartest!" I would blush and duck my head. I would tell her that I did impressions, too, and then I make her beg me to do one. In real life I didn't do impressions, but in my fantasy I could do impressions of nearly anyone. And so I would do impressions of celebrities first—Johnny Carson, the Skipper from *Gilligan's Island*, Scooby-Doo—before moving on to impressions of people we both knew—Mr. Santoro, Gina Morales, Ralph. But even in the fantasy, I felt bad about doing an impression of Ralph.

Miss Martz would say, "What's wrong, Hank?" and when I wouldn't answer, she'd take hold of my chin, pinch it gently, and say, "Oh, what's wrong with my little Hankaroo?"

I suddenly got shy about being naked in front of her. I knew that it was a fantasy and that being naked in front of her was the whole point of it, but I couldn't help my shyness and tried to cover myself.

The following Wednesday, I found Mr. Santoro waiting for me at my locker.

"Mr. Boyd," he said, and I looked behind me, expecting to find my father. Mr. Santoro said, "This way," and started walking.

I followed the principal into his office, a place I'd never been. At first I thought we were alone, but then I saw Miss Martz sitting in a darkened corner, partially hidden by a coat rack, and my heart began to thump wildly. I wanted so much to see her crooked tooth at that moment. I forced a smile to show her mine, but she didn't smile back.

Mr. Santoro sat down on the corner of his desk. He said, "I suppose you know why you're here."

I shook my head. I felt like weeping. Of course I knew.

The door pushed open, and old Pete the janitor shuffled inside, the swivel bookcase cradled in his arms. All the books had been removed from its shelves, causing it to look naked and cheap on Mr. Santoro's desk. Old Pete swiveled it around so all four of us could clearly see the offending sentence: *Miss Martz has a hairy twat.*

I wanted to swivel it the other way. I didn't want Miss Martz to see those evil words, especially with Mr. Santoro and old Pete here in the room with her. They looked like the sort who might wonder if it was true.

Mr. Santoro said, "What can you tell us about this, Hank Boyd?"

There were many things I could tell them, the most important of which was that I wasn't the one who'd carved those words into the wood, but for some reason I couldn't bring myself to speak up. It had all started seeming crazy, how only a handful of weeks ago I had found the graffiti and now I was here, in the principal's office, being interrogated.

Mr. Santoro nodded. He said, "Since you're not going to say anything, let me tell you what we think. We think *Ralph* did this. This certainly *looks* like Ralph's work. Classic Ralph, if you ask me."

A pain shot through my chest, as if someone had pulled free my heart and started squeezing it. I knew I should have defended Ralph, but to defend Ralph meant convicting myself, even though neither of us had done anything wrong. My hope was that remaining silent would keep open the possibility that someone else was guilty.

"Okay," Mr. Santoro said. "We figured this might happen. Ralph probably threatened you, didn't he? He probably warned you not to speak. Am I right?"

I kept quiet. Tears glazed over my eyes, but I fought them back.

Mr. Santoro sighed. He said, "You need to be careful about who you protect, Hank. You're a good kid. I'd hate to see you throw your future away."

I nodded. I imagined my diorama stuffed inside a trash can. "Okay," I choked out. "I'm sorry."

Later that day, during library hour, Ralph looked around the room and then whispered, "Hey, what happened to our bookcase? I'm feeling a little *exposed* here."

I didn't say anything.

Ralph said, "You think someone stole it?"

I frowned, shook my head.

Ralph said, "I'd hate to think there's a kleptomaniac on the loose. You know what I mean?"

I nodded.

Midway through the hour, Mr. Santoro opened the library door and walked inside. A janitor with a flattened nose came in behind him. "Ralph!" Santoro yelled. "Over here. And bring your things."

Ralph didn't have any things. He stood up. "They must've found some new digs for me. Well," he said, socking my arm, "it's been a riot."

Ralph waved at some of our classmates on his way out, slapping a few backs for good measure. No one looked at him. The janitor, hands on his hips and rotating his head the way boxers do before the first bell, sized Ralph up. After the three had filed out of the library, Gina Morales peeked up from her notebook and whispered, *"Thank you, thank you, thank you!"* She let go a deep sigh she'd been holding in her lungs. She looked like an eighty-year-old woman reflecting on her long-gone youth. She lifted the cross that hung around her neck and, shutting her eyes, pressed it to her dry lips.

By the end of recess, everyone on the playground knew the story of what had happened. Ralph, I had learned, would ride out his fifth-grade career in the principal's office under close supervision. Each time I heard the story, my stomach contracted and I let out a grunt. "Ugh!" I said at least a dozen times. *"Ugh!"* Even if I had confessed, they'd have thought Ralph had forced me to confess, that Ralph had threatened me, and I knew this would mean even more punishment for him. I couldn't think of any reasonable solution to the problem, so I tried to act like it had never happened.

To forget about Ralph, I threw myself into schoolwork. Our dioramas were due the following week, so I constructed more tinfoil-wrapped buildings, populated the neighborhood with more green cotton balls, parked Hot Wheels along the streets. Last year our history teacher had shown us a street map of Paris, how the roads were like spokes attached to a main hub, so I patterned my city on Paris, putting our grade school—a shiny cylindrical building—at the center, with several shiny streets shooting out from it.

On the playground one morning before school, Ralph motioned me over. I didn't want to go near him, but I knew I wouldn't be able to avoid him forever. Sooner or later he'd find me—possibly at night, the two of us alone. And then what?

"Pssssst. C'mere," he said, jerking his head sharply to the side. "*You,*" he said. "C'mere."

Ralph made sure no one was watching. Leaves dropped from trees, swirling in large circles around us each time the wind whipped past. Everyone was wearing a windbreaker or a light jacket except for Ralph. He had on a short-sleeved T-shirt and jeans with holes in the knees.

"Stop," he said before I reached him. He regarded me, as if trying to get a fix on what sort of a character I might be. I wasn't sure what he would do. Anything seemed possible.

"Don't worry," he finally said, "I didn't rat you out."

"What?"

"Guys like us," he said, "we need to stick up for each other. We need to watch each other's backs." When Mr. Santoro started walking across the blacktop, Ralph said, "You better get outta here. Don't let 'em see you talking to me."

"Thanks," I said. "Thank you."

Ralph smiled. From the corner of his mouth, like an old-time gangster, he said, "Not a problem, bub."

On the day our dioramas were due, I stood on the playground and, along with a few dozen other kids from Miss Martz's class, held my future neighborhood before me. Miss Martz had asked us to cover our dioramas so we could unveil them one at a time; mine was hidden by the only thing I could find, a torn and faded Rocky and Bullwinkle bed-sheet.

A gold car that looked as though it had been spray-painted with a fire hose roared up in front of the school, parking half on, half off, the curb. Smoke rolled from the tailpipe with the force of a factory smokestack. Kids bent over coughing. I wasn't anywhere near the car, but my eyes were burning. The car's front doors opened, and two men stepped out. Next came Ralph, sliding off the front seat. They all strolled over to the trunk, popped it open, and pulled free something huge and draped with a blanket. Ralph's diorama.

The two men—Ralph's cousins, I suspected—started swearing at each other. "Grab *that* end, peckerhead." "Quit trying to grab *my* end, dickweed." *"Jesus H. Christ!"* Diorama in hand, one cousin tried walking backward while the other walked sideways, like a crab. Mr. Santoro marched over to them, blowing his whistle. After exchanging a few words with them, Santoro took hold of the diorama. Ralph stayed put, watching the three men carry his project away.

From where I stood, I could see through the library's windows. I watched the silent movie of Mr. Santoro and Ralph's cousins trying to fit the blanketed diorama through the library's entrance. It was so big, they had to tilt it. Once it was inside, Miss Martz pushed two tables together so they could set it down. While Miss Martz and Mr. Santoro spoke to each other, one of Ralph's cousins tucked a book into his coat. The other stuffed a stapler down the front of his pants. A few seconds later, all three men left the library, the cousins heading for their car, Santoro for the playground.

Lately, every time I conjured up Miss Martz, Mr. Santoro appeared in the far corner of the fantasy. He always stood in the dark, and from the best I could tell, he was naked, too, but he kept the whistle firmly be-tween his lips, and his unblinking eyes stayed on both me and Miss Martz, occasionally lighting up like a possum's at night.

"Who do you keep looking at, Hank?" Miss Martz would ask. "Why won't you look at me, my love?"

I carried my diorama into the library. I eased it onto the circulation desk. With dioramas covering every available flat surface, no one could sit at an assigned table.

Miss Martz said, "Why don't we go around the room and unveil the cities one at a time?" She turned to me. "Hank? Would you care to unveil your city and tell us a little bit about it?"

Tugging the bedsheet slowly, trying to prolong the mystery, I revealed my diorama. At the sight of my vision of the future, my classmates grew quiet. A few girls covered their mouths with their palms. This was exactly the reaction I had imagined. I took a moment to admire my own project.

Tall and short skyscrapers reflected the fluorescent lights above, causing the entire city to sparkle. Plush green cotton shrubs lined the wide, clean silver streets. The city looked truly magical, the sort of place where I would have loved growing up, a city I could look forward to living in.

I said, "My future city will look like this. Buildings will be round. *Like these!*" I pointed. "And they won't have elevators. Each person'll have a giant egg in their office, and they can walk into their egg and get blasted wherever they want to go." At this I added a sound effect: "*Buh-zhooooooooooom.*" Once I began talking, I didn't want to stop. I started to say other things, important things, *necessary* things, about my city, but Miss Martz cut me off.

"Thank you, Hank, but we really need to move on."

"Oh. Okay."

"Gina? Would you like to go next?"

Gina Morales, her face eerily blank, yanked away her bedsheet, and I gasped. Her city looked like my city—toilet paper and napkin rolls wrapped in tinfoil, cotton balls for shrubs. Had she been peeking in my window at night? Had she broken into my locker and seen my sketches? One by one, my classmates revealed their cities, and each city looked exactly like the one that had come before it. The only difference was in the way the streets had been laid out. Some were on grids. Some were shaped like an S. Some had no streets, the entire city an improbable cluster of tinfoil-covered tubes.

"Very nice," Miss Martz added after each one.

At the end of the hour, Wes Papadakis pointed and said, "Whose is *that* one?"

"Oh," Miss Martz said. "Yes. Well, that one's Ralph's."

Wes checked to see that Ralph wasn't present. "Can we see it?" he asked.

Miss Martz said, "Ralph is no longer a member of this class." She cleared her throat. "But I suppose since he took the time to finish it, he wouldn't mind us looking at it."

She tugged on the sheet hesitantly, as if she were in a morgue and about to unveil the corpse of Ralph himself. Because everyone had huddled around, I couldn't at first see Ralph's diorama, but when I wedged my head between two others, I couldn't believe what I was looking at.

"Wow," I said.

Ralph's diorama was an exact replica of our neighborhood as it looked today. I could easily identify Duke's, where my parents bought beef sandwiches; the Sheridan Drive-in, where my parents had been taking me and my sister for years to watch movies; New Castle Park, with all its sizzling power-line towers; South Side Records, which sold the cheapest albums in town; Red's, the only place nearby to get an ice-cream cone; and Ford City Shopping Center, the oldest mall in the entire Chicago area. I could even locate Jacqueline Bouvier Kennedy Grade School, in which I was now standing.

Miss Martz let out a long, disappointed sigh. She said, "You see, children? This is a perfect example of what happens when you don't pay attention. Apparently Ralph was too busy vandalizing school property to hear the word *future*." With the bedsheet wadded under her arm, she shook her head.

I was the sort of student who spoke only when called upon. The idea of volunteering to talk made my tongue go numb, my hands and feet grow cold. But something overtook me, a force beyond my control, and I did something I'd never done before: I spoke before thinking. I said, "But Ralph's the one who asked what year it should be!"

Miss Martz turned to face me, teeth clenched. Pausing to catch her breath between every few words, as if she'd been running laps with us in gym class, she said, "Ralph is the sort of person who talks for the sake of talking. Obviously he forgot the answer to his own question." When no one said anything, she allowed her features to soften.

I wanted to say more, but my good sense had returned, and with it, the fear of speech. The tone of Miss Martz's voice and the way she'd clenched her teeth had made my heart pound. I wasn't even aware that I was holding a pencil until I snapped it in half. I glared at Miss Martz, trying to send her a mental thought, the way people in the future would speak to one another—telepathically. I tried to pierce her head with my brain waves, thinking the same thought over and over, hoping she would hear it.

The school bell rang. At first no one moved. "Go on," Miss Martz said. "Go to your next class."

I paused before Ralph's diorama for a closer look. I located my own street, and on it, my own house. It was tiny, but there it stood. In one corner, in the smallest of handwriting, Ralph had written, *Scale. 2,450:1.* In another corner he'd written *The Year 2001,* with his name signed below. On the edge of the plywood, using a marker that practically blended in to the many glued-together sheets of wood, he'd written, *A Diagram of the Future.*

Everyone had left the library except me and Miss Martz. I was still trying to send my message to her. I peered into her eyes to see if she was hearing what I was thinking. *Miss Martz has a hairy twat,* I thought, biting down and tightening my jaw. *Miss Martz has a hairy twat,* I thought again and again, but there was no evidence that she was hearing anything I was thinking.

Miss Martz placed a warm palm on top of my head. "Go on, Hank," she said. "You don't want to be late to your next class."

The rest of that day in school I could feel the imprint of Miss Martz's hand. I tried to continue my fantasy of the two of us together, but the images were full of static, like bad TV reception.

At the end of the day, standing at my locker, I turned to Wes Papadakis and said, "What do you think about Miss Martz?"

Wes said, "I kinda like her."

"Really?" I said.

Wes grinned. Two of his permanent teeth were finally starting to grow in, and because of that, there appeared to be something profoundly wrong with him. I studied his ears. The lobes were attached to his head.

"I love her," he confessed.

"You do?" I asked.

Wes nodded. "I love Miss Martz," he said. "I'm in love with her. I'm going to marry her."

I couldn't bear to look at Wes anymore. I had to turn away.

All the way home I kicked rocks, spit on wooden fences, dragged the tips of my shoes through dirt. A car honked, and I realized I was in the middle of an intersection without quite knowing how I'd ended up there. But the car wasn't just any car. It was Ralph's cousins' car.

I squinted, trying to see through the tinted windows, but couldn't. After I had crossed the street, the car pulled up and a window lowered. Ralph, squeezed between his two cousins, said, "Hey, chief. How'd my diagram go over?"

"Everyone loved it," I said.

Ralph nodded. "Yeah, I figured they would. Well, I guess we'll be seeing you later, hoss."

"Tomorrow," I reminded him.

Ralph saluted me. "Tomorrow it is," he said, and then he grinned. "The future!" he announced.

"The future!" I said.

One cousin, the passenger, raised a beer from between his legs and took a deep swig. He raised the can and said, "Here's to the future, little man." He handed his beer to me. The other cousin, the driver, took a cigarette from between his lips and an M80 out of his shirt pocket. He waggled his eyebrows at me, then held the lit cigarette to the firecracker's wick. The moment the wick started to sizzle, he tossed the M80 out the window and into an aluminum trash can. The explosion deafened me. Smoke twisted from the trash can, and several people opened their front doors to look out. The tinted passenger window rose, and the car, blowing exhaust like a rocket blasting from earth, peeled away. As I stood at the curb, unable to hear what anyone was saying, a warm beer clutched in my hand, my heart swelled in anticipation of what lay ahead.

# THE FUTURE: 2001

# BRAINS OF THE OPERATION

## I

**KNEW IF I** poked it once I'd have to poke it again, but knowing this didn't stop me. I reached up under my new White Sox ball cap and poked my head. I was in a law firm, waiting to talk to an attorney about injuries I'd sustained as a passenger in a taxicab; injuries, most notably, to my head. The top of my head was still puffy one full day after the accident, which was why I couldn't help myself. I poked it once more. It was like touching something that was a part of me and not a part of me at the same time—what I imagined Siamese twins experienced when they touched each other's heads.

I had done this sort of thing as a kid, too. I'd discover some oddity of my body, some heretofore unexamined part, and I wouldn't leave it alone, *couldn't* leave it alone. I had discovered my cuticles while sitting in a third-grade classroom—*What are these?* I wondered—and began picking at one, reshaping it, then flattening it like putty. A few years later, I discovered that the knuckles on my fist had a layer of something over them—a band of cartilage?—and each band moved over the knuckle when I pushed on it. I kept making a fist so I could move the odd lumps back and forth. I did this for weeks, months. The body was a world unto itself, and as its host, I felt the need to explore it. In the lawyer's office, each time I poked the lump that covered the entire top of my head, I thought, *What the hell's under there? Water? Blood? Some kind of brain fluid?*

When I saw the secretary watching me, I slid my fingers out from under my cap and smiled at her, but as soon as she returned to her work, my fingers rose to my head.

The lawyer's name was Jerome Krazowski. He was a fat man who, using a pen cap, excavated wax from his ear while he spoke. I told him the whole story. The reason I had come back to Chicago after all these years, the only reason, was for a job interview. On my way to the interview, the cabdriver turned in front of a speeding car, and the head-on impact catapulted me from the backseat, causing my head to smash against the bulletproof divider. A pair of homeless men pulled me free of the cab and helped me to the curb.

"And then," I said, "one of the guys, he went back to the cab, found my briefcase, and took off running with it."

"He stole your briefcase?"

I nodded.

"You're shitting me," Krazowski said. "Tell me you're shitting me."

I shook my head. "I'm not shitting you," I said.

The raw memory of it still made me shiver—not so much the theft as the aftermath of the theft. The accident happened on Chicago's South Side, surrounded by housing projects, the shell of a scorched car across the street. After my briefcase was stolen, I had expected a certain amount of sympathy from the bystanders, but the eyes that peered back were either too dull or too shiny, and no one made a move to chase down the perpetrator. I was a stranger to these parts, an interloper, and all the passersby, every rubbernecker slowing down, knew it. Whatever gratitude I'd felt toward the men who'd pulled me from the car instantly blurred into fear.

Krazowski leaned forward and said, "Fucking humanity in a nutshell. Now, listen. About that head of yours. About your injuries. If you were *paralyzed* as a result of the accident, if you were unable to do your *job*, if you had suffered more *serious* and *permanent* head trauma, we'd have ourselves a multimillion-dollar case on our hands. As it is, we're looking at maybe five thousand. Eight if we're lucky."

"Good enough," I said. "I'll be in touch."

I made a move to stand, but Krazowski wasn't done and motioned for me to sit. He pointed the pen cap at me. "What kinds of tests did they run at the hospital? Maybe you *do* have brain damage and don't know it. In which case we could sue the shorts off the hospital. That could be sweet—*real* sweet. I'd welcome the opportunity. Just remember," he said, jabbing the pen cap into his ear again, "the more neurological damage you have, the higher the dollar figure!"

Outside, exhausted from listening to Krazowski, I leaned against a plate-glass window, reached up under my cap, and poked at my head some more. According to the emergency-room physician, there had been no bleeding inside my brain, no fractured skull, though he suspected a concussion. I couldn't help thinking that the doctors had missed something. Two days later, and the way I felt reminded me of Roadrunner cartoons, the ones in which Wile E. Coyote ends up accordion-shaped after a boulder, falling from a great height, flattens him. The main difference in our recoveries was that I didn't instantly spring back into shape. I had a constant longing to be stretched, my head and feet strapped to a medieval rack, a hooded doctor cranking the device until I yelled for him to stop.

The front door of the law office opened, and a man on crutches, his right leg in a cast, swung himself onto the sidewalk, overshooting his intended landing by about four feet.

"Oh shit!" he said, his hands, still clutching the crutches, far behind him.

"Need some help?" I asked.

He inched the crutches forward, first one and then the other. When they were parallel with his legs, he pivoted around and said, "Nuh-uh. But thanks, bub."

I nodded, but the man was staring into my eyes. I was about to look away when I recognized him. He smiled, and then I smiled.

"Ralph?" I said.

Ralph nodded. "Hank?"

"It *is* you," I said.

"I hope so," he said.

"Unbelievable!" I said. We shook hands. Ralph looked like a carica-ture of his younger self: His features were slightly exaggerated, and his voice was deeper, but otherwise, the old Ralph, the Ralph I used to know, was still visible. The only curious detail was that his facial hair, which had so impressed and scared us in grade school, must have stopped growing when he was a teenager. It was no thicker than it had been all those years ago.

"Jesus," I said. "What've you been up to?"

"Same ol', same ol'," he said. I hadn't talked to Ralph since the sum-mer after eighth grade, twenty-one years ago. I expected him to elabo-rate, but he didn't. "What about you?" he asked. "What's new with the Hankster?"

I told him about leaving Boulder, about the taxi accident, about my stolen briefcase, my head, the *pain,* about the job interview I never made it to, about the two-mile walk from the motel to the law office.

"You *walked?*"

"I wasn't up for another cab ride," I said.

"Let's see the old egg," he said. I raised my cap. He nodded and said, "Okay, you can put the lid back down now, John Merrick." He saw my confusion and added, "John Merrick. The Elephant Man. He had a name, you know."

"I didn't know."

"Where're you staying?"

"Motel Six. By Midway."

"Motel Sex?"

"*Six.* Motel Six."

"That's what I said. Motel Sex." Ralph waited for me to correct him again, but when I didn't, he grinned and winked, then socked my arm. "Listen," he said. "Why don't you stay at my place until you get on your feet?"

On the one hand, the prospect scared me—God only knew what Ralph was doing with his life these days—but on the other hand, it would keep me afloat: I was charging my room to a credit card on which I couldn't afford to make the minimum payment. Plus, there was the monthly storage-locker fee in Boulder.

"I wouldn't want to put you out," I said.

I waited for Ralph to insist, but when I added that I would probably be in his way, he shrugged and said, "Yeah; well; I see your point. Do you need a ride, at least?" He lifted a crutch and pointed to an El Camino.

"Sure," I said. He crutched over to his car. "How can you drive with that cast?" I asked.

Ralph leaned against his door and ripped away his pant leg. I saw that Velcro had been keeping the pant leg attached; he was wearing a pair of cutoffs. The cast, now fully exposed, had a clasp on one side and a hinge on the other. After unsnapping the clasp, Ralph eased open the cast as if lifting the lid of a coffin, revealing a pale and dusty leg. He tossed the cast into the car's bed. Carefully, he reattached the denim leg to his cutoffs. I didn't ask. When it came to Ralph, my desire not to know had always overshadowed my desire to know.

After we'd both settled into his car, I couldn't stop stealing peeks at him. *Ralph!* I thought. *After all these years!* I couldn't remember why we'd fallen out of touch. Had he gone to a different high school? Had he dropped out? Those years were all a blur.

Ralph wheeled the El Camino onto Cicero Avenue. Each time he changed lanes without checking his rearview mirror, my neck tightened. The tightening of my neck triggered a pain in my head that was not unlike a drill bit grinding into me. Ralph ran a yellow light. I opened my mouth to scream, but nothing came out. I had wanted to scream when the cabdriver turned in front of the speeding car, but I didn't then, either. Politeness, I knew, would be the death of me.

"When you're a kid," Ralph said, "you think school's a waste of time, but when you get older, you discover that you can actually use a lot of what you learned. Remember all those papier-mâché projects in art class? I used to say to myself, now when the hell would I ever use papier-mâché when I grew up? Well, my friend, that leg cast is living proof that no knowledge is worthless. Application of knowledge. That's the key. Hey," he said. "You okay? You look a little, I don't know, *sick*."

"I'm fine," I said.

"Hang on," Ralph said. "We're almost there."

My chest tightened at the thought of returning to the motel. It wasn't cheap being poor. With money and a job, I could have rented a studio apartment for five hundred dollars a month. Living in Motel 6 for a month, however, would cost me sixteen hundred dollars. There were motels that charged weekly rates, dives, mostly, where you brought the last of your belongings, a box or two, plus maybe a lawn chair so you could sit outside the room and drink a tall boy, watching the sun go down while you smoked your last cigarette. And then what? A shelter? The streets? The fall would be swift, and I saw myself in a year, bearded and stinking, wearing a two-piece suit made out of burlap coffee sacks, all the while pushing a squeaky-wheeled shopping cart down the street, yelling about the government's conspiracy to plant computer chips in all of us.

"You know," I said to Ralph, "that was awfully generous of you, offering to let me stay at your place."

"Which way to the Motel Sex?" he asked.

"Huh? Oh. South on Cicero. But I was thinking, if you don't mind—"

"Cicero?" he asked. "Are you sure it's not on Harlem?"

"No," I said. "It's definitely on Cicero. But what I was thinking was, if it's no sweat off your back, I'd like to take you up on that offer."

"What offer?"

"The one you made about me staying at your place."

Ralph said, "I offered that? Are you sure?"

"After we left the lawyer's office," I said. "Don't you remember?"

Ralph said, "I'm thinking I offered something else, but if you *want* to stay with me, I guess it wouldn't be a problem."

"Are you sure?"

Ralph made a noise that was neither assent nor dissent.

"Great," I said. "I really appreciate it, Ralph. You're a lifesaver."

At a stoplight, Ralph turned to me and said, "You know what? I knew I'd bump into you again one of these days. I always said you were like a bad penny. You'd keep showing up in my life whether I wanted you to or not. It just took a few years longer than I thought it would."

"Really," I said. I didn't have the heart to tell him that the feeling was mutual.

When people ask me how I ended up in Chicago again after all these years, I tell them the story of the flattened squirrel. The fact is, the squirrel had little to do with my leaving Boulder. The tailspin of my own disastrous life had already picked up momentum by the time the squirrel made its appearance. Furthermore, only *half* the squirrel was flattened. But I don't feel bad about distorting the truth. The squirrel makes for a nice starting point, a place to enter the story, and it's a way to keep the conversation rolling. And in the end, it's the squirrel that everyone remembers, not my problems, which is how I prefer it.

But even now, when I think back on those final days in Colorado, it's the squirrel I return to, and how Karen, my fiancée, had begun packing her things that morning, and how I couldn't bring myself to tell her what I really wanted, for us to stay together but not get married. I'd kept begging off marriage, bumping the date, but since Karen wanted marriage or nothing, she had decided it was time to opt for the latter—nothing.

"You don't have to *leave*," I told her.

"We *both* have to leave, Hank," she said.

This was true: Mr. Stark, our landlord, was turning the apartments into condos, and once the lease was up, we couldn't renew it. Furthermore, the dot-com industry had just gone belly-up, including the speck of a dot-com that I worked for, and my severance package wasn't going to stretch very far in a city as expensive as Boulder. Even if the condo conversion wasn't taking place, I couldn't have afforded to stay.

While Karen packed another box, I walked outside. And that's when I saw him. I always think of the squirrel as *him;* I don't know why. Maybe I saw him as some squirrel version of myself, the poor bastard suffering the physical equivalent of what I was feeling emotionally. Anyway, I thought he was dead. His entire back half had been flattened. A car, I'm sure, had run over him. His fur had turned white, as if the rough times he'd been through had prematurely aged him. But then I saw he was alive, and amazingly, he was still going about his business.

With his two front paws, he dragged himself across the parking lot, heading toward a fountain in our courtyard. The fountain was a popular watering hole for birds and squirrels. He didn't notice me, even though I was sitting only a few feet from the fountain. The base of the fountain was level to the sidewalk, so the squirrel needed simply to lower his head to drink. I was moved by his will to live. If he hadn't wanted to live, he wouldn't have searched out a drink of water. But I couldn't imagine that he was in anything but the most excruciating pain, and even if he wasn't in pain—if he was paralyzed—he surely wouldn't live much longer. He was *flat*. I wasn't even sure how he was managing to remain alive. The logistics were mind-boggling. The decision, as I saw it, rested with me: Let him live and, most likely, suffer, or take him out of his misery.

I didn't notice I was weeping until, back inside the apartment, Karen stopped what she was doing and said, "Oh, Hank, baby. Don't cry."

I opened the closet door and pulled out what I thought would be the best implement for tending to the squirrel.

Karen said, "What are you doing with that shovel, Hank?" It was summer. There was no practical use for an aluminum snow shovel.

The squirrel was where I had left him, holding on to an apple core and nibbling at it, but slumped with his elbows on the ground, the way a drunk man sitting at a bar might eat a sandwich. Eating the apple was further proof of his will to live, but I could no longer see the squirrel's point. *Why go on?* I thought. *Why do this to yourself?*

I lifted the shovel over my head. My eyes were so wet from tears that my vision had blurred. I could barely see the damned squirrel. I knew, however, that I needed to take care of him with a single blow, so I stood in that position for quite some time, shovel in the air, waiting for the perfect moment to present itself.

This is the point in my telling of the story where people like to jump in with their own opinions. The reactions nearly always split along gender lines. Women will say, "No, you didn't! How *could* you?" while men jump to my defense: "I'd've done the same thing. Take the poor son of a bitch out of his misery. It'd be cruel *not* to." Both women and men want to know what happened next. They no longer care how I ended up in Chicago. They want me to hurry to the end. They want to learn the squirrel's fate.

"That poor squirrel," I begin, and then I tell them how I was standing there, shovel raised, on the brink of bringing it down on the squirrel's head, when Mrs. Stark, the landlord's wife, stepped outside and saw me. She first looked up at the shovel's blade, unable to figure out what I could possibly be doing, but when she saw the squirrel, saw that half of it was already flattened, she screamed as if she were the one, and not the squirrel, whom I intended to kill.

"Mrs. Stark," I said, "it's not what you think." When I took a step toward her, she screamed again. She was nearly fifty, bottom-heavy with a sagging face, and prone to hysterics. Tenants peered out their windows to see what the trouble was. A few rushed outside to help.

"Look at what he did to that poor squirrel!" Mrs. Stark yelled. "Look! He *crushed* it."

The squirrel inched away, making his painfully slow trek across the parking lot, most likely where he had gotten run over in the first place. Mrs. Stark told her story to anyone who would listen, turning conjecture into fact. The entire time she spoke, everyone kept their eyes on me, sizing me up. "I'll call the police," someone said, and disappeared. I looked up at our apartment and shaded my eyes. Karen was peering down from our bedroom window, folded panties in one hand, a book in the other, and I couldn't help thinking how much, with her arms aloft, she resembled the very figure of Justice herself, and although deep down I knew better, I was holding out hope that the scales would tip in my favor one last time.

When Ralph pulled up in front of his childhood home, a house I'd never been invited inside, I assumed he was making a pit stop to visit his mother while I waited in the car. I'd never been allowed to meet Ralph's mother, and I was certain I wouldn't be meeting her today. For me to be allowed inside, his mother would need to have been dead. But when Ralph lifted my luggage from the bed of the El Camino and said, "Let's go," I thought, *Holy shit! He still lives at home!*

Ralph's house was the sole aberration on the block, obviously the oldest, built before the developers came and put up cookie-cutter brick homes whose only differences were superficial. Ralph's house was covered on all sides by pebbly shingles instead of brick. Where the other houses were surrounded by fences made of chain link, Ralph's fence was wrought iron with lethal Gothic spikes aimed at the sky. When I was a kid, it had seemed like a junky, run-down house, a poor person's house, but now I could see that it had more character than any other house around, despite the years of neglect.

I hesitated at the threshold. I'd fantasized about this moment so many times when Ralph and I were friends. In my overactive imagination, the house was always haunted, but in the way that houses in Abbott and Costello or Three Stooges movies were haunted. Candelabras would slide across tables. Eyes in family portraits would follow me. A white-sheeted ghost would chase me from room to room.

I stepped inside.

The house, as I'd imagined, was dark and dusty, the smell of mildew immediately lodging itself inside my nose. But where my imagination had failed was with the decor. I'd always conjured up heavy velvet curtains, not miniblinds; Oriental rugs, not plastic runners; a fainting couch, not a beanbag chair; and, in the guest bedroom, a four-poster bed with a canopy, not the futon that lay like a sack of cement on the floor. Ralph tossed my luggage on the futon.

"It may not be the Motel Sex," he said, "but it's cheap."

"It's perfect," I said.

"You're probably tired, what with your deformed head and all."

I reached under my cap and poked the bloated wound, then touched it a second time. "I could use a nap."

"All right, hoss. Find me when you emerge from your crypt."

"Will do," I said, trying not to touch my head anymore, trying to wait until Ralph had left the room, but failing miserably.

I hadn't had a good night's sleep in over a week, not since leaving Boulder, so when I took the painkillers before my nap, I didn't wake up for fifteen hours. The blessed pharmaceuticals had turned Ralph's house into an oasis. When I opened my eyes, two men were standing at the foot of the futon, staring down at me.

"Jesus!" I said, and sat up.

One man had a Fu Manchu mustache and a long, thin braided beard. He was wearing wraparound sunglasses that skiers in Aspen use. The other guy's head was shaved. Tattoos of English ivy twined up his arms, as if his flesh were tree bark. The man with the Fu Manchu said, "Remember us?"

"Kenny?" I guessed. Kenny smiled and nodded, reaching up and yanking on his long beard. "Norm?" I said to the shaved-headed man, and he grunted.

"Look at you," Kenny said. "I remember when you didn't even know how to wipe your own ass."

Norm crossed his ivy-laced arms and said, "Who says he knows now?" He kicked the sole of my foot hard enough to make my eyes tear up, and then he winked at me.

"Ralph called and told us about your head," Kenny said. "We had to come by and take a look for ourselves."

Norm nodded. "It looks like shit," he said.

Kenny reached over, cuffed my shoulder. "It's been a long time, pal. *Too* long."

The way Kenny was talking, it sounded like we'd all been good friends back in the day, as if we'd served a tour of duty together, bonding in the way that only men who'd seen the best and worst of one another could bond, but due to circumstances beyond our control, we had been forced to go our separate ways. In point of fact, I was thirteen years old the last time that I had seen either of them, and they'd been in their mid-twenties. I wondered if I was forgetting some key moment in our mutual histories.

"Great seeing you two, too," I said, but without much conviction.

Norm nodded again. He turned to Kenny and said, "What do you call Irish pussy?"

Kenny said, "Oh no. Here come the jokes."

"McMuffin," Norm said, then tossed a sack from McDonald's at me. "Enjoy," he said. Without another word, they walked out of the room and down the stairs.

I pulled the McMuffin out of the sack but didn't unwrap it. I had a strong suspicion that they had found the sandwich under their car seat and then microwaved it in Ralph's kitchen. I knew the kind of guys they were. I waited until I heard them drive away before heading downstairs.

Ralph was in the living room, leaning back in an old swivel chair that squeaked every time he moved. He was surrounded by several cardboard boxes, each one overflowing with assorted knickknacks and utensils. The only common denominator, as far as I could see, was that everything was made of wood.

"Rip Van Winkle," Ralph declared. "Welcome to the year 2032!"

"What's new in the year 2032?"

"Same old shit," Ralph said. "Only difference is, there are only four of us left on the planet—me, you, Kenny, and Norm."

"Oh God," I said, and sat down.

A wooden jewelry box in the shape of a treasure chest sat in Ralph's lap. He turned it upside down, picked up a rubber stamp, and stamped the box, then set it aside.

"What's that?" I asked.

"*That*, my friend, is an extra one hundred dollars. You see this stamp? It says, *Made in Occupied Japan*."

I waited for an explanation, but when none came, I said, "I don't get it."

Ralph snorted. "And you're an accountant?" He told me then of his latest project—buying worthless crap from Goodwill, stamping all of it *Made in Occupied Japan,* then listing it on eBay. According to Ralph, his new enterprise brought in five hundred dollars a month. "And that's a modest estimate," he added.

"Isn't there something, I don't know, *wrong* with that?" I asked.

Ralph seemed to be genuinely considering the nature of his behavior, but then, poking out his bottom lip and shaking his head, he said, "Nuh-uh. Hey, look, I'm not *saying* it's worth hundreds of dollars. I'm not even saying that the stamp is genuine. People have to take a little responsibility, do their own legwork. There are price guides out there that list what's really valuable. If consumers took the time to look at one of those guides, they'd see that my stuff isn't in them." He poked his lip out again. "Nah . . . I'm in the clear. No one can get me for fraud. That was your question, wasn't it? If someone might catch me for fraud?"

It wasn't my question, but I said, "I guess." I stood, and Ralph followed me into the kitchen.

"Besides," Ralph said, "I'm only able to sell a small percentage of what I buy. Hell, I'm probably *losing* money."

I pulled a mug from the cupboard and poured myself some coffee. Only after lifting the mug to my mouth did I see the words SHIT HAPPENS wrapped around it.

"So, what's the big plan today?" Ralph asked.

"I'm heading over to Manpower," I said, "to sign up for temp work until my head heals."

Ralph stood. "What? *Manpower?* Are you crazy?" He plopped down and sighed. "You don't want to work for them."

"Do you have a better idea?"

"Absolutely. Work with *me.*"

*Work with Ralph.* The words hit like electricity, a jolt of pain that instantly numbed me. I took a sip of coffee and nearly spit it out. It tasted like the very last dregs, even though the pot itself was full, the coffee presumably fresh.

"Where do you work?"

"I didn't tell you?" Ralph said. "I work for Kenny and Norm. They own their own business."

"Really?" I said. "And what business is that?"

"They clean up crime scenes. Well, *they* don't. Not technically. *I* do."

"Crime scenes? What do you mean? You sweep up glass? Fix broken doors? That kind of thing?"

Ralph laughed, then got himself an apple from the fridge. He polished the apple on his shirt. "Naw, I clean up after dead bodies. Homicides," he said. "When a person takes a bullet to the head, someone's got to wipe down the wall, pick up the bone and brain, get the stains out of the carpet. Basically I clean up whatever's left behind after the coroner takes the body away."

"You're kidding."

Ralph peeled a sticker from the apple. He said, "We're getting more and more suicides these days. Death by self-inflicted gunshot. It used to be all murder, but we're expanding."

"People *hire* you to do that?"

"You'd be surprised," Ralph said. "It's big business."

I was thinking Ralph meant by *big business* that his cousins could finally afford to move out of their parents' houses, that they could afford to get their cars repaired, their teeth cleaned, but when he told me that Kenny and Norm had recently moved their office downtown to Michigan Avenue, across the street from the Art Institute, I asked just how big *big* was.

"They're worth, oh, I don't know, about a million each," Ralph said. "They've got the market cornered."

Kenny and Norm, *millionaires?* How could that be? *How?*

"Maybe more," Ralph said. "The business is just getting off the ground. They have crews in Milwaukee, Detroit, Indianapolis. A few other places, too. Kenny, he's the brains of the operation. He's sort of the PR guy, too. Norm, I'm not sure what he does. Maybe the whole thing was his idea. I should probably ask." He touched his finger to where the sticker had been on the apple and then pulled it away. "Still sticky," he said.

I looked around Ralph's place, his mother's old house, with its missing drawer knobs, listing fridge, and microwave so large and old it should have been in a museum.

"What about you?" I asked. "How're you doing?"

"Me?" Ralph opened a cabinet and pulled out a bottle of Goo Gone. He squirted some onto a napkin and started rubbing the adhesive from the apple. He said, "I'm not a partner. I'm an employee. But the pay's good. Twenty-five bucks an hour. Benefits. Retirement."

"Twenty-five an hour?"

"Only half of that's reported to the IRS, of course. The rest is under the table. You're an accountant. You know how that works." He winked at me.

I nodded, but the implication disturbed me, that accountants become accountants only to run their own scams. "So, what's the name of this business?"

"Drop Dead Clean," Ralph said. He put away the Goo Gone, threw the napkin in the trash.

"That stuff is toxic," I said. "I don't think you're supposed to use it on food."

Ralph took a bite of the apple. "Well?" he said, his mouth full.

"Well?"

"Want to join the family business until you're back on your feet?"

"Me?" I said. "Cleaning up murder scenes?" I laughed. "I don't think so."

Ralph, talking and chewing at the same time, said, "I know what's going through that bloated head of yours. How the hell can you do that? And the first time you walk into a homicide, you look around and think, I'm not touching a damn thing. No way. But after the second or third time, it's no different than washing windows. You start finding yourself looking for challenges, like figuring out what sort of cleaning solvent will remove the blood from a velvet portrait without removing the paint. You learn little tricks, like what kind of vacuum attachment works best on bone splinters, how to soak up blood from shag carpeting with the wet-dry vac, that sort of thing. Eventually you start taking pride in your work. You finish a job, you look around and think, No one would ever know that someone got their brains blown out all over this room less than forty-eight hours ago. And it gives you goose bumps. I'm as serious as a pile of shit." Ralph tossed the skinny apple core into the trash. "So? What do you say?"

"I'll give Manpower a call," I said.

Ralph shrugged. "It's your life," he said.

While Ralph stayed home, logging fraudulent goods onto eBay, I borrowed his El Camino. Before I could leave the house, he handed over a stack of business cards for Drop Dead Clean and said, "Here, maybe you could hand these out at Manpower. A lot of desperate people probably go there. Who knows? You could be sitting across from a future customer." I glanced at the top card. The company's symbol was a hand wiping away a red Rorschach blotch with a rag.

On my way to Manpower, I popped in the cassette that was already perched in the deck. I wasn't sure what it was. It wasn't any kind of music that I was familiar with. I popped it out at the next stoplight and read, *The Soothing Sounds of the Humpback Whale*. "Ralph, Ralph, Ralph," I said. "What the hell's this?" I turned on the radio but couldn't pick up any stations. The antenna, I realized, was a wire hanger.

I hadn't ever been to a temp agency, so I was unprepared for the battery of tests—typing, logic, urine. I took some of the tests at Manpower and was told to make appointments elsewhere for the others, like the urine test. Mr. Kubo, my Manpower counselor, spoke to me as though confronted with a dilemma: how to conceal the fact that his life would never turn out like mine, that the world had glorious things in store for him, things I couldn't possibly ever imagine. He spoke slowly, carefully, articulating every word. When I told him I needed employment where I could wear a baseball cap, he frowned. I took off my cap to show him my head, but he averted his eyes as if I had pulled down my pants.

On my way back to Ralph's, I listened to *The Soothing Sounds of the*

*Humpback Whale,* and after a few blocks, the muscles in my shoulders loosened. It *was* soothing. I rolled my head from side to side, easing the knots in my neck. I felt as though I were driving underwater, the El Camino floating from block to block. While the car sailed pleasantly along, I imagined myself humming while wearing long rubber gloves, picking up brains and bone with tweezers. I imagined myself scrubbing bloodstains with a solvent. *How bad could it be?* I wondered. *How bad could it possibly be?*

## II

Ralph and I waited that week for a phone call from Norm or Kenny, telling us where we should go, but it never came.

"That's odd," Ralph said. "Summer's usually our best time."

"Why's that?"

"The hotter it gets," Ralph said, "the higher the murder rate. Temperature breaks a hundred, and people start killing each other left and right."

"Is that a statistical fact?"

Ralph rolled his eyes. "What, are you a census taker? Do you work for the Department of Weights and Measures? Are you compiling data?" He shook his head, disgusted with me. "It's a *hunch,* Hank. And let me tell you, this country would run a hell of a lot smoother if we had a Department of Hunches and Guesstimates. It'd be a bunch of people scratching their heads and shrugging. And it would be the only honest department in government."

"Okay, okay," I said. "Easy."

At the end of the week I suggested that I go back to Manpower to see if they'd found anything for me.

"Go if you want," Ralph said, "but I don't think anyone will hire you with that bean of yours."

My head wasn't really swollen anymore, and I no longer felt the urge to poke it, but I wasn't sure I could bear the humiliation of returning to Manpower. That night Ralph knocked on my bedroom door.

"Kenny and Norm are here. They want to interview you."

"Interview me? I thought I had the job."

"Yeah; well," Ralph said. "You *do*. But they just want to make it official."

"You're kidding."

"You ever get a job without interviewing for it?" Ralph asked. "I didn't think so. It's no big deal."

Ralph left the room. A few seconds later, the door swung open, and Norm and Kenny strutted inside. Norm crossed his ivy-laced arms and studied me. Kenny pulled on one and then the other tip of his Fu Manchu and said, "I knew you'd join us sooner or later."

He spoke like a swami, as though he'd been having daily visions of me joining them and my arrival in town was fated. I suppose I should have been flattered, but looking at the two of them, I couldn't help feeling overwhelming outrage. I had earned a BA and an MBA; I had put myself into serious, backbreaking debt to go to college; I had studied hard for the CPA exam, the sort of studying that neither Kenny nor Norm could ever fathom; in the past ten years, I'd put together hundreds of résumés; I had worked fourteen- and fifteen-hour days, worked weekends, worked holidays for every job I'd ever taken. For all of this, I had nothing to show. Kenny and Norm were nearly kicked out of high school; they took the first jobs they found, in the Tootsie Roll factory on Cicero Avenue; and now, by some fluke, some glitch in the laws of how things in the world were supposed to work, they had stumbled upon an idea and turned it into a multimillion-dollar business. It wasn't fair. It wasn't fair, and with them standing in front of me, evaluating my qualifications, I could taste my own bile.

Kenny said, "You ever done anything like this?"

"Clean up crime scenes?"

Kenny nodded.

"Nope," I said.

"What line of work were you in before?" Kenny asked.

"I'm an accountant."

"Oh," Norm said, speaking for the first time. "You know math?" He scratched some of the ivy on his arms as if it were poisonous.

I nodded.

"That'll come in handy. Me, I was never any good at math."

Kenny said, "And why are you no longer in that line of work?"

I couldn't believe I was having to explain—to *justify*—myself to these two thugs. "I worked for a *number* of companies these past ten years," I said. "But then I got into the IT field and—"

"Whoa. Hold on, chief. IT? What's that?"

"Information technology?" I said. "*Computers?*"

"Oh. Okay. Go on."

"And I hooked up with a dot-com. This was during the boom years, but then it all fell apart. It went bust. With a few exceptions, the dot-coms all died."

Norm said, "Dot-com," and snorted. "The *service* industry. You'll never go wrong offering the public a little elbow grease."

"I guess you know what we're going to ask next," Kenny said.

"Actually, no. I don't."

Kenny crouched down, looked deep into my eyes, and said, "What brings you to our company? Why the career change?"

"Look," I said, "I thought Ralph explained all of this to you. The cab accident? He didn't mention that? My head? My—"

Kenny and Norm started laughing. Kenny said, "Easy, easy. I'm just yanking your chain, little guy." *Little guy.* It was what he had called me when I was thirteen years old. Kenny reached over, squeezed my shoulder, and said, "Of *course* you got the job. We're all family here."

I forced a smile, though I'm sure it looked like a death rictus. They laughed all the way downstairs, repeating some of what I'd said. From the bedroom window, I watched Kenny and Norm get into their respective cars, a matching pair of black '78 Monte Carlos. They each had a vanity license plate: KENNY, said Kenny's, and Norm's said NORM.

"Hankaroo," Ralph said, causing me to jump. I turned around. He said, "Just spoke to the bosses, and they told me that you passed the mustard."

"Glad to hear it," I said.

Ralph nodded gravely. "Not that I was worried. Not *too* much, at least."

I called Karen's mother in Denver from a pay phone in the White Hen Pantry parking lot.

"I heard what you did to that squirrel," she said, but reluctantly, she gave me Karen's new number.

I hadn't spoken to Karen since that night. No doubt when she caught me holding the shovel over my head, she saw the man she had always feared, a man who would one day snap and take out all of life's misery on her—with a shovel, if necessary. What she didn't see was the compassionate man, a man willing to put her out of her misery if she was suffering, a man willing to pay the consequences for such action; though the longer I let this scenario play out in my head, the more uncertain I became about whether she'd have wanted me to put her out of her misery if she was suffering. And maybe this was what she saw: a man who so misunderstood her that in her most vulnerable moment, he'd do the exact opposite of what she really wanted. And how awful would that have been?

Since arriving in Chicago, I had tried not to give in to my urge to call Karen—I had thought that giving her some distance would make her realize what a mistake she'd made—but every time I passed a pay phone, I felt compelled to use it.

I wasn't sure what I was going to say, but I was hoping to elicit a few sympathetic moans when I told her about the cab accident, maybe even an "Oh Hank, oh sweetie" when I described the recent proportions of my head, perhaps a "Why don't you fly back here so we can talk?" when I told her about my new grisly job of vacuuming up bone splinters—not that I'd started doing that yet.

It was two in the morning. The phone rang four times, and then a man picked up and grunted into the mouthpiece.

I hung up and redialed the number. A man—the same man—answered again.

"I'm sorry," I said. "I dialed the wrong number."

A squad car pulled into the parking lot across the street, and though I couldn't see the cop's face, I was sure he had stopped to watch me. After being informed that my calling card had only four remaining minutes, I flattened the sheet of paper with Karen's new number. The man, more coherent this time, answered yet again.

"I'm really sorry," I said. "I must have been given the wrong number."

I heard the bed squeak, a squeak so familiar it twisted my guts, and then a voice. "What's he saying?" It was Karen. And then Karen was on the phone. "How did you get this number? Was it my mother? Of *course* it was my mother. Why am I even asking? What do you want, Hank? Do you know what time it is?"

I tried talking, but I was nervous, grief-stricken, and shy all at once, and I jumbled all that I had meant to say. "My head," I began. "There's something wrong." I sniffled. "Remember Ralph? There's this job. Cleaning up dead people." I was crying now, unable to stop. I wanted to ask her who had answered the phone, but I couldn't bring myself to face it. Not just now. "The cabdriver," I said, "he pulled in front of this car, and WHAM. I thought I was dying. Oh, and my briefcase! Jesus, my briefcase!"

"Are you drunk?" Karen asked. "Is that how you think you'll win me back, getting shitty drunk and calling me late at night?"

I heard the man in the background—"Just hang up on him!"—followed by creaking bed springs and then footsteps. "You need anything, poo?" he called out.

Karen said, "Now that everyone's awake, you might as well say what you want to say. Get it out of your system so we can all go back to bed." She waited. Then she said, "Oh, Jesus, Hank, are you crying?"

I didn't say anything. *Poo?* I thought.

"You're crying," she said.

I sniffled.

The cop's lights came on, a swirl of red and blue blades scissoring the black sky, followed by the heart-clenching siren. The car squealed out of the lot, and I was certain it was heading my way, but it turned onto Seventy-ninth Street and sped away.

"Where are you?" Karen asked.

"I'm home," I said, and hung up.

Saturday night, driving us to a party that I was being forced to attend, humpback whales singing to us the whole way there, Ralph asked how my folks were doing.

"They've passed on," I said.

Ralph abruptly slowed the El Camino as if pulling up the rear of the funeral procession. "*Both* of them?" he asked.

"Dad's liver gave out, and Mom had a brain tumor. They went less than a year apart."

"What about your sister?"

"Kelly? Oh, she's alive." I wasn't sure how to give the narrative of Kelly's life without making it sound as sordid as it actually was. To talk about Kelly meant talking about sex, and you had to give either too many details or no details at all. I opted for the latter. "She's up in Madison."

"Doing what?"

"You know. This and that," I said.

Ralph snorted. "*Hitler* did this and that. *Stalin* did this and that. *Debbie* did this and that."

"Debbie?"

"*Debbie Does Dallas*," Ralph said. Then he grinned and waggled his eyebrows at me. "*Debbie Does Ralph*," he said.

"Oh," I said. "*That* Debbie."

Kelly's name had become synonymous with an infinite variety of romantic entanglements. Until her senior year of high school, she had been uptight, a prude, the sort of girl boys didn't ask out because they knew they'd never get anywhere, not even a copped feel in passing. But then something happened. During her freshman year at Illinois State University in Normal, she started therapy, and while other girls sunbathed on the quad or stumbled bleary-eyed into frat parties or sneaked boys into their all-girls' dorms at night, Kelly fell in love with her therapist, a man twenty years her senior. He was married with two kids, but when the virgin Kelly swooped in with her talons, the therapist, unable to resist temptation, left everything behind, risking his job, moving out of his subdivision split level and, with Kelly, into a one-bedroom apartment near campus. By spring Kelly had already left him. Fresh with my new driver's license, I drove all of two hours downstate to visit her, knowing nothing of Kelly's life except her address. I had knocked on her door, expecting to see Kelly, but the therapist answered. His name was André or Antoine or Alex, and he wanted to talk to me about her, so we strolled the narrow streets of Normal, but all I remembered from our walk was the familiar sounds of dripping icicles and melting snow running down the street and trickling into drains. Birds, too. I heard birds for the first time that year. And college students. They lived in houses without any screens over their windows, and they sat on upholstered sofas on their front lawns, and they drank beer out in broad daylight. I'd never seen anything like it. Kelly, I learned, had moved into a frat house off campus and was dating a new boy each week. This knowledge pushed the therapist over the edge, prompting him to quit his job and move out of town. For Kelly, that year marked the beginning of her life of entanglements. She had moved from the frat house to the athletic center, from professors' offices to TAs' efficiencies, from the freshman dorm to the International Center. She'd even had a fling with a high school boy she'd met at the mall arcade, and, according to Kelly, he'd given her his school ring to wear.

It would take hours to document the whole story, though to Kelly's credit, she'd managed to amass more advanced degrees than anyone I knew. She was presently hard at work on her second Ph.D. at the University of Wisconsin. Her first Ph.D. was in philosophy; her current one was in women's studies. She already had at least three master's degrees. The last time I saw her, a year before, she was wearing camouflage army pants and a camouflage T-shirt and was dating one of her students, a budding feminist named Rebecca. They had tattooed each other's names on their biceps.

"I liked Kelly," Ralph said. "I always thought we'd've made a good team."

"If you ever get a chance to join the team," I said, "you'll probably want to wear a helmet and a jock."

Ralph nodded thoughtfully. "I'll keep that in mind."

When we arrived at the party, cars were parked on the front lawn, a grown couple were making out in a pickup truck, and a man, hands on his knees, was vomiting loudly into a shrub. Glassy-eyed, the man peeked up. His entire face, strained from his assault to the shrub, drooped as if in the first stages of melting. He turned his head, spat, then squinted at us through his tears. "Ralph?" he asked. "Is that you? You're late, man."

Ralph said, "Did I miss much?" He nudged me and said, "Remember him?"

"Who? The guy puking?"

"*That,* my friend, is not just some guy puking. That's Jeff Nitz. Falcons basketball MVP. Remember?"

"We had a basketball team in eighth grade?"

"You never went to any of the games?" Ralph asked.

"You *did?*"

"Are you crazy?" Ralph said. "*Everyone* was there. Remember the pep rallies?"

"No! There were pep rallies?"

"Where were you?" Ralph said. "I thought you had perfect attendance."

"I *did.*" I stopped walking. "How'd you know I had perfect attendance?"

"I spent a lot of time alone in the principal's office. I helped myself to some of the files."

"Those are confidential," I said.

Ralph nodded. "I know."

We walked into the backyard. The party was at Bob Slomski's house. Bob was in our eighth-grade class, but all I could recall was his eighth-grade photo—long hair parted in the middle, chipped front tooth, nose out of whack. Above the garage's side door hung a sign: SLOMSKI'S PLAYHOUSE. MEN ONLY. And men it was, all of them clumped around the keg. A man wearing a Judas Priest T-shirt sipped a beer and pumped the keg with the determination of a man who needed to keep himself breathing, as if the keg were a manual life-support system and to quit pumping would mean certain death. And so he pumped and pumped while others came to fill plastic cups, pitchers, punch bowls, beer bongs, and even the extra-large cups of some poor woman's brassiere.

"Holy moly!" someone said. "Whose is *that?*"

"You can't guess?" the man with the bra said.

I turned to Ralph. "Do we have to stay long?"

"We just got here," Ralph said. "Besides, you know most everyone here."

"I do?"

"This party," Ralph said, "it's for *you!* In honor of ol' Hank Boyd. The prodigal son! These are your old classmates. Don't you recognize them?"

I looked around. I didn't recognize a soul.

"Ralph," I said. "I haven't seen a lot of these people since 1979. And the ones I went to high school with, I haven't seen since 1983. We're talking twenty years, give or take a few."

"Seems like yesterday, though, doesn't it?"

"Not really," I said. "No."

Ralph smiled at a couple walking by—a woman with painted, arched eyebrows who breathed smoke while berating a red-faced man; with his distended belly, he looked six months pregnant. Was it possible that *any* of these people had once been kids? That they had been my classmates? Were these really the same boys and girls with whom I so desperately wanted to be friends, from whom I wanted nothing more than to be liked? Was it true that I had sat next to these same people day after day, year after year, that we had huddled together under desks during tornado drills, that I had craved, in my prepubescence, any of the women here?

While Ralph pointed me out to various partygoers, I looked for a place to hide but couldn't find any. Standing under the porch's yellow lightbulb, a halo of winged insects circling my head, I felt as conspicuous in my striped polo shirt and khakis as I had all those years ago lingering at the far edge of the playground, wearing my stiff back-to-school clothes, hands jammed in my pockets, waiting for a sign from someone, anyone, to join them.

Every fall it was the same: the queasiness, the uncertainty of how things might go this year, the inevitable shifting of friends during summer break. I knew the pecking order well—the slow-in-the-head kids and the fatsos at the very bottom, the physically weak and nonathletes one tier up, the too-smart-for-their-own-good slightly above them, and so on. I fell somewhere in the middle. I was smart but not too smart. I didn't follow sports, but I knew how to play. I was never overweight, never too skinny. While not the toughest kid in school, not by a long shot, I knew which kids I could, if need be, push around. Not that I ever pushed anyone around. Over summer, though, the pecking order's shifts would cause occasional rumbling; rarely would they ever be earth-shattering. But that knowledge didn't stop me from worrying that I had somehow dropped down, pushed from my slot by a fat kid who'd lost weight, or by one of the uncoordinated who'd miraculously bloomed in the outfield, catching what the rest of us would have let fly out of the park. Years later, I would think how silly it all was, how overblown my fears were, but now, at Bob Slomski's party, an outsider dressed entirely wrong for the occasion, I couldn't help evaluating where I stood in their eyes, and like an audit that was going sour, I kept calculating and recalculating the conclusions, hoping for better results, but each assessment left me clinging to the very bottom rung.

I was feeling sorry for myself when a man standing next to Ralph pointed at me and yelled, "*That's* Hank? Hey, everyone, *look:* It's Hank Boyd!"

"Hank!" people called out. And then they wandered over to shake my hand or slap my back, to ask me how the hell I was doing.

"You're looking good, old man," said a guy with a ZZ Top beard. Three women dressed like mud wrestlers before a match stood with him. One of them gave me the once-over and said, "He sure does," and then meowed like an angry cat.

People brought me one foamy beer after another. I did shots with a group of men inside Slomski's Playhouse. When I stepped back outside, a woman who looked vaguely familiar gave me a toke on her joint. The spirit of generosity was enough to bring tears to my eyes. True, I didn't remember most of them. True, I didn't even know my own grade school had had a basketball team. True, I was initially appalled by being here. But all of that had changed in a matter of minutes. These men and women from my youth, they were offering their love to me, and who was I to turn that down?

"You look like you're having a good time." I heard the words first. Then Ralph appeared from behind a woodpile, cradling a possum.

"Aren't those things rabid?"

"What? *This?*" he asked, stroking its back.

I was drunk, and everything was blurry. "You found it behind that woodpile?" I asked.

"Naw. I was taking a whiz back there. I found this someplace else."

"Oh." I tried imagining Ralph taking a whiz while holding a possum but couldn't.

"Look at you," Ralph said. "I bet this is the best time you've ever had."

I hated to admit it, but he was right: This *was* the best time I'd ever had. I hadn't realized it until Ralph said so. Either my life had been a pathetic one, or this party was truly a transcendent experience. I wasn't sure which.

Ralph said, "Did you see Mary Polaski?"

"No!" Mary Polaski had broken my heart more than once. I had pined for her, off and on, from early grade school up until she went away to Queen of Peace, the all-girls' Catholic high school. Occasionally I'd see her waiting for the bus, wearing her plaid skirt and starched white blouse with its stiff collar, and I would get the irrational desire to grab her around the waist and start kissing every exposed part of her body, biting her neck, maybe even sinking my teeth into her as if she were a slab of pork. My notions of romance were informed by years of watching Bela Lugosi and Peter Cushing as Dracula, and I would have loved nothing more than to walk into Mary Polaski's bedroom one foggy night, raise my arms out so that my black cape looked like wings, and then descend upon her, puncturing her soft pale neck with my fangs. "Where is she?" I asked.

Ralph pointed, but all I saw was a heavyset woman standing on the porch, smoking and flapping her arms dramatically while she talked.

"I don't see her," I said.

"The one smoking," Ralph said. "The one gesturing."

"*Her?*"

"Mary frickin' Polaski," Ralph said. "The one and only."

I squinted, then turned away. I couldn't reconcile the Mary Polaski of my youth with the Mary Polaski on the porch. Once, in eighth grade, Ralph made me put on a blindfold and told me to guess which glass held Coke and which one Pepsi, but then he handed me a glass of milk. The look on my face, I suspected, wasn't much different tonight.

"Anyone else I should know about?" I asked.

"There's Pete Elmazi," Ralph said, pointing to a guy wearing an overly

tight Vietnam-era army jacket. "And there's Wes Papadakis." He pointed
to the man with the ZZ Top beard. "Oh," Ralph said, "and there's Janet
the Planet."

I braced myself. I had liked Janet, but she'd been a large girl twenty
years ago. Given the night's empirical evidence, I feared the worst for her.
Little girls, I'd heard, could be crueler than little boys, and Janet, given
her size, had worked harder than anyone else to assimilate, to join the inner sanctum of the most popular girls, which meant that she had to
compensate for her weight by being an extraordinary wit, a charmer, a
seducer. She also had to prove that she possessed the capacity to be mer-
cilessly cruel to those who didn't make it into the inner sanctum, who'd
never make it. But the woman Ralph pointed at was slender, with long,
thick jet-black hair. Beer in hand, she stood alone, and something about
her posture, the slight slump, allowed me to see with perfect clarity the
plump little Janet from all those years ago, back when her family had
moved to town: Janet on her very first day at the new school, standing on
the periphery of the playground, holding her lunch bag in one hand, her
box of school supplies in the other. It would take poor Janet years to secure her place among the charmed.

"Janet!" I called out. When I heard my own voice, its pitch higher
than usual, I realized how drunk I really was. I waved. Janet smiled, and
Ralph prodded me toward her. I couldn't see Ralph—he was behind
me—but I swore he nudged my spine with the possum's nose.

"Janet!" I said.

"Hello, Hank."

"Janet!" I wasn't sure what else to say, so I blurted out, "I'd have recognized you anywhere." Instead of saying what she had probably heard a
thousand times before—*You've lost so much weight!*—I said what I
hoped might cheer her, something that might compliment her inner
beauty while highlighting my own keen perceptiveness, but my com-
ment only caused her to frown. "What I mean," I said, "is that you still
have that same *glow!*" I wasn't even sure what I was trying to say now.
*Glow* was a word thrown recklessly at pregnant women.

"Thanks," Janet said. "I guess." She was quite attractive—a natural
beauty—and I was stunned at how poor a judge we'd all been in grade

school, how shortsighted, how no one back then, teachers included, could have imagined the Janet of today. Janet said, "I always liked you. You were always kind to me."

I wanted to tell her that though I had liked her, too—and I *had* liked her—I had called her Janet the Planet, same as everyone else.

"Why *wouldn't* I have been kind to you?" I said, and smiled.

"Kids are monsters," she said without hesitation.

"I'm not fond of kids, either," I said.

"No," she said. "*They're* monsters." She nodded generally toward the party. "Look at them."

I looked. I tried to imagine what their monster names might be. Bloated Man. The Creature from Slomski's Backyard. Count Kegula.

Janet said, "I only came here tonight to see you."

"Really?"

She nodded. "I wanted to see how you'd turned out."

"Well? What do you think?"

"You don't fit in here," she said. "That's a point in your favor."

I nodded.

"But you came here with Ralph," she said. "So you lose that point."

"Oh, Ralph's not bad."

An almost imperceptible shiver ran through Janet, as if someone, somewhere, had started to electrocute her but then thought better of it.

"What do you do now?" I asked.

She told me about her job at Columbia College downtown, in the Office of Faculty Research, where she helped faculty write their grant and fellowship applications. What she truly wanted was to become a writer, the kind of writer who could write anything—plays, poems, stories, how-to articles. What she wanted were her own grants and fellowships.

"Have you written anything?" I asked.

"Nothing I'd show you," she said. She was staring into my eyes, boring holes into my soul. "What about you? What brings you back here?"

*Karen,* I thought, and the memory of my phone call, the man who answered, the two of them in bed together, was like a spear rammed through my heart. "Oh, you'll love this," I said, but instead of telling her about Karen, I told her about the squirrel. "*Flattened,*" I said. "*Squashed* but still alive." And I could see that, as much as the image of the flattened squirrel repulsed her, I had her. She was hooked.

At the side of Bob Slomski's house, we kissed, Janet and I. The house's electric meter dug into my back, but the vibration of the spinning disc inside was soothing, and I could tell each time someone turned something on or off by the intensity of the pulse against my spine. I was kissing Janet's neck, biting it gently, as I'd imagined biting Mary Polaski's, and I was about to suggest that we go elsewhere when someone yelled our names. I looked up. It was Bob Slomski. He was staring down at us from an upstairs window.

"Have you two seen Ralph?" he asked.

"No," I said. "Not lately."

Bob shook his head. "He stole my possum, the son of a bitch."

"What do you mean?"

"My possum, my possum," he said. I expected him to offer up the possum's Latin name, its genus, for clarification. "It's a hobby of mine," he said. "Taxidermy. But every time I finish up a new roadkill, Ralph comes over and steals it."

At the mention of roadkill, Janet reached down and massaged between my legs. I couldn't tell if Bob could see what she was doing. I imagined Ralph taking the possum home, stamping it *Made in Occupied Japan*, and selling it on eBay.

"If I run into Ralph," I said, "I'll ask about your possum."

Janet massaged harder.

"Good enough," Bob said. "You two having a good time?"

"You bet!" I said—too loud. A neighbor opened up her window and yelled, "Keep it down, or I'm calling the police!"

Bob said, "Ah, go to hell, you windbag."

The neighbor, an elderly woman with wilting white hair, slammed her window shut.

"I'd like to taxidermy that old broad," Bob said. "And then I'd mount her to my roof so that everyone in the neighborhood could throw rocks at her." He saw that I was peeking up but no longer giving him my full attention. "Okay," he said. "You two have fun." Bob shut his window so hard, I expected broken glass to shower us, but with all the alcohol charging through my bloodstream, and with Janet so skillfully using her hand, I wouldn't have felt a thing, nothing at all.

I woke up in intense pain, the sort of hangover pain that debilitates, ice-pick-through-the-frontal-lobe pain, the pain of cyanide poisoning, shivering and convulsing pain, pain that would send atheists kneeling in dark churches, pain that lifts rock after rock off long-buried secrets, indiscretions, transgressions, pain that spits in your face and says, *Look at what a terrible person you are—liar! Cheat! Bad son! Bad boyfriend! Bad human!*

"Oh God," I said, and rolled over, curling up, a textbook fetus. I wasn't sure what I was lying upon—it was hard, uneven, cold—but I couldn't open my eyes to see: They were glued shut.

Someone touched me, said, "Poor baby," in a woman's voice, and draped an arm over me. It was a small comfort, tucked inside the larger blanket of my misery, that someone was with me, even though I wasn't sure who it was. Still, I held on to that arm for dear life, as if it were my only hope.

"Get up!" Someone kicked the sole of my shoe.

"Look at him," another voice said. "Pathetic."

"Get up!" Another kick.

I opened my eyes. The sun, though blighted by clouds, blinded me. I squinted, shielded my eyes as if saluting my guests. They were Kenny and Norm. I looked around. I was in the bed of somebody's pickup truck, still at Bob Slomski's house, and Janet was lying next to me, sound asleep and snoring.

"You looking for Ralph?" I asked.

"No," Norm said. "We're looking for *you*."

Kenny tugged his long braided beard. "Ralph's already on his way to the scene."

"What scene?"

"The murder scene," Kenny said, and Norm smiled. "Ralph told us we'd probably find you here," Kenny added.

"And here you are," Norm said, but he was looking at Janet, sizing her up—*Janet the Planet*, I couldn't help thinking, *I spent the night with Janet the Planet in the bed of a pickup!*

"Oh, man," I said, "I don't think I can do this today. You have no idea the hangover I have." I tried sitting up, but the pain shooting through my head was too intense, and I fell back to my side.

Norm said, "People don't get killed just when it's convenient for you."

"I think there's some Pepto-Bismol in my glove compartment," Kenny said.

Norm nodded toward Janet and said, "Kiss your sweetie good-bye." The way he said it made me think he was going to shoot her.

"Okay," I said. "Give me a sec."

Kenny said, "I'll drive you there."

Norm, climbing over the truck's gate, then hopping from the bumper to the ground, said, "Chop-chop, Casanova."

Kenny winked and said, "Don't worry. I know how you feel. You'll live. You always do."

Kenny drove me to an apartment along the city's Gold Coast, Norm following close behind. I had to keep the window down and not think too much about anything, but the traffic on Lake Shore Drive was fast, the curves were tight, and it took all the willpower I possessed not to heave. I had no idea how alcoholics did it day after day: the searing hot-poker pain through the head, the uncontrollable DTs, feeling overheated one minute, suffering chills the next. My eyes felt like two lightbulbs screwed into sockets that couldn't handle the wattage. They pulsed, and my vision kept fading in and out.

"Here she is," Kenny said, zipping into the parking garage of a dark Gothic monstrosity. The monthly rent here was probably more than I had ever made in a year.

Norm parked in a fire lane and left his hazards blinking. He was the sort of person who treated every event as an emergency. Slicing off his thumb and picking up a pizza would carry the same sense of urgency.

The way Norm saw things, no one's time was more precious than his own.

We took the elevator up twenty-nine floors. The doors creaked open. Yellow police tape blocked off one of the apartments.

"Are you sure Ralph needs help?" I asked, but Norm poked me in the back with something he was holding, and I continued walking as if at gunpoint.

The apartment's door was ajar. Kenny pushed it open. "Go on," he said, and I swung first my right leg and then my left over the yellow tape. I had to push the door open even farther before I could see Ralph.

Ralph was wearing rubber waders, the kind fly fishermen wear, and a butcher's long white jacket. A mask—a disposable respirator—was strapped over his mouth. Bottles and spray cans of cleansers surrounded him. Balanced on his trowel was something rubbery. I squinted. When Ralph saw me, he nodded. "Brain," he said. Then he dumped it from his trowel into the bucket, and the sound it made, the plop and splash, caused me to clutch at Kenny, who said, "Easy, now, easy."

Later that night, over several pitchers, Kenny laughed and said, "You should've seen the look on your face. If I hadn't been there when you fainted, I'd've thought it was *you* we were cleaning up after." It was true: Everything had gone black for a few seconds, and after grabbing at Kenny, I'd fallen to my knees.

Norm wagged his head. "College boy," he said, and smiled, but he was staring into my eyes and wouldn't look away. I tried peering back into Norm's eyes, but they were fathomless, and the deeper I looked, the blacker it got.

### III

Ralph's theory—the higher the temperature, the more work we'd have—proved frighteningly accurate. After the short drought of murders, the temperature rose, and we found ourselves with seven or eight jobs a week. I became a regular at Sam's Club, where I could buy household cleaners in bulk. Since the poor couldn't afford to hire us, we spent most of our days in lavish homes where the air-conditioning felt good and where, during a break, we could catch part of a Cubs game on a big-screen TV. At least half our work came from suicides, and these were the messiest. More often than not, they were men who'd used a gun with too large a caliber at close range. By the time we reached a job, the body already had been taken away, and I could pretend I was cleaning something other than what I *was* cleaning. If that didn't work, I could wear a Walkman and lose myself to music, bobbing my head to Bruce Springsteen or John Mellencamp. We worked alone. No one bothered us. The deceased's relatives had no desire to hang out with us, to supervise. What they wanted was for their lives to go backward, a curling up of time, and for all evidence of pain and death to be erased from the room. To that end, we did our best.

Three weeks into the job, at a CEO's home in Evanston, I was scrubbing a wall near the point of impact when Ralph called me over. I set down my bucket. My hands and arms were sweating inside rubber gloves that went all the way up to my elbows.

"Look at this," he said. He was holding a magnifying glass in one hand and tweezers in the other. Pinched between the tweezers' prongs was a shard of bone. "My guess is, it traveled with the bullet, then shot off on its own. I found it inside this here coffee mug." He raised the mug as if to toast me.

"You're a regular Sherlock Holmes," I said.

"More like *Johnny* Holmes," Ralph said. "Not that you need to know that." He dropped the pinched bone shard back into the mug.

On Friday afternoons the four of us—me, Ralph, Kenny, and Norm—met at Durbin's for the week's postmortem.

"Okay, girls," Norm said one Friday. "Who wants to give us the postscrotum?"

I cringed. I still wasn't sure what Norm did to earn his keep. While Ralph delivered news from the front line, I kicked back and sipped my beer. There was nothing particularly special about Durbin's, no discernible atmosphere, nothing interesting about the lighting or the decor, no apparent theme, nothing to brag about on the jukebox, and yet it was a popular hangout for the locals—locals, in this case, meaning people who lived within a half-mile radius. This was my fifth time here, and I was starting to recognize the regulars. One regular intrigued me because she always came alone, and because my assessment of her had changed radically since the first time I had seen her. She reminded me of the famous study in perception that I had seen in both art and psychology books, a line drawing that looked like an old woman until you shifted your view of what was what—nose for chin, eye for ear—and then, miraculously, you could see the young woman. The woman at the bar (the bartenders called her Ruth) had at first seemed in her fifties, but now I could see that she was my age—mid-thirties. More often than not, her own cigarette smoke masked her face, and she seemed in a perpetual state of appearing from thin air, a woman who couldn't materialize, a glitch in whatever magic she possessed.

"Look who's here!" Kenny said.

One strand of Kenny's Fu Manchu was soaking in his mug of beer, like a dog whose tail drooped in its own water bowl, but I didn't say anything. I looked where he was looking. It was Janet. *Janet the Planet*, I thought, not unkindly. I had thought of her as Janet the Planet for so many years, I couldn't see her now and *not* think that, but I viewed it now as a term of endearment, not unlike *sweetie pie* or *dearest*. Of course, it wasn't the sort of endearment I ever said aloud. I knew better.

"Janet!" I said. I stood and hugged her. Janet's hugs were intense, bruising, squeezing all the wind out of me. "Okay, okay," I whispered, and reluctantly, she released me. Still, she always kept one hand on me, resting on my thigh, gently tugging my earlobe, twisting a lock of hair, tapping my kneecap.

I pulled up a chair for her.

Norm said, "You're here just in time. Ralph was telling us about new techniques for getting entrails out of shag carpet. What kind of carpet you got at your place, Janet?"

"I don't have carpet," Janet said evenly. "I have hardwood floors."

"Oh," Norm said. "One of *them*."

I touched Janet's thigh, squeezed it.

Ralph said, "Anyone singing karaoke tonight? They're starting any minute now."

Kenny said, "Naw. Not tonight."

Norm said, "If they had any Motörhead, I'd seriously consider it."

Ralph looked at us. "How about you two? Maybe a duet? 'You Don't Bring Me Flowers'? 'Endless Love'? 'Ebony and Ivory'?"

"I don't think so," I said. Janet shook her head. "What about you, Ralph?" I asked.

Ralph said, "I may give it a whirl." He looked to be turning the idea over in his head, but I knew Ralph well enough to know that he wouldn't do it, either.

And so the five of us sat there, drinking well into the night. Kenny pulled out a wad of cash and paid me and Ralph for our week's work. Other than Norm booing some poor karaoke singer whose song he found objectionable—as it turned out, any song that wasn't heavy metal was objectionable—we sank into silence, but there were flashes when I felt that we weren't the only four at the table. During those split-second flickers, I sensed the presence of ghosts from this past week, all the dead we'd cleaned up after, as if they'd come to join us for one final beer, one final shot, before drifting either to heaven or hell.

On nights when I didn't have to work the next day, I slept over at Janet's. Even in sleep she clung to me. One morning I told her that it was okay to let go.

"You don't like it?" she asked. She scooted to the edge of the bed and wouldn't look at me.

"Sure I like it!" I said. "But my ribs, they *hurt*."

Janet said, "Okay. If you don't want me to touch you . . ."

"It's not that," I said. "It's not about touching."

Janet frowned, nodded. Whenever she made this face, I saw the Janet I knew in eighth grade, the fat girl who worked ten times harder than everyone else to be loved.

One afternoon after we'd made love, Janet said, "Would you be with me right now if I was still heavy?"

"But you're not heavy," I said, "so it's a moot point."

Janet said, "You can use your imagination, though, can't you? Let's say I *am* heavy. Would you still want to be with me?"

"This is ridiculous," I said.

Janet covered her bare body with the bedsheet and then, keeping her flesh out of my sight, began dressing.

"You're being silly," I said.

"But you wouldn't, would you?"

I didn't want to lie, but I didn't like where this was heading, so I said, "Of course I would. I don't care if you're heavy or thin. You'd still be the same person."

Janet quit putting on her clothes. She said, "You're just saying that."

"Hell, no, I'm not just saying that. I wouldn't care. Really!"

Janet hugged me to her, and when I returned the hug, I felt Janet growing in my arms, getting larger, and I thought, *Uh-oh*, but it was only her deep breaths that were causing her to expand, it was just poor Janet crying, and I hated myself for being grateful.

Karen had left me because I wouldn't set a firm date for marriage. For four years, I had pushed the date ahead, postponing it a month, a season, a whole year once. "You don't want to get married," Karen had said, and I'd said, "I do want to get married, I *do*." And I *did*. But something kept me from committing—a force, a wall—and each time we got within striking distance of the date, my body and my mind would start to manifest a series of tics, the most notable of which was that I would start to itch like mad. We could barely watch videos together because I'd start scratching at the first preview and wouldn't stop until the final credits rolled. I scratched in restaurants, in the shower, in bed. "Did mosquitos bite you?" Karen asked the first time. "No," I said. "Did you step in poison ivy?" she asked. "No," I said, "it's just, I don't know, nerves. I can't seem to stop." But as soon as we agreed to push back the date, the itching went away, and I stopped scratching.

One sweltering day, while working in a house whose air conditioner was on the blink, I told this story to Ralph.

"Maybe you've got eczema," he said.

"No, no," I said, "you're missing the point. The second we moved the date, I quit itching. And the further we pushed the date, the less I itched."

Ralph looked up from his bucket. "Do I look like a dermatologist?"

"That's the thing," I said. "It wasn't a dermatological problem. It was psychological."

Ralph said, "Listen, Freud, I don't know about you, but I'm sweating my ass off, and this place is starting to stink. The sooner we get done, the better."

"Okay, okay," I said, and continued scrubbing my stained wall.

Ralph and I had taken to referring to the dead—the ones we cleaned up after—as the Unfortunates. When the Unfortunates were alive, they probably never imagined someone such as Ralph or me in their homes, doing what we were doing. To pass the time, we sometimes tried piecing together a history for the Unfortunate at hand. My hypotheses were always mundane (men who suffered from depression and couldn't find a reasonable solution out of a relatively commonplace conflict, like credit-card debt), while Ralph's veered toward the outlandish (men sleeping with married but long-closeted presidential candidates after local stump speeches).

After work we'd head back to Ralph's. Sometimes I fell fast asleep, waking up in time for a late dinner. Other times I sat mindlessly on the sofa in front of a television set that was as old as Ralph. It was a black-and-white model, knobless, with reception that wasn't any better than what you'd see through a pair of night-vision goggles, everything tinted green, nothing distinct. Despite this, I watched it, for even in its green-fog state, the TV eased my pulsing brain; the blurred, pixeled images were as soothing as a shot of morphine.

I fell asleep tonight on the sofa with the TV softly hissing at me. I had no idea how long I'd been asleep when someone started squeezing my foot. I opened my eyes. Kenny, clutching my big toe, was eating a Slim Jim and looking down at me.

"You awake?" he asked.

I nodded.

"I think I got Slim Jim caught between my teeth. Jesus, it's driving me nuts." He rubbed his tongue over his teeth a few times. I was dozing off when Kenny squeezed my toe again and said, "I need your help. We need to get Norm."

"Can't Ralph help you?"

Kenny shook his head. "Ralph's asleep."

"Two seconds ago, *I* was asleep."

"Yeah, but Ralph was in *bed*."

"Oh." It had never occurred to me that a hierarchy existed for places to sleep, that people took some places more seriously than others. Naturally, bed was sacred, the highest on the hierarchy; a couch, where I happened to be, was a frivolous place to snooze, a place from which you should expect to get woken.

Kenny said, "C'mon. Think of all the times I've helped *you*."

I sat up, rubbed a hand over my face and through my hair. With the exception of his giving me a terrible job, I couldn't think of any. "Okay, okay," I said. "All right."

We floated through the Chicago night, the skyline shimmering, hypnotic. I wanted to enjoy it, but this afternoon's job, the smell of death, was still lodged in my nose. I'd heard that the worst part of cleaning up John Gacy's crime scene—removing all those bodies—was the smell. The police had hired nineteen-year-olds to help, but they lasted only a day or two. It wasn't the sight of decomposing bodies that got to them. It was the stench. They knew that if they didn't quit, the smell would follow them around, the mournful ghosts of tortured men and boys haunting them the rest of their lives.

"Where are we going?" I asked.

Kenny said, "I've got a question for you." I waited, but Kenny didn't say anything. Just when I thought he wasn't going to ask the question, he said, "When do you think Boston's coming out with a new album?" When I didn't answer, he said, "Tell me something. Are you happy?"

"Happy?"

"You know. Are you happy with your life?"

"No," I said.

"Really? *No?*"

I wanted to ask him what I could possibly be happy about, especially now that I was working for him cleaning up blood and brains. Would a happy person take a job like that? His answer should have been self-evident.

"What about you?" I asked. "Are *you* happy?"

"Me? Fuck, yeah. Why wouldn't I be? I'm a millionaire." He lifted a fist and rubbed his right eye with it. It was the first time I could picture Kenny as a child: little Kenny getting up in the middle of the night, wearing PJs and booties, rubbing both eyes with his tiny fists. He cut his eyes my way and, mocking me, said, "Am I *happy*." He laughed as if the question was the most preposterous thing he'd ever heard. "Name one millionaire who's *not* happy."

"Howard Hughes."

Kenny thought about it. He said, "I could be mistaken, but I think Howard Hughes was a billionaire. Am I wrong about that? He was a billionaire, wasn't he?"

"Point taken," I said.

We drove in silence the rest of the way. I thought about poor old Howard Hughes, how he'd quit clipping his nails, quit socializing, quit trusting anyone. I fell asleep. I was dreaming about Howard Hughes and my sister, Kelly, both wearing camouflage and shooting at me with AK-47s, when I woke up sweating from the nightmare and saw Kenny snarling at himself in the rearview mirror, baring his teeth to see if he could find the stringy remnant of Slim Jim that was driving him berserk.

"Fuck!" he yelled. "You ever get something caught between your teeth, and that's all you can think about? Jesus fucking Christ, I'm losing my mind. Do you see anything?" He turned to me, and I was forced to look inside his mouth. When I shook my head, he said, "Oh, man, something like this'll be the end of me, I swear."

"Where are we?" I asked.

Kenny said, "Where *are* we?" He leaned so close, our noses almost touched. "We're the last place you ever want to be." He got out of the car and started walking.

"What do you mean?" I asked when I'd caught up to him. We walked together down an alley to a back door. I was practically clutching his arm.

"Shhhh." Kenny knocked at the door with one knuckle in an approximation of the opening of Zeppelin's "Rock and Roll." He even started bobbing his head. Did some inner music always play for Kenny, songs he'd heard so many times he could have picked up a guitar for the very first time in his life and played them cold?

The door opened, and a bodybuilder regarded us. He was wearing a Gold's Gym tank top and sweatpants so tight I could easily identify each muscle. He motioned us inside, then led the way to a small room with a black leather couch, where Norm was sound asleep.

The bodybuilder said, "Get 'im the fuck outta here."

Kenny lifted Norm under his armpits, and I lifted him by the ankles. I was surprised at how difficult it was to carry someone, particularly navigating through doorways and around corners. Walking backward, I couldn't see where I was stepping. When I stepped on a rock that was large enough to make my ankle cave in, I dropped my end of Norm. Amazingly, Norm didn't wake up, and Kenny didn't seem to care that I had dropped him.

"You okay?" Kenny asked me.

"I think so," I said.

Kenny opened the Monte Carlo's back door, and together we shoved Norm across the seat.

On our way home, I asked again where we'd gone, but Kenny, staring more often into the rearview mirror than through the front windshield, was distracted by Norm's presence.

"Is he still breathing?" Kenny asked.

I put my arm on Norm's rib cage, felt it rise and fall. "Yep."

Kenny nodded but seemed disappointed.

Kenny showed up at Ralph's house the following three nights, each time insisting on my help. Ralph was always asleep, so the burden of assisting continued to fall on me. The first night Norm was passed out in the back room of an Italian restaurant in the town of Cicero, Al Capone's old neighborhood. Someone had fashioned a string of spaghetti on Norm's upper lip into a cartoon mustache with an outrageous curl on either end. Despite this, the men who led us to Norm were not comedians by profession. In fact, the spaghetti mustache was more likely a warning, a mob signature, their polite way of saying, *Next time you won't be so lucky.*

The second night Kenny received a mysterious phone call directing him to an alley. In that alley, Kenny was told, he would find Norm. When we arrived, a homeless man was lacing up a new pair of high-tops. The man nodded at us, stood, picked up two overflowing shopping bags, and limped away. Kenny and I walked into the heart of the alley, toward the Dumpster, and sure enough, there was Norm. Someone had propped him up against the Dumpster. Kenny shone a flashlight at him. Norm's shoes were gone. "That homeless guy," I said. Kenny nodded. On the third night we picked Norm up from the place with the bodybuilder, only this time a purple welt was blooming around Norm's eye, and dried blood caked his lips.

That last night, on our way back to the southwest side, Kenny popped in a cassette. I expected Boston or Jethro Tull to blare through the speakers, woofers and tweeters pulsing like a heart under stress, but it was the eerie sound of humpback whales. Instead of calming me, as they appeared to be doing for Kenny, the whales made me conscious of just how far I had allowed my life to drift off course, of how much I shouldn't have been here at all, and of how only one year ago, while sleeping peacefully next to Karen, I never could have predicted a night like tonight— me back in Chicago, a city to which I had vowed never to return, riding in a car with two men I hadn't seen in over twenty years, whales singing to us.

I didn't mention to Ralph my nights out with Kenny. On the morning after the last night, Ralph was downstairs packaging up items he'd sold on eBay, getting ready to ship them all off to their new, unsuspecting owners.

"My best month ever," Ralph said. "Cleared a thousand buckaroos."

"Occupied Japan has treated you well," I said.

"Occupied Japan hasn't done jack for me," Ralph said. "I'll tell you who's been good to me. The rubber-stamp industry. I paid ten bucks for this stamp, and according to the company, I should be able to get ten thousand imprints out of it. I'm keeping track, too. Seven thousand four hundred fifty-two to go." He reached over to stamp my forehead, but I moved out of his reach. "Hey, you want to take a drive? I have to see my lawyer this afternoon."

"I think I'll pass." I wasn't in the mood to see Krazowski, especially since the damage to my head hadn't been so bad after all, and since I'd decided to deal directly with the insurance companies for reimbursement. "What's your business with the lawyer, anyway?" I asked.

"What do you mean, what's my business with the lawyer? My on-the-job leg injury. *That's* what my business is."

"What job? Where were you working?"

"Wal-Mart."

"You worked at Wal-Mart?"

"For a day, yes, I worked at Wal-Mart."

"And you hurt your leg? The first day?"

Ralph nodded.

I smiled at him; I knew what kind of scam he was running. "You seem to be walking just fine to me," I said.

"Oh, really? I do?" Ralph stood up and put his hands on his hips. I was about to tell him to take it easy, that I was just ribbing him, but he said, "What, are you an orthopedic surgeon? Have you seen X rays of my leg?" He stepped closer to me. "Do you know my case history? Have you interviewed me extensively? Have you seen the security-camera footage of my fall? Have you spoken to the witnesses?" He started pacing the room, goose-stepping one way, turning, then goose-stepping the other way. "Are you," he said, "or have you ever been employed by Wal-Mart? Have you ever lived in Bentonville, Arkansas, home of Wal-Mart head-quarters? Are you related to the Walton family? Do you own stock in Wal-Mart, and if so, how much?" He stopped pacing. He took hold of his chin and looked down at me. "Are you familiar with the term *hairline fracture?* What about *sciatic nerve?* What about *myopic?* Are these words familiar to you? Do you speak Latin? Have you read *Gray's Anatomy* from cover to cover? Can you tell me how many bones there are in the human body? When you dissect a frog, how do you tell the male from the female? Where did you go to medical school? Where did you do your residency? Are you board-certified?" I started to tell him to cool down, but Ralph raised his palm for me to hold my thought. "Have you ever spent time in an institution?" he asked. "Are you currently taking any medications? Are you presently seeing a psychiatrist or any other mental-health specialist?" He picked up a butter knife and pointed it at me. "What's your political affiliation? When was the last time you voted? Are you an American? Were your parents American? Would you say that your sexual proclivities are normal? Would you please define *normal* to me? Can you answer any of these questions?" Here he laughed derisively and wagged his head. "Why should your opinion mean anything to me?" he asked. "Why? *Why?*"

"Jesus," I said. "Calm down, Ralph. I guess I was mistaken."

"Damn right you were mistaken!" Ralph sighed loudly and shook his head. After an uncomfortable silence, he said, "Naw, you're right. My leg's fine. In fact, I've never felt better in my entire life." He sat down and took a sip of coffee. "Actually," he said, "I've been thinking about going to law school. What did you think of my cross-examination?"

As far as I knew, Ralph hadn't even graduated from high school. Law school, thankfully, would be many, many years away.

"Nice," I said. "Real nice."

Ralph nodded. "And I was just warming up," he said.

While I was patching a bullet hole in a wall, using the edge of a putty knife to smooth the filling, my cell phone rang.

"Mr. Boyd?" a man said. He cleared phlegm from his throat.

"Yes?"

"Chicago police. Detective Bielski."

I waited for more, but nothing followed. "Hello?" I said.

"Yes," he said. "Is this a cell-phone number?"

"Yes, it is."

"I thought so. I hate cell phones. Do you own a briefcase?"

"You found my briefcase?" I said.

"Depends," he said. "Would you please describe it to me?"

"Sure." I told him it was a Mark Cross, and then I described what the leather looked like, the various fittings, its hinges and clasps, its many features as described on the Mark Cross website. "Is it mine?" I asked.

"We'll need you to come down here. You'd have to come down here anyway, to claim the property, but we'd really like to hear more about this briefcase."

"Not a problem," I said.

At the police station I was led to Detective Bielski's empty office. Photos, pinned willy-nilly, covered an entire corkboard wall, the way photos of murder scenes are pinned to police-station walls in movies, but Detective Bielski's photos were of his family, which gave me the uneasy feeling that they were all dead and that he, the only person from the photos who was still alive, was the killer. I'd done this sort of thing as a kid, getting myself worked up over a situation that didn't pose a threat, turning a coat rack in a dark room into a werewolf, a yowling cat outside into someone getting stabbed with an ice pick, seeing just how much I could scare myself. It worked, too. When Bielski walked into the office, the hair on my arms rose.

"You Boyd?" he asked. He was holding a coffee mug in one hand, a hot dog in the other. He had a scar on his chin. A knife fight, I imagined.

"Yep. I'm here for the briefcase."

"Not so fast," he said, and sat down. He looked longingly at his hot dog, then pushed it aside, next to his stapler. "Tell me something, Boyd. Why do you think we found your briefcase in a crack house full of cocaine? And what is your connection to the now deceased James P. Little, Junior?"

"Who?"

"James P. Little, Junior."

"Look. I don't know anyone named James P. Little, Junior. I was in a cab accident when I arrived in Chicago, and one of the guys who helped me out of the cab stole my briefcase."

Bielski said, "What's your line of work?"

"At the moment," I said, "I'm in the cleaning business. Before that I was an accountant."

"The cleaning business and accounting," Bielski said. "Sounds like a money laundering operation to me."

"*What?*"

Satisfied with his conclusion, Bielski helped himself to the hot dog, turning his head sideways and taking a deep bite. After each accusation, most of which were about some hypothetical partnership between myself and Mr. Little, Bielski would turn his head sideways and take another bite. He ran out of accusations only after he'd run out of hot dog.

"I'll be keeping an eye on you, Boyd." He pulled from behind his desk a briefcase that didn't look like anything I'd ever owned. This briefcase had been run over by a car, the leather had been sliced with a razor, the brass fittings were either bent or scratched, and the handle was missing. I took it from Bielski, turned it over a few times. Opening it was like popping the hood on a car that had been sideswiped; I could barely get it shut again. The only proof that it was mine was the name tag inside.

Bielski said, "I'm giving this back to you for one reason and one reason alone."

"Why's that?"

"So I could get a good look at you." He ran the tip of his forefinger over his scar. "And you know what?"

"What?"

"I don't like what I see."

I carried my briefcase under my arm into Durbin's that night.

Ralph said, "Thrift-store shopping? You should've told me. I'm running low on stock for eBay."

Kenny said, "I hope you didn't pay too much for that piece of shit."

Norm's chair was empty. I was glad. I didn't need his input tonight.

Ruth, the regular at Durbin's with whom I was most fascinated, was sitting in her usual place at the bar, wrapped in a smoky cocoon of her own making. A small funneled light from inside the bartender's workstation shone on Ruth, illuminating her the way headlights illuminate a foggy night, everything shrouded by mist and hard to see, yet alluring and hypnotic, dreamlike. No one acknowledged her when they stepped up to the bar. She was a ghost, an apparition. She'd stare directly at them, puffing on her cigarette, jiggling the ice in her drink. When they walked away, she'd laugh to herself and shake her head.

"You afraid someone's going to steal that hunk o' junk?" Kenny asked.

I looked down. My briefcase was clutched to my stomach.

Ralph turned to Kenny and said, "Don't mind him. He's on Planet Hank tonight. It's a boring planet populated by dull people. Accountants, mostly. They're all named Hank."

Kenny shivered. "Sounds awful, man. Planet Kenny, on the other hand, it's just me and a bunch of hot chicks."

"The tragedy of Planet Kenny," Ralph said, "is that there's no oxygen, so you have to wear spacesuits all the time. You can never take them off."

Kenny said, "Okay, smart guy, let's hear about Planet Ralph."

Ralph clasped his fingers behind his head. "Welcome to Planet Ralph, my friends. The next round's on me." He tilted his head at the entrance. "Speaking of planets," he said, "here comes Janet."

"Shhhh," I said. "Don't let her hear you say that."

Janet, wearing a Laura Ashley dress and dark cat's-eye sunglasses, sauntered over and sat down. She looked at Norm's empty chair and said, "Where's the MacArthur fellow tonight?"

"Who?" Kenny asked.

"Norm."

Kenny shrugged.

Janet and I had already fallen into the familiar routine of a married couple, a routine as predictable as the tide. It wasn't altogether unpleasant. In fact, it helped to ground my otherwise unpredictable and hair-raising days with Ralph. Without Janet, I might very well have been out pricing El Caminos or Monte Carlos, stamping everything *Made in Occupied Japan,* and filing dubious lawsuits. I put my arm around Janet, and she rested her warm palm on my thigh.

Between the four of us, we polished off eight pitchers. Waiting for the arrival of the ninth, Ralph pointed across the bar to a woman I'd never seen here before and said, "How much do you think she weighs? Four hundred pounds?"

I cut my eyes toward Janet, but it was too late: She was ready for a fight. "What *difference* does it make how much she weighs, Ralph?" she said.

"It doesn't," Ralph said. "It's a math problem. That's all."

"It's *not* a math problem," Janet said. "You don't wonder how much skinny people weigh. Just people with *weight* problems."

"Naw," Ralph said. "Just *her.*" He pointed again. "There are other fat people here. I don't care how much they weigh."

There was no room in this argument for me. I looked over at Kenny, but he was somewhere on Planet Kenny, trying to figure out a way to survive without his spacesuit.

Ralph said, "Listen. I like fat people. I spent one year trying to get fat myself so I could meet more fat people. I ate six huge meals a day, thousands upon thousands of calories, fatty cuts of meat, lots of candy, milk shakes out the wazoo, Ding Dongs, Ho Hos, peanuts by the can, and guess what? I didn't gain an ounce. In fact, I lost two pounds. I think there's something wrong with my metabolism. I drank six liters of Coke every day, I carried around fried pork rinds to munch on, I bought whole cakes. Chocolate. German chocolate. Nothing worked. Fat people are special. I discovered that when I was trying to get fat. I mean, most people think that fat people are fat because they don't have any self-control. That's not true. We talk about born athletes, born actors, born leaders. If you ask me, there are born fat people, too, and we should honor them. Shit, Janet, if I were you, I'd get a tattoo on my arm, *Born To Be Fat,* and be proud of it. We have a long way to go in this nation, let me tell you, a *long* way when it comes to respecting, understanding, and celebrating fat people."

Janet tugged on her dress, then took a deep breath. "You're so patronizing, Ralph."

"What?" Ralph said. He turned to me.

"Leave me out of this," I said.

Janet shot me a look that began in surprise but quickly melted into disgust. She picked up her purse, stood, and headed for the exit. I followed, even though I knew it wasn't going to be pretty.

"Janet!" I yelled in the parking lot. "Hold on!" Eerie shadows circled her feet. Two bats were flapping around the parking lot's sole light. Seeing bats in Chicago always startled me, so I was momentarily mesmerized, but looking at them was really a ploy to avoid looking at Janet. When I did look at her, she was glaring at me, tapping her foot. "What did *I* do?" I asked.

"Nothing," she said. "Absolutely nothing." Janet tugged on her dress again, and this time I recognized the gesture: It was what she did as a kid, tugging at clothes that were too tight, clothes that highlighted all her ripples and bulges. The Laura Ashley dress fit her beautifully, though. There was no need to tug. "You sat there," she said, "and you didn't say a word."

"It's only Ralph," I said. "You know how he gets."

"I expected you to be on my side," she said.

"I didn't realize we were taking sides. I thought you two were just talking."

Janet surveyed me head to toe. She said, "You've always been thin, Hank. You don't know what it's like."

I couldn't argue with her. I didn't know what it was like.

Back inside Durbin's without Janet, I finished my beer and then ordered another pitcher, another round of shots.

Ralph said, "Okay, everyone, let's keep our eye on the ball this time. That woman over there. How much do you think she weighs?"

I turned to look, but it was Ruth who caught my eye, a ghost in blue-gray cigarette smoke, seemingly trapped in limbo between earth and the afterlife. She nodded at me, and I nodded back, and when the drinks came, our waitress told me that the woman sitting alone at the bar had sent them over. "Really?" I said. I stood to walk over and thank Ruth, but her stool was empty. Only smoke remained.

I didn't have to work the next day, but spending the night at Janet's wasn't an option. Ralph and I stopped at a late-night sandwich shop on our way home, and I made the mistake of pouring too much hot sauce on my food, a skinny bottle of something called Triple Diablo with three devils leering from the label. I suffered for it later, rolling all over the futon, clutching my stomach, sweating, gritting my teeth. I considered praying. I let out a series of low moans, like a man who had just learned of his wife's sudden demise: "*Oooooooooooooooooooh. Oooooooooooooooooooh.*"

Sleep came in spurts. After waking from a dream in which Karen found me and Janet in a compromising position, a dream in which Janet was as large as the four-hundred-pound woman in Durbin's, I rolled out of bed and touch-felt my way to the bathroom. I flipped the light switch and screamed. "Holy shit!" I said.

An old woman with an electric toothbrush was standing in front of me. She was wearing a terry-cloth robe. Her hair stuck out at every possible angle.

I couldn't help it. I screamed again. But it wasn't really a scream. It was more like an off-key note played through my nose, and for a moment I wasn't even sure that the noise was coming from me. I clutched my chest and stumbled back. "Oh, *fuck,*" I said. "Jesus *Christ.*"

The woman, cinching the robe's belt, glared at me.

I headed for my bedroom, shutting and locking the door behind me. My stomach felt as though it had ruptured, and when sleep finally came, I wasn't so sure it wasn't death itself coming for me, an invitation I'd have gladly accepted, death's heavy cloak of terminal darkness a comfort, at least, a relief.

The next morning, with last night's daggers still poking my intestines, I found Ralph sitting at the kitchen table, his *Made in Occupied Japan* stamp in one hand, a cup of steaming coffee in the other. I was certain that I had hallucinated the woman from last night, that Triple Diablo had caused me to conjure the old crone. I poured myself a cup of coffee and sat down.

Ralph examined his hand for a moment, then stamped it *Made in Occupied Japan*. He studied it, pleased with himself. When he looked up, he said, "You scared the hell out of my mother last night."

"Who?"

"My mom. You nearly gave the poor woman a heart attack."

"Your *mother?*"

Ralph said, "Jesus, Hank, how long have you been living here?"

The first sip of coffee hit my stomach like a splash of battery acid. I got up and poured the rest of it down the drain.

"I'm sorry," I said. "I guess I thought she was, uh, you know . . ."

"What?"

"Dead."

"Are you crazy? Just because she doesn't get out of her room much doesn't mean she's dead." He squinted up at me and said, "You've been acting sort of funny lately. If you ask me, I think it's Janet. She's planting all sorts of fat ideas in your head. Fat people are like that. Once they get their meat hooks into you, they'll brainwash you with all their fat-people theories. They think everything's a conspiracy."

"Where do you get this stuff?"

Ralph said, "It's true. Prove to me that I'm wrong."

"How can I prove to you that you're wrong?"

"Exactly," Ralph said.

I drove the El Camino to White Hen Pantry. I bought a 7UP, a bottle of Pepto-Bismol, and a roll of Tums. On my way back to the car, I couldn't stop staring at the pay phone. It beckoned to me. It was like a scene from a horror movie, an inanimate object calling out to one of the minor characters, the one stupidly walking toward it, considering it, and then reaching out to touch it. From that point on, his fate would be a foregone conclusion. Despite my deep understanding of B horror movies, I couldn't help myself. I picked up the receiver. I stared at the buttons as if expecting the whole thing to blow up. After punching in my calling-card info, I tried Karen's number, the one her mother had given to me. She answered on the first ring.

"Karen?"

"Hank?"

"Yeah, it's me," I said.

"Oh, Hank," she said. "I miss you."

"You do?"

There was silence. I unraveled one end of the Tums roll. I popped two in my mouth.

"Hank?" she said. "Sweetie?"

"Yes?"

"Are you coming back here?"

"I don't know," I said. Karen then told me all that she'd been thinking in my absence—how much I meant to her, how marriage wasn't her top priority anymore, how she missed all the little things I did, things that had started to annoy the hell out of her but now seemed to define me as *me*. She continued saying all the things I'd hoped she would say, but an odd thing happened. I stopped listening. I couldn't shake loose our last conversation, the man who'd answered the phone, the squeaking bed, the irritation in her voice.

"Karen," I said, interrupting her litany of regrets. "Who was that guy?"

"What guy?"

"*You* know what guy," I said. "The one who answered the phone last time." I took a slug of 7UP, waiting.

"Oh. *Him*. He's nobody. Don't worry about him."

The fact that he was nobody gave me an even worse pain in my gut, far worse than if he'd actually been somebody. I wasn't sure why. Maybe it was that I hadn't ever thought of Karen as the sort of person who'd fall so easily into bed with a stranger, a man who meant nothing to her.

"Hank?"

"Yeah?"

"Are you okay?"

"I don't think so. I ate something called Triple Diablo last night. My stomach is killing me. I think I need to go."

"Will you call me later?"

"Sure," I said, but I wasn't sure.

"I love you," Karen said. "I don't care anymore what you did to that squirrel. You were under a lot of stress."

"Bye-bye." I hung up. When I turned, I nearly knocked Janet over. She was standing behind me, waiting for me to finish.

"Janet!" I yelled.

"Hank, I'm sorry about last night. I'm not normally that sensitive."

"What're you doing here?"

"I was driving by and saw you. Listen, what are you doing tonight? Do you want to come over and watch a movie?"

"Maybe," I said.

Janet touched my face with the side of her hand. She stepped forward, pressing herself against me. She kissed my cheek. "We don't have to watch the movie," she whispered.

"Really?" I said.

"Hank?"

"Yeah?"

"Who were you talking to?"

"Who was I talking to?" I smiled. "I was talking to Norm. Why?"

Janet shrugged. "Where was he?"

"Home. I called him at home."

"No. Last night. Where was he last night? Why wasn't he at Durbin's?"

"Oh. He wasn't feeling well. Stomach flu."

"I don't like Norm," Janet said. "Kenny's okay. I mean, I don't like Kenny, either, but if I had to be stranded on an island with one or the other, I'd choose Kenny."

"Do you think about this often?" I asked. "Being stranded on an island with Kenny?" I smiled again and touched her chin with my forefinger.

Janet was smiling now, too. She took hold of my wrist and led my finger into her mouth. It was nine in the morning, we were standing outside White Hen Pantry, and Janet was sucking my finger. If not for the

Triple Diablo, I might have gotten worked up, too, but I was experiencing the kind of pain that eclipses everything, including desire, the kind of pain where nearly-impossible-to-carry-out pacts are made with God, a God I may even have renounced. I pulled my finger out from the suction of Janet's mouth.

"Give me a call later," I said.

"I will," Janet said.

On my way home, I thought, *Janet, Janet, Janet. Janet the goddamned Planet.* Who'd have thought it, the two of us an item? I imagined myself in the eighth grade projecting myself twenty-one years into the future. Could I have imagined it back then? The answer was no, most definitely not.

I felt—I don't know—*relief* after talking to Karen. I felt that things were finally coming to a close. Back at Ralph's, I opened the door and, doing my best Ricky Ricardo impression, yelled, "HONEY, I'M HOME!"

Kenny and Ralph were slumped at the kitchen table. Ralph's mother was there, too, dabbing her eyes with a handkerchief. She was wearing the terry-cloth robe I'd seen her in the night before. She frowned at the sight of me.

"What's up?" I asked.

"It's Norm," Kenny said.

"What about him?"

"He's dead."

"Murdered," Ralph added. He brought his SHIT HAPPENS mug to his lips for a sip but decided against it, lowering the mug and shaking his head woefully.

Ralph's mother creaked up off the chair, then shuffled out of the room.

"What happened?" I asked.

Ralph said, "We don't know yet. Kenny just found out. The police called him."

"Jesus," I said. I pulled the Pepto-Bismol out of the bag, uncapped it, and took a long swig. Kenny motioned for me to pass it to him so he could take a snort, too. Then Ralph knocked back some. By the time the bottle made it back to me, it was empty.

"Do they know *when* it happened?" I asked.

"Day before yesterday, they think," Kenny said. "They don't know for sure." His lips were pink from the Pepto. He shook his head and said, "Fucking cops. I hate dealing with those sons of bitches."

"Pigs," Ralph said.

I nodded.

Ralph said, "They want us to make a statement."

"Who?"

"Who else?" Ralph asked. "The cops."

"A statement? From us? Why?"

Ralph said, "They need to know where we were when we last saw Norm."

Kenny said, "I'll kill whoever killed him."

Ralph patted Kenny on the back, and Kenny collapsed onto the table, weeping. I was having a difficult time processing it all, particularly the implications of the investigation. The police wanted to question me? Why?

I sneaked upstairs to hide in my room, but when I reached for the doorknob, I could sense someone watching me. I turned. It was Ralph's mother.

"I told Ralph not to let you inside our house," she said. "I told him that even when you were a little boy." Her knotty hand had trouble gripping the doorknob. I reached to help, but she swatted at me. "I knew there'd be trouble," she said. "I knew it the minute I first laid eyes on you." Since I hadn't laid eyes on Ralph's mother until recently, I was about to ask her when it was that she first laid eyes on me, but before I could say a word, she walked into her room and shut the door between us.

Over the next twenty-four hours, information became more readily available. Norm had been killed in his high-rise apartment downtown. He was shot six times at point-blank range—twice in the head, four times through the heart. No trace of a struggle. No evidence of a break-in.

Ralph and I drove down to the police station, the same station where I had retrieved my briefcase. As I had feared, Detective Bielski was in charge of the investigation.

"I knew I'd see you back here," Bielski said upon seeing me. "You're what we call a boomerang suspect. We throw you out, but you come right back. You can't help it. It's your nature. It's who you are."

Ralph said, "Sir, I've known Hank here since grade school. I admit, I failed two grades, so I should have been ahead of Hank, but as fate would have it, we were classmates. Except, if memory serves me, we were in just one class together. Is that right, Hank? And I believe that lasted for only a month or two." Detective Bielski cocked his head, as if he'd heard a shrill whistle. Nothing Ralph was saying made sense. Ralph forged ahead. "You get the idea, though, right? Anyway, let me tell you up front, Hank is the most honest, decent, and trustworthy person I know. I hate to see accusations flung at him."

I was nodding the whole while, looking back and forth from Ralph to Detective Bielski.

"If it turns out," Ralph continued, "that Hank had a hand in Norm's death, I can tell you that it's because he was criminally insane. That's the only way I could possibly see him doing it."

"What are you talking about?" I asked. "Of *course* I didn't have a hand in Norm's death."

"I know, I know," Ralph said. "I'm just saying *if*."

Bielski said, "Hank Boyd. I want you to wait in the hall. I'd like to talk to Ralph. Alone."

Ralph whispered, "Don't worry. I know how to handle situations like these."

My legs were weak. I knew Ralph meant well, but I also knew how others saw Ralph and how easily it would be to misinterpret the things he said. I knew this to be possible because I knew how *I* saw him and how easily *I* misinterpreted what he said. I waited in the hall for an hour. When Ralph emerged, his cheeks were bright red. His shirt was covered with ridiculously large sweat stains. I expected him to tell me not to worry, that everything was okay, but he merely glanced my way before walking to a drinking fountain and running an arc of water over his face.

"Boyd!" Bielski yelled from his office. "Your turn."

I shut my eyes to clear my head, but what I saw in the darkness of my own thoughts were the times I had stepped into the viewing room at a funeral home to see first my father and then, eight months later, my mother. Both times I could barely breathe. Walking into Bielski's office triggered the same response. It was like sucking in carbon dioxide and breathing out oxygen, the earth's logic turned inside out, as if I had found myself on a planet where what's supposed to be isn't, and what you'd always hoped wouldn't happen does.

Two days after learning about Norm's murder, Ralph said, "Let's do it."

"You sure?"

Ralph nodded.

The El Camino, whales singing, carried us to Norm's apartment. I barely remembered the ride. One minute we were on the city's southwest side; the next we were downtown. We lugged our buckets of equipment to the elevator and rode it up to Norm's floor.

Ralph inserted the key.

"Masks," I said, and we each put on a disposable respirator. Ralph's eyes were already glassy, but nothing was going to stop him from tackling this job. He turned the key and opened the door, and together we walked inside. Blood was everywhere—soaked up by the carpet, speckling windows, smeared across the futon—but blood didn't disturb me anymore. What disturbed me about Norm's was how the apartment had been decorated. Painted on all of the walls and ceiling, covering every square inch, were thick ropes of English ivy. The illusion was such that the ivy had grown straight up through the floor and taken over the entire apartment. As a result, the place was as dark as a forest, and it was impossible not to think of Norm's arms, his ivy tattoos, how stepping in here was like having Norm himself all around you, on top of you, crushing and suffocating, and how Norm, in death, had become eerily larger than life.

## IV

Detective Bielski called me back to the station several times that week, but even he admitted that my involvement didn't make sense.

"There's a missing piece to the puzzle," he said. "What I can't figure out is how our friend James P. Little, Junior, fits into all of this."

"Who?"

"The guy who had your briefcase. The dead man."

"That's easy," I said. "He *doesn't* fit into it. One thing has nothing to do with the other."

Bielski snorted. "Except that *you* are the common denominator. Listen, Boyd, let me tell you something. If I see someone two times in less than two weeks, someone I've never seen before, it's connected. I've been a cop for over twenty years. You don't even have to think about whether they're connected. They just are. That's how things work."

"You're wasting your time," I said.

"Am I? Is that it? I'm barking up the wrong tree? I'm heading down the wrong alley?" Bielski nodded and grinned, but it was the sort of grin that meant, *I'm going to get you, you son of a bitch, and don't you forget it, I'm going to hunt you down, you filthy dog.* The last time I saw that grin was in the sixth grade, when Charlie Beshulis, the class bully, caught me joking with some friends during recess. He stopped me in the hallway between classes and said, "You think you're funny?" I shrugged. Then he grinned at me, the same grin Bielski was giving me. I wouldn't have been so worried about Bielski—I was, after all, innocent—except that Charlie Beshulis, hiding behind a shrub after school, had jumped me and given me the beating of my life. I learned the hard way that being innocent had nothing to do with how punishment was parceled out.

For a week I tried calling Janet, but she was never home, so I stopped by her house after one of my trips to Bielski's office. She answered the door but kept the screen door locked between us.

"Come out," I said. I tapped the wire mesh. "I can't see you."

"*You* know what I look like," she said. "You don't need to see me."

"What's wrong? I thought everything was fine when I saw you at the White Hen."

"Nothing's wrong," she said, but she cleared her throat after saying it, a telltale sign that something was wrong.

"Hey, did you hear about Norm?" I asked. I squinted. "Are you nodding or shaking your head? I can't tell with this damned screen."

"Yes," she said, "I heard."

"Weird," I said.

"He was killed on a Thursday, right?"

"I think so. Yeah, that sounds right."

"And I saw you at the White Hen on Saturday morning?"

"That's right." While I waited for her to say something more, she shut and locked the door. "Goddamn it," I said. "What? What's wrong?" And then it came to me, the problem: At the White Hen, I had told Janet that I was talking to Norm on the phone. That would have been two days after he was killed.

"JANET!" I yelled. I pounded on her door. "JANET, WE NEED TO TALK! I KNOW WHY YOU'RE FRIGHTENED OF ME!" I waited. Nothing. "JANET, GODDAMN IT, OPEN THE DOOR!"

Her neighbors had begun to peer out their windows. I feared they would call the police, and though I was nowhere near Detective Bielski's territory, I was sure word would float back to him, further cementing his resolve. I thought of the flattened squirrel, and how easily an act of mercy could be perceived as an act of torture. It was best to let some things go, if for no other reason than self-preservation.

And so I did. I let Janet go. "Good-bye, Janet," I called out, and then whispered, "Good-bye, Janet the Planet." *Good-bye, good-bye.*

All night I flopped about the futon. The air conditioner wasn't working, and during those few seconds when I actually drifted to sleep, I dreamed I was swimming in my own thick and murky sweat. And then I woke up, mummified in my bedsheet, unable to move my arms or legs.

When I gave up the delusion of a good night's sleep, with the long hours till morning ticking ahead, I began to fixate on every terrible thing I'd ever done. I hadn't done anything so terrible, but nighttime magnified each small infraction, each deviated action, until, taking them together, I was a worthy candidate for the gas chamber. Guilty thoughts were midnight's children, a chorus of whispers: *You're bad, you're bad, you're bad.* To top off the guilt, I started worrying about the little bit of sex I'd had with Janet, all of it unprotected. We'd talked about it, we'd told each other we were safe, that we had been in nothing but monogamous relationships, but why should I have believed her? And who was to say that all of *her* lovers had been monogamous?

I snuck downstairs and booted up Ralph's computer. Using a search engine, I typed in *STD symptoms.* I scrolled down, closely scrutinizing the screen. One recurring symptom was that there were sometimes no symptoms, and I was convinced that these were the diseases that I had. *Of course!* I thought. *My symptoms are no symptoms!* Since I'd never had any symptoms of any kind, ever, it was possible I'd been harboring all of these diseases for years, that I had contracted them from Karen, who then passed them on to the man who answered the phone when I called. We were walking time bombs, all of us, lugging around these awful diseases without even knowing it. From now on I would use protection and, if possible, get tested after every sexual encounter. I would find a clinic that would let me in their back door, whisking me through upon arrival. I would attend church again. I would go to confession for the first time in twenty years. I would demand anonymity. No one would ever know.

"What the hell are you doing?"

I spun around. Ralph loomed over me.

"'Symptoms for sexually transmitted diseases'?" Ralph read from the screen. "Jesus, don't tell me you got the *clap.*"

My heart tried jackhammering its way out of my chest. "No, no," I said, attempting to shut down the website without any success. "I'm doing research." I clicked the mouse several times, but nothing happened. The screen had frozen.

"You don't have crabs, do you?"

"No," I said. "Of course not. This has nothing to do with me."

Ralph nodded. "Well, listen, I couldn't sleep. I thought I'd check my eBay account, see how much money I made tonight."

"Sure," I said. "Here." I stood.

Ralph made to sit but then changed his mind. "I can't concentrate," he said. "I keep thinking about Norm. Why would anyone kill him? Why?"

I could think of a dozen reasons why someone might kill Norm, but Ralph wasn't looking for answers; he was limping through the necessary stages of grief.

"That cop downtown," I said, "he thinks I had something to do with it."

Ralph said, "Naw, you didn't. I already considered that."

"What do you mean you considered it?"

"It's nothing personal. I'm just trying to eliminate people who absolutely didn't have anything to do with it."

"Well, thanks, Ralph. I'm really glad to hear I've been eliminated."

"Me, too," Ralph said. "Me, too."

Detective Bielski called me back to the station.

"Boyd," he said. "Sit down. Listen, I made some inquiries. Colorado. You lived there, right? Boulder?"

I nodded.

"You know a Mrs. Stark?"

"My landlady?" I said. "You talked to *her*?"

"Getting nervous?" Bielski asked. He grinned. "Tell you what. Why don't you tell me the story about that poor little squirrel? Maybe I should inform you, before you begin, that I love the little buggers. I love all animals, in fact. Each night before going to sleep, I read James Herriot. I'm sure you know his books. *All Creatures Great and Small. All Things Bright and Beautiful.* According to Mrs. Stark, there are over a dozen witnesses, including your fiancée, Karen Candellara. And from what I've been told, Miss Candellara kicked your sorry ass out after that episode. I imagine you're pretty angry about that, aren't you?"

I shook my head. "You don't know what you're talking about."

"I don't?" Bielski asked. "Listen, I already had that snow shovel inventoried as evidence. We're testing it, even as you and I sit here, for fingerprints and squirrel blood."

"You had someone go to Karen's place to get the shovel? In *Boulder?*"

Bielski nodded. He said, "Do you know what one of the early signs is for a serial killer? Torturing animals, my friend. Do you know the profile for a serial killer? White male in his thirties or forties. Have you looked in the mirror lately?"

"I don't believe this."

Bielski pointed at me with his pinkie. "I'll give you this, pal. You're good. If I didn't know any better, I'd think you really didn't know what the hell I'm talking about. Yessiree, you've got that act down cold. But so do most serial killers. Look at Ted Bundy. Cool as a frickin' cucumber, that one." He laughed. "Yep, yep, you're good, all right."

Across the street from the police station sat Kenny's Monte Carlo. Kenny was slouched down inside. When he saw me squinting at him, he started up the car. It lurched forward, but when I yelled, Kenny hit the brakes.

"What're you doing here?" I asked. "Did you have a meeting with Bielski, too?"

"Not today," he said. "Nope."

"You look different," I said. I tried figuring out what he'd done, but I couldn't put my finger on it. "What about all those places we had to go to get Norm?" I said. "Do you think any of those people had anything to do with Norm's death?"

"Could be," Kenny said. "But I wouldn't say anything to that cop about it. Let the pigs figure it out for themselves. Those people, they'd probably kill us for saying anything to the cops."

"Yeah," I said, "but Bielski thinks *I* had something to do with it. *Me!*" The reality of such accusations—the possible consequences—hadn't hit me until this moment. It had all seemed ridiculous. But innocent people went to jail every day; some even made it to death row. No one ever claimed that the justice system was fault-free. I'd just never thought I would be one of the unlucky ones who fell through the cracks.

Kenny reached up to touch something, but his hand stopped before reaching his face. And then I saw it. The Fu Manchu mustache was gone.

"Listen," he said. "Let me tell you a story." Kenny's story was about a man on the lam for killing his girlfriend, and when the cops caught him, halfway across the country, they found a receipt in his pocket. The receipt was for an ax that he had rented from a tool-rental company. The police took a trip to the rental company, found the ax, and tested it on the spot for blood but didn't find any. So they took it to a lab, where they removed the head of the ax. Underneath the head, on the wood itself, they found more than enough dried blood. Not only did they find blood, but it was most definitely the girlfriend's. The boyfriend had chopped off her head, her hands, and her feet to conceal her identity, then tossed the body in a forest. The blood and the receipt were enough to put the boyfriend away for life, but the parents of the girlfriend wanted to know what he had done with the head—and, to a lesser but no less morbid extent, the hands and feet. The parents couldn't sleep at night; the mother claimed that every time she slipped into sleep, she saw the disembodied head calling out to her. So, the defense attorney cut a deal with the prosecutor. The boyfriend would tell the parents where the head, feet, and hands were in exchange for a lesser sentence. The parents took the deal. The boyfriend, instead of getting life, got thirty-three years.

"Where was the head?" I asked.

"In a Dumpster," Kenny said, "behind a grocery store. You may not know this, but garbage is carefully tracked. The refuse business is very organized, even down to the dump site, which is on a grid that tells you which truck dumped what, when, and where. They found the head, the feet, and hands. It wasn't pretty, but they found them." Kenny reached up and touched his own head as if making sure it was still there. He said, "And you know what?"

"What?"

"The girl's head still called out for the mother. It didn't make one goddamn bit of difference." Kenny reached up to tug on his phantom Fu Manchu again, grasped the air where it should have been, and said, "I gotta go, man. I wish I could help you, but I can't."

On my way home, I tried sorting through Kenny's story, searching for a lesson, but the only lesson I could cull from the mess was, Don't cut off your girlfriend's head. It wasn't a pretty lesson, and it should have gone without saying, but apparently people still needed to be reminded, some more than others. The problem was, I wasn't one of them.

Ralph and I trudged on with our lives. Kenny would call to tell us where we needed to go, and then Ralph and I would load up the El Camino and head over. It never ceased to amaze me how quickly people adapted to their situations, how what would have seemed unimaginable to me even three months ago—picking up bits of brain with tweezers, sopping up human blood—now carried as much gravity as doing the dishes.

Ralph, wearing his lab coat and peering through his magnifying glass, said, "You ever get rid of those crabs?"

"I never had crabs," I said.

Ralph looked up at me. His right eye was magnified to four times the size of his left. "Whatever you say, Watson," he said.

"Hey, Ralph," I said. "Why don't *you* have a girlfriend?"

"I do," he said. "But she's in Russia. A bona fide Russkie. Former communist. Atheist. A tattoo of Karl Marx on her ass."

"Where'd you meet her?"

"I haven't yet," he said. "I ordered her off the Internet. She should be here any day now."

I decided to drop it. I knew I'd never get anywhere with this line of questioning.

After work we headed to Durbin's, but these days it was just me and Ralph. Ruth had probably spent the past dozen or so years watching this very phenomenon: large groups convening at regular intervals until one person slipped away, then another and another, leaving only one or two, and then, alas, one. It was possible that Ruth had once belonged to such a group. I could see it, too—a much younger Ruth, her head thrown back, laughing, drinking only beer, pacing herself, the cigarette in her hand more affectation than necessity. How could she possibly have predicted the way one thing would lead to another? How could she have seen that she would be the sole survivor of the group? I sure as hell couldn't have seen how getting a shovel from Karen's closet to put a squirrel out of its misery would keep coming back to haunt me.

"I need to make a call," I said.

Ralph saluted me.

I stumbled across the bar, bumping into unsuspecting patrons. From a pay phone near the restroom, I called Karen.

"Hank? Is that you? Where are you?"

"I'm in a bar," I said.

"I can barely hear you. Are you standing next to the jukebox?"

"No," I said. "Listen, why did you give the cops that shovel?"

"I don't know," Karen said. "They told me what happened. What was his name? Nick?"

"Norm."

"They said he was murdered. They said you were involved."

I didn't say anything. Ruth came up behind me to use the phone.

"Hank? Are you still there?"

"Yes," I said. "I didn't hit that squirrel. I didn't even touch it."

"Hank," Karen said. "I saw that poor squirrel. I *saw* it."

"Did you see me hit it?"

"Oh, Hank," Karen said. "I didn't *have* to see."

Ruth's eyes were dark, intense, almond-shaped. I reached toward her and removed a fleck of paper from her blouse. I showed it to her, then flicked it from my fingers.

"I'm not coming back," I said. There was silence. And then I hung up. "I'm done," I said to Ruth. "All yours."

"Are you?" she asked.

"What?"

"Done?"

When I nodded toward the phone, Ruth smiled. She slipped her finger into the coin return, checked for change, then removed her finger, pinching a quarter against her thumb. "My lucky day," she said, and headed for the jukebox.

A voice said, "I know who did it."

"Huh? What?" I woke up. I wasn't even sure where I was. I reached over, turned on the lamp. I'd been sound asleep, dreaming about Kelly throwing grenades down at me while I stood at the bottom of a deep canyon.

"Ralph," I said. "It's you. What did you say?"

"I know who did it."

"Did what?"

"Killed Norm."

I rubbed my eyes. I scooted up in bed, propping pillows against the backboard. "Ralph," I said. "You're thinking about this too much. You should get some sleep, pal. I understand that Norm was your cousin. And I suppose he wasn't such a bad guy." A shiver ran through me even at the suggestion. "But Ralph, you're going to have to let it go. You know what I mean?"

Ralph said, "Kenny killed him."

"What? That's crazy. Kenny didn't kill Norm."

"Listen," Ralph said, and he pulled up a chair. "Kenny killed Norm." And then, over the next two hours, as the morning's light sucked away the night's blood, Ralph told me the whole story, from beginning to end.

## V

At the Goodwill, in one of the far corners, I found a shopping cart overflowing with bowling balls. I lifted the one on top, checked its size, saw how my fingers fit, then set it on the floor. I did this with one after the other, not fully aware of the mess I was making, or the hazard that the mess caused—particularly to children who'd come careening around a corner only to find two dozen bowling balls in their path—until a manager asked me to keep the mess contained.

"Not a problem," I said.

Ralph, pushing a cart up and down each aisle, was beefing up his eBay stock. He tossed one thing after another into the cart, his mind clearly elsewhere. Ralph's dilemma had morphed from "Who killed Norm?" to "What should be done about Kenny?"—a far more complex question.

The story Ralph told was a long one, but the gist of it was short: Norm had drained his and Kenny's business of every last penny, leaving Kenny with a pile of unpaid bills. Kenny had begged Norm to quit gambling, to stop dipping into their collective accounts, but Norm wouldn't relent, continuing to siphon dollar after dollar, until one day it was all gone, every last penny of it. To make matters worse, the answer to my question—*What did Norm do to earn his keep?*—was nothing. Apparently, late one night at Durbin's, Norm had come up with the idea and thereafter clung to the belief that he was owed 50 percent of all earnings. It was a shaky premise, but Kenny, both amazed and grateful when money started pouring in, never questioned the arrangement. Then Norm got to be unhappy with 50 percent. Before long, he was taking 60 percent, and then 70, 80, and 90 percent. In the last few months, Norm had been taking over 100 percent.

Ralph knew most of his cousin's friends, so he conducted his own investigation. It wasn't difficult. In fact, most everyone seemed to know what Norm was doing—everyone, that is, except Ralph. It wasn't until Ralph, after spilling a bowl of salsa on his crotch while watching a Cubs game at Kenny's place, came across a blood-splattered shirt in the closet that he figured it out.

"And I know what bloodstains look like," Ralph had said to me. "It's my job."

I carried my bowling ball—black as tar, chipped and gouged, with the name NANCY engraved across it—over to Ralph's shopping cart.

"Jesus," I said. "You've gone nuts. Look at all that junk!"

Ralph said, "I can't help it. I'm possessed."

"I was going to put my bowling ball in there, but there's no room."

"Here," Ralph said. He took the ball from my arms and set it in the baby seat. "Happy?" he asked.

The bowling ball cost $3.42. Ralph's entire shopping cart of goodies cost under twenty bucks.

In the car, I kept the bowling ball up front with me, resting between my thighs.

"You look like you're enjoying that," Ralph said.

"Maybe I am."

"At least the holes look big enough for you," he said.

I glanced at Ralph, but he wasn't smiling. He could insult me in his sleep, if he wanted, and he might as well have been doing just that. His mind was projecting into the future, his and Kenny's.

Back at home, Ralph set to work stamping each and every new item *Made in Occupied Japan.* "The key," he said, "is to buy only things made of wood. Anything else and the stamp might smear." He stamped a salad bowl, a hand-carved elk, and tongs. He stamped a picnic basket, a cane, and a pair of wooden shoes already stamped *Made in Holland.*

I picked up a wooden chest with a gold clasp and gold hinges. Carvings of temples, suns, sacrifices, and swords decorated all of its sides. I said, "This looks like it might actually be valuable. What do you think?"

Ralph took it from me. He said, "Could be. Something like this, I'd make sure to get what it's worth."

"How would you do that?"

"I'd claim it was even rarer than it is, just to be on the safe side. I'd give it an elaborate history. People love stories. I'd tell them it's one of a kind, that it belonged to some famous pirate, that it's stained with his blood."

"Maybe some things don't need to be more valuable than they're really worth."

Ralph shook his head. "Don't underestimate the price of persuasion. My ability to make people spend more than something's worth is worth money in and of itself."

I stared at Ralph. "You're serious," I said.

"Serious as a heart attack."

Despite my recurring dreams of being assaulted by her, I called my sister in Madison. I needed to talk to someone, and I couldn't think of anyone else. My pool of confidants had always been rather shallow, but lately it had all but evaporated. Before launching into my own problems, I asked her about the feminist she'd been dating. I was told, in no uncertain terms, that I should never mention the woman again, in any context, *ever*.

"That bad?" I asked.

Kelly sighed. "What did I just say?"

"I'm sorry. I didn't realize the moratorium began this very second."

"You never listen, do you?"

"I guess not," I said. "No, I don't. I've been having a dream about you trying to kill me."

"Still having it?"

"What do you mean?"

"You had that dream when we were kids, too."

"Did I?"

"Every night," Kelly said. "So tell me something new."

I told Kelly all that had been happening to me, beginning with Karen and the squirrel, through the murder of Norm, and ending with Ralph's present dilemma with Kenny.

"You know where I am right now?" she asked.

"No."

"I'm on my cell phone, and I'm looking into one of the lakes here in Madison. Do you want to know why?"

"Sure. Hit me with it."

"Otis Redding's plane crashed here in this lake, and they never recovered his body. I was thinking that if I looked hard enough, I might see some of his bones." I didn't say anything. "I'll take the bus," she said. "I'll be there tonight."

"What? Wait a second. You don't have to come down here, Kelly. I just needed to unload all of this on somebody, and I couldn't think of anyone except you."

"I'll be there. No need to pick me up. I'll take a cab to Ralph's."

"You remember where he lives?" I couldn't recall Kelly ever having anything to do with Ralph, let alone knowing his address.

"Of course I do," Kelly said. "I remember everything. It's my curse."

I'd been thinking a lot about Charlie Beshulis lately, and how his jumping out from behind a shrub was one of the most startling things that had ever happened to me. But what I'd really been mulling over was the idea of one person merely looking at another person and hating him enough to want to punch him, to do bodily harm. I was grateful to Charlie Beshulis because I never again took my safety for granted. I was still fearful of shrubs. I always expected someone to jump out from behind whatever I was passing—a motorcycle, a couple of trash cans, a U.S. mailbox. No one ever did, but Charlie opened up the possibility of that world, a world in which people squatted behind objects only slightly larger than themselves, lying in wait, ready to pounce.

I'd been thinking about all of this so much that, distracted, I had let down my guard. I was out taking a walk when Kenny stood up from behind a baby carriage. "Oh, shit," I said. "Oh, fuck." The baby inside the carriage started crying, and the woman pushing the carriage stepped in front of her toddler, blocking me from doing whatever it was I would do to it.

"Kenny," I said. "I didn't see you down there."

Kenny said, "One of the wheels fell off. Can you imagine that? A wheel falling off a baby carriage? If I were this poor woman, I'd sue the shit out of the manufacturer. I'd soak every last penny out of the sons of bitches. Pardon my French. But really, you need to make peckerheads like that pay through the nose." Kenny reached into the carriage, tickled the baby's cheek, and said, "Anyway, the pin that held the wheel in place must've fallen off. So I took one of her hairpins"—he pointed at the mother—"and now it's as good as new."

"A hairpin?" I said. I was so relieved that Kenny wasn't here to kill me that I started pouring on the compliments. "That's ingenious, Kenny. I'd never have thought of that. Brilliant!"

Kenny smiled. He raised his eyebrows at the woman, tipped his head at me, and said, "College boy," then snorted. It was exactly the sort of thing Norm would have said, and it triggered a sickening hollowness in my gut, as if the murderer's curse in life was to have his soul invaded by the person murdered—a passing of the spiritual torch.

"Cute baby," I said, but the woman again blocked my view. She was wearing too much hair spray, blue eye shadow, and a shirt that exposed her midriff. Her belly button and bottom lip were both pierced and adorned with costume jewelry. When she bent over the carriage to tend to the crying child, the top of a tattoo crept out of her pants, and though I couldn't fully identify it, I saw feathered wings, and I imagined an eagle swooping down to perch on the woman's too-big butt.

"Ralph home?" Kenny asked.

"He had to go out," I said.

Kenny nodded. "I'll try back later."

"Good enough," I said.

Only later did I realize that I had failed to ask Kenny where he'd parked his car or what he was doing two blocks from Ralph's. His sudden appearance from behind the carriage had momentarily eclipsed all logic, and it wasn't until he had walked away with the baby's mother, disappearing around a corner, that the world of order came back into focus, leaving me with far more questions than answers.

The doorbell rang, and I sat bolt upright on the couch. It was the first time I'd ever heard the doorbell here. Someone had rigged it so that both traditional chimes and a buzzer sounded at once, but in my deep sleep, the noise came like a visit from the reaper himself. I composed myself and then answered the door. A woman with long blond hair, wearing a white blouse and a plaid skirt, stood on the front porch.

"Yes?" I said.

"Hank," she said. "You could give your sister a hug, if you were so inclined."

"Kelly?"

She rolled her eyes.

Kelly had always been a brunette, and I hadn't seen her wear a white blouse or a skirt since her confirmation at St. Fabian's when she was in the eighth grade. I wasn't sure what I'd expected. Full military regalia would have seemed more in keeping with the spirit of Kelly.

"What happened to your shaved head?"

"It's hair, Hank. It grows."

I nodded. People tended to remain static in my mind, which went a long way in explaining why I was comforted by Ralph's presence. In twenty-one years, he'd barely changed.

Kelly said, "Can I come in, at least?"

Once she was inside, I meant only to pat her on the back, but I pulled her to me, tightening my grip, and nearly started weeping on her shoulder. "It's so good to see you, Kelly. Thanks for coming. You don't know what this means to me."

When I let go, Kelly took a step back. "Jesus, Hank, are you okay?"

"No," I said. "No, no, I don't think so. It's been a stressful couple of months."

Kelly said, "Your life has been entirely way too easy until now. You may not see it yet, but these past few months have been good for you. Stress will build your character."

"Now, wait just a minute," I began, already regretting having called Kelly, but before I could say another word, Ralph came bounding down the stairs.

"Kelly!" he yelled, as if able to see through the scrim of time, finding the essence of the girl she used to be.

Kelly grinned as if they'd been old friends, when they'd been anything but. "Look at you, Ralph. All grown up!"

"I'm a big boy now," Ralph said.

"You look good," Kelly said.

Ralph's expression grew serious. He said, "The body is a temple, Kelly. I eat well. I take care of myself. I don't put anything into my body that I can't purge in a four-hour period. I have a regimented eating schedule. Lots of fruits, lots of grains. Hank, on the other hand . . . *whoo*. You should see what this boy eats. You wouldn't believe how much beer he can consume in an eight-hour period." Ralph turned to me. "Hank," he said. "I noticed you've been spending a lot of time in the bathroom lately. How're the old bowels treating you?"

"I don't think anyone wants to hear about my bowels," I said.

"At least thirty-three percent of the people in this room are interested," Ralph said.

The three of us stood silent for a moment. "Let's drop it," I said.

Ralph turned to Kelly. "I think Hank's resistance speaks volumes."

Ralph had a point. Cheap beer and fast food were killing me. What came out of my body these days was looking more and more extraterrestrial.

Kelly said, "So, folks, what's this I hear about Kenny killing Norm?"

Ralph cut his eyes toward me; I shrugged. "She knows," I said.

Ralph nodded. "Now what?" he asked.

"We should talk," Kelly said. "I'm the perfect person to include in this dialogue. I'm anti–death penalty. I'm anti-cop. I'm anti-authority. But we've got a problem on our hands."

Ralph looked at me and said, "I always did say your sister was the one with the brains in your family. Didn't I always say that?"

I couldn't remember Ralph ever saying anything like that.

"Okay, fellas," Kelly said, "sit your butts down. We need to take a look at this Kenny issue from a variety of different angles."

People always did what Kelly told them to do. We sat. We sat and waited for her next command.

Around noon the next day, I staggered downstairs to fix myself coffee. I was regretting the midnight beer run. I was regretting some of what I'd said and done. At one point I had started bawling, muttering something about Karen. Fortunately, Ralph and Kelly were so deep into negotiations about Kenny that they ignored me. From what I could remember, Ralph had wanted to send a letter to Detective Bielski that implicated Kenny, but he wanted to sign one of his own enemies' names to the letter. That way, if Kenny didn't get convicted, the person he'd most likely kill next would be someone Ralph wouldn't mind seeing dead. Kelly, on the other hand, had thought we should convince Kenny that by turning himself in, he would be doing what was best for everyone in the long run, and he'd benefit when a sentence was handed down. The last compromise I could recall, shortly before I headed to bed, was made by Ralph—that he, *Ralph*, should send a letter to Kenny signed by one of Ralph's enemies, trying to convince Kenny to turn himself in, maybe by blackmailing him.

I slept with one foot touching the floor to keep the room from spinning. By morning the room had become stationary, but my head felt as though it had been lightly tapped all night with a ball-peen hammer. As I sipped my coffee, I was beginning to regain a sense of equilibrium when Kelly walked into the kitchen wearing one of Ralph's T-shirts. The T-shirt said, I'M GOD. WHO ARE YOU?

I said, "Oh, please tell me that you just borrowed that."

"I did," Kelly said.

"You know what I mean. Please tell me that you didn't, you know, spend the night with Ralph."

Kelly, master of the poker face, said nothing.

"Okay," I said. "Let me rephrase that. You didn't spend the night with him, did you?"

"Answer just one question for me," Kelly said. "How's old Janet the Planet in the sack? Hm? I bet the boys don't call her the Planet for nothing. I'll bet she does a pretty good around-the-world, doesn't she? Or don't you know what an around-the-world entails? Maybe you've already been around the world and don't even know it. Poor Hank. Poor, poor Hank. Where did our parents go so wrong with you?"

"Oh God," I said. I covered my face with my hands. I wasn't sure what was worse—my sister and Ralph having sex, or my sister and Ralph talking about *me* having sex after they themselves had had sex.

Kelly said, "I don't know why people make such a big deal about it."

"Because it's *sex*, Kelly. Because in some parts of the world, people get killed for who they have sex *with*." I had a hunch. "What're you studying right now?" I asked.

"What?"

"What classes are you taking?"

Kelly said, "Labor politics."

"Aha!" I said. "Say no more." Ralph, the ultimate proletarian, was Kelly's latest conquest. She probably figured it would be easier to absorb the content of a course if she bedded one of the subject's representatives. I was starting to see a pattern to her life. I didn't know why I hadn't seen it earlier. It was obvious. *Too* obvious. Poor Ralph. Exploited by an academic. I was almost feeling sorry for him when he burst into the kitchen, wearing tube socks, boxers, and a T-shirt that said, MY MOM AND DAD WENT TO THE BERMUDA TRIANGLE, AND THEY WERE GOING TO BUY ME THIS CRUMMY T-SHIRT, BUT THEY NEVER CAME BACK. His smile, wider than ever, curdled what little sympathy I was trying to muster for him.

He said, "Man oh man, I could use a cup o' joe." He used his SHIT HAPPENS mug. He picked up two spoons and started hammering out a solo on the dirty dishes.

"Hey, Keith Moon," I said. "Take it easy with the spoons. Some of us are hung over."

"Maybe some of us are jealous," Ralph said. He put down the spoons and joined Kelly and me at the table.

"What the hell's *that* supposed to mean?" I asked. "What are you implying?"

Kelly looked from me to Ralph and settled on Ralph. "Don't mind him," she said. "He's in a bad mood today. He was like this as a kid, too. Always bringing everyone else down."

I chugged the rest of my coffee. "Okay. Let's forget about me. Why don't you tell me what you two decided last night. What did you two brainiacs come up with?"

Ralph scratched the BERMUDA on his shirt. His face went slack, and for the first time since I'd been here, Ralph looked his age. Kelly said, "It's not going to be pretty." She reached over and took Ralph's hand. Under normal circumstances, I'd have been mildly disturbed by such a level of intimacy between the two of them, but given this new and unholy union, I shivered.

"So?" I said. "Tell me the plan."

"The plan . . ." Ralph began.

Kelly nodded. "The plan," she said.

Ralph, nodding solemnly, said, "Here's the plan."

Kenny, having been evicted from his high-rise condo on the Gold Coast, was living only four blocks away from us. This explained why I'd seen him trolling the neighborhood the day before. Naturally, no one had told me.

"It slipped my mind," Ralph said. "It's not like you're all that interested in my family, anyway."

"How could you possibly say I'm not interested in your family? I'm a prime suspect in the death of your cousin. Jesus, Ralph. It seems to me I couldn't be any *more* interested."

Ralph huffed. "Yeah, but see what it takes to get you interested? Now, *me*," Ralph added, "I've always taken a keen interest in *your* family."

"I don't want to hear about it," I said.

The apartment building Kenny lived in now was a boxy three-story, twelve-unit complex. Dozens of these eyesores went up in the '60s and '70s, one looking more or less like the other. I'd been inside a number of them when I was younger, visiting fellow classmates, but I was startled now at how cramped everything was—the narrow hallways, the absurdly low ceilings, a foyer hardly large enough to accommodate me and Ralph standing side by side. From floor to floor, you could smell what everyone had cooked the night before, and none of it was particularly appetizing.

Kenny lived on the third floor. The plan was for me to wait out in the hallway while Ralph talked to Kenny. And that's what I did. Gladly. Kenny opened the door, Ralph walked inside, and the two of them spoke for a good hour. When they stepped out of the apartment together, I followed behind. Kenny didn't acknowledge me, and I didn't say anything to him. I saw for the first time that Ralph and Kenny had the exact same walk, with a slight bounce to their steps, like little boys, and how their heads were the same odd shape, as if someone had inflated each one too much, adding an extra pound or two of air.

Our plan was shortsighted when it came to getting Kenny to the police station. Kenny, broke, had sold his car. That meant the three of us had to ride in the El Camino, which had only the one bench seat. Kenny squeezed between us, promising a long and uncomfortable drive to Detective Bielski's.

Kenny, after a few uneasy miles of silence, sighed and said, "Shit. Why did Norm have to go and fuck up everything?" He shook his head. "Even when we were kids, he'd pull me down. Why do you think that is? Huh?" He looked from me to Ralph and then back to me. I wasn't sure he really wanted an answer, so I didn't offer one. Kenny said, "Maybe if I knew the answer, he'd still be alive. Maybe that's the problem. All those years of *not* knowing, they finally did something to me."

At the police station, Ralph told me to wait in the car. I rolled down the window. Kenny bent forward and said, "He couldn't have been too surprised to see me with a gun. He didn't *look* surprised." He was staring through my eyes, as if trying to see what was behind them. "You went to college," he said. "What do *you* think?"

"I don't know," I said.

He smiled. "Me neither," he said. "Remember that story I told you? The one about the parents who cut the deal with the attorney so they could find their daughter's head?"

I nodded.

"I just want you to know, I'm not turning myself in because of you two clowns. I'm turning myself in because I keep seeing Norm's head. It comes to me every night, and it looks like it did right after I shot him. I can't take it anymore."

Ralph said, "Shit, Kenny. Does he speak to you?"

Kenny shook his head. "No, he just stares at me."

I decided not to remind him that the mother, even after learning where the killer had put her daughter's head, had still been visited by the gory sight. "I'm sorry," I said. Kenny squeezed my shoulder, then turned and crossed the street with Ralph.

# VI

Ralph drove up to Madison with Kelly to load her belongings into the bed of his El Camino and lug it all back to Ralph's house. Kelly took a temporary leave from her Ph.D. program, though I suspected she would try to get credit for her time with Ralph. Nothing about Kelly surprised me, not even that she'd hooked up, albeit a few decades later, with the boy she had found most loathsome on this planet. What *did* surprise me was Ralph. Being with Kelly transformed him into the one thing I never could have imagined Ralph: a romantic. He cautioned her about sinkholes in his front yard. When it rained, he raised an umbrella over her head. He held her hand even when they were inside the house.

"You feeling okay, Ralph?" I asked. "You don't seem yourself."

"What're you talking about?" he said. "I've never felt better."

"What about the woman you ordered from Russia? The Internet bride?"

"Oh, her," Ralph said. "I stopped payment. I lost my deposit, but I don't mind. It gave me a chance to bone up on my Tolstoy. What about you, old man? You've been looking a little peaked lately. You running a temperature? Feel free to use my mother's thermometer, if you like."

I shivered at the thought. "I'm fine."

Over the next few weeks, the three of us brainstormed about how to pay for Kenny's attorney.

"What we *don't* want," Kelly said, "is for him to get a state-appointed defense attorney. That's a guaranteed fast track to the gas chamber."

"But we're *broke*," I reminded her.

"I know, I know," Kelly said. "But the more you say that, the bigger my headache gets. And the bigger my headache, the harder it is for me to concentrate."

Ralph reached over and patted Kelly's thigh. "That's my girl. You tell him."

"Ralph!" I said. "We're not taking sides here. I'm just giving you the facts."

Ralph scooted his chair closer to Kelly.

Since Kenny had handed over Drop Dead Clean to Ralph, Ralph enlisted me as its accountant. I had put off looking over the books, but when I pulled out Norm's and Kenny's financial records, I was surprised at how easily I fell back into the mode of accountant. I was even more surprised at how much I had missed it. I felt at home in the world of numbers. The books were a disaster—missing entries, miscalculations, basic subtraction errors—but once I saw how badly they'd screwed up, my heart started to thump wildly at how much more money they could have made if they'd been more prudent. The main problem was unnecessary overhead, and even if Norm hadn't run the company into the ground, they'd been set to crash-land in a few short years. Kenny and Norm weren't businessmen; they were thugs who'd stumbled upon a good idea.

I put together a proposal on how not only to salvage the business but how to start turning a profit that would make Kenny and Norm's earnings look paltry. My first suggestion was to have Kenny file for bankruptcy, while Ralph and I resurrected the same business under a new name, applying for small-business grants and loans.

I presented my proposal to Ralph. He nodded at all the key points. When I'd finished, Ralph drummed the proposal with his fingers. He said, "Well, it's not *The Joy of Sex*." He poured himself a bowl of Count Chocula.

"What's *that* supposed to mean?" I asked.

Ralph, spoon aloft, said, "Listen. When I run across a particular number in *The Joy of Sex*, it gets me revved up because I can put a face to the number. Two faces, in fact. I get a visual image, if you will. But your proposal, it's full of numbers, and I can't see anything. I'm not even sure what you're talking about. No offense, of course."

For each spoonful of Count Chocula, Ralph would slurp all the milk from the spoon, then insert the rest of the spoonful into his mouth, tightening his lips around the spoon's neck and then pulling it free. He did this spoonful after spoonful, without variation. I didn't realize I was glaring at Ralph's mouth until he furrowed his thick brow at me. When he'd finished the bowl, he said, "There's more Count C in the cupboard, buddy, if that's what you want. Help yourself. I'd better get back upstairs, though. Big K's waiting."

"Count C? Big K?"

"You've been under a lot of stress lately. Why don't we all go out tonight so you can let your hair down." Ralph headed for the stairwell, then turned and said, "I never thought we'd be brothers-in-law. I mean, we may *not* ever be brothers-in-law, but I have to tell you, I'd never thought about it until these past few days. And you know what, Little H?"

"What?"

"It's scary." Ralph headed upstairs.

I felt better knowing that such notions scared Ralph. We may not have been reading the same book, but we were at least on the same page, and I could take some small comfort in that.

Another part of my proposal was that Ralph and I would no longer be directly involved in cleanup. Ralph would oversee crews, hire and fire, delegate, perfect more efficient methods of stain removal. I would handle the budget, keep the books accurate, start making investments for us, take bids for services we could subcontract, negotiate prices for bulk supplies, implement a better payroll system—in short, deal with all things having to do with money. I continued outlining the business plans over pitchers at Durbin's.

At one point Ralph turned to Kelly and said, "Look at him. The dullest man on earth. Who'd have thought we'd end up at the same table with him? What are the odds?"

Kelly said, "Don't ask him the odds. He'll probably whip out his Texas Instrument and start calculating them."

Ralph snickered. "The odds are pretty good that I'll be whipping out *my* Texas Instrument later tonight, if you know what I mean."

"*Please,*" I said. "I don't want to hear what the two of you do in the privacy of your bedroom. It's bad enough I have to live under the same roof."

Kelly, a snifter of port in one hand and an unlit cigar in the other, said, "You're not a *Republican,* are you? Please tell me that you haven't become a Republican."

"Jesus, Kelly, what kind of question is that? No, I'm not a Republican."

Ralph said, "I always write in my own candidate. What's that make me?"

"An idealist," Kelly said, and kissed Ralph's cheek.

"A fool," I said.

I excused myself. It was Friday night. Everyone was unwinding for the weekend. Smoke rose to the ceiling as if from the mouths of so many dragons. In the glare of the bathroom mirror, I could see precisely how drunk I was. I pressed my nose against the glass and stared so long that I looked like an impostor of myself. There was something slightly wrong about the shapes of my nose, my eyes, my mouth. Did I really look like this? I wondered. Had I *always* looked like this? I stared until I started to think I was nose-to-nose with a stranger, that there was no mirror between us, and that he, this stranger, was mimicking my every move. I contorted my mouth; he contorted his mouth. I raised an eyebrow; he raised an eyebrow. I flared my nostrils; he flared his. I had just poked my tongue out, alternating between making it puffy and making it flat, when a man walked into the restroom, stopped when he saw me, and said, "You don't have a lot of friends, do you?"

I headed back into the main bar. "Lights" by Journey came on, and the bartender turned it up. "Lights" had been the final song of every high school dance I'd ever gone to, the quintessential slow song, and I couldn't resist: I walked over to the bar and offered my hand to Ruth. She hoisted herself up off the stool, and I led her to the dance floor.

"I'm Hank," I said.

"I know," she said. "We went to school together."

"We did?"

"Grade school. But then my parents moved away."

I tried remembering her but couldn't. She put her arms around my neck, and I put mine around her waist. And then we began to dance, weaving from side to side while rotating clockwise. She rested her chin on my shoulder blade. When I leaned my cheek against Ruth's hair, it could have been 1979 all over again, tinfoil stars blinking from the gymnasium's top rafters. Eighth-Grade Dinner Dance. Of course. *Ruth.* We had danced that night. I had kissed her ear. I had kissed all the girls' ears that night. Through heavy clouds of cigarette smoke, I spotted Ralph and gave him a two-finger salute. He shook his head as if he couldn't believe what he was seeing, and the truth was, I couldn't believe it myself.

Ralph, Kelly, and I huddled around Ralph's computer. It was three in the morning. We were drunk.

"What's he doing?" I asked Kelly.

"He figured out how to pay for Kenny's defense," Kelly said.

"How?"

"Shhhh," she said. "For once in your life, just watch."

I watched. Ralph had the hand-carved chest, the only thing from Goodwill that looked like it might actually have been worth something, the chest with carvings of temples, suns, sacrifices, swords on it. He turned it upside down and stamped it *Made in Occupied Japan.* Next he removed from his closet a cardboard box large enough to hold four pounds of coffee. On the side of the box was a sticker: *Norman "Norm" Wilson. 1954-2001.*

I said, "Are these . . . ?"

Ralph nodded. *Norm's remains.* Carefully, he poured Norm's ashes from the cardboard box into the wooden one. When he was done, he lowered the wooden box's lid and turned the hasp so the ashes wouldn't leak out. Kelly patted Ralph's back.

Ralph logged on to eBay. For the description of what he was selling, Ralph typed, *Remains of Saigo Takamori, legendary Japanese samurai, hero of the Japanese people, who led his warriors into the infamous battle of Satsuma. Saigo, wounded, committed suicide in the samurai tradition. His ashes are laid to rest in a beautiful, one-of-a-kind, hand-carved chest, stamped* Made in Occupied Japan. *There is no limit to the value of this item.*

After submitting the information, Ralph pushed back his ancient swivel chair, the cast-iron wheels squeaking. And then we sat in silence, hunched forward, lit only by the glow of the computer screen. We waited for the first bid to come in, eager to see how much—given Norm's new exalted and unlikely stature—the market would bear for the sum total of a man's life, this wooden box full of ashes and lies.

# ABOUT THE AUTHOR

John McNally is the author of *Troublemakers,* an award-winning story collection. The recipient of a Chesterfield screenwriting fellowship, sponsored by Paramount Pictures, and a Thomas Williams fellowship from the Isherwood Foundation, John was recently chosen as one of Fiction's New Luminaries by *Virginia Quarterly Review*. A native of Chicago's southwest side, he and his wife divide their time between North Carolina and Los Angeles. To contact John, visit www.bookofralph.com.

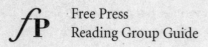

Free Press
Reading Group Guide

*The Book of Ralph*

1. Ralph is the title character, and Hank is the book's narrator. Of the two, who would you say is the main character? Why do you think the author chose to tell the story from Hank's perspective and not Ralph's? With Hank as the narrator, the reader is privy to his view of the people in his life—Ralph, Kenny, Norm, Kelly, his parents, his teachers. How do they, in turn, view Hank?

2. In what ways do Hank and Ralph change during their eighth-grade year? Why, at the end of the summer, do they not speak again until they're reacquainted by chance more than two decades later? Did reading about Hank and Ralph in their youth give you a better understanding of them as adults?

3. On more than one occasion Hank admits that he has no idea why he and Ralph are friends. What draws them together? Is Ralph a good influence on Hank in any way?

4. Setting plays an important role in *The Book of Ralph*. In what ways does setting function as a character? Does Chicago's South Side setting give us a better understanding of Hank and Ralph, and if so, how?

5. Discuss the second part of the book, "The Past: 1975." What does this section add to your understanding of Hank and Ralph?

6. When Hank reconnects with Ralph as an adult, he falls into a similar role he played as a kid—Ralph's sidekick, not standing up for himself, going along with Kenny and Norm's schemes. Why do you suppose this happens to him?

7. When Hank stays in Ralph's house after arriving back in Chicago, he says, "When I was a kid, it had seemed like a junky, run-down house, a poor person's house, but now I could see that it had more character than any other house around, despite the years of neglect" (217). What else does Hank see differently now that he's looking through adult eyes?

8. Discuss how family is portrayed in *The Book of Ralph*. Is Hank's a typical family? Why does Ralph's mother appear only briefly in the book? Is there any significance to Ralph never having left his childhood home?

9. To what extent are the lives of the characters shaped by their economic circumstances, and by the time and place in which they live—the South Side of Chicago in the 1970s? After vowing "never to return" (249) to Chicago, why does Hank not only return but decide to stay?

10. Discuss Hank's relationships with Karen and Janet. Why is he unable to fully commit to Karen? How would you describe his relationship with his sister, Kelly, both in childhood and adulthood? And his relationship with his mother?

11. In one instance Hank says, "What *did* surprise me was Ralph. Being with Kelly transformed him into the one thing I never would have imagined Ralph: a romantic" (283). What attracts Ralph and Kelly to each other? Were you surprised that they ended up as a couple?

12. What is Hank's fascination with telling the story about the squirrel he almost killed? How does this incident, as he says, "keep coming back to haunt" him?

13. What do you think is the most compelling scene in *The Book of Ralph*? Which scene reveals the most about Ralph? How about Hank?

14. When Hank and Ralph both admit that the prospect of being brothers-in-law is scary, Hank reasons, "We may not have been reading the same book, but we were at least on the same page" (285). Have he and Ralph been more on the same page than Hank has been able to admit?

15. Author Haven Kimmel described *The Book of Ralph* as being "populated by unlikely heroes." Who is she referring to as the "unlikely heroes," and why?